VOID BREAKER

THE KEEPERS: BOOK THREE

DAVID DALGLISH

orbitbooks.net

ORBIT

First published in Great Britain in 2021 by Orbit

1 3 5 7 9 10 8 6 4 2

Map by Tim Paul

A CIP catalogue record for this book is available from the British Library.

ISBN 978-0-356-51161-0

Printed and bound in Great Britain by Clays Ltd, Elcograf S.p.A.

Papers used by Orbit are from well-managed forests and other responsible sources.

Orbit
An imprint of
Little, Brown Book Group
Carmelite House
50 Victoria Embankment
London EC4Y 0DZ

An Hachette UK Company
www.hachette.co.uk

www.orbitbooks.net

VOID BREAKER

Clouds roiled and split, making way for the dragon's passage as it descended toward the great field beyond the western gates. The front legs touched ground, and they made not a sound, for the dragon's arrival was gentle. Its body slithered and curled as it settled, like smoke making a home, or a living fog given scales and a pulse.

Nihil's physical body landed with its feline face grinning at the crawling mountain, and then its ruby eyes closed, and its marble teeth hid behind sealed lips as it slowly lowered to the ground. Outside the gates of Londheim, the tops of their towering bodies the only part now visible to Evelyn from her perch, the two dragons faced one another. Evelyn could not shake the feeling that the demigods were opposed in more than mere cardinal directions.

"And so you arrive at last," Evelyn whispered to the wind. "Such conflict was bound to draw you in like flies to honey."

The Dragon of Conflict reared back its head, and it let loose a tremendous roar. It was no cry of an animal or monster. It was a crack of thunder, and it rumbled, and rumbled, a mighty herald of war.

Praise for
David Dalglish

"Fans will love the second installment of this dark fantasy about very human characters beset by inhuman dangers"

Kirkus on *Ravencaller*

"With strong world building, imaginative monsters, and a capable system of magic, this series will please readers who enjoy dark epic fantasy with engaging characters"

Booklist on *Ravencaller*

"A fast-paced, page-turning ride with a great, likeable main character in Devin Eveson. It's the definition of entertaining"

John Gwynne, author of *Malice*, on *Soulkeeper*

"A dark and lush epic fantasy brimming with magical creatures and terrifying evil . . . Dalglish's world building is subtle and fluid, and he weaves the history, magical workings, and governance of his world within the conversations and camaraderie of his characters. Readers of George R. R. Martin and Patrick Rothfuss will find much to enjoy here"

Booklist on *Soulkeeper*

"A soaring tale that nails the high notes. *Skyborn* had me gazing heavenward, imagining what could be"

Jay Posey, author of *Three*

"Dalglish raises the stakes and magnitude, demonstrating his knack for no-holds-barred, wildly imaginative storytelling and worldbuilding"

Publishers Weekly on *Shadowborn*

"Fast, furious, and fabulous"

Michael J. Sullivan, author of
Theft of Swords, on *A Dance of Cloaks*

By David Dalglish

The Keepers

Soulkeeper

Ravencaller

Voidbreaker

Seraphim

Skyborn

Fireborn

Shadowborn

Shadowdance

A Dance of Cloaks

A Dance of Blades

A Dance of Mirrors

A Dance of Shadows

A Dance of Ghosts

A Dance of Chaos

Cloak and Spider *(novella)*

To the recast among us—I hope I did all right

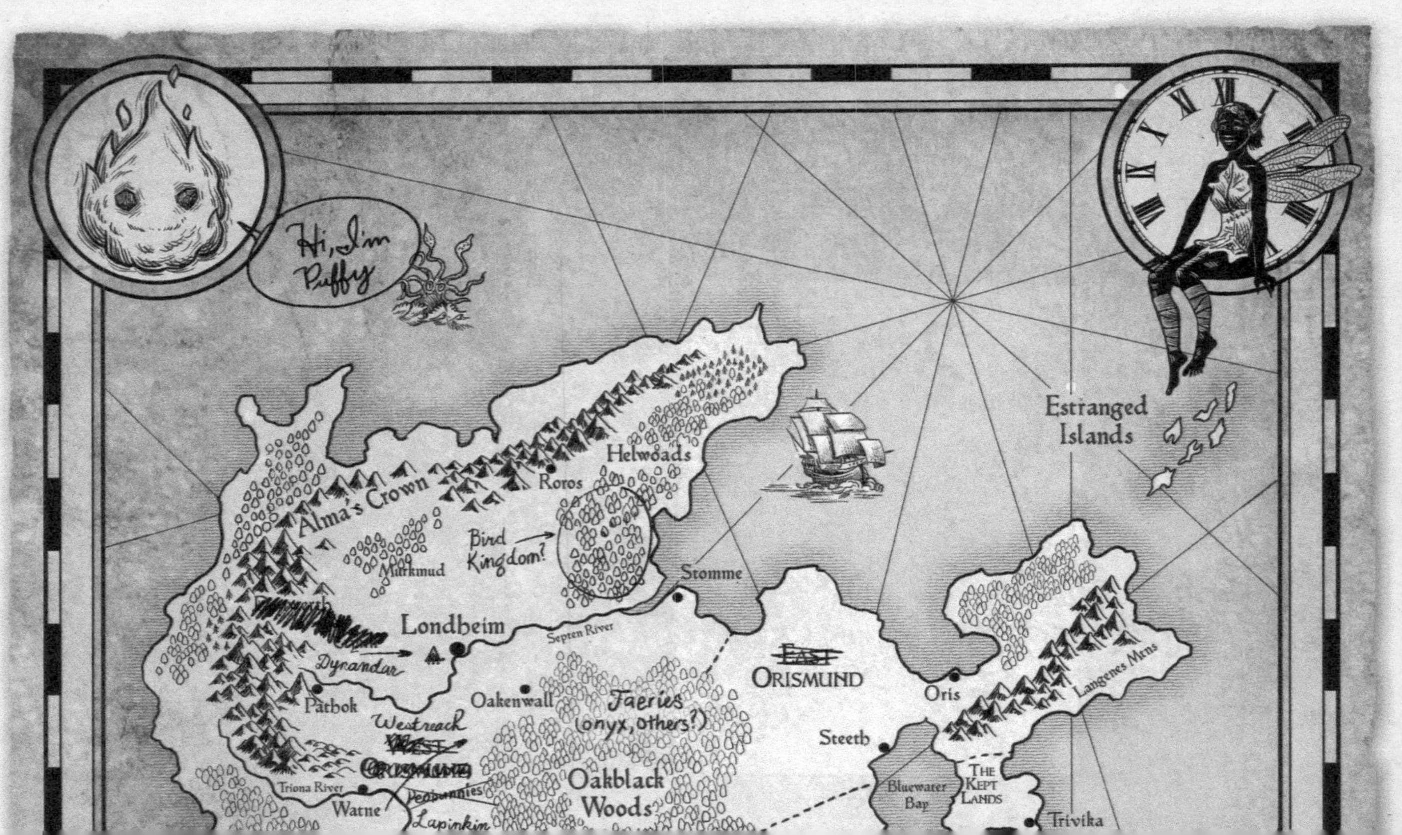

Hi, I'm Puffy
Estranged Islands
Alma's Crown
Roros
Helwoads
Bird Kingdom?
Murkmud
Stomme
Londheim
Septen River
Dyrandar
Pathok
Oakenwall
Faeries (onyx, others?)
East
ORISMUND
Oris
Langenes Mtns
Westreach
West
ORISMUND
Steeth
Triona River
Watne
Peabunnies
Lapinkin
Oakblack Woods
Bluewater Bay
The Kept Lands
Trivika

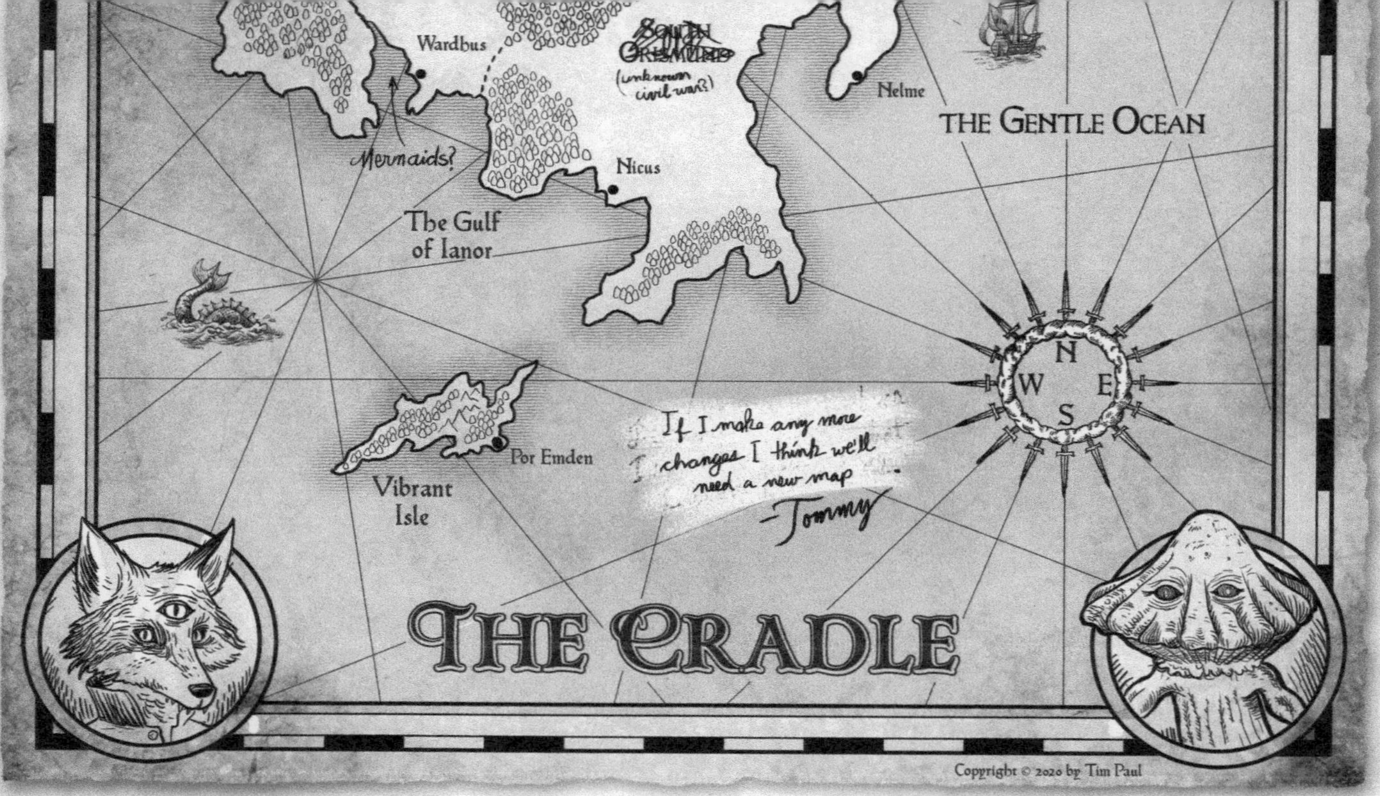
Wardbus
(unknown civil war?)
Nelme
THE GENTLE OCEAN
Mermaids?
Nicus
The Gulf of Ianor
N
W
E
S
If I make any more changes I think we'll need a new map
-Tommy
Por Emden
Vibrant Isle
THE CRADLE

CHAPTER 1

Sweat rolled down Brittany Eveson's neck and forehead, little rivulets stinging her eyes on their way to the tip of her nose. With her every push-up, the growing drops would shake and fall to join the puddle beneath her.

Fifty-eight. Fifty-nine. Sixty.

Her arms burned like fire. Her heart hammered inside her chest. Both sensations kept her body rising and lowering above the stone floor of her room. More drops fell, growing the puddle. She'd have wiped her face with her shirt, but it'd be pointless. The cloth was already soaked through with sweat.

Sixty-five. Sixty-six.

On sixty-seven, her shaking arms collapsed. She landed chest first upon the floor with a thud. With her eyes closed and her cheek pressed to the cold stone, she softly groaned. Just a little break, she told herself. Just a moment to catch her breath.

A knock on the door opened her eyes. Had she slept? She honestly didn't know. Time seemed to flow weirdly in this room of hers.

"One moment," she said.

Vertigo washed over her the moment she spoke. Brittany clenched her hands into fists and rode it out. Things had improved over the past week, but it still unnerved her when she spoke and heard a distinctly foreign voice coming from her throat.

You'll get used to it in time, Adria had told her during one of their many private sessions. Maybe so, but never completely. One didn't forget the sound of their own voice.

It took longer than she'd anticipated to get to her feet. Her arms didn't want to cooperate. Sixty-seven push-ups and already her body was ready to call it quits. What a joke.

"Come in," Brittany said when she finally opened the door. Adria stood on the other side with her hands clasped behind her back. Even with her face hidden behind her black-and-white mask, there was no mistaking her. An elaborate jewel-encrusted silver pendant hung from her neck, a triangle with a bright daytime sun in the top-right corner. That pendant marked her as Vikar of the Day, a rank she was temporarily filling while Londheim awaited the election of a new Deakon to appoint an official replacement.

"Shouldn't you be wearing a white suit?" Brittany asked. She turned from the door and pulled off her soaked shirt. The church's novices kept a small basket in the corner for her dirty clothes, and she tossed her shirt into it while opening a drawer of her lone dresser. Her options weren't many, just a few pieces in various shades of gray. Adria kept offering to take her on a trip to some clothing shops, which Brittany flatly refused. She'd not left this small, square room since her very first day back from...from her own grave, really. Was there any other way to put it?

"I only recently had my measurements taken with a church-approved tailor," Adria said. "It will take some time, and truthfully, I'm not sure how happy I will be to leave my dress behind."

Brittany grabbed a shirt at random and turned. Adria's eyes quickly looked to the floor, which earned her a derisive snort as Brittany pulled it over her head.

"They're just tits, Adria. For Sisters' sake, they're not even mine."

Those brown eyes snapped back up to hers.

"You shouldn't refer to your physical body as belonging to another. I believe it will slow your integration."

"Acknowledging this isn't my body is the only thing keeping me sane," Brittany argued. "*My* body was capable of one hundred push-ups and sit-ups without rest. This one is skinny, weak, and better suited to wielding a dagger than my axe. Speaking of, have you made any progress in bringing me a replacement? It'd help with my practice."

Adria gestured to the cramped room. It was four walls, a bed, a lidded chamber pot, a dirty clothes basket, and a dresser. Nothing fancy, but given the purported destruction of the Cathedral of the Sacred Mother, everyone was making do with significantly less finery these days.

"And how would you swing it without carving grooves into the walls?" the Vikar asked.

Brittany shrugged.

"Fine. Get me a sword, and maybe I'll leave this room more often. That's what you want, isn't it?"

"What I want is for you to start living."

"And how exactly do I go about that when I'm stuck with these?" She gestured to the chain tattoos across her throat, placed upon the body when the woman was a young soulless. "How might I explain away this? Sorry, inquisitive guard, I'm not soulless. I'm actually a recently deceased person hopping into a new body, but I understand the confusion."

"Must you sound so bitter? I'm looking into solutions. Surely something minor as wearing a scarf or disguise is worth this new chance at life?"

Brittany's mind flicked through ideas of what that new life might even mean. Patrolling as a Soulkeeper again? Moving back in with Devin in the home they'd shared? Or perhaps joining Bailey and Hanna on their trip to the Winding Gardens, obediently carrying her younger siblings' things while...

No, wrong, wrong, she thought, her insides churning hard enough that she grabbed the dresser to steady herself. *Tommy is your brother. Tommy, not Bailey, not Hanna.*

Her spell did not go unnoticed. Adria reached for her hand, only to have it brushed away.

"Are the memories still confusing you?" she asked, showing no sign of being upset by the rejection.

"It's getting better," Brittany said. She rubbed at her eyes, as if she could scrub away her frustrations. "Not at night, though. When I dream, I dream of this body's past. She might have been soulless, but she had a name, and a family. I can almost feel myself going numb and falling into that past persona. It's . . . disconcerting."

"The physical body creates and stores memories and emotions," Adria said. "The soul does likewise, but for a permanent remembrance, and therefore it is much stronger. The life your soul lived will slowly burn out the old existence."

"You make it sound like I'm murdering the previous owner. Don't talk like that again. It's creepy." She glared at the mask. "And take that thing off. I'm family, not one of your subjects needing prayers."

Adria put a hand to the bottom of her porcelain mask but then hesitated. Brittany crossed her arms, and her expression made it clear there'd be no more conversation until it was gone.

"If it will make you feel better," her sister-in-law said at last. She pulled the mask off, revealing her pale face and shadowed eyes. Errant strands of hair clung to her cheek and neck. Brittany fought to suppress a reflexive wince.

"You're not sleeping well, are you?"

"Is it your turn to aid me?" Adria asked, a small smile curling the sides of her mouth.

"If not me, I hope someone else is. You look worse than I do, and I'm recently back from the dead."

"It's merely stress. Others suffer far worse than I."

"Others suffering doesn't mean you should also suffer."

"You're right. It means I should work that much harder to stop those others from suffering."

Brittany laughed.

"I was thinking it meant you should take a nap every now and then, but you've always been the hardest worker among us. No wonder you're acting Vikar. Well, that, and the ability to resurrect people probably played a hand in it."

Adria visibly cringed at the remark. For whatever reason, she didn't like it when Brittany commented on her newfound abilities. There was surely a reason for that, but Adria was more elusive than a barn mouse about how or why. On the third day of Brittany's renewed life, Adria had spent several hours detailing some of the changes that had happened upon the Cradle. The stories sounded insane, of gargoyles and lapinkin, crawling mountains and time-controlling faeries living in forest villages. Wildest of all, her younger brother supposedly could wield magical spells. The image of her kindhearted Tommy roasting enemies with fire seemed so ridiculous, she couldn't help but laugh when Adria told her.

"It's true," Adria had insisted.

"Oh, I know," Brittany had told her. "Any other time, I might have doubted you, but I'm sitting here in a stranger's body. There's not much room to doubt."

Adria had spent the fourth day discussing the more recent events in Londheim, and of the newly renamed Westreach in general. She spoke of the madman named Janus, a magical renegade group known as the Forgotten Children conquering the district of Low Dock, and of the grand cathedral's burning. In all these stories, Adria remained vague about her own capabilities, suggesting that her prayers to the Goddesses were more powerful than the other keepers'.

Her self-imposed break over, Brittany returned to the floor. She bent her knees, put her hands behind her head, and began her sit-ups. It hurt like the void, and it might take multiple sessions, but damn it, she was going to hit her one hundred before the day's end. Adria watched quietly for a minute, the silence not entirely unwelcome. Sometimes Brittany caught her tired sister-in-law whispering little prayers whenever she thought it unnoticed. Anxiety Brittany didn't even know she had would ease, and it'd seem like her memories would clear from the fog surrounding them. It never lasted more than an hour or two, but it was a welcome reprieve despite the guilt she felt for needing help from her exhausted, overworked sister-in-law.

"Is there anything else you need?" Adria asked once her hidden prayer was finished.

"Some books might be nice. Are the Tomms Brothers still printing their weekly news leaflets?"

"They are."

Brittany's body shook for a moment and then she collapsed onto her side, having not yet reached fifty. She gasped in lungfuls of air while wishing for the millionth time that the previous owner had commanded the soulless to run the occasional mile to keep in shape.

"I wouldn't mind a few of those to read," she said after collecting herself. "It'd be nice to catch up on what's been happening while I lingered in a grave for... how long was I dead, actually?"

"I'll look into acquiring some," Adria said, pointedly ignoring the question. "As for your axe, I suppose I could ask Devin if he kept your old one after... well..."

"My what? My first death? My temporary funeral? What should we call it, Adria? It'd help if we settled on a term so you stopped dancing around it like I'm some fragile child. I was dead. Now I'm not. It won't hurt my feelings to acknowledge that fact."

A hard smirk crossed Adria's face.

"Fine. I will ask Devin if he kept your axe after he buried you, or if he returned it to the sacred division because he couldn't bear the sight of it. Is that better?"

"Much."

Brittany shifted so she was sideways. Too much time focusing on her arms and abdominal muscles lately. Had to work the rest of her as well. She balanced on one foot and hand, then lifted and lowered her hips. Within seconds her sides were burning.

"You haven't told Devin, have you?" she asked. Her gaze lingered on the dirty space beneath her bed, as if she weren't interested in the answer. She didn't know who she was fooling, though. The only thing keeping her going over the past week of nonstop drills and exercises was the thought of seeing him again... yet perversely an overwhelming fear of meeting him was why she had not left her room.

"It is not my place to do so," Adria said. She slipped her mask over her face and tightened the strings behind her head. "Take all the time you need, and don't rush yourself."

Brittany switched to her other side. Lift and lower. Steady, rhythmic movements. The only part of life still under her control.

"You're yet to give me an answer," she said. "How long was I dead?"

Adria crossed her arms, no doubt frowning behind that black-and-white porcelain mask.

"I think you should be in a better mind-set before learning this."

"I've seen your face, Adria. I know it's been years. I just want to know how many."

The woman sighed.

"Six. Six years."

Even braced for the knowledge, she still felt stabbed in the gut. Six long years for everyone she'd known, and yet only the blink of an eye for her. Precious Goddesses above, Tommy was almost as old as she, in a sense. And if that much time had passed...

"Has he moved on?" she asked, halting her exercises. She struggled to force the question out in the foreign voice created by the stranger's tongue inside her mouth. "Has he found someone else?"

The soft fall of Adria's shoulders gave the answer long before her words confirmed it.

"Yes," she said. "I believe he has."

Brittany swallowed down a sudden lump in her throat.

"Good," she said. "Good for him." Damn it, these stupid tears. She didn't want them. She didn't want any of this. "Does...does he know how I died?"

Adria's head tilted the slightest amount.

"We were told you died of heart failure."

Still a secret, then. Brittany couldn't decide if that was a blessing or a curse. Perhaps both.

"I'd like to be alone for a while," she said, pointedly dropping the subject.

"Of course." Adria dipped as if bowing to a superior and then turned for the door. Helpless frustration pushed Brittany to ask one last question before her sister-in-law might leave.

"Why did you bring me back?" she asked. "Why give me this body, this life, if he doesn't even need me anymore? My time was done, Adria. My life, my pain, my loving and living and dying, it was *done*."

Even with her mask to hide behind, Adria could not bring herself to turn and face her.

"I thought it was the right thing to do," she said.

"Do you still believe that?"

Adria said the only answer Brittany would have accepted.

She said nothing.

CHAPTER 2

Devin's optimism dropped into his shoes as he stepped through the door. Though it had once been a bedroom, the four-poster bed had been removed and replaced with a long oak table. Vikar Caria and Vikar Forrest sat at the table's opposite side, neither one looking particularly pleased. The sight of silk curtains, ornate dressers, and a towering mirror behind them would have been comical if not for the dire expression on their faces. If Devin looked out the curtained window, he could catch a glimpse of the charred walls that had surrounded the cathedral's exterior.

"Have a seat, Devin," Forrest said.

An empty padded chair waited for him directly across from the Vikars.

"Given how this feels more akin to a tribunal, I think I'd rather stand." He kept his hands burrowed into the pockets of his leather coat, feigning relaxed confidence. Ever since the cathedral fire, the leadership of the church had been scattered among a handful of homes and buildings generously offered to them by Londheim's wealthy. Devin currently met with the Vikars in a mansion belonging to a family who made their wealth from rope and leather factories near the docks. The mansion's proximity to the destroyed cathedral made it a convenient headquarters for the leadership of the church to use as they organized their rebuilding efforts.

"It wasn't a suggestion."

Devin flinched. It was never pleasant being on Forrest's bad side. But now his Vikar had turned the situation into a direct challenge. He could refuse it, of course, a scenario unthinkable a few weeks ago. But now his sister was acting Vikar of the Day, and more importantly, she was practically worshipped by the people of Londheim. Neither Vikar could afford to have Adria as an enemy if they were to maintain the city's precarious peace.

"If you insist," Devin said, and he slid into the chair. He shifted his coat so that his sword and pistol were clearly visible. Proper behavior would have had him disarm himself before an official meeting with his superiors. Given how said superiors had kept the reason for the meeting a secret when sending a novice requesting his presence, Devin felt it was a small but satisfying disregard of tradition.

He leaned back in the chair and said nothing as the silence stretched on and on, growing increasingly uncomfortable. He had no intention of making this easy on his Vikars. His gut told him exactly what this meeting would be about, and he didn't like it one bit.

"I understand your feelings will be complicated in regards to this matter," Forrest said after coughing to clear his throat. His blond hair, normally kept back in a neat ponytail, hung loose about his face. The muscular man wore the traditional Soulkeeper uniform instead of the black suit worn by a Vikar. It certainly hung easier on his muscled frame. *Was his suit lost in the cathedral fire?* Devin wondered. Or did he anticipate a battle with Devin and need the freedom of movement? Devin's eyes flicked to the enormous axe leaning against the table beside Forrest. Not a good sign.

" 'Complicated' is one way to describe it," Devin said. "I assume we are to talk about Adria?"

"We are," Vikar Caria said. She looked even worse off than

Forrest. The circles underneath her eyes darkened her brown skin so that she looked like she'd lost a bare-knuckle fight. "Given everything we've both heard and witnessed, it's clear we are ignorant of much about your sister's abilities. We'd like you to remedy that as best you can."

Devin dug his heels into the carpet so he could rock his chair back and forth a few inches.

"There's an easier way to obtain this information," he said. "You could ask Adria herself, yet you haven't. Why is that, my Vikars? Do you believe she'd lie to you? Or... are you afraid of her?"

"One of our Faithkeepers is resurrecting the dead," Forrest said. "Curiosity is only natural. Now less attitude and more answers, Devin."

The chair creaked as he lowered it.

"If you want answers, you're not getting them from me, for I haven't any to give. Her power bewilders me as well."

"Where did it come from?" Caria asked. "The spectacle we witnessed at the cathedral was far beyond any healing or protective prayers other keepers have exhibited. Did it emerge naturally with the newly awakened world, or was it given to her?"

"More like forced upon her," Devin said. "Unasked for, and unwanted, I assure you. The monster we hunted by the name of Janus captured her, and it was by his magic she received this power."

The eyes of both Vikars lit up. It seemed neither had believed he would share as much as he already had.

"So it was given to her by the dragon-sired," Caria said. "Not the Sisters?"

And now Devin realized why he should just keep his mouth shut. That fact alone could be used against his sister.

"So far as I understand it," he said. "Which isn't much. The power to manipulate souls belongs solely to the Sisters, and nothing I have seen contradicts that belief. Though the gift was given to her by a dragon-sired, Adria wields the power of the Goddesses in some shape or form. Of that, I am certain."

"But to what end?" Forrest asked. "And for what purpose?"

"Is that rhetorical?"

"None of this is rhetorical," Caria snapped. "Your sister is already acting Vikar of the Day after Thaddeus's death, and will likely keep that post once we elect a new Deakon. Knowing what she is, and what she's become, is of vital importance. If you were truly loyal in your faith to the church, you'd understand that."

Devin ground his teeth together to halt his initial response, which would have been far too crude for addressing his superiors.

"So my faith is now in question," he said. "Any other surprises you'd like to spring on me while the day is young?"

"Ditch the attitude," Forrest said. "We witnessed the resurrection of one hundred lives. Our flocks are hailing it as a modern miracle, worthy of praise alongside the Sisters themselves. Thousands flirt with the edges of blasphemy. Our people are frightened, our city under siege, and our sacred buildings aflame. This time is ripe for false prophets to steal glory from the Sisters and cast it upon themselves. So if Adria views herself as a bringer of some new holy scriptures, we'd like to know, preferably *before* she becomes appointed to lead the entire church of West Orismund."

"You mean Westreach," Devin said, unable to help himself.

Forrest's glare could melt steel.

"Unbelievable," he muttered.

"Listen well," Caria said, forging on in an attempt at diplomacy. "We are merely curious as to your sister's intentions. Will she be placated with an appointment as Vikar, or will she press to become the new Deakon of Londheim? It's unheard of someone receiving either position at so young an age, but these are hardly normal times, and Adria is no normal candidate."

"You use subterfuge and whispers when a straightforward approach would suffice," Devin said. "I hate to repeat myself, but if you want to know my sister's intentions, then ask her. I am not her keeper, and she is not one to lie. If I may be so bold, this meeting, and your questions, lead me to believe you fear her power, you fear her ambitions, and you are looking for reasons to act against her. So forgive me, my Vikars, but I will give you none."

Forrest's chair creaked as he stood. His hand drifted to the handle of his axe.

"May I remind you that we could send you back to prison if we wished," he said quietly. "You have been given no formal trial, and your current freedom is conditional only on our good graces."

Devin hated this, hated everything about his current situation, but he couldn't show weakness. If he were honest with himself, he was also sick of all the horseshit.

"Then do it," he said, rising to his feet. "I've bled and killed to protect Londheim and its people, and I fought alongside both of you when the dragon-sired burned down the cathedral. Your accusations of treason are false, and you both know it. But please, by all means, toss me in prison for crimes I haven't committed. Let us see how long it is until Adria smashes down its walls to set me free."

Vikar Caria slammed her gloved hands atop the table.

"You would flaunt our authority due to your sister's popularity?" she asked.

"The positions of Vikar and Deakon have always been based on popularity," Devin said. "Consider me upholding tradition."

He spun and stormed for the door.

"Halt," Forrest ordered. Devin's hands settled atop his weapons as he turned back to the Vikars.

"Yes, my Vikar?" he asked softly.

"Your dalliances with dragon-sired may be forgivable, but the actions of your apparent lover, Jacaranda, are not," Caria said. "She must still undergo trial for the murders at the Gentle Rose Brothel. You may be found innocent, but will she?"

Devin's jaw twitched. His hands tightened about his pistol and sword. Memories flashed through his mind of an injured Jacaranda stumbling into his home, her clothes splashed with blood that wasn't hers.

"If you come for her," he said, his voice ice, "it won't just be Adria standing in your way."

"Noted," Forrest snapped. "Consider yourself on leave for the time being, Devin. I don't want to count someone so insolent among my Soulkeepers' ranks."

Devin bowed long and low to the both of them.

"Fucking fine with me."

CHAPTER 3

Jacaranda was caught off guard by the anger in Devin's movements as he slammed shut the door to his home and stormed immediately into the kitchen. Puffy elongated within the fireplace and lifted one beady eye higher than the other.

I don't know, she mouthed to the firekin as she rose from the couch. She found Devin in the kitchen ripping the cork out of a bottle of wine, not caring for the mess that splashed across his floor.

"What's wrong?" she asked, putting a hand on his arm.

"I'm currently on leave," he said. "And I deserve it, too, for being an idiot and threatening my own Vikar."

"You threatened him?" she asked. "Why?"

"Because of you," he said, and she winced. His tone immediately softened. "Sorry, sorry. It's not your fault. This whole situation's gone diving into the gutter and I'm desperately trying to tread water lest I be drowned in shit."

Devin put the bottle to his lips and drank. Wine dripped out the sides of his mouth and ran down his neck. Jacaranda bit her tongue to prevent herself from scolding him. Something had gone terribly wrong, and she would let him blow off steam however he needed to.

"Better," he said after pulling back the bottle and gasping in a breath. "Not much, but better."

He retreated to his chair by the fireplace, and Jacaranda followed.

"I'm all right, I promise," Devin said upon seeing Puffy's worried head poke out from the fireplace.

"I'm not sure either of us believe you," Jacaranda said as she leaned against the wall with her arms crossed. "How about you start from the beginning before that bottle's empty and your memory is shot?"

"If you insist," he said. She listened as he recalled the surprise meeting with his two Vikars, and he spared no kind words for his opinion on that matter. Less amusing was when he switched to Devin's and Jacaranda's arrests prior to the dragon-sired attack on the cathedral.

"Do you think they're bluffing?" she asked. "Or will they risk Adria's anger and come for us both?"

"I think I'm in the clear," Devin said. He tipped the bottle her way. "Besides being Adria's brother, it's ridiculous to claim I conspired with the dragon-sired after fighting against them during the attack. You, on the other hand, are in a far trickier situation."

"I shouldn't be. Adria can prove the existence of my soul in mere moments."

"I'm not talking about that," he said. "No, much more damning now are the accusations of you murdering people at the Gentle Rose Brothel. Normally I'd scoff, but I remember the shape you were in when you came home. What happened that night? I've tried to respect your privacy, but at some point my Vikars will force this situation to a head. I'd like to know I'm on the right side."

"You'll be on *my* side," she said. "Why would that not be enough?"

"Jac, I love you, but that doesn't mean I'll turn a blind eye to everything you do. Not if you're murdering innocent people."

Jacaranda tried to see things from his angle, but she couldn't shake the feeling she was being judged. Of course he'd be upset if she were wantonly killing. Would it be right to expect him to cover for her? To sacrifice his beliefs to protect her? No, she didn't think it would be, but no matter how much she told herself that, it remained bitter in her stomach, and the words rang hollow.

"Yes, I was there at that brothel," she said. She hesitated, wanting to know how Devin would react. "Yes, I performed the killings."

She should have never doubted.

"What did they do to you?" he asked softly.

"One of the bed warmers," she said. "He worked with Gerag by testing the soulless to keep their training sharp after they were sold. The other two were guards who tried to stop me from fleeing."

She left out the parts of her going to the brothel to work out her fears and paranoias about intimacy. Devin didn't need to know any of that, certainly not while he was angry and halfway through a wine bottle.

"I swear Gerag's rottenness seeped everywhere," he said with a sigh, and slumped deeper into his chair.

You have no idea, thought Jacaranda, her mind flashing to the dark corridor beneath the Sisters' Remembrance, and the hideous, cursed form imprisoned there.

"Will the Vikars bring me to trial?" she asked.

"I don't know. They're threatening it. Based on what you've told me, I think there's a decent chance that, if you admit to everything, they would be willing to extend mercy given the bed warmer's involvement in Gerag's crimes. There's still the guards, though, the poor bastards."

Jacaranda took the bottle from Devin's grasp and downed a few burning chugs of her own. She needed to keep her guilt at bay, and both alcohol and anger were wonders in that regard.

"I will admit nothing to them," she said upon handing it back. "I hold no faith in your Vikars' judgments."

"They're good, honorable people," Devin said, suddenly defensive. The shift in his behavior was quick and subtle. There was a degree of separation between them, she a person outside the church, criticizing those like him within. Did he even realize it, she wondered, or was it merely a reflex built up over a lifetime of service to the Sisters?

"Good people," Jacaranda said. A mirthless laugh escaped her lips. "Devin, do you know why I wasn't imprisoned in the room next to yours when the cathedral battle started? Vikar Thaddeus had me brought to his chambers in secret, where he then offered me drugged tea."

Devin's entire body froze as if he had been carved of marble. "Thaddeus tried to drug you?"

Jacaranda hesitated. She'd not told Devin of how she'd escaped the cathedral, of Thaddeus's betrayal, and of killing Gerag's cursed form underneath the Sisters' Remembrance. That moment of sliding the knife along his wrists, of taking the life from the sick, twisted master who had dominated so much of her existence, had felt deeply personal to her. She'd only told Devin one night that she'd found Gerag. All else she promised to tell in time, once she was ready.

It seemed now she was.

"Your sick Vikar tried more than that," she said. Her stomach clenched at the foul memory. "He tried to curse me with the Book of Ravens. Thaddeus was the hidden link we were looking for. He was the wealthy buyer that kidnapped Gerag. One of your good and honorable Vikars tried to drug and execute me to hide the fact he bought soulless from Gerag to serve as his little sexual playthings. I cut his throat for it, and then I went below the Sisters' Remembrance, where a mutilated Gerag was being held prisoner, and I bled him out as well."

"Thaddeus, working with Gerag?" Devin asked. His mind appeared to have ceased functioning properly. "Why... why didn't you tell me any of this?"

"Because I feared how you would react," she said. "I killed

Thaddeus to escape, killed one of the highest members of your church. At what point do you stop forgiving me, Devin? Lucky for me, the fire claimed that bastard's body, though I consider that a tainted blessing. It has been a special form of torture listening to the faithful praying in the streets for Thaddeus's 'kind soul,' his 'devout nature,' and his 'honorable sacrifice.'" She spat the words out with greater and greater relish. "No one will know the true extent of his perversions. Lucky him, I suppose. He dies pure in the eyes of the church, the same church that would have me punished for killing a bed warmer in league with Gerag's underground trade."

Her blood was boiling now, the words tumbling out of her mouth as fast as they entered her mind. She found her hands clenched into fists, and they shook at her sides.

"I don't care what your Vikars think," she said. "I don't care if they're upset, or if they want to imprison me a second time. I know you rely on the Sisters and the church for strength, but so far they have only brought me misery. I guess that's to be expected, though, isn't it? Until a few weeks ago, the Sisters didn't even know I existed."

"That's not true," Devin started, but she would not be there to hear the rest of his argument. Jacaranda grabbed a thick coat by the door and flung it on as she burst out into the cold. At least her white scarf wouldn't stand out. Jacaranda walked without a destination, only needing the movement to keep the fuming frustration from overwhelming her entire body.

Once she exited the Church District, and more and more people joined her upon the cold cobblestone, she felt her nerves cooling. Devin was in an impossible situation and, by his own admission, had just cursed out his superior for threatening her. What more could she expect of him? Actual bloodshed?

"It's not his fault," she muttered as she walked between shuttered stores and boarded-up doorways. "You're the one who killed the bed warmer, not him. You could have left. You could have let him live." An older woman bundled in layers cast her a strange look as she walked past. Jacaranda's hand slipped to her scarf on instinct, confirming its presence.

You're talking to yourself, that's all, she thought. She wondered if her suspicion and fear would ever truly subside, or if she'd spend the rest of her life waiting for her chain tattoo to be exposed.

Jacaranda checked her pocket for coins and found them empty. Damn it, a bite of warm food sounded amazing right now, but it was either steal it or return home to grab her coin purse from her room. Her frown deepened at the thought of either action. Stealing from those themselves struggling with the besieged Londheim felt wrong, yet returning to Devin? That likely meant apologizing for storming out, but damn it, was it wrong for her to be angry? Couldn't she rage? Devin had come home smashing apart a bottle to drown himself in alcohol, and he wasn't even the one the church was threatening with imprisonment.

Jacaranda's gait quickened. Forget it. Let the cold air cool her temper. Despite the lack of money, she drifted to the nearest little market, pretending to be interested in what few wares were available. When she'd finished there, she moved on to the next, letting the hours pass in solitude. The time allowed her to digest the news, and frustrating as it might be knowing the church would use her against Devin and Adria, they'd need to prepare for another arrest. They couldn't rely on Adria's popularity and authority forever.

Perhaps it was her training, perhaps it was her constant paranoia, but within moments she realized she was being followed. The young, dark-skinned woman was eyeing her while trying to pretend otherwise. Whenever Jacaranda moved to the next stall, this woman inevitably moved on within moments. Jacaranda stole a single glance, but what little she could see of the woman's face brought back no memories.

What game are you playing?

Jacaranda had not grabbed her weapons before leaving, a misstep that weighed heavily on her as she shifted her path. That meant relying on surprise to be her weapon. She pretended to be finished shopping and made for the exit. Sure enough, the woman followed. Instead of returning home, Jacaranda continued westward for another two blocks, picking locations carefully.

There, a relatively wide alleyway and without too much clutter so she could move about. She turned and slowed her steps. It was quiet here, and far from prying eyes. If the woman tailing her planned an attack, it'd be here and now. The sound of Jacaranda's boots upon the stone echoed in her ears, her every sense flaring active in anticipation. Closer now, she could feel her unwelcome shadow hurrying closer, the hairs on her neck lifting up as she heard another pair of footsteps dashing in.

At the last possible second she spun, her left hand shooting out to catch the assailant's wrist, halting the striking motion of her dagger. Her shadow let out a frightened cry just before Jacaranda's other arm smashed into her throat. The woman staggered backward, or at least, she tried. Jacaranda refused to release her other hand, not while it still held a dagger. A quick jerk, a painful twist, and the weapon fell to the cobblestones.

"Damn you," the woman croaked as she stumbled backward. "Let me go!"

Jacaranda did, not at her request, but out of shock. Her elbow to the throat had dislodged her attacker's cloak wrapping about her neck, revealing the tattooed skin beneath.

The *chain* tattoos beneath.

"You were soulless," Jacaranda said.

"You should know," the woman spat. She looked torn between fleeing and lunging in an attack with her balled fists. "You dragged me to my new owner."

This woman was one of Gerag's, she realized. One of the soulless she herself had trained and escorted during her time as the bastard's special chosen.

"You don't understand," Jacaranda insisted. "I didn't have a choice."

"Liar," the woman snapped. "You always had a choice."

"No," Jacaranda said, and she pulled down her scarf to reveal her own tattoos. "*I didn't.*"

With Londheim battened down as if expecting a siege, it wasn't difficult for the two to find a quiet place to talk. Devin would likely have approved of the location, for it was atop the flattened roof of a home adjacent to the market district. Unlike Devin's roof, this place was meant for visitors, with faded tarp drawn across thick wood poles to form an awning. Jacaranda sat in one of the wood stools while her ambusher paced on the opposite side of the weathered square table.

"I didn't think it was possible," her ambusher, Wren, said with a heavy shake of her head. She'd introduced herself once they'd found their spot. "I kept an ear open for any rumors of other soulless awakening, but I never heard much beyond a few strange occurrences in the east. Certainly nothing here in Londheim."

"That's because the church worked to keep it that way," Jacaranda said. She suppressed a bitter wave of bile that crawled up her throat upon remembering Thaddeus's grotesque speech when he thought her paralyzed from her tea. She forced her thoughts to the woman pacing before her. Wren was small, even for a woman, and her round face looked destined to forever be described as baby-like, a fact not helped by her enormous umber eyes. Her pale shirt was tightly buttoned and tucked into a thick gray skirt that hung down to her ankles. She wore a thin cloak of similar color, which was fastened at the top to hide her tattoos.

It had confused Jacaranda at first that she didn't remember bringing a younger Wren to her owner. After a few minutes of watching her pace, she'd realized Wren was a recast woman, and that her long, tightly braided hair was a wig. *What had her name been back then?* Jacaranda wondered. Aaren? Warren? Something like that. Knowing this allowed her to remember that trip to a small house tucked into the southwest corner of Londheim, to an old man with graying hair and a white frosting of stubble across his cheeks and chin.

"What did your..." Jacaranda caught herself before she finished the thought. She'd meant to say "owner," but she knew all too well how much that description would burn. "What did your former controller do when it happened?"

"Grandpa was mostly just confused," she said. She stumbled over the word "Grandpa," not to Jacaranda's surprise.

"Did he want you to call him Grandpa?"

Wren answered with a nod.

"From what I've put together since awakening, he didn't take his grandson's death all too well. One of his children bought me to play-act as a replacement. Gra...Kennet's mind is not sound. Within a day or two of my playing the part, he believed I was his grandson, Warren. When my soul returned, he thought I was having some sort of seizure. When I refused to act the role of his grandson, it nearly broke him. He accused me of being a gremlin who stole away his boy so I might take his place."

Jacaranda listened intently, intrigued by Wren's emotions. Wren lacked the rage Jacaranda had felt for her previous master. When she spoke of her grandpa, her words were mostly filled with pity. Of course, she'd been treated like a beloved grandson. Not like Jacaranda. Not like a personal, sexual plaything.

"Is he still alive?" she asked.

Wren leaned against one of the awning poles. Her fingers absently traced the curls of her black hair. It was a very fine wig, Jacaranda thought, and almost certainly stolen based on the cheap quality of Wren's other clothing.

"Kennet never hurt me," Wren said softly. "I doubt he knew I was soulless. I was just his grandson, his perfect little well-behaved grandson..." Her eyes flicked up to meet Jacaranda's. "My anger isn't for him. It's for those who sold me. Who trained me. I thought you one of them, but I was wrong. That still leaves Gerag. Where is he, Jacaranda? Where is that miserable prick?"

"Why is it you hate him so?" Jacaranda asked. She couldn't help but compare Wren's situation to hers. A coddled life confused for a dead grandson, versus her time as a sexual teacher and plaything? How could Wren's situation compare? "The fate he sold you to was a kindness compared to what most of us experienced."

Wren froze for a moment, then exploded. Her heel smashed the side of the table between them, toppling it.

"A kindness?" she asked, her voice cracking. "A *kindness*? Do you think my training was so innocent as that? Do you think Gerag ever gave a shit about what I was meant for, or who I was going to? Oh, he knew, Jacaranda, he knew, and it only made him that much worse."

She crossed the gap and grabbed Jacaranda's shirt with shaking fingers. Jacaranda's spine went rigid, and she clenched her jaw to prevent herself from reacting. Wren leaned closer, their noses nearly touching. Her voice dropped to a strained whisper.

"'*What a pretty boy*,' he told me. '*I'd hate for such a pretty boy to go to waste*.' It may have just been once, but I remember it, Jacaranda. I remember it with a searing clarity that won't go away no matter how hard I try. I remember it when I sleep. I remember it when I get dressed. I remember it when I walk about Londheim with my tattoos hidden beneath my cloak. *What a pretty boy.* I want him dead. I *need* him dead. Where is he, Jacaranda? His mansion's burned down, and I hear he's gone missing, but I know he's hiding somewhere. So where is he? Tell me. Tell me, so I can kill him!"

"I can't," Jacaranda said softly.

"Why not? Why would you protect him from me?"

"Because he's already dead. *I* killed him."

Jacaranda had not lifted a finger in defense, yet Wren staggered away as if struck.

"Dead?" she asked. "Then... what about Belford?"

Belford had been Gerag's personal butler and assistant to the training. Jacaranda had shot him through the mouth during her and Devin's failed attempt to rescue another awakened soulless, Marigold.

"Dead as well," she said. "Both at my hand."

Wren's hands balled into fists and then released. Her head swept side to side. Finally she settled into the chair she'd neglected the entire conversation. Her pent-up energy seeped out of her with a visible relaxation of her muscles from head to toe.

"Both dead," she said. "So then there's no one left."

"I'm sorry," Jacaranda said. "I understand your need for revenge. I felt it myself. Gerag died horribly cursed and disfigured, if you find comfort in knowing that."

"Comfort," Wren said. She spat the word out like a joke. "Imagining what I'd do to them is what kept me going. To find you, and learn that everyone's dead and gone... it's like the world moved on and didn't bother to tell me."

Jacaranda wished she could offer comfort. She'd been so lucky to have Devin when she awakened. Poor Wren had no one but a mentally ill old man who couldn't possibly understand what was happening.

"I'm sorry for... well, everything," Jacaranda said, and she chuckled. "Not that it'll do much good. Where are you staying at now? Please tell me you're not sleeping on the street."

"No," Wren said. "I mean, I did, but not anymore. A recast man found me and offered me a home while I needed it."

"That was decent of him. I have a feeling we former soulless will be relying on the kindness of others for many years to come. I'm glad someone lent you aid. And Wren..."

Jacaranda slowly reached across the table, knowing she had to offer Wren plenty of time to refuse. Even after all this time had passed, Jacaranda knew how difficult accepting physical touch could be for a soulless like them. How important offering that choice was. Her hands wrapped around Wren's, and when she squeezed, the other woman squeezed back.

"I'm happy to meet another," Jacaranda said. "So happy, and I will do whatever you need to help you acclimate. We're bound in a way no one else in all the Cradle understands, and I will honor it as best I know how. There may be no blood between us, but you are my sister, do you understand?"

The emotional outpouring was more than Wren was capable of handling. Little tears swelled underneath her eyes.

"Do you mean that?" Wren asked.

"I do."

"Good." She wiped her sleeve across her face. "Then will you teach me to fight?"

"To fight?" Jacaranda laughed out her surprise. "Why is that?"

"When I decided to kill Gerag, I started teaching myself how to wield a knife, and for all my training, you disarmed me and knocked me down in seconds. I want to fight like you do. And if someone ever sees my tattoos, I want to know how to defend myself. So will you?"

Jacaranda rocked her chair back and wondered what she'd gotten herself into.

"It's a deal," she said. "From this day on, consider yourself my apprentice."

CHAPTER 4

Evelyn walked the streets of Belvua, and though she often believed her heart hardened against memories of the past, she found herself lost in nostalgia as she looked upon the changes that had overcome that little corner of Londheim. Hardly a single human house remained, each and every structure having returned to the original shape before the human Goddesses cast their illusory blanket across the Cradle.

"Was it so terrible for us to live among you?" she wondered aloud as she stopped before a collection of avenria homes. They were tall black stone, the tops open and full of wide windows and gaps. They still bore a traditional door for visitors of other races, a common occurrence in those long-ago days. Evelyn stepped over the little stream of water that ran from the center of the street to the side of the home. The flowing water was a wonder that took nearly three years to build, and only with constant supervision of the normally flighty waterkin. It was a marvel of engineering, fresh drinking water flowing from a shallow groove in the center of the street to every home in Belvua. Evelyn remembered hearing how the humans had turned down offers for similar constructions throughout their city. Even during times of peace, their distrust had run deep.

A cluster of foxkin homes was next, half underground, half

above. The masters of illusion had begun re-creating the magic that had once bathed their homes, turning stone walls to thatched reeds and cracked cobbles to blooming flowers and tall brush. The whole block resembled a sudden country paradise lodged into the normally dour city. Despite the heavy covering of clouds in the sky, the garden sparkled as if it were a bright spring day. Evelyn knew it was fake but stopped to brush a collection of blue roses with her gloved fingers anyway. The cold arrival of winter meant nothing to the illusions, nor did the snow that covered much of the ground. Here it was spring, and would forever be spring so long as the owners desired it.

"My grandchildren once played here," a woman's voice said. Evelyn turned to find an old friend standing with her arms crossed over her tanned leather coat. She wore shoes similar to a human's, though the toes were cut at the ends to make room for her thick, stubby claws. Her triangular hat was pulled low over the foxkin's face, keeping hidden her closed third eye.

"As did mine," Evelyn told Aerreth Crimshield, the phantom death of Nicus. "Sometimes it seems I lived two lives, one of peace, and one of war."

"They are the same lives, for peace and war are never so separate as we wish to believe."

Aerreth joined Evelyn's side, and she knelt before the illusory garden of roses. The foxkin removed her glove, exposing her red-furred hand. The faint hint of gray claws slid across the petals. Dew fell from the disturbance, but upon hitting the ground, it faded into nothing. The illusion could only be maintained for so long.

"My family bore deep roots in the southeast," the foxkin continued. Her yellow eyes glazed over with memories. "The reason I came to Londheim was to participate in those doomed attempts at diplomacy prior to when the real bloodshed began. My grandson came with me, and he ran up and down these streets like a monster let loose. There was so much life here, even then. He'd buy a candied apple from a human vendor, he'd swim the rivers for hours, laughing with the fishermen and pretending to be caught by their nets. Queen Arondel's owls were never fond of the city, but sometimes one or two would arrive for a meeting, and my grandson would always beg for a ride above the rooftops, and no matter how noble or proud those owls were, they'd always give in to his charms."

"Your grandson sounds like a wonderful pup," Evelyn said.

"He was," the foxkin said. She stood and pulled her glove back over her hand. "The day diplomacy failed was the day humans hung him from a rope at the entrance to the city gates. Living here meant we lived among monsters. It was never wise, and it cost us dearly."

A memory of her granddaughter's lifeless form came unbidden to Evelyn's mind, and she shook it away.

"I'm sorry about your grandson," she said.

"You lost your own flesh and blood, too, Evelyn. Let us not weep for each other's losses. We will lose the entire day. Walk with me instead. There is something I would like to discuss with the bearer of Whisper-Song."

The two women traveled eastward along the road. They passed several fountains meant to house waterkin as well as feed water into the system of tributaries throughout the district. Evelyn paused for a drink, and she wondered what illusory form humanity had seen these fountains as instead. What the Goddesses could not change, they covered with illusions, if not blinded the eyes of humanity to them completely. Did the humans see a normal well? Or perhaps a more basic fountain than the grand series of interlocking pools held up by swirling marble funnels?

"The avenria were instrumental in taking Belvua back from humanity," Aerreth said after taking her own drink. "But you refused to join them. Instead you left the responsibility to your son."

"Yes, my son," Evelyn said, committing nothing.

"Whom you killed."

"You're not one for tact, are you?"

"We're both too old for that. So is it true, Evelyn? Did you kill your own son for the crime of warring against humanity?"

Evelyn rested her hands atop the hilts of Whisper and Song, an act she knew the perceptive foxkin would notice.

"I killed him for threatening to sacrifice the entire city to the void," she said. "Do not presume to know everything, Aerreth. I will not be judged by the phantom death of Nicus."

Aerreth met her gaze for the briefest moment. The foxkin woman was sharpened steel hidden beneath fur and cloth. If it came to blows, Evelyn wasn't sure who would emerge the victor. They both bore a list of victims a thousand miles long.

"Logarius held together the Forgotten Children with the strength of his personality alone," Aerreth said. "And upon his death, my son tried to take up that mantle. His reward was murder at the hands of the abomination known as Adria Eveson. The young are meant to inherit the Cradle, yet here we are, two old women thrust back into leadership. Perhaps that is the worst crime the humans committed, the theft of our future. Now only us elderly are left to weep over the loss."

"So now you lead the Forgotten Children?"

"Who else will? I had hoped my time killing was over. Perhaps it soon will be. The dragons are furious, and the Goddesses weak and absent. This isn't like the old days, Evelyn. Something new approaches. Whether we live to see it, well...we've never been guaranteed anything in this world, have we?"

It seemed the moment had passed. Evelyn withdrew her hands from her weapons, and the two resumed walking the streets of Belvua.

"Rumors claim Shinnoc approaches with an army of dragonsired," Evelyn said, shifting the subject. "What will your Forgotten

Children do when they arrive? Will you aid the attackers? Pretend at neutrality? Or will you defend the walls from your own fellow dragon-sired? You've sacrificed much to claim your corner of Londheim, yet now the Dyrandar King seeks to burn it all to the ground."

There was no hiding Aerreth's frustration as she led the way.

"I will not blame Shinnoc for his rage. Cannac's death was a tragedy, but it was a necessary tragedy. The peace he sought, and the peace he would have achieved, would only forestall the inevitable war. Will we aid Shinnoc? Perhaps, if he is willing to listen to reason. Londheim must not be destroyed, for it is not a human city, but one of dragon-sired as well. We must *claim* it. All of it. Let every brick and plank within these walls become Belvua as a message to the rest of humanity that we will have a place to call our own." The woman shook her head. "Sometimes I wonder if all the Cradle would be better if humanity kindly died off, but then I wonder if we dragon-sired would cooperate so easily if not united against humanity's gross inadequacies."

"Perhaps it is not the fault of humanity, but of the Goddesses who bless them and raise them," Evelyn said. They stopped before their apparent destination. On the outside it seemed a simple, dilapidated shed. In reality it was one of the hidden entryways into the tunnels underneath Londheim, and the machinery that the dragons had secretly built to grant power over souls to the humans. Aerreth gestured to the shed, and her voice dropped to barely above a whisper.

"There is much we do not know," the foxkin said. "But even I can sense the deep magic emanating from this place. Logarius and his avenria ventured here often, but they would not tell us the reason. You spoke of the void, and I sense its stench from these tunnels. What is it your son meddled in before his death, Evelyn? Might you tell me?"

Evelyn clicked her beak together as she thought. Aerreth was one of the finest women she'd known in her whole life. Her moniker, the phantom death, was one she'd earned over a decade in the human city of Nicus. Every night, every single damn night without fail, she had used her magic to sneak past the guards stationed at the gates, broken into the home of a powerful noble or politician, and executed them with a single cut across the throat. Never more than that one kill, but day after day, year after year, she'd killed thousands. She'd single-handedly made every human in Nicus terrified to wield a modicum of power lest they find themselves her next victim. If she commanded the Forgotten Children, then whatever goal they set upon themselves, they would achieve.

"Down in those tunnels are machinery and magic crafted by dragons," Evelyn said, deciding to share at least a portion of the truth. "It was meant to free humanity from the Goddesses, but all it did was condemn us dragon-sired. Do not go down there, Aerreth. It was not made for us. If it were in my power, I would collapse the tunnels and destroy everything they hide."

The foxkin woman nodded as she listened, and it seemed she believed her.

"Very well," she said. "I shall trust your judgment, old friend. As much as I would prefer you as my ally in this coming war, I will accept your reasons for remaining separate. Forgive me, though, if I hope you someday change your mind before humanity wipes us clean from the Cradle's surface. Until then, do as your heart guides you. I will lead our people in Belvua as best I can, and whatever legacy of your son's I carry out, I hope it is one you will bless."

"Thank you, Aerreth."

They parted, but Evelyn did not return home immediately. Though she'd seen no eyes watching her during her meeting with the foxkin leader, she highly doubted they were alone. Once enough time had passed, she sprinted toward the nearest home, wrapped her wings about her, and passed straight through the wall. She did the same for the next two homes, passing through empty rooms and barren bedrooms with the best speed her old legs could manage. She used the cover of these homes to switch directions, and once she'd darted through two more, she again paused to watch out a slender bedroom window.

Sure enough, she spotted two hooded foxkin pass by, their noses low to the ground. Foxkin noses were hardly the sharpest, which meant they were desperate in their search for any hint at her passage. Evelyn bristled the feathers of her wings. The fools. As if she could be followed so easily.

A few more leaps through walls and she was on her way through the dark corners of Belvua. She had indulged in her nostalgia, and after her banter with Aerreth, she wanted nothing more than to return home. The black tower was not far, and she did not bother with the door on the first floor, instead using her wings and her sharp claws to climb up to the second and then pass through the wall.

Evelyn emerged into her bedroom, which bore a hanging basket bed in its center. Within that bed, knees curled to his chest and his wings curled about his body, rested her injured son, Logarius.

"Have you slept well?" she asked as she removed her gloves and pulled down her hood. Logarius did not look at her, nor did he answer. A sigh escaped Evelyn's thick beak. Ever since she'd dragged his bleeding body to her home in secret, he'd refused to say a word to her. Not that she should be surprised. She'd seen the heartbreak in his eyes after she buried her dagger into his back. She'd seen that betrayal break him. Still, she wished he would curse her name instead of silently sulk. It pained her to see him so weak, so defeated.

"Your strength will return in time," she said, chatting away as if he were merely sick with a flu. "Perhaps when you are feeling better, you will finally speak with your mother?"

Logarius shook his right leg, rattling the heavy steel chain attached to his ankle. She'd tightened it so that it dug into his black, scaled skin. There would be no escape, not even with the help of his wings. His meaning was clear, even if he would not speak a word to communicate it.

"I do what must be done," she said in response. "Think on your actions, my son. You were willing to release the void upon the Cradle. There is no greater crime in this land. To betray the existence of life itself in such a way is criminal, and you know this."

Again the rattle of his chains. Evelyn reached for him but he turned away, the motion spinning his bed so his wings were toward her, blocking out all sight of his weak, injured form.

"Would you prefer I killed you?" she asked him softly. "Would you prefer my dagger punctured your liver or your lungs? I'm sorry, my son. My heart is not as strong as yours. I would have you live. That is my crime."

No rattle of the chains. No movement of the wings. She thought he'd ignore her completely, but for the first time since waking up in that bed, he spoke to her. Three soft words, and then silence.

"Nihil has come."

Evelyn's feathers ruffled as if touched by a cold wind. She pulsed her wings and leapt, carrying her upward from floor to floor until emerging through the rooftop. Her claws clung to the shingles as she stared west from the top of her high spire, praying her son was wrong. It was a futile prayer, for she could feel the nearby presence of her maker just as easily as her son. Viciss would no longer be the lone demigod meddling in the affairs of Londheim. Nihil, the Dragon of Conflict, had arrived.

Viciss was the crawling mountain, his physical form enormous and weighty, and dragged along with gargantuan legs made of both flesh and steel. Nihil was just as enormous, but it bore none of that weight, for it was not a being of stone. It was a creature of clouds, of wind and air, and it flew high in the sky above the city. Its body resembled a serpent with four legs, its scales blindingly white, its body impossibly long. It bore no wings, yet still it flew with mere undulations of its long form. Clouds roiled and split, making way for the dragon's passage as it descended toward the great field beyond the western gates. The front legs touched ground, and they made not a sound, for the dragon's arrival was gentle. Its body slithered and curled as it settled, like smoke making a home, or a living fog given scales and a pulse.

Nihil's physical body landed with its feline face grinning at the crawling mountain, and then its ruby eyes closed, and its marble teeth hid behind sealed lips as it slowly lowered to the ground. Outside the gates of Londheim, the tops of their towering bodies the only part now visible to Evelyn from her perch, the two dragons faced one another. Evelyn could not shake the feeling that the demigods were opposed in more than mere cardinal directions.

"And so you arrive at last," Evelyn whispered to the wind. "Such conflict was bound to draw you in like flies to honey."

The Dragon of Conflict reared back its head, and it let loose a tremendous roar. It was no cry of an animal or monster. It was a crack of thunder, and it rumbled, and rumbled, a mighty herald of war.

CHAPTER 5

Surely you agree," High Excellence Albert Downing asked Adria as he paced before her in one of his mansion's luxurious rooms, "that your public support would help greatly in transitioning Westreach into a new era?"

Adria sat up in her cushioned chair. The fabric was overly stuffed with feathers, and it felt like it was actively trying to push her to her feet.

"Indeed, I do, which is why I must be cautious with how I use my influence," she said. "My servitude is to the three Sisters, and it is to them I remain loyal. What you're asking for is distinctly political."

"As if the church has qualms interfering with politics," Mayor Soren muttered from a nearby couch. This earned a surprising glare from his son, Dierk, who lurked behind him with his hands resting atop the couch back.

"There is a difference between advisement and interference," Dierk countered.

"If the Royal Overseer wished only for advice, I would have already offered it," Adria said.

"High Excellence, please," Albert gently corrected.

"My apologies." It had been two weeks since the announcement had swept through Londheim, given as a joint statement from Soren Becher, Albert Downing, and Vikar Caria. In it they'd finally revealed information that had been kept secret for the past month: Queen Woadthyn the Ninth had abandoned all claim to lands outside East Orismund. The joint proclamation announced the foundation of a new nation, and declared West Orismund to be renamed Westreach. Albert rescinded his old title, and instead branded himself the High Excellence. He promised to uphold the values he'd been elected to protect, and made clear he carried Soren's approval as well as that of both Vikars. It was a bold gambit, but at least in Londheim, it appeared successful.

But appearances could be deceiving, hence Albert calling Adria to his mansion to sweet-talk her for aid.

"You read far too much into my position," Adria continued after taking a sip of the tea they'd brought her. The honey stuck to her tongue, and she savored its sweetness. She'd barely spent any time eating or drinking for an eternity, it seemed. To her parched tongue, the tea was a divine treat. "I am not even officially a Vikar, merely an acting one."

"For now," Dierk said. "Will you be content remaining just a Vikar?"

"The boy echoes the rumors we all hear," Albert added. He halted his pacing to face her. His dark skin was noticeably paler, and she swore there were more gray strands scattered throughout his hair than there were a year ago. "Many believe you could easily win a vote for Deakon if you announced your candidacy."

"And if I did?" she asked.

"Then I'd greatly appreciate the new Deakon's support for my position. I want peace for Westreach. If we can maintain that here in Londheim, the lords in Wardhus and Stomme should be amicable to remaining in the fold."

"It's that or what used to be West Orismund be carved up into a hundred little fiefdoms and city-states," Dierk said. "And if that happens, none of them will stand a chance against the dragons and their armies of dragon-sired."

Adria frowned behind her mask. She'd heard the rumors of the dragon-sired army marching toward Londheim, as had the rest of the city. What exactly that army entailed, or its overall goals, were mere guesses. The only concrete knowledge was of their leader, Shinnoc, who had appeared to the city leaders in a rage-filled vision upon learning of his father's death.

"Are we certain they seek conquest?" she asked. "The dragon I believe called Nihil landed yesterday, and has so far committed no aggressive act."

"The Dyrandar King promised to burn Londheim to the ground, albeit in more flowery words," Albert said. "I don't think there's any other way to interpret what is happening. We will need to make a stand against the horde come to our gates. As for Nihil, who is to say he doesn't wait for his minions to arrive before joining in the slaughter?"

Soren started to say something but then flinched as if he'd pricked his finger.

"Fleeing now would be foolhardy," the Mayor said after collecting himself. "Making a stand is our best option, even if we now face two dragons instead of one. The question is, will the Sacred Mother reborn be there with us in that fight?"

This time it was Adria's turn to flinch. She hated being called the Sacred Mother reborn. The Sacred Mother was a nameless entity, the first-ever human gifted with a soul by Alma. It was her offspring that elevated humanity from its humble origins as mere animals to the leaders of the Cradle. Adria was not a reborn version, nor was she gifted with any particular unique soul by the Sisters. If her power came from anyone, it was the dragons and their strange machinery hidden deep below Londheim.

"I will do everything in my power to protect the innocent people of this city," she said. "Of that, you have my promise."

"Excellent," Albert said, clapping his hands. "It is good to know at least that. I understand you are reluctant to make a public statement supporting my position as High Excellence, but know that I wish nothing but the best for our people."

Adria stood to leave, the meeting clearly at an end. It'd begun with Albert relaying fears from farmers that the bread created by the Faithkeepers' prayers would destroy their own livelihoods, but the complaint had merely been a pretext for the recruitment attempt. She was eager to leave the mansion's confines, for after so many years in Low Dock, she was never truly comfortable amid such wealth. Two goddess-damned dragons sat outside their city walls. Bickering and positioning for politics felt asinine under such circumstances.

Sadly escape did not yet appear possible. Dierk lingered by the door, and once Albert and Soren had left, he approached.

"So, um, how are you doing, Adria?" he asked. "I can't see your face, not with your mask, but I can see your, you know. Your soul. And you seem tired. Drained."

"I *am* tired and drained," Adria admitted. "It seems everywhere I go, people ask for miracles, and those who don't want miracles want blessings, prayers, or favors."

"Like Albert."

"Yes, like our *High Excellence*." She shook her head. "Who came up with that title?"

"I did, actually," Dierk said, and he puffed his chest up with pride. "Just one of many suggestions of mine that Albert has adopted. He's listening to me like he always should have. And he'll listen to you, too, if you speak."

"I don't want to speak. I want to sleep for a hundred days and wake up in a far saner world."

Dierk crossed his arms and glanced away. He was such a nervous boy, and she'd noticed that even making eye contact was difficult for him.

"I could help you," he said. "Like I did at the cathedral."

Repulsion flooded through Adria's veins. Dierk had destroyed

Vikar Thaddeus's soul and used its remnants to flood Adria with power, allowing her to resurrect one hundred people back from the dead. At the time it had felt a worthy cause, and Thaddeus a truly despicable sacrifice. The passage of time had saddled her with doubts, and the idea of her choosing new souls to condemn to be eternally forgotten felt like one step too far.

"No," she said. "That was a singular event. I won't destroy souls to alleviate my own struggles."

"Not like that," Dierk insisted. "I would use my own soul, and my own energy. Just a little, not enough to cause myself any harm. All you have to do is ask. I want to help. I'd love to help. Really, I would."

Adria tried not to dive into people's minds unbidden, but with Dierk, she could not help herself. Emotions were pouring out of the young man's soul like water leaking over the top of a swaying bucket. She could feel his nervousness, his uncertainty, and his lack of confidence. Yes, there was a yearning for her, too, an awkward sexuality common for anyone his age. She did her best to ignore it and focus on Dierk's potential goodness. He was so alone. What might he become if shown friendship and kindness?

"There's someone I feel you should meet," she said. "A former Mindkeeper by the name of Tamerlane Swift. He has studied the Book of Ravens, and his religious knowledge is both extensive and nontraditional."

"Tamerlane?" Dierk asked. "How do you know him?"

"He's a good friend," she said. "He helped open my eyes to the changing world, and he might be able to help you, too."

A new emotion spiraled into the little wispy strands of Dierk's soul: jealousy.

"Sure," Dierk said, his stance growing stiff. "I'd love to meet him."

Together they two exited the mansion. She watched him out of the corner of her eye as they walked. Part of her wondered if the young man would benefit from a mask like her own porcelain face. He was always at war with himself, his newly blossomed confidence fighting against his lifelong belief in his own worthlessness.

"The church has given me a small home to stay not far from here, House 27 in Windswept District," she said. "Come by tomorrow afternoon. I will introduce you to him. You both might learn greatly from one another."

"Sure, sure, I'd love to," he said, the poorly told lie convincing neither of them. Adria stopped just shy of the mansion entrance, needing to change the subject quickly lest the awkward silence take hold. Without thinking, she slid her mask above her forehead so she might plainly address the young man.

"I know times have been difficult, but I fear they will only grow harder," she said. "Stay strong. We both have our parts to play."

Dierk's neck flushed, but she could tell he was flattered.

"Of course," he said. "You know I'll always be here for you. And if you must fight the dragon-sired, I'll give you whatever power you need to win. That's a promise."

"Will it come to that?" she asked. "I wasn't there for Shinnoc's vision, but if Shinnoc is anything like his father, he will be kind at heart and prefer peace over war. Are you sure there isn't another way to avoid this coming conflict?"

"You didn't feel his rage," Dierk said. "He towered over us like we were... like we were ants. Little bugs for him to step on. His grief and fury painted the whole world red. There will be no peace. The loss of his father cut far too deep."

"Cannac would not want this war."

"And now Cannac is dead. What lesson do you think his son took from that?"

Adria sighed and pulled her mask back over her face, needing its comfort before returning to the streets of Londheim, and the small crowd waiting to beg her for prayers and miracles.

"When given a choice between peace and bloodshed, we humans never choose peace." She shivered at the thought of lapinkin armed with spears leaping over Londheim's walls and owls diving with avenria riding atop their backs. Her eyes flicked to the sky, and thick trails of smoke rising from the direction of Belvua.

"And so we prepare for bloodshed," she said softly as she hurried that way. Dierk hesitated a few steps behind her until he, too, saw the smoke and began jogging to catch up. Adria very much wished he'd remain behind as she dashed through districts toward Belvua. Dierk could be many things, but a peacemaker he was not.

On the night of the cathedral attack, Viciss had stirred from his apparent slumber to bathe the city with his black water. His aim had been expertly precise, the water falling only on the stone wall that marked Belvua's borders. The Dragon of Change had warped the stone into living matter, creating a mesmerizing row of strange, enormous trees similar to the one that had lived in the heart of Londheim until an angry mob had cut it down. It was as if the trees had grown right up through the wall, so that gray brick and black bark intertwined with mesmerizing patterns. Their branches rose to the heavens, sealing off the district and hiding the buildings within behind living leaves that could flutter and glow a rainbow of colors. Those leaves had taken flight like a million butterflies, and they flashed red in alarm at the fire burning in the district entrance.

Adria did not know who had caused the fire, but she could guess. The district entrance was blocked off by a massive pile of furniture stolen from the homes within, and it seemed someone had attempted to set it ablaze with a bit of oil or alcohol as a starter. The fire burned unevenly, and did not appear that it would consume the blockade, but that wasn't the real problem now. No, what frightened Adria were the several hundred people gathering in a ring about the entrance, shouting curses and waving makeshift weapons. A trio of foxkin stood atop the gate, crossbows held in hand, their forms shrouded in smoke. Adria felt a shiver of remembrance at the last time foxkin had aimed those crossbows upon her. She'd crushed them all, and it'd been so easy, so pleasurable. They glared at her, but they dared not aim their weapons her way.

"Calm your wretched!" one of the foxkin shouted as Adria pushed to the front. "Or we'll do it for you!"

Calm them, the foxkin demanded, as if it would be so easy. Adria scanned the crowd, and she saw lit torches funneling forward. Whatever troublemaker had started this, it seemed others were eager to finish it. And what then? When the barricade was burned, would they charge into Belvua with some foolish goal of conquering it? She doubted anyone had a true plan. Instinct was taking over, violent, fearful instinct. Two men rushed forward, torches in hand. The first flung the torch onto the burning barricade. The other fell dead, three crossbow bolts thudding together into a tight cluster at the center of his neck.

"Oh shit, they've made a mess of things now," Dierk said as the crowd roared for blood. With a wall and a fire between them, there wasn't much they could do yet beyond vent their rage, but vent they did. Curses and swears filled the air. The anger sickened Adria's stomach, and she felt panic start to creep along her spine. Countless people found what stones they could and flung them toward the top of the gate. The foxkin ducked low as they reloaded their crossbows. How long until they charged the barricade? Adria didn't know, nor did she want to know. Things were spiraling out of control, and if she were to stop it, it must be now.

To counter this rage without loss of life required a spectacle, and so she gave them one. The power of souls was the power to remake the world, and she drew the tiniest sliver into her from the gathered crowd. It wasn't much, just a little wisp of memory from each and every person present, but it flooded her mind with possibilities. Adria lifted her hands as light swirled around her body, the stolen power made manifest. She felt the pull of gravity holding her down, and she denied it. Her body rose, guided upward so effortlessly, she wondered why she had waited so long to try. Just as effortless was snuffing out the fire with a mere wave of her hand. The crowd gasped as she hovered above them, her eyes gleaming with white light.

"Leave this place!" her voice thundered throughout the district. "Let no further blood be shed."

Clubs, knives, and swords lowered. The bloodlust withered beneath her divine rage. A few grumbled, but they were the minority as the people turned to go about their lives. Adria released the power she had taken, and with its passage she floated back to the ground. Her feet touched the cold cobbles, and she breathed out a long, heavy sigh of relief.

"Idiots, all of them," Dierk grumbled as he watched them disperse. "Why would they be so stupid?"

"They're frightened," Adria said. She touched her forehead, dreading the telltale signs of a headache that pulsed pain along her temples and behind her eyes. "Two dragons lurk outside our gates, and dragon-sired hold a portion of our city."

"A portion of the city we've failed to take back," Dierk said. "A portion, mind you, I've had my father decree officially theirs in the name of peace."

"Peace," Adria said, the word a mockery upon her tongue. She stretched her fingers to the soul of the man killed by crossbow bolts and lifted his soul to the heavens, sending it into the beyond despite the midday hour. "This is peace? What happens when Shinnoc's army arrives? Do you think we will still have peace?"

Dierk glared at the dispersing crowd.

"I think the people will do as they are told if their leaders are strong enough."

Adria could feel the emotions leaking off the people's souls, and with but a thought, she pulled them into herself. A small fire had burned for mere moments, and already it drew hundreds of people eager for blood and retribution. What might happen if Londheim were put under siege? Belvua had withstood a few hundred soldiers, but the rage of an entire city? Was she strong enough to prevent such a disaster? Was *anyone?*

"Lyra help us if a true riot begins," she whispered, for the only victor would be the carrion crows.

CHAPTER 6

Devin jolted upright in his bed with his heart punching an urgent rhythm into his rib cage. Sweat bathed his limbs. The night was deep, but his mind raced without a hint of sleepiness. In a vivid dream he'd received an invitation, and it refused to fade now that he was awake.

"All right, all right," he muttered, sweeping errant bangs off his forehead as he staggered to his dresser. "I'm coming."

He quietly dressed, careful not to wake Jacaranda sleeping in the next room. She'd come home tired and quiet, and though she had accepted his apology, he had a feeling it'd take a few days for things to mend between them. It seemed even after his death, Gerag would haunt them with his memory.

Once he'd donned his coat and weapons, Devin slipped out into the cold air of a Londheim night. On his walk he passed a dead cat lying with its back legs twisted. Two rats fed on its entrails.

A pleasant sign, Devin thought.

He spared it only a glance, his eyes locked on the sky. It was habit now, and he was surprised how quickly he'd learned it since the owls began their attacks. No incidents had been reported since the grand cathedral's burning, but that didn't erase the paranoia. If not owls, there always might be a gargoyle leering down, seeking a bigger meal than some rats. Uneven clouds blocked much of the sky, but Devin tried to find comfort in the starlight that shone through the gaps. Now more than ever, it felt like their protection from the void was thin and fraying.

Devin's dream had been simple but overwhelming. He'd stood alone before a dried-up well a quarter mile from his home. At first there'd been silence in the dream, but then the flow of time had upended. The entire world had aged, the sun and moon dancing thousands of times across the sky in the mere blink of an eye. Words echoed in his mind, and those words had stayed with him after the dream's end.

I await you.

And so upon waking, he dressed himself and ventured out into Londheim's dark night, and walked to the place his dream had summoned him: a secluded alcove surrounded on three sides by moss-covered brick walls. Part of him had hoped it would be empty. That part of him was so very wrong.

"You are fearful," the Goddess Lyra said. She sat on the edge of the well with her legs daintily crossed. Stars sparkled in the folds of her dress, which ran down to her ankles. Her long hair wrapped once around her waist before spooling together at her feet. Her dark skin was so smooth and unblemished, it more resembled stone than flesh. Unblinking eyes watched his every move. Devin tried not to look into them. Instead of irises, a starscape of things he could not identify softly rotated about her pupils, as if entire worlds were trapped inside those white orbs. The image sent his stomach into loops, and chills danced along his spine.

"I fear the task you would set before me," Devin said, and he slowly dropped to one knee. Seeing the Goddess before him was so surreal, he felt like his mind wasn't fully grasping the weight of the moment. "History is not kind to prophets and sages."

"Does that mean you would refuse me?"

Her voice was so beautiful, but that beauty carried an edge. In nature, the brighter the colors, the more dangerous the bearer.

Before him was the creator of nature herself, and none was brighter, nor more dangerous.

"You are my beloved Goddess," he said, bowing his head. "How could I refuse?"

"We are refused every day, every hour, and every minute," she said. "By the wise and the foolish, by the rich and the poor. Humanity is cruel when I ask them to be kind. They are vindictive when I ask them to be forgiving. You ask how? With ease, Soulkeeper. With practiced, effortless ease we are denied."

Devin's neck flushed at the correction. A needed reminder that empty platitudes would mean little here, and he should spend more time on his answers. Whatever his Goddess desired, it would not be easy or simple.

"Forgive me my foolishness," he said.

"There is nothing to forgive. Stand, child. We must speak."

Devin rose to his feet. Lyra was watching with those unblinking eyes of hers. What did she see, he wondered. Did she see his entire life, all his collected deeds both good and ill like the church told children on their ninth-day classes? If Adria could look into the contents of a soul and witness its memories, surely a Goddess could do so in an infinitely superior capacity?

Adria . . .

Devin's stomach tightened, and he feared he knew why he was in this abandoned alcove under the cover of night. He begged that weren't the case as a biting panic nibbled along his neck and spine.

"Please, tell me why you summoned me," he said. "I will do my very best to listen and obey."

Long seconds passed in intolerable silence. Devin felt naked and isolated. Could she hear his thoughts? Did she know his every worry? And damn it, were those actual stars twinkling in her dress, or a mere approximation of them? Everything about meeting the Goddess felt . . . wrong, like an unwritten rule of the Cradle was being broken.

"Please," Devin repeated when it seemed she might never talk. "I must know."

"Your sister is an abomination."

Each syllable was a knife thrust to his heart.

"How so?" he whispered.

"She was created by the dragons to upend the proper order of all things. Alma is to bring souls from the Aether to the Cradle. I am to watch over them, protect them from the consuming touch of the void, and deliver them into Anwyn's hands. Anwyn guides the souls back to the Aether, to re-enter the eternal flow beyond the stars."

Her cosmic eyes bored into his. Her every word shook with indignation.

"Humanity is not to interfere."

Devin wanted to argue, to challenge her accusations against his sister, but this wasn't some stranger. This was Lyra. This was one of the three Goddesses to whom he'd spent his whole life praying. Who was he to contest a single word she spoke? But damn it all, this was his sister she so savagely condemned.

"With every funeral rite we aid souls on their passage into Anwyn's arms," Devin gently said. "Do we not already interfere?"

"You are a child holding the hand of a parent on a walk through a forest," she said. "Your rites and prayers are not interference. But what the dragons built, and what they have crafted your sister into being, is a blasphemy so dangerous, we cannot allow it to continue."

There were very few ways to interpret such a statement. Devin tried to remain calm. He failed.

"Twice I asked, and twice you refused," he said. "But though I fear the answer, I must know it. Please, beloved Goddess, what is it you require of me?"

Lyra softly set her feet upon the rocky ground and rose from the well's edge. She crossed the distance between them in perfect silence. Was she really there, he wondered, or just a divine image? His body froze in place. Her every move mesmerized him with its fluidity. She touched his cheek with her fingertips, and though it was an act of love, his skin burned like fire.

"Only one action will prevent a complete upending of the balance we three Sisters have created. If I am to live, you must take your sister's life."

Devin wanted to scream out his refusal, but the Goddess's words haunted him.

With ease, Soulkeeper. With practiced, effortless ease we are denied.

"Why must you ask this of me?" he pleaded, deciding to respond with naked honesty instead of rage or argument. "I don't understand. You are Adria's most beloved Goddess. She has sung your praises with every day of her life as a Faithkeeper. It is your symbol that hangs from a pendant about her neck. If her… if her life must be taken, can it not be at your hands instead of mine?"

Lyra put her back to him. Her hair formed a shroud hiding every inch of her body. Scattered starlight that pierced through the clouds sparkled off the strands packed so densely together, they seemed to move and flow like water. Though it made no sense, it seemed like her hair continued on forever, pooling at her feet without any apparent end before curling across the dirt, about the well, and down into its black depths.

"We cannot kill," the Goddess said over her shoulder.

"Cannot?" Devin asked. "You made the mountains. You shaped the world. How could you not snuff out something so frail as a human life?"

"We ourselves were spun from the great Aether flow," she said. "And there are laws older than ourselves which we cannot break lest our very identities be made forfeit. We cannot kill, only create and guide."

Devin thought of the many stories he'd grown up reading as a child. There was no shortage of them where the Sisters punished the wicked, but there was a common thread running through them, and suddenly he knew all too well why Lyra had summoned him that night.

"You need champions," he said.

She faced him, her eyes settling on his. The galaxies within them turned and turned.

"We do," she said. "I would have you be mine."

"I am not worthy," he said. A meager complaint, but he had to think of something to say. His entire body was locked down in panic.

"Neither are our current champions," Lyra said. "We never told humanity, but there was a world before yours. Our creations were…flawed. We wished to start anew, but we could not wipe away the lives we made no matter how limited and unfulfilling they might be. And so we created the dragons. We spun them from ourselves like a spider weaves silk from her own spinnerets. We gave them our power, and they washed away the old so we might, together, build a glorious new Cradle."

The Goddess turned away, and Devin felt his insides tremble. For the briefest moment he'd seen rage building upon Lyra's perfect face, and he feared his mind would break at the sight.

"The dragons *betrayed* us," she said. "They sought to deny our authority, and to make a mockery of our love. The dragons would have humanity live a life free of our influence, and for that, we imprisoned them and their children beneath the ground. It was akin to slicing off our own arm, but we did what we thought we must. It cost us dearly, Soulkeeper. Every day we bled to deny the part of ourselves we imprisoned. We did not slumber, but we viewed the world through a haze, and as the centuries passed, our power drew back into us. We faltered in our duties, and so emerged what you call the soulless. The void began chewing its way into the Cradle. Reaping rituals, once merely symbolic, became necessary to aid Anwyn in reclaiming souls to the heavens. It could not continue, Soulkeeper. The price of imprisoning the dragons was too great for us three to bear."

Lyra shook her head.

"And so we released the dragons and their children. They now walk the Cradle, free of their prison, and already they resume the blasphemy that caused their banishment. Nihil and Viciss sit outside these city walls, plotting and planning as they always did. Adria Eveson is the fruit of their labors, and her existence is a threat to our own. She must die, Devin. I do not say this out of malice, or envy, or anger. I only require that what must be done, be done."

"Then talk to her! Convince her of the danger!"

The Goddess lifted her gaze to the stars.

"In time, I will try, but I fear it will matter not. If I look to the future, I see a thousand possibilities, and in far too many, her meddling will destroy the protection of the stars. She will break the very existence of my Sisters and I. In other fates, the void will wash over the Cradle, undoing our work and snuffing out the light of each and every soul. Rarer still, I see her becoming a Goddess herself, cruel in power and ruthless in her desires to create a perfect world that will only mirror our first failed creation. My Sisters and I cannot accept such risks. Can you?"

Lyra spoke of the end of the world, of the deaths of every last human life. Of course he would do anything to prevent that... but to kill his own sister?

"Why me?" he asked that unending river of black silk that was her hair. The strands shimmered as with a life of their own. "Why put this cruelty upon my shoulders?"

"Because she trusts you."

"She trusts you as well."

The look his Goddess gave him spiked chills through his blood.

"Does she?"

The night darkened. Devin blinked, and Lyra was gone. No sign of her remained, nor any proof she had ever existed. No stones were shifted or turned from her hair, nor were there signs of her waiting at the well. The tension that had built up in his muscles eased, and it suddenly felt like he could breathe easier. Was it a vision he'd experienced, or had the Goddess truly conversed with him?

There was a time, when he was a much younger man, that he'd fantasized about meeting one of the Goddesses, or of hearing their words in a prophetic dream. He'd relished the idea of being given a greater purpose to guide his actions. Hearing the words of the three Sisters surely meant the banishing of his doubts and a reinforcement of his faith, or so he'd believed. Now older, weary, and alone, Devin knew otherwise. He shivered as if ice were lodged deep beneath his ribs. His faith was wounded, not strengthened. His doubts were emboldened, not slain. He wanted nothing more than to pretend the past few minutes were a lie.

"It doesn't have to be this way," he whispered as he walked back to his house. He could feel panic clawing at every frayed edge of his mind, eager to consume him completely. "If Adria's power is a risk, then we can talk to her, we can change her mind. Don't ask me to do this, Lyra. Please, I can't do this..."

"Devin?"

He turned to discover a woman rooted in place in the center of the street. Her clothes were plain and gray, her long blond hair wound into a ponytail that hung off her left shoulder. *Just like Brittany used to*, he thought, surprised by the strength of the memory. The woman held both hands before her as if clasped in prayer, and it seemed she struggled for words.

"Yes?" he asked, his distracted mind scrambling to put a name to her face. The woman paused, and it seemed she could not meet his gaze. The turn in her head allowed moonlight to shine upon her neck, revealing a row of chain tattoos.

"If you have a message, deliver it," he said, but her hesitance seemed counter to a normal soulless's behavior. "Unless... unless you are awakened?"

Finally she met his eyes. Green eyes, and speckled with tears. Definitely not soulless, but why would she come to him? Did she somehow know he'd helped Jacaranda go through the same?

"I can help," he said, doing all he could to keep his tone gentle. He offered her a hand. "Tell me, what is your name?"

The woman turned and ran. Devin watched her go, and he prayed Lyra give her comfort and guidance. The world was a cruel place to those awakening to it. Would Lyra listen, though?

If I am to live, you must take your sister's life.

"You ask too much," he whispered as he watched the woman vanish into the dark distance, and he envied her, for there was nowhere for him to run that a Goddess could not find.

CHAPTER 7

Brittany ran until her lungs were aflame and her legs felt like jelly, and only when Devin was a good mile in the distance did she slump onto the porch of a closed-down shop and bury her face in her arms. In her former life she could run from one side of Londheim to the other without stopping, yet now a single district was a test. The anger at her physical limitations helped chase away the panic that had overtaken her when her husband had looked at her with those brown eyes of his and asked for her name.

"Adeline," she'd nearly said, the name her body had possessed before her soul had been thrust into it. When the confusion had passed, she'd realized Devin was standing there, waiting, his hand outstretched, offering kindness that had always been his hallmark in her mind. That desire to help the downtrodden had brought him into the ranks of the Soulkeepers, and now years later and much older looking, there he was, offering her aid despite not knowing her true identity. She could have accepted. It would have been so easy. All she had to do was reach out and touch his hand, let their fingers clasp together, let a thousand memories spark to life inside a body that had not been there for a single one of them.

"Brittany," she whispered. She thumped the back of her head against the storefront, using the pain to focus. "My name is

Brittany Moore Eveson. My body doesn't matter. What I look like doesn't matter. I'm Brittany. *Brittany.*"

Was it cowardice that kept her from telling Devin? She didn't know. He'd looked so different, and yet so similar. The worry lines around his mouth had deepened. His hair was a bit longer and more disheveled compared to the tight, short trim he'd kept it in when they were married. Even his voice was slightly off, as if the passing six years had added an invisible weight to each syllable.

Or perhaps...were her memories wrong? Damaged, even? She'd been dead for six years, with her soul trapped beneath the dirt while awaiting the end of the world. Perhaps it wasn't Devin that had changed, but her faulty remembrances of him.

Brittany slammed a fist against the porch. Pain spiked up her wrist to her elbow, and she let out a soft cry.

"Brittany...Moore...Eveson," she said through clenched teeth. She had to remember who she was, and Goddesses damn it, a weepy out-of-breath woman was decidedly not it. She'd been one of the best Soulkeepers to grace the halls of the Keeping Church. As much as it irked her to take Adria's advice (she had her stubborn pride, after all), it was time to start looking at establishing her new life.

Brittany buttoned the top of her coat to hide her neck. Things would go smoother if no one could see the chain tattoos. Adria had told her of the grand cathedral's burning, and of the mansion nearby that the church leadership was currently using as its new headquarters. Brittany broke into a light jog, something just enough to keep her heart rate going as a sort of penance toward her lack of endurance. She crossed through several districts as she wound her way north toward the center of the city.

Despite the late hour, two novices stood guard at the door to the mansion with clubs strapped to their belts. Faint candlelight flickered through little cracks where the tall curtains met behind the windows. An iron fence surrounded the tiny few steps of grass that were its front lawn.

"I wish to speak with Vikar Forrest," Brittany told them.

"Vikar Forrest?" one novice repeated, as if he couldn't believe he heard her right. "Now? In the middle of the night?"

"I'm sure as shit not waiting out here in the cold."

Both novices looked to be in their first year of Soulkeepers training by her guess. They'd be given few, simple directions to follow, and the idea of disturbing a sleeping Vikar would seem blasphemous to them.

"I don't, um, I don't think I will," one said, his face unfortunately covered with wide swathes of acne. "I can't. Let me go find..."

"Listen to me carefully," Brittany said, adopting the tone she'd always used whenever she were tasked with teaching at the Soulkeeper Sanctuary. "I need to speak with Forrest, and only Forrest. Tell him one of his Soulkeepers from afar has come home. Can you do that?"

"I can," the other novice said, the girl smiling pleasantly enough and trying to be helpful. "Um, but who, exactly? Your name, I mean? He'll want to know."

Brittany bit her lower lip as she briefly thought.

"Susanna Raynard."

"All right, I'll go. Stay right here."

She ducked into the home, and Brittany heard the click of a lock from the other side. She stomped her feet and swayed side to side, trying to reawaken some warmth into her extremities. Her chest still hurt from her sprint, and for the hundredth time she wondered how long it'd take for this new body to reach the finely tuned athleticism of her old. No matter what the actual length of time, the correct answer was "too damn long."

"So you've traveled from outside West Orismund?" the acne-covered novice asked.

"I thought it was Westreach now."

He blushed, and his immediate response was nonsensical.

"Just curious about what things are like back east is all," he finally muttered.

"Things are shit everywhere," she said as the door reopened. "Just how and why seems to vary."

The second novice stepped out. Her skin seemed to have paled in color by half.

"Vikar Forrest has agreed to meet with you," she said. "And, uh, he seemed rather angry. Good luck."

Brittany followed the novice into the mansion. There was a vague familiarity about the place, perhaps from a party or event hosted by whoever the owner was. The wealthy were always dining with the church's elite as an attempt to create blind spots toward their own crimes and inadequacies. More often than not, it worked, too. Brittany walked on an overly thick carpet past rows of paintings, closed mahogany doors, and random rooms that seemed to contain no reason to exist beyond being filled with expensive furniture.

"Forrest's bedroom is also his office," the novice explained as she stopped before a door. "I didn't want you surprised is all."

She opened the door and then gestured for her to enter first. Brittany stepped into a quaint room with a plain bed shoved into a corner, the dresser butted directly up against the bottom half to make room for a wildly out-of-place oak desk in the center. A neat stack of papers lay in its center. A freshly lit lantern burned at one corner. Vikar Forrest stood behind the desk, his arms crossed and his expression foul.

"Get out," Forrest told the novice. The young woman was all too pleased to do so. Brittany leaned against the door once it closed. Unlike Devin, Vikar Forrest had changed significantly less over the past six years. He was still a bear of a man, and his muscles seemed determined to push against the fabric of his bed robe. His blond hair was tied back into a ponytail, though a half-dozen strands had escaped its hold and hung loose between his bloodshot eyes.

"Well then, *Susanna Raynard*," the Vikar said as he slumped into his desk's chair. The act was highly exaggerated, and meant to hide how his hand closed around the handle of his enormous axe that leaned against the desk beside him. "Care to explain who you really are, because you sure as shit don't look like my dead wife."

"I meant no offense," Brittany said. "But I knew you would meet with me if I used your wife's name, and I am yet unwilling to share my own with anyone other than yourself."

"That so?" he grunted. "Couldn't it have waited until morning?"

"I'd rather no other Soulkeeper see my arrival."

"Aren't you the suspicious one?" he said, his eyes narrowing. "Are you a shapeshifting foxkin come to kill me, perhaps? Those brats at the door seemed dumb enough to let one inside."

Brittany laughed. No, Forrest had definitely not changed at all.

"You're not going to believe what I have to tell you," she said. "But I'm going to tell it anyway. Though I do not look it, I am Brittany Eveson, back from the dead."

"You're right. I don't believe it."

Though he still appeared relaxed, she could see the tension in his legs, the white-knuckle grip on his axe. She had but a moment before he attacked.

"Worms," she said.

Forrest froze in place.

"Excuse me?" he asked.

"Before you were named Vikar, you went with me to Suroy to help rebuild after a tornado destroyed half the town. On our trip there, you told me your biggest fear wasn't spiders or heights or drowning, but long, fat earthworms."

The giant man leaned back into his creaking chair.

"You didn't believe me," he said, testing her.

"No, I didn't," she said, cracking a grin. "So I snuck several into my pack for the return trip to Londheim and put them on your face while you slept. I thought you'd cut my head clean off my shoulders after you woke up howling."

"A story Brittany could have told dozens of times before she died," Forrest said. She could sense his disbelief cracking. He just needed once last little push.

"After you got the worms off, you were stupid enough to throw a punch at me," she said. "By the time we were finished, I'd broken two of your fingers and you'd knocked loose one of my teeth. We vowed to never tell a soul, you because you were embarrassed about the worms and I because I hated the idea of people thinking I lost a fight. Which I didn't. We called it right before I broke another two fingers, if I remember correctly."

"That's because my elbow was going to permanently leave your nose as a flattened pancake," Forrest said. "All right, I'm starting to believe, but you need to give me an explanation of how in the void you're standing here before me and why you look like that."

"Adria took my soul from the graveyard and placed it into a soulless's body."

The Vikar let out a soft grunt.

"You know if you opened with that, I might have believed quicker."

"Yes, but it wouldn't have been as fun," she said, and this time when she smiled, he mirrored it with his own. His chair groaned as he pushed up and opened his arms wide for a hug, accidentally exposing himself as his robe slipped.

"You're indecent," she said as she returned the hug.

"You saw worse when we traveled together. Damn, I've missed you, Brittany. Instead I've been saddled with that wet blanket of a husband of yours, and he's just not as fun."

"I'm not sure he's my husband anymore," she said, her amusement faltering. "Our vows are until death, after all." The need to know overwhelmed her hesitation. "I know this is awkward and sudden, but did you... did you tell Devin about where I was when I died?"

Forrest retied the sash to his robe and took a step back.

"Where?" he asked. "You mean 'who with,' don't you?"

Her neck flushed.

"Yes. That."

The Vikar let out a long sigh.

"No, Brittany, I didn't. Devin had just lost his wife. The last thing he needed to know was that she'd been, well, *you'd* been having an affair. Unnecessary cruelty, that's how I viewed it. Plus with how foul a mood your husband was in, I couldn't guarantee he wouldn't try to put a lead shot through Havelock's forehead. All it took was a few words, some pulled strings, and I made it seem like you were alone in your room when your heart gave out."

That was some relief, but not much. Part of her had hoped Devin discovered the affair upon her death, and that he'd have had six years to move on. Instead the truth was buried, and if he were to know, it'd be from her own lips. Could she tell him? Should she tell him?

"Where is Havelock anyway?" she asked. She'd not even considered searching for him since returning to life. The affair had been a brief dalliance, a distraction from the loneliness while Devin was out and about on one of his many required visits to tiny villages that dotted the west. Havelock had meant nothing to her other than as a warm body in close proximity.

"Right, you wouldn't know," Forrest said. "Havelock died two years ago. He pissed off a bunch of bandits that had stolen some rifles on delivery from Roros. Took a shot to the gut, which turned fatal after a few days. Ugly way to go, but there wasn't much we could do for him."

Brittany bit her lower lip and looked to the floor. She didn't know how to feel. Sorrow filled her, but not for Havelock. She'd not been close to him, and every Soulkeeper knew that a violent death lurked in their future. No, it was just another reminder that the whole world had moved on without her. She'd become a fading memory. Was it even right to re-enter their worlds? Tommy, Devin, Adria . . . what was she to them? And yet it felt so unfair. To them, six years had passed, yet for her, it'd been but the blink of an eye. One blink, and all was shifted and lost.

"I see," she said as the silence stretched on long enough to become uncomfortable. "Thank you for not telling Devin. I'm sure that was a tough decision."

Forrest shrugged as if it'd been nothing.

"Relationships get messy. You obviously knew that. No reason to hurt Devin when nothing good could come of it, and I sure wasn't one to judge. I wasn't always faithful to Susanna, either. This shit's hard."

"Marriage, or being a Soulkeeper?"

"Goddess-damned both. I'm guessing since you're asking me about Havelock, then you haven't told Devin you're back yet."

Brittany struggled to meet his gaze.

"You're right, Devin doesn't know. I'm . . . waiting until I'm ready."

"Well, wait as long as you need, but why come to me before him?"

"I thought it'd be obvious. I want my old position back."

His eyebrows nearly rose off his forehead.

"Do you, now?"

"It's not like I've forgotten my training," she said. "Nor will I sit idly by while those I know and love are in danger. If that cloud dragon attacks our walls, I want to be out there fighting alongside the rest of you. Besides, for my own sanity, it's better I be helping people than sitting alone in a room with Adria babysitting me like a child."

Forrest mentally debated for a half-second before acquiescing.

"All right," he said, gesturing to his robes. "Let me get dressed first."

When he returned, he was wearing a pair of worn trousers, a

gray sweater, and his long dark leather coat. He wordlessly gestured for her to follow as they together exited the mansion.

"Should we give you a new name?" he asked as they walked the empty streets. "Unless you feel like explaining your dead-but-not-dead status to everyone you meet, it might be better to have you assume a new identity."

"Let's stick with Brit," she said. "I have enough things to adjust to with a new body, and it's not like people will immediately assume any connection between myself and a dead Soulkeeper."

"It's your skin, not mine. I'll say you were traveling west from Stomme when all this mess with the black water started, and that you arrived in Londheim just before that second dragon showed up. That should let you integrate into our ranks without too much fuss. But to do that, you need to be properly dressed. We lost most everything in the cathedral fire, but thankfully we had some older uniforms stored off-site."

They arrived at their destination, which had been a Mindkeeper office until recently. Forrest unlocked the door with a key and then led her inside, pausing only a moment to light a candle with a tinder box positioned upon a table by the door. The dim glow revealed stacks upon stacks of crates crammed into the various rooms. Much of it appeared salvaged from the fire, with a cursory glance in one crate revealing a mishmash of pistol parts stained by smoke. Atop a table were over two dozen matching shirts forming a gray hill. Coats hung from wood poles propped up on even more crates.

"This is everything we could save from the Soulkeeper Sanctuary," Forrest explained. "Take what you need. I'll help you search if need be. There's not much organization to it yet."

Brittany wandered about, collecting bits of clothing to create her uniform, though to call it a uniform was a bit of a misnomer. There was no official Soulkeeper uniform, a concession made decades ago to accommodate the variety of climates Soulkeepers trekked through as part of their duties. The triangle and moon pendant they wore around their necks, and the matching symbol decorating their pistols, was all that was required. An unofficial uniform had emerged over the years, particular in West Orismund. Thick, dark pants able to withstand hours of riding and hiking, plus a matching shirt that could keep the bitter cold out in winter. She even lucked out to find a pair of boots that matched the size of her feet.

"I think that's everything but the coat," she said after locating a set of burnt leather gloves. She gave Forrest a moment to turn around before she stripped down to change.

"Flamestones are being kept in a warehouse near Greenwich Lane," Forrest said as he perused through a crate. "But you still need yourself a pistol."

He found one and offered it to her once she was dressed. Brittany hesitantly accepted. Feeling the smooth handle in her grip awakened a thousand memories, and this time they felt entirely hers, this new body be damned. Forrest gave her the gun belt he held in his other hand, and she quickly strapped it about her waist. Next came a heavy coat, and feeling its weight settle upon her shoulders filled her with a peace she hadn't believed she could experience since returning. She was herself again. A Soulkeeper of Anwyn. A woman of the people.

"Last, but not least," Forrest said, and he placed a hat atop her head. She had no mirror, but a glance down at herself was enough to thrill her. As much as she'd scoffed at Adria's desire to go out and re-establish her life, it did indeed feel amazing to be wearing her Soulkeeper attire and have a pistol strapped to her thigh. There was, however, one key part missing.

"Whatever happened to my axe? Was it lost in the armory during the fire?"

Forrest blushed.

"Not exactly," he said.

"Did you give it to a different Soulkeeper?" she asked, perplexed by his reaction.

"Not that, either." He pushed through the piles toward one of the far corners. "Truth be told, Brittany, I didn't have the heart to see anyone else wielding it. I knew if I returned it to the armory, it'd be reassigned, so I stashed it away. A blessing in disguise, it'd seem."

Brit lost sight of him for a moment in the deep shadows, and when he returned, she couldn't hold back her pleased grin. Held in the giant man's meaty fists was her enormous double-headed axe. She accepted it graciously. The texture of the black leather handle beneath her gloves felt more right than anything else in the world. A grunt escaped her lips as she traced her fingers along the smoothly polished steel head.

"If only Adria had chosen a stronger body," she said. "How did I never notice how heavy this damn thing is?"

Forrest laughed.

"I doubt Adria could have found any woman in all of Londheim with muscles like you had, let alone a soulless. Do you know how many silver crowns I won betting on your arm-wrestling matches whenever we visited a new tavern or bar?"

"More than enough to cover this new set of gear, I'd wager?"

"You wager correctly." Forrest crossed his arms, muttered something, and then shook his head. "Aw, piss on it, come here, you."

He buried her in a hug with his enormous frame, this second embrace far more warm and vulnerable than the first. Brittany barely had enough time to shift her axe out of the way, lest he cut himself on its edges. She laughed even as a few of her tears wet the front of her Vikar's shirt.

"New body or not, it's good to have you back, Brittany," Forrest said. "Our travels out west were some of the best years of my life."

"Then you've had a shitty life," she said, but she couldn't stop the grin spreading across her face. "Hey, could you do me one last favor? Don't tell Devin anything about me being back. I feel like I should be the one to do it."

Forrest gently released her frame and shot her a wink in the candlelight.

"I kept your secret before, and I'll keep your secret now," he said. "Welcome back, Brit. You're officially a Soulkeeper of Londheim. Again."

CHAPTER 8

Humans were shit at sanitation. This was Janus's favorite point to prove the species' overall ineptitude in his rare discussions with other dragon-sired. Londheim's sewer system was scattershot, with most of the overwhelmed gutters flowing straight into the Septen River. There were a few smaller tunnels that flowed westward to dump their refuse through grates in the wall surrounding the city to collect in a foul pond of shit and piss. It was at one such grate Janus knelt. The smell did not bother him, for he'd smoothed his face completely so it lacked a nose. As for the texture, it was still matter like all other matter, and did not bother him like feces bothered most other living creatures. Why worry about a bit of waste when he could turn the entire sludge flow into sparkling gold?

"You'd probably prefer that course of action, wouldn't you?" Janus muttered as he stared at the crawling mountain in the distance. "Better I spend my time slaving away turning their shit to gold than making true art with their bones and blood."

No other species in existence had been coddled like humanity had been coddled, but it seemed those gentle times were coming to an end. Nihil had arrived. The cloud dragon settled opposite the mountain in the great field beyond Londheim's walls, and there was no doubt in Janus's mind that Nihil directly faced Viciss as a challenge. In many ways, the Dragons of Conflict and Change were bosom brothers, each aiding the other during their days of creation in manipulating the Cradle into becoming something better than the glass world the Sisters first built. But when it came to humanity, and their ultimate fate, the two no longer saw eye to eye.

So far their disagreements had remained polite, but Shinnoc's army approached. When the siege began, would either remain neutral?

Janus banished the grate with a touch of his hand and hopped down. The city was on high alert, with every wall and entrance crawling with soldiers. That sewer tunnel was one of the few ways he could ensure he exited the city completely unnoticed. He landed ankle deep in the filth below. He walked through it naked. Once his feet touched dry land, he focused on his skin, shedding a singular outer layer like a snake might its scales, so that he walked pristine through the grass. A quick brush of the dirt with his fingers pulled a black coat up for him to wear. Blades of grass became trousers and a belt. Of all the gifts granted to him, Janus was most thankful that he wanted for nothing. Sometimes he wondered if similar gifts should have been granted to humanity. If they could feed themselves without the need to farm and butcher, would they still squabble like children? Or would they, now free from their daily toil, simply have that much more time to focus on being cruel to their neighbors? If armies no longer needed to be fed, would there ever be an end to the armies?

Bah. Such questions were beyond Janus's interest. The night was young, and two dragons were near. Best to keep his mind on things that mattered, and what mattered most was the Chainbreaker.

The spiritual cores of the dragons had left their physical shells to meet atop a nearby hill marked by a dwindling campfire. Again, it gave the feeling of opposing forces meeting on neutral ground. Did either Viciss or Nihil understand the significance? Or were they, in their own timeless way, ignorant of the growing disparity between them? Over his centuries of life, Janus had grown rather unimpressed with Goddesses and dragons. It seemed they spent so long observing potential futures and the consequences of their divine actions, they often missed what was happening right underneath their noses.

Janus halted at the foot of the hill, crossed his arms, and waited. He would not interrupt a meeting between demigods without an invite. As much as he liked to flaunt their will, he also had no desire to have his atoms ripped apart one by one. Thankfully he did not have to wait long. Viciss's voice floated down the hill, carried by the wind.

Approach.

Neither dragon bothered with their humanoid disguises. Viciss hovered on one side of the fire, a swirling starscape of flowing black water. Nihil stood opposite him, its body significantly more translucent than its physical dragon shell. Starlight shone through it, refracted, and became something strange and distorted. One did not see Nihil, not quite. One more saw where Nihil's existence warped and changed things, so that the grass beneath its feet disassembled into brown and orange color, starlight became noise, and the wind took on a watery form that trickled down Nihil's shoulder's like silver rain.

"Welcome among us," Nihil said. Its voice was that of three children, all girls. When it next spoke, it was of an elderly man on his deathbed. "We discuss the Chainbreaker, and your input is warranted."

"I've kept an eye on her, yes," Janus said. He thought of his collection of artwork in the tunnels underneath Londheim, paintings and sculptures and models of Adria Eveson numbering in the hundreds, and felt a sudden flush of shame. Hopefully the dragons were unaware of his recent "hobby."

"Nihil insists Adria's actions have proven her unsuitable for peace," Viciss said. His voice floated out of him like a soft kiss. "Do you agree?"

"I don't know," Janus said. "What makes you think peace is far from her mind? Is it the slaughter of our brethren at their ruined cathedral? Is it when she killed every single dragon-sired within several hundred feet during an ambush at a market two weeks ago? Or is there something new she's done to warrant this uncertainty?"

"Your sarcasm and wit are unappreciated," Nihil said. A smoke-like haze washed over its form, and its voice took on the growl of wild animals. "Speak with wisdom and humility, or I shall render you forever without a tongue with which to speak."

Perhaps Janus could devise himself a new tongue, or find an alternate way to speak, but of all five dragons, Nihil was the one that frightened him most. If Nihil wanted him to suffer, then Janus would suffer, his own cleverness be damned.

"Forgive me," Janus said instead, and he slowly sank to his knees. "Ask what you wish, and I shall answer as best I can."

"What we wish to know is if Adria would be capable of accepting peace between humans and dragon-sired if the Sisters were no longer a factor," Viciss asked.

Janus suppressed a smile.

"I did not think executing the Sisters was an option you were yet considering."

"Answer the question, avatar," Nihil demanded.

"It depends on what you mean by 'no longer a factor,'" Janus said with a shrug of his shoulders. "If the Sisters were slain, the impact it would have on her faith would be difficult to determine. As things are right now? I struggle to believe Adria will ever consider the lives of dragon-sired equal to or above her attachment to humanity."

"We do not need her to believe the dragon-sired are superior," Viciss said. "Only for her to accept our children as equals."

"Forgive me, dragons, but you worry over the wrong matter. It doesn't matter if Adria wants peace. The problem isn't the Sisters. It's humanity itself, and the flaws given to them by the Sisters when they were made. Even if the Chainbreaker tried for peace, there is no guarantee we will find it. The fear of the unknown is too strong."

"A message of forgiveness and acceptance preached since birth could change the next generation," Viciss insisted.

"They already hear sermons of forgiveness and acceptance," Janus said, and he bitterly laughed. "They just never think to apply them to anyone different than themselves."

He rose to his feet, and he felt the eyes of both dragons upon him. That they sought his opinion amused him greatly. Despite wanting peace with humanity, neither dragon had spent much time with the insipid race. Janus, due to his desire to slaughter as many humans as possible, had spent far more time immersed in their society than either of them. Perhaps he should be given the powers of the Chainbreaker, he thought dryly. Perhaps it was the murderers of humanity that understood the wretched beings best.

"You speak to me of peace," he said, and he gestured westward. In the far distance, like a thousand gathered fireflies, were the campfires of Shinnoc's forces, now mere miles away from reaching the city. "Yet an army approaches seeking war. What will you do, dragons? Will you sit idly by when a siege begins? Will you send our forces home, or will you shatter the walls with a single breath to ensure victory?"

Nihil turned away from Viciss, that alone giving him a clearer answer than the deep, baritone voice the dragon spoke with next.

"If we are to correct the mistakes of the past, we must let our children live out the consequences of their actions," Nihil said. "If Shinnoc seeks to conquer Londheim, we must let him."

"I disagree," Viciss said. "This is the precipice we stand upon. The Chainbreaker is still ignorant of her full potential. She is close, so very close, to accepting her role as a replacement cog in humanity's cycle of souls. To allow a war would jeopardize everything. We lose all hope of peace with Londheim's destruction. It is not too late for us to order Shinnoc to take his army and leave."

"I will give no such order," Nihil said. "Our children are just that, our children, not our slaves. It is the Goddesses who expect slavering obedience, not us."

That the dragons could so starkly disagree frightened Janus in a deep, unsettling way he did not anticipate. There had been previous disagreements between them, of that he had no doubt, but that was before the Sisters had imprisoned them. Now they were awake, and the Sisters' power seemingly diminished, there was no one keeping an eye on their actions. Should they battle, would anyone stop them? *Could* anyone or anything on the Cradle stop them? He thought of Viciss and Nihil clawing at each other's physical forms, and he felt his stomach tighten.

"Adria will never accept a position to replace the Sisters while the Sisters yet live," Janus said. "But if the Sisters were slain, she would feel forced to take up their mantle. You are right, Viciss, she is close. And when she takes up that mantle, I fully believe she will disregard secular rule entirely. That is your best hope for peace, one where Adria gives a divine mandate to all the bickering, childish leaders in power, one they have no choice but to obey. Help me kill the Sisters, and you will have your peace."

The discordant chaos that was Nihil turned back to face them. Janus could just barely see the outline of eyes and a mouth, formed from the refracted light of Shinnoc's distant campfires.

"Perhaps we are wrong to put our hope in Adria," Nihil said. "Perhaps we need a second Chainbreaker, one who better understands the role they are meant to play."

Panic spiked through Janus.

"It's not too late for her," he said. "Let me talk to Adria. Let me give her one last push in the right direction."

"It is odd to see you caring so much for peace," Viciss said. The swirling starscape briefly hardened into humanoid form, then spread back out into an oval. "I would think you would prefer Shinnoc to raze Londheim to the ground, and the Chainbreaker with it."

"Or perhaps I would hate to see yet another human given power they should never have," Janus weakly countered. He would never dare admit his newfound fascination with Adria, but that left him with pitifully little to argue his position.

"Enough," Nihil said with the voice of a tired, broken mother. "I have made my position clear. Shinnoc's army shall do as it wishes when it arrives. We will not interfere with their free will. Am I clear, Viciss? If you wish to prevent a war, find a way to prevent it that does not bind the hands of either humans or dragon-sired."

"The Dragon of Conflict seeks war?" Viciss said. "I suppose it is your nature."

"Life does not bloom atop a plateau," Nihil said. "It blooms in pits and caves, ditches and mountains, the crags of the deep and the carved holes beneath the plains. Let them fight. Let them die. Peace is a goal foreign to our nature. That was the Sisters' desire, not ours. If the Sisters would replace our children with their own, then let them earn that right, not inherit it through coddling and manipulation."

The Dragon of Conflict had finished his piece, and he abruptly turned and descended the hill toward his physical form resting beyond the gates of the city. Janus watched and waited, for he would not leave until his own creator dismissed him.

"Nihil grows overconfident," Viciss seethed after an interminable wait. "It no longer feels our undertaking necessary given the weakened state of the Goddesses. Perhaps it is right. Perhaps not. But that risk is not worth taking, not when we might accomplish so much more without the need of countless bloodshed."

"You have a fondness for humanity that the others do not share," Janus said.

"Perhaps with their short lives, they embody my essence more than most," Viciss said, and he turned his gaze toward Janus. "I know what it is you want, avatar, and you may have it. Go practice your art. I see little reason in protecting the people of Londheim from your tendencies when Shinnoc's army shall soon burn them all to ash. Consider only Adria forbidden from your cruel instincts. I will remain hopeful humanity may still be freed from their enslavement to the Goddesses' whims."

This was hardly the way he'd hoped for such permission, but Janus felt a skip in his heart nonetheless at those words. Even the lone restriction meant little, for harming Adria was the furthest thing from his mind.

"You are too kind," he said, and he bowed low to his maker.

Janus felt paralyzed by the choices as he sprinted back to the city. For what felt like an eternity he'd been stifled, even if it'd been only a few weeks in reality. The ache to create burned hot in his chest, of that there was no doubt. But create what? Art, but in what form, what manner? He didn't know, but he trusted it would come to him, no different than the ability to swim came to a dog tossed into water. Perhaps, through creation, he might decipher what his own confusing thoughts were for Londheim's future.

The surrounding wall was a minor obstacle. He formed a door with a moment's thought, then returned it to flat stone behind him. A grin spread across his face as he scrambled to the rooftops and began hopping from home to home with feet that shifted to resemble those of the lapinkin. He hunted no specific person or place, merely sought out the very first soul foolish enough to wander at night.

Janus found it in a middle-aged woman hustling along with a small knapsack clutched between her wrinkled fingers. He stalked her for a minute, wondering what could be so important that she'd risk the owls and the gargoyles. Was she one of their night women? Perhaps, but men came to them in Londheim, not the other way around.

He'd never learn, he decided, but what did it matter? She was materials. She was substance. She was paint and clay and marble. He dove on her from the rooftop, and he landed with his elbow directly atop her head. Her eyes crossed, and she let out a slight "Oh" as her knees went weak. Janus swept her into his arms as she fell, cradling her as if she were his lover.

"You are both blessed and cursed," he whispered. "Lament your death as you must, but know that I shall create something beautiful through it."

He grabbed the woman and slammed her against the brick wall that segmented two divisions of the city. Her head hit a second time, and it was enough to induce a bout of vomiting. Janus carefully sidestepped the mess, then gently wiped a bit of the filth off her lips with his thumb.

"Shush now," he said, his touch sealing the flesh together. "This will not take long."

She likely didn't understand him with how glazed over her eyes were. Her legs were weak, but that was fine. A bit of pressure on her shoulders and she stood, her weight braced against the wall. Janus observed her in the moonlight. A bit pudgy, with a flat nose, painted cheeks, and her hair cut short at the neck. Her eyes were an uninspired shade of green, a far cry from the vibrancy Janus put into his own pupils. *What was her name?* he wondered. What crimes had she committed in her life, both little and grand? He could peel back her skin to reveal her organs, her bones, blood and teeth, but he knew nothing of who she believed herself to be.

A grunt signified her realization of her predicament, followed by a scream squelched by the sealing of her lips. Janus split his arms in two lengthwise, the thumbs of the upper halves sharpening and becoming jagged points. He thrust them deep into the woman's shoulders, pinning her to the wall. The lower halves of his arms reshaped, becoming slightly thinner, skinnier hands, with bits of his bones still protruding through the milky skin.

"Not long," he insisted as he brushed her curly red hair. "Though forgive me if I am as of yet uncertain."

He felt a disturbing fear growing in his belly. Yes, he must create. It was a need deeper inside him than humanity's sexual desires that often enslaved them. But... create what? What message did he have to convey to this doomed city? He had mocked them when he first arrived. He had put them in their place with his display at the market. But what now? His past few weeks floated through his mind, and for a brief moment he felt afraid.

"What have I to say?" he asked aloud. The helpless woman was crying, he noticed. Her tears rolled down her face, and snot started to drip from her nostrils. So disgusting, the human design. He sealed the nostrils as well. What did it matter if she couldn't breathe? Death was her inevitable fate. How it happened didn't matter.

The color left her face. Her chest heaved, and she struggled against bonds her body could not fathom. Janus's bony secondary extrusions kept her firmly pinned in place. He thought he'd feel something as he watched her die. He thought it would light a creative spark within him. It had been so long since he'd crafted, damn it, how could he feel nothing? But when her life passed, he felt only frustration and sorrow at this empty shell. Her soul remained within her skull. Whatever this woman had been, good or foul, kind or rotten, it was inside that soul, and it would soon rise to the heavens to be forever remembered. Such permanence was forever denied to him, a member of the dragon-sired.

What did he have to say? What message might he offer people who, no matter how horrid or pathetic their existence, could still escape it to an eternity that would forever welcome them? Their suffering was ephemeral, as was their joy. He envied them. He hated them.

Janus didn't even realize he was changing the woman's body before it was already halfway transitioned. The curly red hair darkened. Her face thinned, and the deathly paleness filled with a calmer, more beautiful white. The woman's simple dress became transitory monochrome. The features of her face shifted, not that it mattered. With but a thought he sealed it over with a porcelain mask, left side white, right side black. It was so effortless turning her into Adria Eveson, it bordered on second nature. Janus melded infinitesimally small pieces of her skin and clothes to the wall so she'd remain upright when he pulled away his jagged extensions and folded them back into his arms like a snake resetting its unhinged jaw.

"What message have I to offer?" he wondered aloud. "What have I to say?"

It was one thing, and one thing only, that he might tell the people of Londheim. It was a message he repeated seven more times that night. Sometimes he started with a man, sometimes a woman, but the end result was always the same. It was the hanged body of the Chainbreaker, her face obscured behind her mask, and with a message scrawled above her in her blood, which sparkled with gold and diamond akin to when Janus first made his presence known to the city. He kept it simple, so that even humans might understand.

NEW MOTHER. NEW GODDESS.

CHAPTER 9

Many believe you're the Sacred Mother reborn," Dierk said as he glanced about the tidy but small home. "You deserve a mansion like mine, not this."

Adria winced at the comparison.

"Multiple bodies resembling mine were found this morning declaring a similar message," she said. "I do not appreciate the comparison. I am no Goddess, and no Sacred Mother reborn."

"Sorry, sorry," he said, realizing he'd touched a sensitive nerve. Adria set out cups for tea for herself, Dierk, and their third member, the man he'd come to meet. Tamerlane Swift reclined in a rocking chair stacked with two pillows for comfort. He was a striking figure, with a broad, handsome face and gold eyes and perfect tanned skin and so many other perfect qualities that made Dierk seethe with a squirmy, formless jealousy. "But I still believe you are of such great importance, you deserve finer accommodations."

"And when someone donates one, I'll stay there while we rebuild the cathedral."

Dierk fought down an impulse to volunteer his own mansion for her to stay in. As much as he loved the idea, he'd hate for her to know about the daily curse he had to cast on his father to maintain control over the estate. Perhaps once he staged an accidental death to enable his official takeover…

"I certainly can't complain," Tamerlane said as he accepted his own cup. "This quaint home is still a mansion compared to my previous abode."

Dierk beamed a smile at Adria as she poured him tea. Supplies were painfully thin, and what remained was often dark and bitter. He sipped it, and was thankful to detect a strong amount of honey within.

"Surely whatever previous home you lived in could not have been too terrible as to make this little shed seem glamorous," he said, trying to keep any bite out of his question. From the moment he stepped inside, it had been painfully obvious Tamerlane lived with Adria inside the home donated for church use after the cathedral's burning. Knowing that someone, anyone, other than himself was living with her set his teeth to grinding.

"It's all perspective," Tamerlane said, and he chuckled. "Before Adria rescued me, I had been imprisoned by Vikar Thaddeus for what I did to the Deakon."

"The Deakon?" he asked. "What did you do to the Deakon?"

The smug look on Tamerlane's face set a fire in Dierk's stomach.

"I afflicted him with the mutilation curse from the first chapter of the Book of Ravens."

Dierk tried, and failed, to hide his admiration. He was reluctant to cast any spell from the Book of Ravens, for all of them carried tremendous power in their words. The mutilation curse in particular had intimidated him with its implications. For this Tamerlane person to have cast the curse on the *Deakon of Londheim* was absolutely absurd.

"Try not to seem too proud about that," Adria said as she joined them in the small living room. The lone two chairs were occupied, so she sat upon a little nest of pillows to the side. She kept her mask on, something that piqued Dierk's curiosity. Would she continue to hide herself from the two of them, or did she even realize she still wore it?

"Well, I'm sure he deserved it," Dierk said, still trying to form an opinion of the man. Adria had wanted them to meet for a reason, and it seemed his knowledge of the Book of Ravens was that reason. Could Tamerlane be a teacher to him, in a way the avenria Logarius could not?

"Without getting too much into the weeds," said Tamerlane, "yes, young Becher, he very much did."

Dierk hated it when people referenced his family name while talking to him. It no doubt was meant to flatter him, but all it did was remind him of his father, and how so much of his life had been shaped and molded by that abusive asshole.

"So, um, who were you before?" Dierk asked as he shifted in his rickety old chair. "Before you were thrown in prison, I mean."

"I was a Mindkeeper assigned to the Cathedral of the Sacred Mother. I mostly helped with lesson plans for the cathedral's various teachers. A thinking man's thinking man is how I liked to view myself, though I see in hindsight how much arrogance was involved in that assessment."

"Arrogant" was certainly a word Dierk would have used to describe Tamerlane. There were others, too. Handsome. Charming. He reminded Dierk of so many suave men who dressed in fine clothes and wowed crowds with speeches during his father's various state functions. Everything about him ignited intense feelings of jealousy and inadequacy deep within Dierk's chest. He tried telling himself to calm down and be mature about things. So far Tamerlane had been nothing but pleasant and respectful to him, so why did he feel so antagonistic toward the man?

Perhaps it was the way Adria hovered about him so casually. The way she had touched his shoulder upon gliding past him to her current perch near the window. The way Tamerlane's eyes lingered on hers as he talked, even when he addressed Dierk. His mind bounced between a thousand lewd thoughts. Did they sleep together? Pray together? Did Tamerlane even know a damn thing about what Adria could truly do, and how Dierk could enable it?

"Adria thinks I could teach you," Tamerlane said, and he seemed reluctant to bring his attention Dierk's way. "So I suppose I should start at the very beginning and ascertain your level of knowledge. Have you read the Book of Ravens?"

Dierk clapped his hands together eagerly. Now they were getting to something he was confident about. He'd devoured the words for years since receiving it as a birthday gift from one of his father's guards.

"Cover to cover," he said.

"Then can you tell me its purpose?"

"Its purpose?" he asked. "That's a bit vague. As in why it was written?"

"As in, what are we to learn from it? How would the Cradle be changed if its truth were known and spread throughout the populace?"

"I can tell you exactly its purpose," Dierk said. "I've met the author, Logarius."

Finally he got to see a bit of surprise on his supposed new teacher's face.

"You have?"

"An avenria," Dierk said, relishing the sudden attention. "And his purpose was simple. Humanity was inferior to the dragon-sired, and so we needed to learn to serve them if we were to coexist without humanity's eventual extinction."

"Is that so?" Tamerlane leaned closer, and his intense gaze made Dierk squirm in his seat. What amusement he'd felt in possessing knowledge the other Mindkeeper lacked was long gone. He felt like a rabbit before a starving wolf.

"Of course," Dierk said. "Why else would the Ravencallers help retake Belvua?"

"And you agree with this analysis?"

He shrugged.

"I don't disagree with what the book says, only the logic that follows. I refuse to be slaves to the dragon-sired. Logarius may believe our defeat is inevitable, but I saw what happened at the grand cathedral. We can still win, especially with Adria on our side."

"I'm not here to win a war for us," Adria said. She'd lurked to the side during the conversation, trying to let the two discuss, and she seemed unhappy to have to interject at all. Dierk felt his neck flush a bit, and he nodded to show he understood and agreed. Meanwhile Tamerlane put his fingers together and tapped them to his lips as he thought for a long moment.

"You were lied to," he said. "This Logarius you met wasn't the author."

Dierk rocked backward at the audacity of such a claim.

"I'm sorry," he said. "But you think that why?"

"Because that's not what the book teaches, nor is it its purpose. The Book of Ravens isn't about humanity's relationship with dragon-sired. The dragon-sired are rarely mentioned, if at all. It is a systematic attempt to re-understand and re-contextualize the Sisters, their relationship with humanity, and how the Keeping Church has bastardized all of it in its quest for power. That's why it includes the curses. How could the church, who insisted the Sisters were pure and without malice or flaw, possess the power to cast something so horrific as the mutilation curse?"

"So Logarius lied to me?"

"Humans lie all the time. Is it so hard to believe these creatures could do the same in a bid for power?"

"But don't you still worship the Sisters?" Dierk asked, baffled. "Why would you learn from and teach a book that hates them so?"

"Because the initial argument is still valid. The Keeping Church is woefully broken and needs mending. The Sisters have been stifled of creativity and wonder, and presented as nothing more than flat caricatures incapable of true emotions, doubts, and risks. What we are, this whole explosion of life upon the Cradle, is a tremendous experiment. But let me be absolutely clear, that experiment was made *for us.* If there is to be any extrapolation toward our position compared to the dragon-sired, it is that our lives will echo for eternity, not theirs. That fact alone positions us as superior."

"You only think that because you've not seen the true power they can wield," Dierk said. "I've witnessed it. I've felt it. These beings, the avenria, the nisse, the dragons, they're *better* than us. If you don't believe that, then you're just being willfully ignorant."

"Willfully ignorant, am I?" Tamerlane asked, his voice as cold as a winter storm.

"If not worse! If humanity is to take our rightful place in this world, we're going to have to take it by force. We'll take it by being smarter, more ruthless, more brutal. It won't be by . . . by . . . pretending to be superior just because we have a soul, as if they give two shits about that fact." Dierk stood up straight, and he felt his wounded pride take control of his tongue. "That's why I will be taking over the city from my father. That's why I will rule our people to a better future. Because I understand what needs to be done, and it won't be by uselessly praying to the Sisters."

"Enough, both of you," Adria snapped.

"No, no, I would hear this," Tamerlane said. His eyes never left Dierk's. "Is that what you are, young Becher? Are you a smarter, more ruthless, more brutal person to rule Londheim? Is that how you will lead us to victory over the dragon-sired?"

Dierk could feel the trap being laid, but how else might he avoid it? To cower was to refuse everything he'd just proudly stated. To agree, though . . .

Agreeing meant declaring himself to be everything he hated about his father, if not worse.

"I'll rule Londheim because I'm the best person to do it," he said, trying to cut the argument off at the knees. "Adria's the only person stronger than I am. Don't you get it? Either of you? You don't need the Goddesses. Adria could replace them in a heartbeat, and become the new mother the city desperately needs! The Goddesses are nothing, and if you're still worshipping them, then you're just a damn fool."

"You're a child with no respect for the Goddesses," Tamerlane said. He rose to his feet as well, and he approached Dierk with calm, steady steps. "You're a fool denying a well's existence while stealing its water. You think you're special. You think you're unique."

Tamerlane was towering over him now, his physical presence so close, so overwhelming. His golden eyes were more intimidating than any glare from an avenria. "Do you know what I think? I think you are a product of your birth, and nothing more."

"I'll kill you, you bastard."

"Try."

Dierk shoved Tamerlane in the chest, but he was smaller, weaker, and it just made him stumble backward instead of moving the disgraced Mindkeeper.

"Anwyn of the Moon, hear me!" they both shouted in unison, but it was Tamerlane's presence that was stronger, his tongue quicker. Dierk felt invisible chains latching across his body as the other man continued, his gaze horrifying in its calmness.

"Hold this serpent so its teeth find no purchase," he continued. "Turn flesh into lawful stone. Turn willful impulse into silent obedience. May the body—"

"I said *enough*."

Adria stepped between them, and with a single wave of her hand, Dierk felt the curse upon him break. He gasped in air as if he'd been holding his breath. Being held helpless for even those few seconds left him feeling deeply violated.

"How dare you!" he shouted.

"No more," Adria said, her voice hardly above a whisper but its intensity unrivaled throughout the Cradle. Her eyes could shoot flames through the holes of her mask. She pointed at Dierk. "I brought you here so you could learn, not engage in a damn pissing contest. Both of you disappoint me immensely. Leave. Now."

"I'm more than happy to get away from that...that prick," Dierk mumbled as he rushed down the stairs and out to the street. He took a straight path back to his mansion. The scowl on his face may as well have been etched from stone. Tamerlane's words echoed again and again in his mind, as if they were carved upon the sides of a wheel that would not stop spinning. Such an insufferable man! That he was both handsome and significantly better educated did not escape Dierk's notice, either. Of course Adria wouldn't bother with someone like Dierk when Tamerlane was clearly infatuated with her.

"Stupid smug little cunt," he muttered as he climbed the steps to his house. "You've not seen what I've seen. I was Vaesalaum's student. I witnessed Logarius split the night sky to reveal the magical realm beyond. You, you're just a...just a stuffed-up asshole Mindkeeper."

Words he wished he had said before storming out of Adria's new home. What did it matter if Tamerlane *was* smarter about religious matters? He wasn't stronger than Dierk. His eyes weren't attuned to the spiritual realm like Dierk's were after his constant contact with a nisse. Adria should have listened. She should have taken his side.

Of course, there'd been that brief moment when Tamerlane had started whispering the words of a Ravencaller curse, when the deep magic had wrapped its tendrils about his body, and Dierk had only stood there. Shocked. Frightened. Helpless.

The hour was late, but sleep felt distant, and he couldn't shake a feeling that he was forgetting something important. Once back home he swung by the kitchen to grab a half-full bottle of ale.

He'd not been much for the stuff prior to taking control of the mansion, but his tongue had gradually welcomed the taste. He didn't bother grabbing a glass. Instead he drank straight from the bottle as he wandered room to room, finally settling beside a fireplace with a dwindling flame. He tossed two fresh logs atop it, then for amusement splashed a bit of his wine over the fire to really get it going.

I think you are a product of your birth, and nothing more.

"Fuck you," Dierk whispered, and he drowned out Tamerlane's words with a huge gulp. "Fuck you, you fucking...fuck."

He slumped into the chair beside the fire. Damn it all, he was crying, wasn't he? He wiped at his face with his sleeve. Why did things have to be so confusing? He'd confessed his heart to Adria at the cathedral. She knew how important she was to him, and how deeply his love pounded for her. Yet she still treated him merely as a friendly acquaintance. Had she ever looked his way like she did toward Tamerlane? Of course not. He'd given her the power to perform miracles, yet it seemed without a firm square jaw and a charismatic smile, he'd still be an afterthought.

Dierk drained the last of the bottle, and when he needed to piss, he pissed on the fire. A thousand ways of murdering Tamerlane danced like faeries in his head. The night dragged on, yet he still couldn't bring himself to return to his bed. Eventually he curled up in his chair and pressed his face into its cushion. Why bother with the effort of going to his room, he thought groggily. The mansion was his. Its every room. Its every chair.

Rough hands grabbed him awake. A fist smashed his face. His lips cut upon his teeth, and blood sprayed across the chair. Dierk's panicked stand ended the moment something hard crashed into his stomach. Last night's ale came rushing back up, and he vomited on the floor. Through blurry vision he saw several pairs of boots. Words pushed through his haze.

"... let him speak..."

Someone pushed a thick wad of cloth into his mouth before he could react. His gag reflex kicked in, but a strap of leather followed, a single loop tightening to hold in the cloth so that his coughs and heaves resulted in nothing. The pulling motion drew back his head, and at last he laid eyes upon his attackers.

Soren Becher stood opposite him with arms crossed and murder in his eyes. Two house guards stood beside him, with an additional two behind Dierk's chair. They bound his arms and buckled the leather strap that prevented him from speaking. If Dierk had anything left in his stomach, he'd have vomited that up, too. That nagging feeling of forgetting something, something important, returned tenfold. The spell he cast on his father to keep him under control, it needed to be refreshed once a night, every night, or it would fade.

Except last night, amid his drunken tantrum, he'd forgotten.

"Take him to the basement," Soren said. "And no matter what you do, do not let him speak."

"Wait!" Dierk screamed into his gag. "Stop!"

His father knelt on one knee and gently cradled Dierk's face in one palm.

"I have never taken a life with my own two hands," he whispered, his deep voice quaking with rage. "As Mayor, I thought such bloodshed beneath me. Surely it was wiser, and safer, to let my men do the necessary dirty work."

He grabbed Dierk by the hair and lifted him up so they might stare eye to eye.

"That all changes with you."

CHAPTER 10

"You're overthinking it," Jacaranda said as Wren missed the parry for the third time in a row. "You have two movements to choose from. Pick the right one, and then do it."

They trained in the tiny square of pale grass that was Devin's "backyard." The house hid the two from the street, which was as much privacy as Jacaranda could hope for. At least she didn't need to wear her scarf to hide her chain tattoos now that the church was aware of her presence and knew she lived with Devin. Wren still kept her cloak wrapped tightly about her throat, clearly uncomfortable with the idea of taking it off regardless of Jacaranda's assurances.

"Pick the right one," Wren said. "As if it's so easy and obvious."

"It *is* easy," Jacaranda said. "You're just bad at it."

Wren laughed. She'd removed her wig for the training, and sweat shone as it trickled down the sides of her head.

"I'm beginning to think you're a shitty teacher."

"I never said I'd be a good one." Jacaranda settled into a stance. "Now lift your dagger. Try again."

It honestly did seem simple to Jacaranda. They both wielded blunted daggers, and the current scenario was an attempt to develop basic defensive instincts for Wren. If Jacaranda did a downward slash, Wren was to parry it with a sweeping motion.

If Jacaranda thrust, she was to take a single step to the right and then bat the thrust aside. Jacaranda had shown her both maneuvers, made her practice them a few times, and then began the trials. All Wren had to do was read the attack and pick the correct of two options. Jacaranda even exaggerated her movements prior to swinging, but yet again it didn't seem to matter.

Jacaranda's dagger thrust poked against Wren's chest, the attempted parry coming in too late so that the other dagger's blunted edge struck Jacaranda's elbow. The sting from the contact made Jac's eyes water but she pretended to be otherwise unhurt. If it were a real fight, Wren would be dead from a stab to the heart. A cut elbow was irrelevant compared to that.

"Damn it," Wren said, stepping back and glaring at the dagger in her hand as if it had betrayed her. "Goddesses and Sisters above, I am completely worthless."

Jacaranda twirled her dagger as she thought. Memories of her own training flashed through her mind, but she'd been honed by the finest duelists that money could buy. Not only that, but she'd learned while soulless, in a state where following orders on how and when to perform various maneuvers was in her nature. Perhaps the way she'd been trained was not applicable when it came to someone who wasn't soulless?

"Don't beat yourself up," Jacaranda said. "I'll talk to Devin about how the Keeping Church trains its novices. I may be going about this entirely the wrong way."

"If you say so," Wren said.

Their training finished, they returned inside Devin's home. Jacaranda swapped out her training clothes for a loose wine-colored sweater and a pair of comfortable trousers. Devin had left for a night of drinking with Tommy to give them privacy, so the two sat before the fire, the heat pleasant on Jacaranda's sweat-soaked skin. Wren had no clothes to change into, but she did replace her wig and then settle into Devin's rocking chair. Jacaranda noted

Puffy lurking inside the fire, its little black eyes perfectly still to not give away its presence. So far she and Wren had not discussed the dragon-sired, and part of her was hesitant to bring the matter up lest she discover Wren harbored hatred toward the creatures.

"It'll get easier, I promise," Jacaranda said. She offered the woman a glass of wine she'd poured in the kitchen. "It'll never be truly easy, because that means you need to push yourself harder, but it will get more bearable."

"Thanks," Wren said as she took the glass. "You really know how to cheer someone up."

"I don't remember agreeing to be your court jester, only your trainer." Jacaranda returned to the couch and sipped the wine. Remembering her initial encounter with Tommy, wine, and a magically summoned phantom penis, she wondered if Wren had consumed alcohol before and asked.

"Once," Wren admitted. "It went... poorly. I might have made a fool of myself by singing in front of an entire tavern. Thankfully Kye was with me and spared me from performing an encore."

"Who is Kye?"

"A recast man I met not long after awakening. He's let me sleep in his spare bedroom, and is the only other person who knows about these damn tattoos." She sipped the wine and seemed surprised by its taste. "Oh, wow, this is much nicer than what I had my first time."

"Devin tends to buy the super-sweet varieties. He may not admit it, being a gruff Soulkeeper and all, but he prefers those over straight liquor and ale."

"Sounds like a smart man to me."

"He is. At times."

They shared a laugh. Jacaranda paced herself as she drank. The last thing she needed was to re-create her first visit with Tommy.

"Where did you meet Kye?" she asked.

"He runs a shop in Watermark District," Wren said. "Have you visited there before?"

"I have," Jacaranda said. The Watermark District housed multiple shops owned and run by recast men and women, and catered specifically to their needs, which were often overlooked elsewhere in Londheim. "I sometimes went there when I needed a disguise for one of Gerag's assignments."

"I'm not wearing a disguise," Wren snapped. Jacaranda lifted her palms.

"I didn't mean to imply such a thing," she said. "Only that they sufficed for such purposes when I was soulless."

"Sorry." Wren rubbed sweat away from her eyes. "I shouldn't be so touchy about my decisions, especially since that's the reason I went there myself. I was looking for my ideas to hide, well..." She gestured to the exposed chain tattoos on her throat now that she'd removed her cloak upon coming inside. "I'm sure you've experienced similar, but the sensation of shopping was exhilarating the first few times. There I was, browsing through items deciding if *I* liked them or not. I didn't even need a specific reason or rationale for it, either. This was pretty. This was ugly. I would wear this, I wouldn't wear that. It's, it's...fun?"

"The first time I dressed myself," Jacaranda said, "I thought Devin would laugh at me, and he probably wanted to. I've gotten better at it since, but that first time, I was a mess of every single color and style, all because it was such a joy to make that decision."

She pointed to the giant wide-brimmed hat hanging by the door.

"Also I took and wore that hat with every outfit regardless if it matched. I sometimes still do."

Wren's guarded nature eased away, and she beamed.

"I was too scared about fitting in and not being found when

I first left Kennet," she said. "But while I was in Watermark, I found myself touching the scarves, the dresses, and on a whim I tried on one of their longer wigs. I told myself the hair might help distract attention from my neck, but the moment I put it on and looked into the seller's little hand mirror…"

She shook her head.

"From the first moment I awoke, I'd felt like my soul was a stranger to my own body. Sometimes I wondered if it were a mistake. Perhaps the Sisters had sent my soul to the wrong soulless? Perhaps I should have even stayed that way, with how every decision and idea felt weird and wrong." She lovingly ran her hands through her hair. "When I saw this, I knew I had to have it. And Kye knew, too, because he pressed me to visit his clothier friend next door and request a dress."

Wren blushed.

"I hate admitting this, but I was so unbelievably stupid. I didn't know why Kye wanted me to buy the dress. That seemed weird. Why did I need a dress? But Kye insisted I try one on, a blue one that complemented my eyes. And so I did."

"See, you're lucky someone was there to help you color coordinate," Jacaranda said, earning herself a pleasant laugh. "I bet you'd look lovely in a deep blue dress."

"I did, to the point where I felt it a problem. I was turning too many heads! But would you believe me that, even when I stepped outside in a robin's-egg dress and this braided wig, I still didn't quite understand why I liked it? I thought maybe it was only because I enjoyed trying new things I'd never tried while in my grandpa's…in Kennet's care?" Wren rolled her eyes. "It took a few weeks, and plenty more trips to Watermark District, before I truly understood. Afterward I changed my name to Wren and made a great show of burning my old clothes Kennet had bought for me. They were the last remnants of the decisions he had made for me, and I would abide them no longer."

Another sentiment Jacaranda had shared. She'd cast aside her old clothing to dress herself at the Oakenwall camp. And afterward, they'd both sought to find and slay Gerag for his crimes. It seemed the only real difference between them was in Jacaranda's brutal training. That, and she'd found Gerag first.

"Well, I'm glad your awakening experience went fairly well, all things considered," Jacaranda said. "I was lucky enough to be with Devin when it happened. He had a decent idea about what was going on, and he hid me from both Gerag and the church while I figured it out myself."

"If only everyone were as lucky as us," Wren said, and she drained the last of her glass. "There *are* others beyond us two, aren't there?"

Marigold's face flashed inside Jac's mind.

I can't die. I never lived.

"Yes," she said. "There are more, and I suspect most will not escape like we have. Gerag himself killed one, and Vikar Thaddeus admitted that the Keeping Church has killed several more to keep the existence of awakened soulless a secret."

"They have?" Wren asked. She shuddered. "But why? Why would they care so much? You'd think the arrival of souls to the soulless would be seen as a good thing, a return of their Goddesses' power and whatnot."

"You'd think," Jacaranda said. She stood and took the glass from Wren's hand. "I need a bit more. How about you?"

"Sure. I could use more wine to forget the embarrassment I made of myself out there."

Jacaranda used the privacy of the kitchen to lean against a wall and close her eyes. A wave of fresh, raw pain assaulted her heart. She had hoped time and distance would lessen the hurt. Gerag had died, damn it, died by her hand. She feared him no longer, but that did not erase the damage. It didn't restore the lives the bastard had ruined. What joy might Marigold have found in her life? Who might she have become free of Gerag and his slavery?

She poured the rest of the cherry wine into the two glasses.

Hold it together, she told herself. *If not for you, then for Wren.* For all of Jacaranda's problems, she felt more comfortable with herself, her life, and her place within it than she ever could have imagined those first few days after awakening. The same could not yet be said for Wren.

"Here you go," she said, handing Wren the other glass and then settling in on the couch. Before either could drink, the door opened without a knock or hesitation. Together they turned to see a Mindkeeper step inside and remove her mask to reveal a very tired, very frustrated Adria Eveson. Adria slammed the door shut behind her, and that uncharacteristic display of frustration and anger surprised Jacaranda so much, it took her a second to react.

"Hello there," she said at last. "Long day?"

Adria's head tilted to one side as if just now realizing she wasn't alone. She broke out into laughter.

"Yes," she said. "Very long, and very full of idiot men. Please tell me you have more of that wine."

"I'll need to open a new bottle."

"Then do it. If Devin complains, I'll yank his soul out of his body and use it as a toss-ball."

Jacaranda stood, and she grinned ear to ear.

"Oh, it's been *that* bad a day, has it?"

Once a new bottle was opened, and all three had glasses, Jacaranda gave Wren a proper introduction.

"It's nice to meet you," Adria said, and she even made it sound convincing as she sat on the floor directly before the fire. Jacaranda glanced at Wren, then bit her lip as she thought.

"Is it all right if I tell her?" Jac asked. Wren's brow furrowed.

"Are you sure?"

"Tell me what?" Adria asked. In response, Wren sighed and

pulled the scarf down from her neck to reveal her chain tattoos. Adria's eyebrows rose toward the top of her head.

"Well now," she said. "What a day for surprises. How did you two meet?"

Jacaranda told Adria the story as best she could, always careful to hesitate prior to personal aspects of Wren's life to give her new friend a chance to protest or fill in the details herself. When Jacaranda had finished, Adria put her hands together and pressed them to her lips as she sank deep in thought.

"If this continues, we need to formalize the Keeping Church's response," she said. "We can't have soulless continue to awaken and suffer under their masters and owners due to public ignorance."

"Is that something you could accomplish?" Wren asked.

"Here in Westreach at least," Adria said. "I'm acting Vikar of the Day, after all."

Wren's eyes widened as she realized who exactly was speaking to her.

"You're the one they call the Sacred Mother reborn," she said.

"Please, don't, I loathe that title," Adria said with a visible shiver. Her relaxed atmosphere was rapidly fading away, her arms and legs stiffening. Wren, however, was growing lively.

"But we've all heard of the messages proclaiming you as such written in gold."

"And people died at the hands of a monster to convey that message," she snapped. "I have denounced them again and again, yet it never seems enough, not for anyone, not for the church, and now apparently not for you."

Wren backed a step, and she dipped her head in quick, half-hearted apology.

"Forgive me for not knowing what I am and am not to believe," she said. "All of Londheim hears stories of you, each more outlandish than the last. Is it true what they say, that you can command souls? That you can even return life to the dead?"

Adria's shoulders sagged. She couldn't look more exhausted and uncomfortable if she tried. Jacaranda thought to reprimand Wren but wasn't sure if it was her place. She was older than Wren, true, and currently her teacher when it came to daggers, but that hardly made her the recast woman's parent or guardian.

"My powers are great," Adria said. "Though I'd rather not speak of them in this house. Out there in Londheim, I am acting Vikar. In here, I seek only to be Devin's sister and Jacaranda's friend."

"I know, I know, but there was a story I heard. A mother brought you a girl, a soulless girl, and you gifted her the soul she was meant to be born with. Is that true? Did that happen?"

Adria glared over her shoulder at Wren. Her hands fumbled into one of her pockets and pulled out her porcelain mask. It wasn't until that mask was comfortably over her face that she answered.

"Yes," she said. "I did."

Wren lurched to her feet, her hands clenched into fists.

"You bitch," she shouted. Jacaranda shot between them, baffled by the sudden outrage.

"Back off, now," she said, her elbow digging into Wren's stomach. "What in the void has gotten into you?"

"She admitted it," Wren said, finally relenting. "Don't you get it? She just admitted she could grant a soul to a soulless. Yet look around Londheim. Piss, just look around the Keeping Church itself. It still has hundreds in the ranks of Alma's Beloved. It still has soulless cleaning their stained glass windows and sweeping their floors. You could grant a life, a soul, to the many soulless in Londheim and you haven't yet? How come, Adria? How come? Too busy being Vikar? Too busy getting everyone to love you than do something for people like us!"

"Enough!" Jacaranda shouted. "I've watched her give everything to protect this city. It is not your place to criticize her."

Adria rose from her seat and said not a word. Her arms crossed over her chest, and she looked aside, deep in thought. Silence hung heavy over the three. Wren's face flushed red, whether from embarrassment or anger, Jacaranda couldn't tell. Both emotions were appropriate as far as she was concerned.

"You have done nothing wrong," Jacaranda told the withdrawn Adria. "Don't tear yourself apart for inaction, not when you've exhausted yourself daily helping others."

"New mother..." Adria whispered, then finally looked up. "But she's right, Jac. I could have helped the soulless, yet not once did I think to do so. I fear my own strength, and it has crippled my ambitions. Here I am healing broken bones and high fevers when I alone possess the power to salvage the soulless from their emptiness and give them the life they were promised. It isn't right, and I won't allow it to continue."

Jacaranda hated the guilt she heard in Adria's voice. The woman had given everything of herself, pushed beyond the point of exhaustion to heal and help others, and yet she was convinced she could do more, that she *should* have done more.

Wren, however, heard the contrition and replaced her anger with cautious optimism.

"You have something in mind," she said, her eyes locked on Adria's behind the mask. "Don't you?"

"I will not sit idly by when a fault has been laid bare before me," Adria said. "Not when I have the power to correct it. If I hurry, I can set things in motion by tonight. When the reaping hour comes and the barrier between worlds is at its thinnest, I will make amends. Would you come with me, Wren, and bear witness? Will both of you be there for me, and more importantly, for them?"

"Them?" Jacaranda asked, so much hope and fear mixed together into that single word.

"Those my fellow keepers bring me from Alma's Beloved," she said. "They will need assistance from someone who knows what they're going through, someone who can guide them when I give them their souls."

"But how will you choose who to awaken and who to leave soulless?" Wren asked.

"I don't think you understand." Adria returned to the door, and she flung it open to the cold outside. "I need to stop being afraid of the power I possess. I won't choose, Wren. I will awaken them all."

CHAPTER 11

Adria stood in the center of a ring of soulless, and she felt pride at how many she had gathered into the graveyard on such short notice. Over sixty men and women bearing the dark cloth of the church stood in a perfect circle, their posture straight, their eyes that soulless combination of alert yet relaxed. Seeing all, yet caring for none of it unless it invoked a previous given order. The moon was high, the stars bright. Adria lifted her arms, and she felt power within her aching to be unleashed.

"I pray you forgive me for taking so long to understand the responsibilities I alone should bear," she told the soulless. "And I pray that when you awaken, you trust me to guide you through this new world you find yourselves walking through."

The soulless did not respond, nor would they. These words were not for them, not in their current state. They were for when they awakened. They were for when their minds struggled to understand their newfound freedom and choice.

"Are you sure you can do this?" Jacaranda asked. She and Wren lurked at the far edges of the ring, their forms hidden underneath thick coats meant to hold back the winter chill. The group amassed in the same graveyard that Brittany had once been buried within, the graveyard in which she'd returned her soul to another body. In Adria's heart, it felt correct to do this act in the same place. She'd focused on righting the wrongs in her own life, and in making Devin happy, while ignoring just how profoundly she could improve the lives of others. This went beyond a cut to the flesh or illness in the body. This was life. True life, new life, made aware. Made whole.

"I can sense them, if I concentrate," Adria answered. "Each and every soulless is like an empty plot of soil, and there is a matching seed crying out for it, a seed that was never brought down by Alma upon birth like it should have been. I believe...no, I *know* that if I call for it, it will come, and it will seek the body it was always meant to be given."

Sixty soulless standing perfectly still. Jacaranda looked at them, men and women of all ages, and she shook her head.

"This is incredible, Adria, if you can do it."

Adria didn't appreciate the doubt, but who could blame her? It seemed everything Adria did lately defied reason and possibility. Then again, Jacaranda didn't know about Brittany's return. She didn't know just how easily it was becoming to defy the supposed order she'd grown up believing in. Adria took in a deep breath and looked to the stars. Those heavenly guardians protected the Cradle, but beyond their reach flowed the great Aether stream of souls. Within that cosmic existence waited the sixty souls meant for the soulless surrounding her, eager seeds desperate to be planted.

If only she'd brought Tamerlane, she thought. He should be here, but after his spat with Dierk, she'd decided she needed a break from the both of them. Perhaps he'd accompany the next batch of soulless, she decided, for there would be more. These sixty were just those employed by the Keeping Church that she could locate on such short notice. How many more soulless lurked throughout the city as guards for the watch, or as servants for the wealthy?

Adria closed her eyes. Within her mind she could see the

shining brilliance of every single soul living in Londheim. If she focused her attention, might she also detect the shadowed gaps of the men and women who were soulless? Could she awaken them as well despite not being physically near them? A frightening yet exciting thought, one she swore to revisit in time.

Deep within her lurked a chasm of power, and she opened her heart to it. One by one her presence swirled through the gathered soulless, touching them with her mind while simultaneously looking to the great Aether flow in the heavens. An emotional yearning overtook her, as if she felt the desperate need of these empty bodies for their missing piece. Among those stars, she could feel those pieces, almost see them as sparkling diamonds amid a dark night sky. Waiting for her to claim them. Waiting for her to grab hold and command them.

Her eyes opened.

"It's time to awaken," she said. Her hands rose heavenward. Pillars of soft blue light shone down upon the sixty, marking the approach of the infinitesimally small seeds screaming across the impossible distance between the Cradle and the realms beyond. Cold sweat beaded across Adria's brow as she felt the wind leave her lungs. Her fingers clenched into clawlike shapes as she forced the souls onward. She would not fail in this. She would awaken these empty shells about her, no matter the cost.

And then she saw them with her own eyes, little beads of light crashing in like falling stars. They streaked down the blue pillars, headed straight for the foreheads of the soulless. Miles crossed within the blink of an eye. Exultation spread a weary smile across Adria's face. Unlike killing the dragon-sired or using the soul of another to resurrect the dead, this was something she knew was good, something pure. That smile broke the moment the souls slammed to a halt mere feet above the perfectly still bodies, and a furious whisper broke the silence of the graveyard.

"Cease this madness."

Adria's heart shuddered. Her mind wilted. It couldn't be. It couldn't.

The Goddess Lyra stood at the edge of the graveyard, her impossibly long hair flowing about her like a river. It settled atop the fence, blanketed the grass, and wove through the stone markers for now-barren graves. Her starlight eyes bore into Adria's, and they were filled with rage. Adria dropped to her knees, and she commanded the soulless to do the same. Wordlessly they obeyed.

"Beloved Goddess," Adria said into the eerie calm. "You honor me."

"And you dishonor me," Lyra said. Her gaze turned to Jacaranda and Wren. The two women were the only ones to remain standing. "Will you not kneel before your Goddess?"

After a moment's debate, Jacaranda slowly lowered to one knee. Wren remained standing, and she clenched her hands into fists.

"*Are* you my Goddess?" Wren asked. "You never cared for me the first thirty years of my life."

Lyra didn't look at her. Didn't address her. She merely waved her hand toward the recast woman, and immediately Wren's legs buckled. Adria lowered her head and looked away, for some reason feeling an intense shame at the forced obedience. Fear pounded through her veins, and all the while, she endured the strain of holding those sixty newborn souls hovering in place.

"I will not have my love, or the love of my Sisters, questioned," Lyra said. She approached the ring of soulless. "And I will not have my role usurped. You meddle in affairs beyond your understanding, Adria Eveson, and you do so with power granted to you by dragons seeking chaos and disruption. Abandon this path at once. Return those souls to the untouched realms beyond."

Adria didn't want to believe what she was hearing. It made no sense. She brushed her mask with her fingers, needing its comforting strength so she might stare her Goddess in the moonlit eye.

"The souls are here," she said. "Right here. With but a thought

I can save these soulless from their abandonment, and yet—yet you would have me return them across the void to the Aether?"

Another calm, careful step of the Goddess. Without command or spoken word, the soulless moved aside so none would stand between her and Adria.

"Were my words not clear?" Lyra asked.

"Your words are clear," Adria said, dimly aware that she was committing heresy by arguing with her own Goddess. "But your intentions are not. If you would deny me this, then take the souls in your own hands. Please, finish this deed with your power instead of my own. Are they not worth it?"

Another step. So close now. Adria felt like her clothes would burn away from the heat of the Goddess's presence. She felt her skin would peel and char, her mask would crack, and her entire physical form break down before a power and presence older than the Cradle itself. Resisting was madness, yet her anger and pride refused to surrender.

"This is good," Adria insisted when Lyra did not respond. "This is just. How can you refuse souls to these shells, souls that were always meant for them that your weakness left them denied?"

Lyra was all Adria could see, an overwhelming presence. The Goddess's skin was as dark as the midnight sky, as smooth as the calmest pond. Her eyes bore not mere stars but slowly rotating collections of planets and moons and celestial beings for which she knew no names.

"Do not mock me," said Lyra. "And do not pretend at wisdom in matters beyond the understanding of mortals. As your Goddess, I command you. Send. Them. Back."

"Don't!" Wren shouted, the woman still forced to her knees. "Look at us, look at us both! I don't care what she says. This is better! This is what's right! Don't leave them like this."

Inside Adria raged a storm of emotions that horrified her. Rebellion. Confusion. Fury. Not love for her Goddess. Not adoration for the being to whom she'd prayed the entirety of her life. Between Lyra and Wren, it was Wren—a near stranger—she wanted to listen to and obey. Only a nagging voice in the back of her mind kept her in check, and it maddeningly spoke with the tone and voice of her deceased Vikar Thaddeus.

Would she really pretend to be wiser than a Goddess?

"As you wish," Adria whispered.

She let them go. All of them. The sixty little seeds of essence flew back to the heavens, the blue pillars of light fading away from the soulless. Adria cast her gaze to the perfectly still bodies, these soulless that knew nothing of their loss nor what they might hope to gain, and her heart broke.

"Either these soulless lives have meaning, or they are empty," she said. "If you would deny them eternity, then they are empty shells without hope or permanence. Let none here pretend otherwise."

Not even a Goddess.

With a simple lifting of her hands, Adria bathed those sixty members of Alma's Beloved with white fire that flowed from her fingertips. Their bodies crumpled to ash. Their bones withered into chalk. The unmatched power of her soul tore apart each and every one of those soulless beings, and she could not deny a sense of grim satisfaction at the destruction.

Wren screamed out a wordless protest. Jacaranda wrapped her arms about her, trying to comfort her and failing. Adria dared not spare a moment's thought to either of them. She kept her eyes locked on her Goddess. If she was to challenge her maker, she would do so with her head held high. If she was to die, she would die proud.

"Why this tantrum?" Lyra asked. Her voice gave away nothing.

"Because you made it clear you would leave them soulless for the rest of their worldly lives," Adria said. "You would deny them the love you promised them, and for what? Pride? Fear of what I can do? You would rather they continue on without purpose than accept the gifts I now possess? If that is how you demand our world continue, then I will be no part of the charade. Soulless will live and die, become ash, and be forgotten. Let it all come to the inevitable end."

The furious Goddess turned to Jacaranda and Wren. She gestured toward the entrance of the graveyard.

"Leave us," she ordered.

Jacaranda helped a sobbing Wren back to her feet, cast one final glare toward the Goddess, and then guided the both of them out. Adria crossed her arms and waited. The graveyard felt remarkably empty. Wind blew in from the east, and it teased away the obliterated remnants of the soulless. Adria watched the ash float on the wind. Was this how Lyra saw them? Was that how she saw all beings who lacked the gift of a soul?

"The dragons granted you power that belongs solely to gods and demigods," Lyra said once they were alone. "Do you not see the great risk that comes with that? Do you not sense the path of heresy you walk? I am your Goddess, Adria, the one that listened to your prayers. I am the one who comforted you as you knelt before your parents' pyre. I am the one who salved your weary heart during your long nights alone in Low Dock. You blame my Sisters and me for the exhaustion we suffered. You blame us for the failures of this world. You succumb to mortal foolishness, yet you wield immortal power. That foolishness cannot be suffered any longer."

Again Adria felt the overwhelming power of the Goddess washing over her. She tried to justify her actions but couldn't shake the feeling that'd she'd acted purely out of frustration.

"What is it you wish of me?" Adria asked softly. "Speak, and I shall listen."

"Will you?"

Lyra turned away. For a brief moment the human visage she adopted flickered. Beneath that pure black skin was a star field of power and magic. Within her trailing dress of hair twinkled stars, actual stars, the same power and essence holding back the furious void that sought to swallow the Cradle in shadow and emptiness. The age and majesty of the Goddess overwhelmed Adria, and she dropped to her knees.

"Yes," she said. "Forgive my pride. Forgive my compulsiveness. I am here, and I will listen."

She meant it, every word. Let her stubbornness and pride be damned. She was a Mindkeeper of the Keeping Church. She was a loyal servant to her Goddess. All her life she'd whispered of the mercy and love the Sisters showed to all their children, and she would not let her newfound power stand in the way of that belief. More than anything, she wanted to feel the warm embrace of the Goddess, and to believe that she could remove the mask that covered her face and be truly loved.

"I hope you do," Lyra said. "You must use the power granted to you by the dragons to destroy the machinery beneath Londheim. There must never be another Chainbreaker."

"I would have destroyed it already if I felt doing so were safe. Won't it risk the release of the void into the Cradle?"

"A temporary release," Lyra said. "The stars will burn it away in time. The loss of life in Londheim is irrelevant compared to saving a thousand future generations from the dragons' influence."

Her Goddess was asking her to kill thousands. There was no other way for her to see it, and her insides twisted into revolted knots.

"Is that all you'd ask of me?" she asked, fearing more. Already her need for her Goddess's embrace was starting to falter. Her humble faith shivered, and when she heard her Goddess's next command, it broke completely.

"No, Adria. I bring one other task. Once the machinery is destroyed, you must take your own life."

Tears flowed behind her porcelain mask. Her love of the Sisters, her dedication to them and their virtues; it could not survive, not this. What did it matter, her countless hours of prayer and servitude? Her entire life, she had believed. It had guided her, defined her, shaped her into who she was and who she wished to be. No longer. The foundations of her heart crumbled, and at last she acknowledged a truth that terrified her. This was it. The last wound her bleeding faith could endure.

It hurt more than she thought possible.

Adria reached out to her Goddess, her hand shaking, her words trembling.

"You would ask this of me? You, my beloved guardian? You, the Goddess I prayed to all my life to watch over my soul?"

Still Lyra would not turn to face her.

"This is not a betrayal," the Goddess insisted. "My Sisters and I call upon you to make the ultimate sacrifice. We do not do so lightly. The dragons and their children meddled in the realms of the eternal, and in doing so they laid this heavy curse upon your soul. Equally drastic measures must be taken if my Sisters and I are to survive. Do not be afraid, my child. Do not despair. We will be with you always, through every step of this journey."

Adria gestured to the circle of ash that surrounded her.

"Like you were with them?"

Lyra shook her head, and Adria realized the Goddess shed her own tears. For what reason did she cry? What loss did she suffer? It was Adria's head she called for. It was her death that she demanded!

"I didn't ask for this," Adria said. Her growing anger made her tears flow all the harder, and her every word fought against a sob. "I asked for none of this! Yet through it all I have tried to help others. I have healed the wounded. I've given life to the dead. And I would have brought souls back to the soulless. All this, and yet you refuse to even *look* at me. How am I to believe you love and cherish me as I walk this awful path?"

Adria ripped the mask from her face.

"Look at me!" she screamed. "Look me in the eye as you ask for my murder!"

Lyra turned. Their eyes did meet. The sorrow that passed between them was both intimate and impossibly foreign.

"I weep for you, my child," the Goddess said. "But my tears do not erase what is necessary. You have heard my command. Follow it faithfully, or rebel against it as humanity is wont to do. It is your choice, for choice was our ultimate gift to our children, one which we will never lament. Not even if it leads to the destruction of the Cradle."

Lyra vanished. Her presence lingered.

"Gift?" Adria whispered as she slid her porcelain mask over her face. "Heavens spare me your gifts."

From the dragons to the Goddesses, it seemed their gifts were nothing but poison, and yet she must swallow it down, choke on it, bear it in her belly as it slowly, inevitably, killed her.

CHAPTER 12

There was only misery and solitude for Dierk in his dark prison, and he feverishly dwelled in both. His father's men had bound his hands and feet, gagged him, and left him on the cold floor of his family's cellar. It was not lost on Dierk that a month ago he'd done the same to a homeless man. With Vaesalaum's aid, Dierk had sacrificed the man to honor the beliefs held within the Book of Ravens. No doubt a similar sacrifice awaited him. It would be to no god, no ideals, and for no higher purpose, but as he wept upon the stone, Dierk knew it would be a sacrifice nonetheless. It'd be at his father's hands, and when the blood flowed, it would be to erase the sins committed against his father's name.

The nisse was right, he thought. *You're nothing. You're wretched. And now Father knows.*

If only he'd remembered to recast the spell. It was Tamerlane's fault, the stupid bastard. If only they'd not fought, if he'd not been distracted when coming home from Adria's, then he might have remembered. Yet as much as Dierk tried to focus on that rage, it felt hollow. Like all his problems, this was Dierk's responsibility. He'd fucked up, just like he'd fucked up everything else in his life.

Hours passed. Dierk heard scurrying from one of the walls, and he wondered if a curious rat would come to nibble on his flesh.

Not yet, little rat, he thought. *Give it time. Father won't let me live, I'm sure of that. You'll get your meal soon.*

From acting as the new Mayor of the city to being rat food in a cellar. What a difference a day made.

The door cracked open, and Dierk felt his heart begin to pound and his pulse quicken. He squirmed against his bonds, as if somehow they'd magically loosened over the hours he'd lain helpless. It was no use. The ropes were bound tight enough to dig into his skin. The only thing he'd managed was to scrape himself raw. Drawing blood would only interest the rats further.

Heavy footfalls marked his father's descent into the basement. Light washed over him from a carried lantern. Dierk endured the pain to stare his father in the eye.

"Good," Soren said. "You're awake."

The older man set the lantern on the floor not far from Dierk's face and then walked out of view. Dierk stared at the lantern, relishing that golden light from the burning oil. He'd had plenty of time to fantasize over what punishment his father would concoct. Beatings? Stabbings? A swift execution? Whatever his ideas, the worst was lifelong imprisonment in the cellar, awash in darkness and left for his mind to crack and his body to slowly wither away. His father was certainly capable of such cruelty, but Dierk consoled himself with the knowledge that Soren was much, much too angry to allow such a patient torment.

His father returned carrying a simple wooden chair from one of the mansion's kitchens. He set it down in front of Dierk, straightened it, and then sat on its green cushion. The lantern lay near his foot, and he picked it up and let it swing from his loose grip. His gray eyes peered down at Dierk, who did his best to glare back, given his awkward position on his stomach.

"I will not remove your gag," Soren said. His voice was remarkably calm as he slowly rolled up the sleeves to his long white shirt. They might as well be discussing the next family outing or a dinner at a family friend's house. "So do not think you will agitate me into doing so. I know you need your voice to perform... whatever trick it is that you performed. Understand that I do not need answers from you. I don't want information. At best, you'll nod or shake your head if asked a question. Is that understood?"

Dierk didn't answer. It was a petty protest, but what else could he do?

In response, Soren slowly stood, set the lantern in the center of his chair, and then pulled his boot back for a swift kick straight into Dierk's gut. Dierk wretched into his gag, and a bit of bile trickled up his throat. He'd not eaten since his captivity, a very meager blessing against the revulsions assaulting his stomach. Pain rolled out from the kick in waves, but before he could even gather his breath, Soren kicked him again. And then again. Always in that same spot, right in the gut. Dierk tried to curl his knees to protect himself but the ropes were too tight, and a long loop connected his wrists to his ankles so that his motions were limited.

Another kick. Another. Dierk rolled onto his back, but that only made it worse, for Soren started to stomp down on him with his heel instead. Again and again, targeting that same spot just below his ribs. Dierk heaved into his gag as he sobbed, his stomach attempting to vomit bile and air. With nowhere to go, the vomit filled his throat, and despite the pain, he had to force himself to swallow it down lest he choke. On and on went the barrage. It wasn't even as hard as his father could manage, nor did it need to be as the swelling began and everything grew increasingly sensitive.

When Soren's leg tired, he dropped to his knees and began using his hands. His savagery turned aimless. Blow after blow, to the face, the chest, his legs, his stomach, wherever the meaty fists landed. The lantern light illuminated Dierk's father in shadows. The look on his face was stone. No emotions. Not even anger. That made it that much worse, and that much more terrifying.

Eventually it stopped. There seemed no particular reason. Soren returned to his feet, straightened the collar to his shirt, and then sat back down in his chair. Dierk wept through the pain. Was this his future now? Goddesses help him, could he endure such beatings every day? Every hour? Just how often would his father manifest his pain into such torture?

"I know how you did what you did," Soren said. His voice was surprisingly winded. "I scoured your room and found your copy of the Book of Ravens. An interesting read, that book. Most of it is drivel regarding the Goddesses, but there is magic in there, too, isn't there? Magic you learned to harness."

Something heavy thudded to the floor beside Dierk's head. He blinked away the tears to see. It was his copy of the book, and opened to the sixth chapter.

"Helplessness," his father continued. "The curse you put upon me. 'Helpless' describes how I felt then. I'm betting it describes how you feel right now, doesn't it, son? But unlike you, I don't need magic to pull it off. My power is real. It comes from my birthright, my wealth, my station, and the reputation brought about by my hard work. All these things might have been yours, if you were patient. You were never patient, though. You'd encounter the slightest difficulty or resistance and give up immediately. A weak child. A pathetic child. And yet somehow of my own blood. What a disgrace."

Dierk bit his tongue. He needed that pain to help him focus against the overwhelming waves that washed over him from the lower half of his body. This loathsome silhouette in the lantern light had no right to judge him. Dierk didn't care what he thought. His words meant nothing. He told himself that, again and again, hoping he might believe it before his mind broke completely.

The chair groaned as Soren leaned back into it. His hands settled atop his knees, his perfectly manicured nails drumming his kneecaps.

"You controlled my household for two weeks, yet your damage is almost irrevocable. Londheim should have been evacuated the moment we learned of the dragon-sired army's approach. When the second dragon landed, it should have been greeted with an empty city! We do not have the forces to withstand an assault. We don't have the food to endure a prolonged siege. Perhaps if the church keepers produce food through their miracles, we might last a bit longer, but sieges don't win solely through empty stomachs, but also sickness, despair, and betrayal. Londheim is fucking *drowning* in all three. Yet what did you do? You burned our boats. You called *me* a coward and declared us staying to fight. Damn it all, your stupidity is baffling in its depth."

"Fuck you," Dierk shouted into his gag. It came out as a garbled "mmffuuu." His father reacted like lightning, bolting out of his chair and slamming the tip of his boot straight into Dierk's face. A massive splatter of blood spewed from his nose.

"Stupid," Soren said, and he scraped his boot onto the stone floor before sitting. "So damn stupid that you don't even know to keep silent while I speak. I admit, evacuating Londheim would be a monumental task, and no matter how many boats were at our disposal, we would have left behind a tremendous amount of wealth to be pillaged by either the poor or the monsters that followed. So for now, let us presume that staying was the best course of action. Even allowing that to be true, why in all the Cradle would you decide that we should acknowledge Belvua?"

A boot tip pressed his face, turning it so he'd look at the blurry, lantern-lit outline of a beast that was his father.

"Is that how much you hate your own kind?" Soren asked. "That's the reason, right? The reason you sided with these monsters, the reason you helped them, even learned from them? The Forgotten Children disguised themselves as our soldiers, rounded up the sick and poor, and then marched them out of their homes so they could declare Low Dock theirs. How could you possibly think they were in the right? And then after those monsters slaughtered our soldiers when we attempted to retake our land, you wiped away the bloodshed and declared the wise course was to *acknowledge* their claims. Why? Because it was theirs a thousand years ago? Who gives a shit, my son. We occupy it now, and only a fool gives up their home without a fight. Only a coward. I'm not a coward, and neither are the people of Londheim. But you?"

He rose from his chair.

"You?"

Dierk rolled onto his back, and he glared up at his father as the boot slowly settled onto his throat. Would this be it? Would this be when his father finally crushed his larynx and choked the air from his lungs? It'd be preferable to the speeches. It'd be better than the rants. Dierk conveyed his contempt and fury with his stare, for he dared not speak another word, not after the painful mess that was his nose.

"I knew about your sick habits," Soren said softly, as if confessing a secret to a lover. "Your skinning of the animals. Your obsession with death. We all have our vices, Dierk, and the wealthy tend to be more extreme than the poor. *I can overlook this*, I thought the first time. *I can turn a blind eye*, I thought the second time. But it never stopped, and it never got better. You took pleasure from corpses. Not sexual pleasure, I believe, but instead having more to do with their mutilation. What was it? Was it the blood? The peeling back of flesh to expose the gruesome innards we keep hidden from the light of day?"

His father knelt over him. His fingers slowly brushed sweat-stained hair away from Dierk's forehead. If it were another man, and another place, the act might be mistaken for one of love.

"I want you to know that as of today, you've been removed from my will," Soren said. "No matter what happens to me, you receive nothing. You inherit nothing. This is mostly symbolic, because I've already begun spreading word of your death. You're a tragic loss to the monsters of Belvua, which means in death you'll accomplish more than you ever did with life. You're a dead man already, no different from a corpse."

Lantern light glinted off the steel of a knife. Dierk never saw him draw it. The cold metal pressed to Dierk's cheek. Not cutting, but close, so close.

"You derived satisfaction from mutilating corpses," his father whispered. "I will do the same, only for me, you'll still be breathing. I won't let you die no matter how badly you wish for it. If you refuse drink, I'll funnel it down your throat. If you try to harm yourself, I'll break your legs and tie you to a chair. I will have my satisfaction. I will peel back your flesh to reveal your own guts and innards, and I will find the inherent rot inside you that kept you from being the son I deserved."

Dierk tilted his head sharply to the left. The knife cut across his cheek, but this time the pain felt good. The pain sent a message. He feared no threat. No blade. No fist. He glared at his father despite the blood that trickled down his face from the cut, blood that joined the river that had flown from his nose. He met his father's gaze, and he did not wither before it. The words of the Book of Ravens flowed through his mind.

I will wait years, he thought as his father put away the knife. *I will live decades in torment if I must. I will pay you back, Father. I will speak the words of another curse. You know it. I know it. Kill me now, or suffer.*

Soren rose to his feet. Did he understand the message? Did he sense the threat, or did he not care? Dierk didn't know. It didn't matter. He was practically delirious from the pain. Every part of his body hurt, but at least he felt a sort of certainty in his soul that gave him purpose. The words of the curse were writ forever in his mind. One slipup. One mistake. That's all he needed.

Soren grabbed Dierk and hoisted him to a seat upon the chair. He checked the ropes, then double-checked the gag sealing Dierk's mouth. Once satisfied, he wiped the knife clean on Dierk's shirt and put it away.

"I'll be back tomorrow," Soren said. "Try not to die until then."

Dierk laughed into his gag, and he swayed side to side amid his pain and fury.

"Mmffuuu."

CHAPTER 13

Hello, Devin," Malik said as he thrust the door open to the Wise tower. "Come in and out of the cold, please. Tommy is currently occupied but I'm sure he'll be happy to see you nonetheless."

Devin kicked freshly fallen snow off his boots before entering the surprisingly warm tower. A healthy fire burned in the fireplace, and guessing by the blankets and glass of wine beside one of the padded chairs, he had a feeling he'd interrupted Malik's relaxation time.

"So what is Tommy up to?" he asked. "Nothing too dangerous, I hope?"

"Of course it's dangerous," Malik said, a bit of frustration leaking into his deep voice. "Tommy wouldn't be doing it if it weren't. He's downstairs. Please tell him I have his dinner prepared if he'd like to come be social."

"I'm guessing he's forgotten to take some breaks?"

"Oh, he's not forgotten, for I've reminded him. He's steadfastly refusing now. I fear he's growing more stubborn as he becomes more certain of himself. It'd be charming if he wielded that maturity for good instead of ill."

Devin laughed as he descended the stairs.

"I'll see what I can do."

The basement to the tower was surprisingly expansive and, by the looks of it, freshly cleaned to allow Tommy to practice his magic. Two lanterns hung from hooks in the ceiling above the basement middle, casting light across an intensely concentrating Tomas. The young man knelt before a collection of lead shot, approximately two dozen based on Devin's quick count. The shots were piled atop one another into a little pyramid, and drawn in chalk around this pyramid were strange runes that Devin vaguely recognized as magical in nature.

"Hey, To—"

"Shhh," Tommy hissed, his eyes not leaving the lead. He lifted a single finger toward him and held it up, emphasizing the shushing request. Devin crossed his arms and choked down an annoyed sigh. Tommy knelt closer to his little pile of lead, and his hands linked above them. It was quiet, hardly above a whisper, but Devin realized his brother-in-law was repeating a chant.

"*Aethos glaeis,*" Tommy chanted.

Devin recognized some of the words. Ice magic, if he remembered correctly. His guess was confirmed by the frost that built across the ground, starting with the runes and then flowing inward like a river. Blue light swelled from the ice, as if a cold fire burned within it. Once the ice encased the lead shot completely, Tommy's chant rapidly switched, becoming louder and more intense.

"Chyron secus aliu, Chyron secus aliu!"

The two dozen lead balls pulsed with blue light, and that light seemed to absorb into their very essence. Their color changed from a dusky black to the color of the ocean. The glow faded, and despite the stillness of the basement air, the chalk that surrounded the pyramid scattered in all directions as if blown by a sudden gust. It was only then that Tommy let out a gasp and crumpled to his rear.

"Thank the dragons and Goddesses alike," the young Wise said. "I thought for sure they were going to explode."

Devin tilted his head and blinked.

"Explode?"

"Well, not technically an explosion since it'd be of ice instead of fire and heat, but I think you get the idea. I haven't tried to produce that many magical shots simultaneously before, but if I'm to make as many as Vikar Forrest requested, then I'm going to need to up my production lest it take me months."

There was so very much wrong with what Devin was hearing, he needed to break it up into multiple thoughts. Once Tommy had scooped the icy balls of lead into a small leather pouch, Devin embraced his brother-in-law, then jammed a finger into his chest.

"Let's start with the obvious," he said. "Would I have been killed if those exploded into ice?"

"I don't know about 'killed,'" Tommy said, and he offered Devin a tired grin. "Maybe frosted a little? With how close I was, I'd be the one who was shredded. But really, you should know that when magic is involved, you should keep a safe distance away. There's always going to be some inherent risk."

Devin decided not to press the issue on what a "safe" distance was when he didn't know there was a chance of an explosion, let alone the size and scope of said explosion. Instead he gestured to the pouch of lead.

"Those are spellstones like you've made for me," he said. "So what's this about Vikar Forrest wanting some?"

"Oh, I assumed he'd have told you," Tommy said.

"The Keeping Church and I aren't exactly getting along right now."

"Oooooh, right, the whole imprisonment and harboring Jacaranda thing. So at the fight at the cathedral, you used some of my spellstones in front of Vikar Caria, and she told Forrest about it. They both agreed that other Soulkeepers should be given similar spellstones to help defend the city, and so they put in an order."

While the basement was mostly empty, a lone wall bore a table stacked with supplies. At least half the table was covered with scrolls and books, but a significant portion contained pouches upon pouches. Devin pointed to them as Tommy laid his two dozen ice shot onto the table.

"Are those all full of spellstones?" he asked incredulously.

"Simple ones, yes. I'm keeping them fairly basic since these are made for all of Londheim's Soulkeepers. There's red ones for a basic fiery explosion, some yellow ones that contain bolts of lightning, and of course, you saw me make the icy ones. Those explode and freeze everything around them. Nice and simple."

Devin counted ten pouches. The amount of power collected together on that single table was horrifying. And if but a single stone broke, what might happen? Would it set the others off? Would the Wise tower even survive?

"We should go upstairs," Devin said, deciding that Tommy's advice about safe distances when it came to magic was suddenly very, very prescient.

"Very well. I could use a break."

That was putting it mildly. Tommy nearly fell over when he tried climbing the stairs. Devin didn't bother asking when he'd last eaten, but when Malik immediately thrust a plate into Tommy's hands at the top of the stairs, the safe assumption was that he hadn't had a bite for the entire day.

When the three settled down before the roaring fire, Devin tried to decide what it meant for the Soulkeepers to have access to Tommy's magic. He knew the power those spellstones possessed. It had allowed him to challenge the dragon-sired in a way he never could have with his regular pistol and sword. But to have dozens of Soulkeepers wielding fire and ice...they could wipe out an entire army. Given the dragon-sired forces reportedly marching toward Londheim's walls, they might even be given the chance.

"Did you consider refusing the Vikar's request?" Devin asked. "I'm not sure how comfortable I am with these spellstones. To arm an entire sacred division seems... dangerous."

"Of course we couldn't refuse," Malik said. He made an ugly face at the memory. "I assure you, I tried, even after Tomas accepted. Forrest heavily insinuated that we might be labeled a valuable asset to the city and brought in for safekeeping."

"You mean held prisoner," Tommy muttered.

"Yes, that is exactly what I mean, and exactly what Forrest meant, and exactly why we agreed to make the Keeping Church their spellstones."

Devin didn't bother to hide his distaste. On another day he might have defended the church's reasons, and brought up the need for magic to protect innocent civilians, but he had neither the heart nor the energy. It was amazing what being imprisoned did to one's opinion of an institution.

"Oh, Devin, I have something for you!" Tommy pulled a single spellstone from his pocket. Devin accepted it, then rolled the lead ball around in his palm. It was a swirling mixture of white and gray with little spots of black intermixed throughout.

"So what wondrous thing does this one do?" he asked.

"Oh, Goddesses help us, you actually made it?" Malik asked before Tommy could answer.

"Yes, I made it," Tommy said, and he looked genuinely hurt. "Everything we do seems to kill and destroy. I—I—I think we should be considering promoting other options in case we need them. That's what that spellstone there is for, to give you a non-lethal option. It's a polymorph shot."

"Polymorph?" Devin asked.

"It turns someone into a sheep," Malik said, and he sipped his wine to hide his grin. Yet again Devin tilted his head to the side and blinked.

"Permanently?"

"No, not permanently," Tommy said. "It wouldn't be that great of a nonlethal option if it were permanent. The spell turns someone into a sheep, but based on the scroll I read, I'm fairly certain it should only be for an hour or two at most."

"Fairly certain? So you haven't tested it?"

"Um. No?"

Devin forced the spellstone back into Tommy's possession, then used his free hand to caress his temple. Malik continued sipping wine and stayed out of the conversation, but there was no hiding that grin of his.

"Tommy, let me say this as gently as possible: I cannot use this spellstone on someone without being absolutely certain that the, uh, 'sheep' change isn't permanent."

"That's reasonable, yes," Tommy said. "So then we test it. What's the problem?"

"We can't test it, either. Not without knowing it will work for certain."

"But we won't know it works for certain until we test it!" Tommy was growing exasperated. "I don't...but...what is the problem again?"

"I'm getting more wine," Malik said, and he fled to the other room. His deep laughter echoed through the doorway.

"Tommy, there are some things that must remain unknown," Devin said. "Let's say you found a book that claimed that if you read it, the entire world would end. Is there any possible way for you to determine if the book is lying or telling the truth?"

"Reading it immediately confirms the truth or not," Tommy said. "This isn't that hard a conundrum."

"And in turn, you end the world if it does work. Do you see what I mean? I'm not testing a sheep spell on someone only to discover they're a sheep forever. I'm serious, Tomas. My foot is down. My mind is set. I have accepted many ridiculous occurrences of magic, but this is my line in the sand."

Tommy looked ready to argue to the death, but a knock on the door interrupted him.

"We shouldn't be having any visitors," he said as he stood. "Did Jacaranda say she'd be joining you?"

"She's training with Wren," Devin said. "That's why I thought I'd stop by, to give them some privacy."

Tommy thrust open the door to the tower. A gust of cold air swirled inside. Devin glanced over his shoulder, then sat up in his chair upon seeing a pale blond-haired woman dressed in Soulkeeper garb. He recognized her, but from where? His mind finally clicked. She was the woman who had tried speaking with him on his way home from Lyra's midnight visitation.

"Dragons help me, I swear I'll get you your spellstones soon," Tommy said. "You Soulkeepers are the worst when it comes to being patient."

"Spellstones?" the woman asked, tilting her head slightly.

"Did Forrest not send you?"

"I'm here for my own business," she said. She glanced into the tower, and the way she reacted upon seeing Devin left him deeply confused. This woman, a Soulkeeper it seemed, definitely knew him, but from where?

"I was hoping you would be alone, but I see Devin's here, too. I guess that's for the best."

"Devin?" Tommy asked, and he glanced back into the tower. "Uh, are you two friends?"

"Not that I'm aware of," he said as he stood. "Though I certainly could be wrong. Have we met on our travels? Are you stationed further east, perhaps?"

"Do you mind if I come in from the cold before I explain?"

"Of course, of course!" Tommy stepped aside so the woman might enter. Devin watched her move, something strangely familiar about her mannerisms in a way he could not define. The tattoos on her throat, combined with her distinctly not-soulless behavior, heavily implied she was awakened like Jacaranda. But an awakened Soulkeeper? What nonsense was this? Did the church have more secrets hiding in its past than he was aware of?

Malik returned from the other room and, upon seeing the stranger, smiled warmly and offered her his glass.

"Would you like a drink, miss?" he asked.

"I would," she said. Though the three men stood about awkwardly, she took the glass and drained its wine in one long series of gulps. When finished, she wiped her chin, sighed, and then stood to her full height.

"No way around this that makes it easier," she said. "Tommy, Devin... I know I look like someone else, but my soul is the same. It's me, Brittany. Brittany Eveson." She grinned. "You can thank Adria for this. I'm back, and I thought I should finally let you two know."

The silence that followed was deeper than any ocean. Devin felt the gears of his mind come to a screeching halt. The words she spoke made perfect sense, but the meaning behind them was absurd. This couldn't be true.

"Bullshit," he said.

"Honestly, it *is* bullshit," this strange woman said. "But I'm here. Would you like to play a game, ask me twenty questions, or maybe hold a quiz? Devin, we first met on the road. I'd killed three bandits preying on travelers making the trip from Watne to Pathok, and when I greeted you, you thanked me for doing your job for you and offered me a drink from your rucksack. It was, quite sadly, the most romantic gesture you ever made in our five years together."

Devin's hands trembled. His lip quivered. He tried to think, to process, but it was too much. It couldn't be. It couldn't.

"Brittany?" Tommy said, and he took a single step toward her. "Big sis? It's... it's..."

And then he buried her in his arms, holding her against him, as he sobbed into her hair. This woman, this person claiming to be Devin's long-dead wife, gently returned the embrace as her own tears fell. Even as she did, she snuck a look at her former husband.

"I see he hasn't changed while I was dead," she said, and it was that sarcasm, that willingness to joke even while crying, that convinced him more than her story ever could.

"Brittany?" Devin said. "It's you. It's really you."

And then it was his turn to embrace her, to wrap the body of a stranger in his arms and welcome the soul of the woman he'd given five years of his life.

CHAPTER 14

Goddesses above, he's gotten so big," Brittany said as she sat next to her former husband on the outside steps to the Wise tower. Former, for it was hard to imagine her still married to him despite mere weeks having passed to her mind. For Devin, it had been years, and the longer she stayed with him, the more apparent the toll of those years became. His hair was longer, more disheveled. His smile came less easy, and though she'd dare not poke him for it, there was an undeniable addition of a few pounds of fat about his waist where there had once been only pure muscle.

"You make it seem like he was a baby when you died," Devin said.

"When I died," she echoed. "It sounds so weird still."

"Weird? Yeah. I think weird is a good starting place to describe . . . this."

They laughed, and it felt so damn good to hear the sound. Wind blew down the snow-capped street, and the chill felt pleasant on Brittany's neck and cheeks. It was so stuffy inside the tower, comfortable if in a loose robe like Tommy or Malik, but too much for the thick sleeves and trousers of a Soulkeeper that both Devin and Brittany wore. She breathed in the cold air and exhaled it in a burst of frost. Outside they may be, but they were alone, the street quiet, and in that privacy Brittany dared lean her head on her husband's shoulder.

Former husband, she immediately corrected in her mind. Perhaps the change was not so easy to remember after all.

"I don't mean to imply Tomas was a little babe," she said once it was clear Devin would not pull away from her. "But he was, what, eighteen, nineteen when I last saw him? He's actually filled out into a grown man compared to the scrawny mouse that he was. I mean, you look pretty close to what I remember, but I'd have needed to glance twice if I passed Tommy on the road."

"So what you're saying is, I'm aging well?"

Brittany poked his side.

"You certainly wish. You've got some new scars, I see."

Devin tapped his cheek with his glove.

"Had a wolf nearly chew my entire face off, but only after it started talking to me. This was when the crawling mountain was first emerging, and black water would wash over hundreds of miles the next day. Simpler times, by comparison, but the first time that wolf told its pack to 'hunt,' I nearly pissed my trousers."

Brittany smiled and nodded along, her cheek rubbing against the hard leather of his coat. The smell of him returned to her, of his sweat, the polishing oil for his sword, of the faint burning scent that lingered from discharged flamestones. They were details that had been second nature to her for so long, but now they stood out to her keen and clear on that cold afternoon.

"I'm sure you handled it better than I would have," she said. "If a wolf had started talking to me, I'd have assumed I accidentally ingested some local mushrooms and found a ditch somewhere to hunker down and wait it out."

"By the time I killed the entire pack, I was bleeding to death, so that wasn't really an option. I lived because some stone creature named Arothk healed my wounds with its blood."

He said nothing, he barely even moved to bring attention to it, but Devin shifted so that she couldn't comfortably lean against him. Brittany accepted it with as much grace as she could muster.

As hard as this was on her, she had to remember it was equally hard on him. Here she was, back from the grave, and in a body he would not recognize. Such familiarity between them was bound to be awkward.

"It sounds like you should go ahead and tell me the whole story," she said, trying to keep her tone light and betray nothing of the little jab of hurt she felt.

"All right, but you have to promise not to make fun of me or Tommy for any of the stupid stuff we did."

"No promises. I've earned at least that right from our years of marriage."

Brittany fought an instinct to hold his hand as he told her of his travels to Dunwerth, his encounter with the wolves, meeting Arothk, and the arrival of the black water. She shuddered when he described the shuffling dead, and she wondered how she might have reacted in similar circumstances. More than that, she wished she could have been there with him during his struggles. She wished she could have watched his back while he slept so he wasn't surprised by the spider-wolves, wished that she could have been the one to rescue him from the strange woman named Lavender. When she heard of the firekin, Puffy, she allowed herself to smile.

"Promise me I get to meet the little guy," she said.

"Everyone wants to meet Puffy," he said.

"He sounds cuter than you. Smarter, too, I'd wager."

"Must you always insult me?"

"Must you always be so insult-able?"

She elbowed his side, and he wrapped her in his arms in return. His touch, his laughter, it was everything to her, and she felt something hard and jagged inside her chest start to crumble and break. The moment didn't last. Devin pulled away, and oddly enough, he blushed with embarrassment.

"Sorry," he said, and though he had nothing to apologize for, she understood his reasons at once.

"It's . . . it's all right, Devin," she said. She tucked her hands into the pockets of her coat. The cold was getting to her, the warmth of the tower behind her growing more attractive by the minute. "I understand this is all bizarre. Years have passed, and here I come, once dead as a ghost to you, claiming to be alive and in another woman's body. I'm not under any delusion that things will return to normal. Even if that were possible, I'm not sure that I . . . I'm not sure that I even want that to happen."

"Normal," Devin said, and he sniffled and wiped at his nose. "What does normal even mean anymore? Brit, I don't, I . . . I'm not sure how to tell you this."

"It's all right, Devin. I know about Jacaranda."

He glanced at her sharply.

"You do?"

"To an extent. Adria's told me what she can. I'm not surprised, and I'm not hurt. It's been six years. You've grieved longer than we were married. If anything, I should be upset it took you this long to move on and find someone else. Did you think my lingering soul wanted you alone and miserable?"

"Of course not," he said. "I didn't grieve for you constantly over those six years, I swear. I'm not that pathetic. But even though the hurt stopped, there was always that fear that someone new could hurt me in the same way. It nearly ruined me once. To love someone as deeply as I did—as I do you—and then to lose them? It'd have broken me, and I don't think I'd have put together the pieces as well as I did the first time. Shit, I didn't do that great a job the first time, either. Adria helped me out immensely, as did Tommy. Tommy, the poor bastard, if anyone needed you back, it's him. Without his sister to watch over him, he was ready to vanish into his tower of books and never leave."

"Well, it's a good thing you two were there for him," she said. Silence settled over the pair, awkward and unwelcome. There were dozens of questions she wanted to ask him, but they all felt surreal to her. There was a gap of time between them, invisible to her, and inescapably wide to him. And even if he could bridge it, this face she bore was not the face he'd fallen in love with. Brittany felt a stranger to her current body. How could she expect Devin to feel any differently?

"Brit," Devin said, breaking the silence with an effort that was clearly gargantuan. "I love you. I still love you. While we figure all this out, I want you to know that and never forget it. I don't want to hurt you. I'm just... very confused right now, and I'm worried I'll say or do something stupid."

"I was married to you for five years, Devin. I know you say and do stupid stuff when you're confused. I wasn't much better. Killing ruffians with my axe always seemed easier than trying to comfort the sick or injured." She reached out for his hand, and after a moment, he took it. She squeezed his fingers, and they felt so much larger than before. Her hands were smaller, she realized. It's why he seemed taller now, too. "I understand that time has passed, and that I cannot occupy that same place I once did. It would be cruel of me to demand that of you. All I ask is that you not be cruel to me. Don't make me pretend my love for you no longer exists, or that I have no right to it."

"I would never," he said, and after a moment he laughed. "Goddesses help us, this shit is so fucked up."

"So very fucked up."

A gentle tug on her hand pulled her back to him, and she rested her cheek on his shoulder like she once had. The warmth was there, not quite the same, but she accepted it with her eyes closed.

"I do want to meet her sometime," she said.

"Who? Jacaranda?"

"Indeed. It only seems fair I meet my replacement. Besides, I need to make sure she's good enough for you."

"It's not a competition."

"Damn right it's not, because I'd win if it was."

"Ever the confident one, aren't you?" he said with a laugh.

"You fell in love with me while I stood over the bodies of my fallen enemies. A lack of confidence has never been a fault of mine."

He elbowed her side just hard enough to make her squirm.

"Fine, fine. I will try to set that up, but give me some time, all right? I need to mull this over myself so I know how exactly I think and feel. It will be doubly difficult for her. Competition or not, she's going to be feel threatened."

Something weird and unwelcome tightened within Brittany's belly.

"You love her, don't you?" she asked softly.

Her former husband squeezed her hands within his own.

"Yeah, I believe I do, Brit. I'm sorry."

Brittany pulled away and kissed his cheek. There was no passion to his reaction, and that alone told her all she needed to know.

"Stop apologizing," she said. A vision of Havelock flashed before her eyes. "You have nothing to apologize for. Now let's go inside. It's freezing out here."

"I should really return home," Devin said. "Where are you staying? With Adria?"

"At a room she's provided in Windswept, with her and Tamerlane."

"You're more than welcome to return home. It's both of ours, after all."

Brittany smiled at her beloved Devin. So wonderful at times, and so stupid in others.

"You mean move in with you and Jacaranda?" she asked.

His face blushed.

"Oh. Right. That might be awkward, wouldn't it?"

Brittany stood, and Devin did likewise. She hated everything about this moment, from the way they kept a few feet apart as if they were strangers, to the way he tried to hide his staring at her new face and body, hated it with every fiber of her being.

"Tommy's already offered to let me stay with him and Malik here in their tower," she said. "I think I'll take him up on that while we get reacquainted. Good night, Devin. I'll see you soon."

"You, too," he said, and he hesitated. She knew what it was that he debated. Was it a good-bye kiss she deserved? A hug? A handshake? She settled it for him by gentling wrapping her arms around his waist and leaning her weight against his chest. His coat folded about her as he returned her embrace. The ache within her heart pounded with new life.

"I love you," she said softly.

"Me, too, Brit."

They separated, and he went on his way. Brittany did not watch him leave. She couldn't bear it. Instead she hurried inside, a gust of warm air from the fireplace greeting her. Tommy lurched up from his seat, eager to attend her. He'd always been like that, adoring her even as a young boy. Somehow he cared not at all about her new body, nor her time gone. Her wonderful brother. He was a lovely soul, far better than she deserved.

"Hey, is everything all right?" he asked. "Need something to drink, some milk, beer, maybe a snack..."

"Everything's fine," she said, and she wiped at her face.

"Are you sure? You're crying."

The simple matter-of-fact statement broke a tired laugh out of her constricted throat. Her little Tommy was so pure, so gentle-hearted. He'd been a late child of their parents, yet in the blink of an eye, the eight years between them had vanished to a mere two. How the void did she make sense of that?

"All right, fine," she said. "I feel like shit, this world is shit, everything is shit. Everything is... everything..."

Brittany slumped her back against the door, and she slid to a sit on the floor. Anger and pain intertwined with confusion and despair, an awful mix that beat against her chest and demanded sobs to flow. Brittany had always considered herself a strong woman, proud, and never one to cry. She and Devin had often joked how he was the softer member of their relationship, the one more prone to tears and malaise. Now she sat there, bawling, hating everything about her new self and this new life, and hating the sheer fact that she was crying over it. It was a vicious cycle, its tracks greased with stupidity, and it only brought forth even more tears.

"Brit, Brit, Brit," Tommy said, and within seconds he was on the floor beside her, his arms about her. "Brit, it's all right, I'm here, I got you."

She took slow breaths in, let slow breaths out. Had to get herself together. Get control.

"I don't know what's worse," she said once she could manage words. "That I thought I could handle this better, or that I wish I had never told him at all."

Tommy kissed her forehead twice, then squeezed her tightly.

"You know you had to tell him eventually. I sure wasn't going to be able to keep it a secret, even if you asked."

"No, secrets were never your thing. I still remember the first time you developed a crush on a boy. I prodded it out of you in less than an hour, and had you two on a lunch date within a day."

"You see? I'm helpless without you. So no being upset you're back, all right? What Adria did was unprecedented, but this is good, we can make this good."

Brittany thought of the power her sister-in-law possessed, and of that first moment her soul had awoken in a body of flesh and blood that had not been its own. Was this good? She didn't know. In those initial hours of screaming, a single sensation had dominated her entire mind, a certainty about the *wrongness* of it all. Her own sorrow, Devin's confusion, the struggles acclimating to a foreign body...maybe it was never meant to be. Maybe some cosmic law was broken, and she would forever suffer the consequences. But she would not dare tell Tommy that. Not when he looked so in love with her, so lost in joy to have her back.

Her emotions finally under control, she patted her brother's shoulder and gave him a wink.

"All right then," she said. "Enough of my drama. It's time for yours. I want to be officially introduced to your new boyfriend. It's not my place to judge who Devin ends up with, but I sure as shit can still watch over my little brother."

CHAPTER 15

I wonder," Wren said, and her voice echoed the fear Jacaranda felt inside her constricted chest. "How long until one of those dragons decides Londheim isn't worth the effort and razes it to the ground?"

Jacaranda crouched on her haunches as the two lurked atop the city's outer wall. Cold wind blew through her hair, and it teased her skin at the edges of her scarf. She held her two short swords drawn despite no enemy in the vicinity. It simply made her feel better.

"Viciss hasn't destroyed us yet," she said. "No reason to think this new dragon will, either."

"I'm not sure that makes total sense, Jac."

"What in this world does?"

This earned a dour laugh. Together the two women stared at the newer of the two dragons. If Viciss was the crawling mountain, this new dragon was a living cloud. The length of its body curled up and about itself for seemingly a full mile. Its scales were pale like mist, its claws hardened marble. Puffs of a substance akin to smoke rose from its body with each gust of wind that swooped in from the northeast. Where Viciss was a towering, undeniable presence, this new dragon, which Tommy had quickly determined was Nihil based on his available research, was like an unwelcome dream. No matter how long they stared, Jacaranda could not shake the disturbing feeling they admired an illusion.

"Maybe it's time to abandon the city altogether," Wren wondered. She stood with her arms crossed over her chest, and her umber eyes openly glared at the two dragons. "The Sisters have already abandoned both it and us. When the army of monsters arrives, we'll be doomed."

"We don't have the food or supplies for such an undertaking," Jacaranda said. "Thousands would die."

"Thousands will die anyway. At least we'd be making an attempt at survival instead of waiting here for our deaths."

Wren had been in a foul mood their entire training session. Her friend was still deeply hurt by Adria's actions, yet Jacaranda had felt awkward even attempting to broach the subject. Eventually Jacaranda had cut the session short and suggested they go for a walk and purchase something sweet to snack on. Their travels had taken them to the western wall, and on a whim, Wren had suggested they take a look at the new dragon. She'd heard it was a marvel to behold, and looking upon the illusory, cloud-like body of Nihil, she had not been wrong.

"Flee or stay, either way we fight," Jacaranda said. "And I still hold hope for peace."

"Peace." Wren shook her head. "We're not destined for peace. We're destined to be a pile of ash and bone." She walked to the wall's edge and leaned on its snow-capped stones. Though she stared at the dragons, her mind was firmly lost in the past. "You haven't said a thing about what Lyra did."

"Is there anything to say?" Jacaranda asked.

"The Goddess your lover's sister follows declared us unworthy of existence. I feel like maybe there's a few things to discuss, yet you've spent all day pretending that everything's normal. I hate it. I hate the pretending, so cut it out. Please."

Jacaranda chewed on her lower lip. What was there to say? That she disagreed? That a Goddess was wrong, and she correct? Did she have the pride to make such a claim? The audacity?

"Wren, ever since I awakened, I've been keenly aware how much harder everything is for me compared to others. The life I live is not the same one Devin lives, nor the same as thousands of others. Only someone who has walked the streets with their chains hidden can truly understand, and you're one of those precious few that I know." Jacaranda did her best to smile. "Just stay with me, all right? Together we'll figure this out, even if it means standing up to a Goddess."

"It wasn't just the Goddess," Wren said. "Adria burned those soulless bodies as if they were nothing. That could have been us, Jac, any one of them in our time before we awakened. What if their souls would return tonight? Tomorrow? Next week, or next year? Yet that hope wasn't worth keeping them alive. Better we were dead, she says. Better dead, says the rising spiritual leader of the church in Westreach. I'm sorry, but it frightens me that Adria knows my name and what I am. How long until she decides you and I deserve the same fate as those sixty Alma's Beloved?"

"She won't."

"You don't know that," Wren said, spinning from the wall to jab a finger at her. "We're not even supposed to exist. How long until someone in the church decides to correct that mistake?"

Jacaranda had to bite her tongue to hold back a retort. The church had decided to correct that mistake before, had it not? Vikar Thaddeus had practically gloated over that fact to her when he thought her helpless in his chambers.

"Change is coming," she insisted. "With Adria in charge, it's only a matter of time before our presence is made official to Londheim, and all of Westreach thereafter. We won't need to hide. We won't be at risk like we are now."

"You're putting your trust in someone who charred sixty soulless to the bone out of petty spite to her Goddess. Forgive me if I think it's pretty damn misplaced."

Jacaranda jammed her short swords into their sheaths and turned from the dragons.

"What do you want from me, Wren?" she asked. "To tell you everything will be fine? To tell you I'll kill Adria? Because I won't tell you either. But yes, I do believe Adria will make things better, assuming we aren't all killed the moment the dragon-sired army besieges Londheim, assuming the cloud dragon doesn't kill us in our sleep, and assuming Lyra doesn't obliterate all of humanity out of spite. Lots of assumptions, yes, but I'm just trying to hold on to some measure of hope."

Wren let out the bitterest of laughs.

"I don't have that hope, Jac. I don't. We made no choice in this. I didn't ask for these tattoos on my throat. I didn't ask to be hated, or forgotten. All I wish is to live my own life, yet the Goddess would claim me an abomination. Worse. She would claim me a *mistake*."

She was crying again. Jacaranda wished she could blame her, but a similar hopelessness clung to her own heart, and it was brutal.

"Lyra considered us unworthy of the souls we now possess," Wren continued. "And our new Vikar charred the soulless of Alma's Beloved to ash lest they continue with their lives. That's all that's waiting for us now, isn't there? Either ash or abandonment. There's no place for us in this world that doesn't want us. What is the point?" She cast her hand toward the western field. "Were we made to suffer? Is that our lot in life? Are we not allowed happiness? Maybe if we're lucky, one of those two dragons will bite Lyra in half. At least then they'd be doing the Cradle a favor."

Wren stormed off, and Jacaranda did not follow. They both could use some quiet time alone. Once she gave Wren a few minutes to gain some distance, Jacaranda descended the stone stairs, having to turn sideways to avoid a couple coming up them to gawk at the dragons themselves. Once back on the streets, she walked without a destination. The movements warmed her body, and they allowed herself to sink into her own mind. Not that she would find any real answers, but chewing over Wren's frustrations was relatively calming. Light snow began to fall halfway through her walk, and she caught a few flakes on her gloved hand. The city was tense and quiet, with people hiding in their homes for more than warmth. They were like rats cornered in a den. If they were lucky, they would be left alone.

Jacaranda did not think they were lucky.

Devin was sitting in his chair by the fire when she returned home, but he quickly lurched to his feet the moment she opened the door.

"Hey, Puffy, do you mind if we have a few minutes alone?" he asked the fireplace. The little firekin's coal eyes rose up from the fireplace center, it formed a hand to wave twice in rapid succession, and then it dashed up the chimney. Jacaranda pulled off her hat and coat. All the while she felt Devin's eyes on her. Something was wrong, but what? Devin felt like a man ready to explode. Whatever it was, it wasn't good news. He looked like he was trying as hard as possible to keep his face calm and neutral.

"How'd training go with Wren?" he asked, pretending at casual conversation. Jacaranda sat on the couch, and she lifted an eyebrow at him. He wasn't sitting. Too nervous? Too preoccupied? Her worry only grew.

"Terribly," she said. "She's worried about your sister, Devin, and I have to admit I'm worried, too. Adria was supposed to legitimize the concept of awakened soulless. Instead a Goddess arrived and demanded she halt her ritual. In return, Adria destroyed the soulless and declared them all a sick joke. It's... not exactly how we were hoping things would go."

Devin nodded, his mind clearly elsewhere.

"That's, yeah, I can see why. Do you want me to talk to her?"

Jacaranda smiled up at him.

"No," she said. "I want *you* to talk to *me*. Something's bothering you, so just say it before you worry a hole in your stomach."

Devin crossed his arms and blushed.

"Am I that obvious?"

"Painfully so."

He tugged at the collar of his wool sweater. His feet tapped the floor. Jacaranda kept her smile firmly in place, hiding her own nervousness. What could possibly be upsetting Devin so?

"Jac, I don't know how else to say this, so I'll say it plain and simple. Adria took Brittany's soul from the graveyard and put it in a soulless body. It... it worked. Brittany's alive."

Jacaranda felt a cold wet slap strike her face and neck.

"Alive?" she parroted. Her mind was incapable of producing its own words. The floor spun beneath her.

"I met her earlier today," he said. "Her body's different, obviously, but she's still the person she was."

"Oh," Jacaranda said. That's it. That's all she could say. The memory of Devin quietly crying over Brittany's grave washed her mind gray.

"Look, I—I understand this is difficult," he said. "And I want you to understand that this changes nothing about how I feel for you."

"Changes nothing?" She shook her head in bewilderment. "Devin, don't treat me like a child. This doesn't even sound real. How could it possibly not change things?"

He slumped into his chair. She noticed for the first time how red his eyes had gotten. He'd been crying during her absence. Guilt stung at her chest, but she choked it down with surprising ease. This was not a time to pity him, not here, not now.

"You still love her," she said. It wasn't a question.

"I never stopped," he admitted. "You know that. But it's been years. I moved on. *You* helped me move on."

Easy to say, harder to believe. She bolted back to her feet, her coat and hat back on in seconds.

"I think I need to go for a walk," she said.

"Are you sure? You just got in, and I'm sure you're cold."

More than anything in the world, Devin didn't want her to leave. She knew that, could tell it easily, but it didn't matter. She needed out. She needed time to think.

"I'll be fine. Good-bye, Devin."

She left the home. Snow fell atop her as she stood outside the door, paralyzed. She looked down the dark street. She looked up to the clouds, blinked against the flakes. Wren's bitter words echoed in her, so prescient, so perfect, that they accompanied a silent sob that tore from her throat with physical pain.

Were we made to suffer? Is that our lot in life?

Her tearful eyes looked to the stars, and she spoke the final words with a voice that shocked her with its vileness. She expected no answer from the falling snow, the absent Goddesses, or the slumbering dragons. Only silence and abandonment.

"Are we not allowed happiness?"

CHAPTER 16

Adria was the last person Devin wanted to see, but he could sense the apprehension hanging like a cloud over his sister when he opened the door to his home, and so he did his best to smile and invite her in. Puffy also popped its head up, but Adria and the firekin weren't particularly close, and it quickly sank back into the flames.

"Is something the matter?" he asked. So far she'd yet to remove her mask, nor did she sit. Instead she stood beside the fire, her gloved hands gently turning above the heat.

"Devin, I don't know who else to turn to," she said. At last she removed her porcelain mask. Devin did his best not to flinch. His sister's eyes were deep black circles sunken into her face. Her skin was pallid, and the worry lines on her face were growing into caverns. "It's about Lyra."

"I'm hardly the best when it comes to theological discussions," Devin said, trying to lighten the mood.

"This isn't theological," she said. "Nor is it hypothetical or spiritual or anything else. This is practical. She came to me, Devin. She came to me and . . . and she asked me to kill myself. My Goddess requests my suicide. My suicide. Fuck."

She nearly collapsed into the rocking chair beside the fire. Devin's first instinct was to rush to her side, but he kept his feet rooted by the door. Adria would not want him fawning over her. She'd want strength and reliability. He wished he had any of that in him, but he did his best to cross his arms and fake it. After his conversation with Brittany, he felt equally drained as Adria looked.

"I'd ask if she gave a reason, but I fear I already know it," Devin said. "She came to me as well, and asked that I end your life."

There was no hiding the betrayal on Adria's face.

"She'd have me murdered by my own brother? Is this the reward the Goddesses offer me for my faith?" She wiped at her eyes. "Why in the world did she think you would say yes?"

Devin slowly joined her by the fire, and in the quiet din broken only by the crackling of the fire, his footfalls were thunderous.

"I don't know. Because of what you did to Tesmarie?" He cleared his throat. "And what you did to Brittany?"

That cleared the fog over her vision. Her head snapped in his direction, and he felt an involuntary desire to shrivel beneath her hard gaze. Goddesses above, her personality, it was so forceful when she wished it to be.

"You know?" she asked.

"Yeah. I know. She came and introduced herself to Tommy and me yesterday."

An awkward silence fell over them. What was there to say? Everything about the situation was unprecedented and absurd.

"I thought it'd make you happy," Adria said carefully, finally breaking the silence. "I thought, after how much I'd hurt you, her return would make up for my failures. I'd be using my gifts to do something good, something amazing. Was I wrong?"

Before he could answer, bells sounded from the nearby alarm tower. Neither knew the reason from their wordless exchange.

"Stay here and warm up," he said, grabbing his coat. "I'll see what is the matter."

The moment the cold air hit Devin's skin, he exhaled a pained breath.

"Damn it all to the void."

He didn't know the answers to the questions his sister asked, yet he sure as shit didn't want to hurt her. Adria remained inside, granting him a momentary reprieve as he trudged across the street, leaving footprints in the thin layer of snow. The nearest alarm tower was only a few blocks away, and manned by a trio of soldiers. Devin pushed past a small gaggle of bleary-eyed gossipers to address the oldest among the soldiers.

"What's the cause?" he asked.

"The monsters' army," the soldier shouted back over the tolling of the bell.

Devin tipped his hat and returned to his home. Adria was dressed and ready by then, and she'd slipped her dual-toned mask over her face.

"Shinnoc's army has finally arrived," Devin said, answering her unspoken question.

"Which means we are needed," Adria said. "We should meet with our Vikars to discuss a proper reaction."

Devin reached for his sword and pistol, sighing as he lifted them from their hooks.

"Perfect," he muttered. "Just perfect."

High Excellence Albert set up a display of power to greet the diplomats during their walk to the mansion. Rows upon rows of soldiers marked the path. First were the few riflemen employed by the city, their weapons expertly cleaned and oiled. After them were the soldiers, most wielding spears and swords and decked out in various amounts of steel and leather. It was through this display the dragon-sired delegation would walk before meeting with Albert at his mansion.

After the squads of soldiers came the arms of the church.

Soulkeepers of Londheim lined opposite sides of the street, and though their melee weapons were buckled and sheathed, each and every one had their pistols drawn, loaded, and held at the ready. The signal was clear enough. One wrong move, and the dragon-sired delegation would be obliterated with lead shot. Devin stood in the middle of the group, and he was glad his stance required he keep his eyes forward at all times. It made it easier to ignore Brittany four keepers to his left. He knew she was in the body of a stranger, but the way she wore her coat, how she folded the ankles of her pants, even the slight angle to her axe on her back, all reminded him of her in ways he never expected to be so vivid.

"Arms at ready!" Vikar Forrest ordered. The Soulkeepers raised their pistols and aimed them at a skyward angle, as if to form a tunnel for the approaching dragon-sired. Tension crackled through the ranks as the delegation arrived. There were seven of them in total, each of a different race. They passed in a tightly clustered group so Devin could see only glimpses of them. The tallest was a dyrandar woman, her hooves clacking against the cobbles like hammer strikes. Red ribbons dusted with snow fluttered from her antlers. A foxkin man led the way, looking sharp in a black suit that could have been tailored anywhere in Londheim's clothing districts. A grasslike viridi walked with him, her body clothed in a blanket of flowers. A lapinkin followed just behind, regal looking in a leather outfit that could easily pass for armor.

Most mesmerizing of all was the woman at the heart of the delegation. Unlike the rest, she wore no clothes. Instead her body was covered with soft scales, far more akin to flower petals than anything reptilian. Her neck and chest were stark white, and from there the color radiated outward to pinks and reds, all but for the hard green loops of vines about her legs and belly. Her hair vaguely resembled dreadlocks, though it appeared to be made of linked scales that sparkled a rainbow of color. This strange woman looked like a blooming flower given humanoid form and sentience, except when she smiled, her teeth were razor sharp and her hands bore long middle fingers like stingers. Devin vividly remembered those stingers, for she'd pierced them into him to drink of his memories while he hung from one of her webs back when the black water first washed over the Cradle.

He prayed he went unnoticed. He was not so lucky.

"Devin?" asked the spidery woman, whose scented name was unpronounceable and so she went by the moniker of "Lavender." "My, my, I did not expect to see you here."

"Why is that?" Devin risked asking. "Hoping I'd be eaten by your pet spider-wolves after I escaped your den?"

Lavender's smile blossomed.

"They desired so, but I ordered them to behave." She extended a long, jagged finger toward him and announced her intentions to all in attendance. "He will accompany us."

Devin glanced at Vikar Forrest at the tail end of the line, who shrugged.

"Go ahead."

Devin slipped from the line and joined Lavender's delegation. His neck flushed red as he felt the judging eyes of his fellow Soulkeepers follow him. Regardless of his actual feelings, he couldn't shake the appearance of being a traitor to Londheim as he approached Albert's mansion.

"So what brought you to our lovely city?" Devin asked, for nervously chatting was better than stewing in silence. It had always been his way. "I thought you meant to dwell in your mountain cave for all eternity."

"Forgive a woman for a bit of drama after finding out the entire world moved on without her," Lavender said. She winked a pastel eye his way. "Truth be told, I grew bored. I was meant to dance with kings and queens, not lurk in murky tunnels."

"Why were you hiding in Alma's Crown in the first place, then?"

"The royalty of that final era wanted nothing to do with me," she said. Her grin spread. "But that royalty is long dead and rotted. I suppose there are some advantages to the passage of time. Now that we have the pleasure of a second meeting, I want to thank you for your help, however unwilling it might have been. Your memories of towns and landscape aided my return east."

"Most welcome," he said dryly, then stumbled as the dyrandar woman behind him not-too-gently bumped his side to keep him walking at a brisk pace. Devin glanced over his shoulder. Her head and antlers towered over his diminutive form by comparison, and there was no hiding her distaste at his presence.

"So how did you hook up with Shinnoc's army here?" he asked Lavender, pretending not to have noticed.

"My uncle found her," the female dyrandar said, revealing her eavesdropping. "And unlike your people, we know how to properly treat an araloro."

"Araloro?"

"My true name," Lavender said. "Your kings and princes always called me a flowerkin, though. An insultingly simple name for what I am, but simple people do tend to need simple names."

They climbed the stairs and passed through doors opened by a squad of four soldiers. Side doors were closed and locked, guiding them along the carpeted hallway to the grand meeting hall. Devin noticed the ballroom had been adjusted to more closely resemble the throne room in Oris, including a hastily constructed dais with an elaborate chair that was obviously never meant to be a throne. All of it coincided with the naming of Westreach, and the attempts to add legitimacy to Albert's rule as the newly created High Excellence. Vikar Caria stood to his left, Mayor Sören Becher to his right. Below them both a step waited Adria with her hands calmly folded before her, and unlike her own Vikar, she hid her face behind her mask. After the door shut behind them, Vikar Forrest took position beside Caria, having followed the delegation as part of the rear guard.

"Welcome to my home," Albert said once it was clear everyone was ready to begin. "As High Excellence of Westreach, I extend my greetings to you and your kind, and I pray that we may speak and debate in a spirit of peace and friendship."

Lavender smoothly separated from the delegation to bow before the dignified yet nervous Albert upon his throne.

"Greetings, High Excellence," she said, and the tone of her voice reminded him of when she had first awakened him in her cave. It was soft, welcoming, as clear as crystal and inviting as a summer day. "My name-scent is beyond human tongue, so you may refer to me as Lavender. I speak on behalf of the dragon-sired army united under the banner of Shinnoc, the Dyrandar King."

"Welcome, Lavender," Albert said. His tone was careful, and guarded. Unlike Lavender, he needed to project strength and control. This meeting would be rapidly retold in stories throughout Londheim in the coming hours. "I wish we could speak as friends, and in an atmosphere of peace, but I fear that is not why you come. Yet still I pray that your army's leader knows peace is the better outcome than a costly siege upon our walls."

The araloro tilted her head ever so slightly. Not her stance, nor her dazzling eyes, nor even her smile gave away the slightest hint to her thoughts. Devin believed her claims that she had flitted from court to court in times past. She seemed more comfortable in Albert's makeshift throne room than Albert did.

"And peace is still yet an option," she said. "But it will come with a cost. We have wept for the loss of King Cannac, a dyrandar most noble and beloved by all our races. He sought peace, and as a reward, his life was cruelly taken. If we are to believe any claims of peace you would whisper our way, we must first achieve a counterbalance to this cowardly crime."

Albert glanced at General Kaelyn standing to the left of the throne as his personal guard. She was in charge of what remained of the royal soldiers stationed in Londheim prior to the Queen's abandonment. If the city was put under siege, it would be she who helmed the defense.

"Of course we are willing to hear any terms or demands," he said. "Though I make no promises should they be grossly unfair."

"I assure you our demands are very fair," Lavender said. Her amusement was unmatched. Her smile was a beacon of joy. "In fact, they are the perfect punishment for the sins committed against us. The people of Londheim took the head from King Cannac's shoulders, and so we demand reciprocation."

"Reciprocation?" Albert asked. "For a beheading?"

"*Your* head, to be precise," Lavender said. "Delivered to us in a basket. You have three days to deliver, and if you do not, we will raze Londheim to the ground and mount your head on a pike above the ashes. Those are your two options, High Excellence. Either way, we will have your head. What matters is how many lives will perish alongside you. Are you willing to sacrifice your life for the lives of hundreds of thousands? Or will your pride and selfishness doom an entire city?"

Whatever semblance of proper court decorum broke with such an outrageous demand. General Kaelyn reached for her sword, Vikar Forrest his axe. Others present hurtled insults or outright mockery of the dragon-sired.

"This is nonsense," Mayor Soren shouted over the sudden din. "To present such conditions proves you hold no honest desire for peace, but to insult and demean a good man..."

"To make such a demand is to give the humans here a chance at life they would not otherwise have," Lavender said. Her voice never raised a shred, but something about its tone and tenor hardened to such a razor edge that all there immediately quieted. She was masterful at commanding attention, in a way that bordered on magical. The araloro stepped closer to Albert, not caring in the slightest that General Kaelyn pointed a sword toward her breast.

"You don't truly fathom the depths of your crime yet, but you will," she said. "The betrayal your kind wrought? The pain and agony it caused the new Dyrandar King? It should have doomed you, every last one of you. I was friends with Cannac, in an age your kind has long forgotten. He was a good man, perhaps the best man to ever walk this bastard creation known as the Cradle. And how did you repay his message of peace?"

She slid two fingers into her mouth, hitched once, and then withdrew a small red marble that had been hidden within her throat.

"You cut off his head."

It was a spellstone, akin to the ones Tommy made, and Devin realized it far too late. He dashed for Lavender's wrist, but she flicked the marble to the ground, shattering it. Red light rolled all directions like a mad ocean wave. Devin felt it crash against his skin, hot like fire, slick like oil. His vision blanked. Foreign thoughts intruded into his mind, and they slashed away sight and sound so that he relived a memory—Shinnoc's memory.

Sorrow. Shock. Loss. They crushed his shoulders and crippled him to his knees. Tears flowed down his face, and he gasped out an incomprehensible sob. Cannac was dead. His father, his beloved mentor and guide, was dead. He saw a shimmering illusion take shape in the flames of a campfire before him, of the mighty dyrandar's body lying on a blood-soaked street. His head was missing. No. Not missing. Taken. Shoved onto a spike. The illusion shifted, becoming the crowd, showing the spike, showing the head bobbing up and down as if it were some sick-minded child's toy. Another sob, but soon his emotions turned red. Devin's fingers dug into the ground, and he felt his fingernails crack. In the vision he clutched dirt, but his real body carved into cold, tiled floor.

That pain, that blood, was only a brief reprieve from the powerful spell, and it quickly overwhelmed him. The visions in the campfire returned and, with them, a new emotion. It smothered his shock. It buried his sorrow. Devin's jaw clenched tightly shut, and he bared his teeth like a wild animal. Cannac was dead, but he was not. His rage was alive. Alive, and ravenous. The illusion in the fire shifted again, becoming three men in a small room, Albert, Soren, and his son, Dierk.

"Overseer?" Devin heard himself roar with the voice of Shinnoc. "Where is the Overseer?"

His eyes fixed on Albert, then the mere Overseer of West Orismund. His rage found an outlet. The cruelty of the world found its justified victim. Amid visions of a desolated Londheim, this one life would be made to suffer a thousandfold beyond.

The memory faded away. The emotions drained from Devin's body as if through a sieve in his foot. The ballroom, which had been painted red in his vision, resumed its cold, pale color. Devin pushed himself back to a stand, and he saw that many others had crumbled to their knees. Only the dragon-sired stood firm. Lavender spun to address them all.

"You knew this day was coming," she said. "You knew there would be a price to pay for this betrayal. You have all felt the rage of the Dyrandar King. What I offer, a single life for a single life, is still a mercy far beyond what your wretched race deserves, and more than your race would ever extend to us." Her focus turned to the High Excellence. "Three days, Albert. Deliver your head, or we come and take it."

The delegation turned to leave, and all there were too stunned to stop them.

"Oh, and so we're clear," Lavender said, halting at the door. "Should your troops make any move on the district known as Belvua, we will launch our attack immediately in retaliation. If you want a fight with dragon-sired, come outside your walls and get one."

CHAPTER 17

The chains were murder on his ankles, but Logarius knew better than to request his mother to loosen them. If anything, it'd make her double-check if they were properly sealed. He lay in his avenria-styled bed and stared out his lone window. The view was hardly impressive. Just two nearby homes with slanted rooftops and wood shingles, but he stared out it nonetheless as time dragged along with the speed of a drunken tortoise.

"Shinnoc's army has come," Evelyn said as she checked the bandages on his side. Logarius pointedly stared out the window instead of acknowledging her. Was he being immature with his silence? Perhaps, but she'd also stabbed him in the back and dragged his bleeding body home for imprisonment. He felt she deserved a bit of immaturity.

"They've not begun any siege preparations," she continued. Her fingers probed the bare flesh where she'd removed his feathers to sew the skin shut. "From what I can tell, they've not blocked the river to prevent anyone from fleeing. No matter his grand pronouncements, I don't believe Shinnoc has the heart for war. If he does have the heart, then it appears he lacks the head for it instead."

Apparently satisfied with the rate of healing, Evelyn returned the bandages and then stepped away. Her arms crossed, and he felt her stare boring into his body.

"You are not twelve," she said. "Behave as an adult, and speak with me, or I shall treat you as a child and begin spoon-feeding you gruel. Or would you have me act as a robin, chew your food for you, and regurgitate it down your throat?"

"Heavens no," Logarius said. At last he turned to face her, and he accepted an end to his petty silence. "I merely wished to avoid your lectures. Was that so wrong of me?"

"Better my lectures than my blade," she said.

"The lectures hurt worse."

His mother squinted, and she let out a soft snort. On a human's face, the expression would have been called a "smirk."

"At least my son is alive in there somewhere. I thought I had lost him forever to the cult leader he became."

Logarius rattled his chains.

"Now that we are pleasantly speaking, might you free me from these? I can barely walk. What purpose is there in keeping me imprisoned?"

"Because I don't trust you." She used her wings to pass through a side wall and returned holding a filled wooden cup. He accepted it, then sniffed to identify the foul liquid inside as a root often used to combat fevers and infection.

"My health is fine," he said. "I have no need of this crud."

"You have no need of it because I've kept your body full of it ever since your injury," she said. "Now stop complaining like a child and drink."

Logarius sighed and did as asked. As much as he hated the bitter taste, it was smart to ensure no late infection settled into his wound. He'd seen his share of infirmaries during their many battles against the human forces. He knew how fatal the tiniest cut could be if left untreated.

"You say Shinnoc hasn't the heart or head for a siege," he said as he returned the cup to her. "But what will you do if he attacks? Hide out here and hope for the best?"

"You and I will remain out of any fight, yes," she said. "We've both done more than enough killing in our lifetimes. Let someone else wet their blades."

She gently lifted him up so she might check the wound on his back. Logarius rolled his eyes.

"Would you like me to just ask outright? Would that make you feel better?"

She lifted the bandages, then grunted unhappily. Instead of returning the bandage, she unrolled a fresh one about her wrist and began applying it over the wound.

"Ask what?"

"What you've been dying for me to ask about ever since I awoke," he said.

"And what is that, my son? Tell me, since you are so wise."

Logarius sighed. He hated that she was playing the fool here, but he sensed what she wanted with every single action she took. She wanted to explain herself, needed to do it so badly, it hurt her. It was the only reason she'd loathed his constant silence. Fine. He could grant his mother this, if only to let her drop her charade.

"Why did you not kill me?" he asked. "Why not bury your blade in my heart instead of my side?"

"Because I still held out hope I could save you," she said softly.

"Save me," he echoed. "From what?"

She returned him to his back and then addressed him face-to-face.

"From yourself. From the hatred and the bloodlust I know all too well. The Cradle has moved on without us, and the humans, forgotten us. The only grudges that remain are ours. The only bitterness still felt is in our hearts, not theirs. We could find peace, if we worked for it. I truly believe that, more than I ever did when I was younger." She dipped the cloth into the basin, wrung it out, and then pressed it to his forehead, slowly cleaning his feathers, which were slick with sweat. "I guess I hoped to convince you of that, too."

Logarius closed his eyes and endured the cleaning. Memories of a smoke-filled forest tugged at his mind, demanding to be relived, and he fought them with greater ferocity than he ever used against a living foe.

"There's no saving me, Mother," he said softly. "Not anymore. My hope for peace died with my daughter in the smoke and ash of the Wardhus Forest. Eileen was my joy. She was my future. Now I have only vengeance."

"'Only vengeance,' he says," Evelyn mocked. "Then why establish Belvua? If you think there's no future, why fight so hard to establish a home for the dragon-sired here in Londheim? Why recruit humans and indoctrinate them with that foolish screed I wrote?"

The memories proved more stubborn than usual. The smell of smoke tickled Logarius's nose. The look of anguish on his mother's face as she cradled Eileen's tiny body. Try as he might, he couldn't dismiss the panic he'd felt constrict his chest as he realized just how calm his little girl's body was, how glassy her eyes, and how empty her lungs.

"I spent years assaulting the human armies," he said. "And what did it accomplish? Nothing. Centuries of their breeding and spreading like roaches erased whatever damage our avenria caused. So when I awoke to discover the entire world conquered by the chosen species of the Sisters, what else was there for me to do? I refuse to surrender, Mother. I refuse to accept this idea that the Cradle belongs solely to them and not us. So Belvua is my final defiant stand against this new world we've awakened to, where we're to be subservient, a minority, a footnote. This little district might be my only accomplishment that lasts beyond my death. It may be a paltry victory against humanity's spread, but it is a victory nonetheless. Must you hate me for this? Must you imprison me and fear what I might do to accomplish it?"

He felt the sorrow afresh. The horrid agony of knowing Eileen's future was stolen. He'd never see her grow, mature, live and love and have children of her own. Forever strangled by the smoke of a thousand fires. Did he rage against the wrong villain? Did he cast his blame too low?

"Maybe coexistence wasn't the mistake," he said. "Existence is."

Evelyn settled her hand atop his. Her scales were dry and cracked, and he was so keenly aware of her age. Time would one day take her from him, too. She squeezed, but he did not squeeze back.

"I will not give up on you," she said. "Even if you are lost in your own sorrowful sea, I will hold out hope for us both. I will be the shelter amid the storm. I will always love you, my son. Always."

She left him to his thoughts, for which he was thankful. Tears had begun to build in his eyes, and he did not want her to see them fall. Solitude, however, was not to be his.

As he stared out his little window, he noticed a cloud gathering, small at first, then larger, thicker, forming into the translucent shape of an avenria. This form manipulated its size so it might slip through the window, then re-formed within a heartbeat. Its surface was like puffy cotton, all but its eyes, which were dead black orbs that pulsed with starlight deep within their centers.

"Hello, Logarius," said Nihil, the Dragon of Conflict. The words emanated with nine voices, each perfectly synchronized. "It appears rumors of your death are greatly exaggerated."

"Nihil, I... I am flattered to be graced with your presence," he said. "I would kneel, if I were not chained."

Logarius was indeed flattered, but also frightened. He had met the demigod only a handful of times prior to their imprisonment by the Sisters. Of all the dragons, Nihil was the one most feared by the humans. They had altered their names in their stories, shifting their concepts in subtle ways to paint them in darker lights. The Dragon of Change became the Dragon of Corruption, the Dragon of Time became the Dragon of Decay, Thought became Heresy, and Elements became Destruction.

As for Nihil, representative of the innate nature of conflict? To the humans, and even to many of the dragon-sired, Nihil was the Dragon of Chaos, and it was to be feared above all.

"I need no displays of respect from you," the white, cloud-like version of an avenria said as it paced. "What I seek are answers. What will those in Belvua do should Shinnoc's army launch an attack upon the walls? These Forgotten Children are your people. Will they remain neutral? Will they assault the human soldiers, or will they turn traitors to their own race and assist with the defense?"

"We Forgotten Children seek a place to call our home," Logarius said, carefully choosing his every word. "If Shinnoc's army assaults the walls, we shall leave him and the humans to fight their battle. If he burns human homes, then so be it. But if he brings his destruction to our district, yes, we will defend ourselves. Above all, we want to be left alone."

"So you want peace, despite your constant shedding of blood?"

Logarius shrugged.

"In a sense, I suppose. Humans are a stupid, stubborn lot. They will not give us what we deserve without a bit of bloodshed."

Nihil stepped closer. The cloud-form that made up its being was starting to break apart. Its wings had already collapsed, and the two legs were merging together into one long, snakelike lower half.

"So tell me, seeker of peace," the dragon asked with the voice of a young child. "Why did you murder Cannac?"

The simple question set his heart to racing, and he flinched despite desperately trying to remain calm and neutral.

"For what reason would you accuse me of such a crime?" he asked.

"You speak with a demigod, avenria. Do not belittle me. Your

Forgotten Children took the former Dyrandar King's life. I seek to know why."

Logarius struggled for a satisfying answer. It'd seemed logical at the time, almost a necessity if they were to hold on to Belvua. Humanity would never accept them, and so they had to take their birthright by force, take it with blood and steel and claw. Cannac, on the other hand, came seeking peace. He wanted nothing to do with Londheim, and he had even declared the Forgotten Children traitors without proper allegiance to the Kings and councils that ruled the various dragon-sired races. With a heavy heart, Logarius had given the order for his death to be carried out by the onyx faery, Gan.

"Cannac did not seek coexistence," Logarius said. "He sought friendship. Humanity will never give us the respect we deserve, yet he failed to understand that key truth. If left to his own devices, I truly believe he would have demanded our exit from Belvua as a concession. As much as it pained me, I saw no other way to ensure our collective survival."

"You murdered a dyrandar who came seeking peace, all in the name of ensuring peace?" asked the bemused dragon.

"I told you, I didn't want peace. We wanted humanity humbled. Peace was to be ours eventually, yes, but not at first. Not before we slaked our thirst for vengeance, burned down the church's cathedral, and murdered those who slavishly obeyed the Sisters' laws. We wanted a conqueror's peace, but Cannac would have brought about a victim's agreement. I took no pleasure in the sacrifice, but it was a necessary sacrifice, nonetheless."

Nihil hardly looked convinced, but Logarius did not trust himself to read the thoughts or expressions of a demigod. Damn it, what he'd give to be healthy and able to properly kneel before the dragon. He felt exposed and vulnerable in his current position on his bed, and humiliated by the chains holding him in place.

"Do you judge me for my actions?" he asked as the silence stretched on.

"I do not judge," Nihil said. "For the decisions you mortals make are rarely your own. You are spheres on a table clattering together and then bouncing off in random directions. Cannac was good, and wise, but many good and wise people die as children, die murdered on their walk to work, die choking on smoke or bleeding from disease. This world is not just. It is not fair. You let your anger and hatred guide your actions, and in that, you are very, very . . . normal."

Hardly a relief to hear himself simplified and dismissed so easily, but it was certainly better than having the demigod angry with him.

"What of Shinnoc?" he asked. "Does he know?"

Nihil shook its head.

"The new King remains in the dark."

"Will you tell him?"

After a long, agonizing moment, the dragon once again shook its head.

"I swore I would remain impartial in this impending battle," it said. "And I will remain true to my promise. These events shall play out as they are meant to play out. My interference will only be to prevent the interference of others."

"Then what is it you need me for?" he asked.

The demigod had lost all sense of coherent form. Its body was pure vapor now, shaped in a mix of over a dozen dragon-sired creatures. All but the head, which had taken on the shape of a human woman.

"You have seen the machinery we built in defiance of the Sisters. You know the gamble we take to preserve the Cradle's future. More is at stake than one meager city, and I would have a champion with values aligned much closer to ours than the current Chainbreaker." The cloud-shape raised its hand. Its voice became crystalline, beautiful and alluring. "Would you be that for us, Logarius? Could you become a new Chainbreaker?"

The blood in his veins chilled. The air about him turned cold. Logarius felt the tantalizing allure of power held before him, power beyond anything he could comprehend. All he had to do was say yes. All he had to do was swear his allegiance to the Dragon of Chaos. He had witnessed firsthand what the current Chainbreaker could accomplish with her undeserved gifts. What might he do if granted those wondrous abilities instead?

But to wield it would be to become Nihil's avatar, a glorified pet in a way that Adria was not. For in their plan, Adria was the catalyst to removing humanity's reliance upon the Sisters. Him, though? He wouldn't even be working for his own dragon-sired people. He'd be pledged to serve humanity, to guide their souls upon birth and restore them to the heavens upon death. The thought of it sickened him.

"We are the Forgotten Children," he said with dry tongue and still heart. "You sought to bestow humanity with a precious gift while we, your own children, suffered and died. And now you would offer that gift to me? I don't want it, dragon. None of us ever did. We wanted your love. We wanted your protection."

"That is what I offer you now," said Nihil.

"You ask that I become a weapon for you to wield. That isn't love. To the void with your gift."

The demigod stepped closer. Logarius shrank into his bed, and his every ounce of courage blasted apart into nothing. Rage dwelt in those star-filled eyes. Feelings of contempt and betrayal blanketed his mind so that he could not form a coherent thought.

"Our every act was done for you, our children," Nihil said. "Insolent wretches. Ungrateful spawn of mine. If you will not accept, I will find another who is willing."

The demigod shrank in upon itself, thickening, becoming a single cloud no larger than Logarius's fist. It floated out the window and to the sky above. Once it was out of sight, Logarius shivered from steadily draining fear and excitement.

"Is that what you'd have wanted from me, Mother?" he asked the emptiness. "Was that the right choice?"

Not so long ago he'd have leapt at the chance to inherit such power. He'd have betrayed his every principle to wield untold destruction against the humans of Londheim. Shinnoc's army would not even be necessary, for he'd have reduced everything to ash and rubble with his own two hands. Now the thought of that much destruction and responsibility resting upon his wings filled him with tired dread.

Perhaps there was hope for him after all.

Or perhaps, just like with Cannac, he would forever regret his decision.

CHAPTER 18

Adria needed no magical powers of reading souls to know anger was spreading throughout Londheim like a ravaging flame. She could see it in the eyes of the fifty men and women gathered outside the Becher family's private mansion. The mass was organized into a loose line by the city guard. No doubt they were waiting for a meeting with the Mayor that would never come. Adria slipped between them, her shoulders back and her head held high, and did her best to let their angry words slide off her.

"You'll tell them, won't you?" an older woman shouted as one of the guards pushed open the gate to allow her passage. "We can't win a siege while the enemy's already got a foot in the door!"

Belvua. Always Belvua. Adria prayed her upcoming meeting with Mayor Becher was about anything other than that. Since Low Dock's takeover, and the subsequent destruction of the Cathedral of the Sacred Mother, she'd used what spare time she had to pray her miracles, heal the sick, and conjure food for the hungry. Yet more and more, the people coming to her knew about what she had done at the battle for the cathedral, and at the marketplace where the Forgotten Children had ambushed her. They knew the power she wielded, and they wanted her to use it to take Belvua back.

Adria's hopes for a simple meeting involving food shortages vanished the moment she stepped into the lounge room and saw the waiting crowd sitting in either the tall-backed chairs or on the edges of the cushions of the two long couches. Mayor Soren stood to greet her, present as expected, though unexpectedly his son was missing. Sitting beside him was High Excellence Albert Downing looking prim and pleasant as could be. Accompanying him on the adjacent couch were Vikar Caria and Vikar Forrest, both dressed in their official black suits. General Kaelyn Rose lurked by the door, her hands resting on her sword's hilt. To see a congregation of Londheim's most powerful figures together, all waiting for her, could not possibly mean anything good.

"Greetings, everyone," she said as she removed her heavy coat and set it on a coat rack beside the roaring fireplace. "I trust the reason for my coming is not what I was originally told?"

"Regrettably not," Soren said, the handsome man smiling at her as he offered her his hand. She shook it, then bowed to the two Vikars. Politeness in this scenario involved removing her mask, but she dared not expose herself in such a way when already on her back foot.

"I pray you forgive us for this mild clandestine affair," the Mayor added.

"We didn't want to cause any concern or alarm," Albert said from his chair. He held a half-full glass of wine, and he gently swished the dark red liquid around, close to but never quite spilling it over the edge. "We also do not know if spies are watching our movements, so I thought it best we hold this meeting here."

"Caution is wise when there is an army camped outside your walls," Adria agreed. The only available spot on the couch, whether left there accidentally or on purpose, would have her surrounded on all four sides. She remained standing. "So why am I here? Have I done something wrong?"

"Not at all," Vikar Forrest said, and he smiled at her in an obvious attempt to calm her nerves. "We just have some questions for Londheim's rising star, that's all."

"Then ask them," she said, not caring that she was behaving rudely to her hosts. "There is much for me to do today, and many who need my aid."

"Indeed, many do," Albert said, and he stood while Soren sat. "And that is why we've called you here. All four of us have heard stories of the power you now wield, and some of us were even fortunate enough to witness it during the cowardly attack on the Keeping Church's most holy cathedral."

Everything rapidly clicked into place. Adria's hands curled into fists, and she clenched them tightly to her sides.

"You want me to fight for you," she said.

"For Londheim," Vikar Caria clarified. The woman looked dashing as ever in her dark suit and vest. She'd even neatly redone the tightly braided bun for her hair, so important was this meeting, apparently. "The army outside our walls has threatened to slaughter every living human within, and to burn all our homes to ash. This is the greatest threat our city has faced in its entire three-hundred-year history, and we must prepare accordingly."

She wasn't wrong, but it felt like she was neglecting to mention how that entire threat could be negated by High Excellence Albert turning himself over to the besieging army.

"I've given a little thought to what I'll do should the dragon-sired attack," Adria admitted. "But I have always assumed it would be my choice as to how I protect the people. Is that not to be the case?"

Albert closed the space between them, and she saw him reach out for her hands briefly before changing his mind. The man was incredibly charismatic, and even with her mask, he could read her emotions with the expertise of a lifelong politician.

"I do not wish to give orders unless I must," he said. "The reason we brought you here is so that we may hear, from your own lips, a confirmation of your allegiance to Londheim, to Westreach, and to your superiors. Normally I would hold faith in someone who has defended Londheim to her utmost abilities, but the spate of murders shaping victims to share your image, and declare you certain . . . titles, has us worried."

Adria glanced at the two Vikars from the corner of her mask's eye slots. This meeting might not have been Soren's or Albert's idea after all, she decided. Right now, she was merely acting Vikar, and she held little doubt that concession was granted to her as a form of appeasement. No one knew when the vote to appoint a replacement Deakon for the deceased Sevold would be held, either. Until then, the other two Vikars effectively ran the entire church organization.

"You speak of the golden bloodstains declaring me a new Sacred Mother," she said. "Have I not denounced them? Have I not told you already they are the work of the monster, Janus, and not my own hand?"

"We just want to know your allegiances," Albert said softly.

"Allegiances. You wish to know my allegiance? Tell me, *High Excellence*, why is it that I should hold allegiance to you in the first place?"

The mood in the room, which had been tense but cordial, rapidly soured.

"Because Albert represents the will of the people," Soren argued.

"Westreach is now an independent nation," Adria said. "But is it even a nation when we barely have contact with any other town or city beyond Londheim? Why is it I should be subservient to the High Excellence? Why should the Keeping Church? In fact, what power does the church now hold? Have we any authority over the common folk, or will the Ecclesiast cast us aside in the same manner as the Queen?"

"Hold your tongue," Vikar Caria snapped. The woman leapt to her feet. "The church and state have reached agreements to maintain all former relationships in Westreach. The people need stability in these troubled times, not confusion or bickering over power."

Adria knew she should control herself, but her frustration boiled over, and for once she felt no fear of these powerful men and women. She could see their souls. She could see, quite clearly, that every single one of them was terrified of her.

"Stay the same," she said. "The world has changed. Are we not to change with it? We are to stay mired in traditions? We are to hold on to power structures built over centuries in an irrelevant world where monsters and magic are mere stories, and the only threats we face are the ones of our own making? This is insanity. We have a chance to build everything anew, to be stronger, to be better. I will not aid in suppressing that much-needed change."

She pointed a finger directly at Albert.

"No, I will not fight for you," she said. "I will not shed blood at your command when you might spare thousands of lives with a single sacrifice of your own."

"Do not speak of that ludicrous offer," Albert snapped, his calm facade breaking for the first time ever in her presence. "I will not subject myself to mockery, torture, and execution on the slight chance those monsters keep their word."

Adria had often feared power and its accompanying responsibility. Now as she stood among the powerful, she realized how foolish she had always been. The powerful were just as afraid as she had always been. They were just as clueless, and just as frantic in their search for the right course of action.

"You are treading on dangerous ground," Vikar Forrest said. The giant man's face had turned as red as a tomato. "Do not force us to take action."

"You have no action to take," Adria said. The sudden lightness in her chest was positively addicting. "You hold no power over me, neither of you. And though the vote has not taken place, we all know who the people of Westreach desire as the next leader of the church. Declare it so, or I will declare it myself. I am Deakon now. If you would keep the structure of power the same, then I shall claim its head. All of you, accept *my* authority, or face my wrathful words to the populace." She pointed at the two Vikars. "You have until tomorrow to publicly declare your loyalty, as well as reaffirm my appointment as Deakon, or I shall have you replaced. There is no shortage of candidates loyal to myself that would be happy to fulfill your roles."

"This is grotesque," Caria stammered. "This is insurrection. We will not stand—"

Adria ripped Vikar Caria's soul right out of her skull and held it over her open palm. Its soft blue-white light shone upon the others. A soft sound like a ringing bell hummed from the soul's burning center, which grew in volume as Adria made the soul twirl and dance just above her grasp.

"I will protect the people of Londheim," she said, her every word powerful in the sudden chilled silence. "Even if it means protecting them from you. Albert, turn yourself in, or I will hand you over to them. Soren, announce yourself in agreement with the decision. Forrest, Caria, you've both heard my terms. I am Deakon now. Make it known."

A flick of her wrist and the soul plunged back into Caria's body. The woman staggered a step, as if she'd just regained her balance. Adria put her back to them and exited the room, a smile blooming behind her porcelain mask.

By the Goddesses and all that was holy, that felt *amazing*.

The angry crowd had grown in size by the time she returned to the front lawn, numbering near seventy or eighty at first glance. Adria approached them without trepidation. They wanted her to save them from Belvua, to save them from the dragon-sired, to save them from hunger and thirst and fear. So be it. Adria was done being paralyzed by indecision. She was done being defined by inaction.

"People of Londheim," she cried as they parted at the gates. Her voice carried, enhanced with a mere thought and a soft, unseen tendril of power drawn from her own soul. "I know you are afraid. I know you are angry. You wish to take action, but I beg of you, do not resort to violence. Do not resort to theft and bloodshed. A better way comes, and it comes now."

Adria harnessed the power of her soul and forced it to flow through her. That ancient power could warp reality itself, and she used the tiniest flicker of its flame to lift herself off the ground so she might levitate above the crowd. All eyes were upon her as the men and women gasped. Some cried out her name. Some just cried.

"Do not be afraid," she told her people. "Give up your anger, and listen instead. Hear me. Trust me. Know in your hearts that whatever fate awaits our grand city, the Chainbreaker shall forever be at your side."

CHAPTER 19

If they fed him, Dierk would have tracked the passage of time through his meals, but they gave him only the occasional sips of water through a straw while a guard ensured a dagger stayed at his throat at all times lest he attempt a curse. If there were windows, he'd have used the sun, but the cellar was pitch black. He slept at random lengths and intervals. Sometimes he passed out, other times he stared into the nothing in a drugged-like daze. Only one thing remained consistent. Only one thing allowed him to track the passage of days, and it was more reliable than any clock or sunrise.

The door opened, light sliced into the dark, and his father's footsteps thumped down the cellar stairs. A new day. A new round of punishment.

As usual, it did not start with beatings, punches, or kicks. Dierk lay in his own filth, his cheek against the cold stone, his entire body a mess of bruises and sores. Soren settled into the lone chair kept down there for such purposes. The wood groaned against his weight. Dierk's father clasped his hands together, and he gathered himself to speak. Every time, he did this. Why? Did it help his father accept the current situation? Did it alleviate his guilt? Whatever the reason, Soren spoke on city matters with a light, businesslike tone.

"It's taken a bit of effort, and even more secrecy, but we have managed to avoid the damage you nearly caused," Soren said. Dierk couldn't see his father's face, only his feet. His legs were crossed, his nearest boot casually bouncing up and down as he sat. "Every single boat in the harbor is now under the possession of a . . . coalition of the wise, one might say. Their cargo holds are full to the brim with our belongings. Only what must be taken, of course. Sadly many heirlooms will remain behind."

Soren rose from the chair, then placed the jacket to his fine suit over its top.

"We'll flee this city and sail south, to Pathok. Once there we'll secure wagons to bring our belongings to Watne. Safely away from the dragon-sired army, we will have a chance to plan out what to do with Westreach's future. Perhaps we'll raise an army. South Orismund was abandoned by the East, same as we were. They're undergoing civil war, so there's a chance we side with a faction and meld Westreach into the newly formed nation of the victor. A lot will be in play these next few years, Dierk. A lot to be decided. The Cradle will need people like us to guide them. Wise people. People with forethought."

His father was rolling up his sleeves. Dierk let out a long sigh through his nose. It'd start soon. The violence. The torture. But at least it meant the talking would cease. He hated the casual one-sided conversations more than he hated the beatings. Each kick to his stomach showed the truth about what his father thought of him. There was no hiding behind charisma, no pretending at a shared humanity. Just pain, blood, and suffering, and Soren was so very good at drawing out all three.

"Not that you'd understand any of this," Soren said. "You'd have left us here to die."

The tip of his boot slammed into Dierk's chest. He tried not to make a noise. He had no indication whether or not his suffering gave his father pleasure. Everything about the torture was so workman-like. So practical. Still, Dierk tried to hide it just in case, though he most often failed. His body was too weak, his spirit too broken. As the kicks started, all focusing on his ribs and stomach, he sobbed against the pain. At least twice he bit his tongue, and blood spilled across his gag. His tears gave him something to focus upon, but for once, it seemed Soren was not done talking.

"You have no *idea* how much this pains me," his father said. Dierk doubted he meant the punishment. "To leave Londheim? To abandon our family paintings, our carefully purchased properties? To be Mayor, and have my last act as Mayor be a midnight flight to safety? Fucking disgraceful, but you left me no choice."

The kicks shifted so that they were aimed at his groin.

"You hear me, Dierk? No. Goddess. Damned. Choice."

Near the end he couldn't contain himself and curled up in a vain attempt to protect his crotch. Soren's kicks came in even harder. One in particular collided with his face, and he jerked to the side while biting down a yelp. Blood flowed from his scraped cheek, but he didn't care. That kick to the face, his mouth and teeth in particular, was something he had been trying for seemingly days now. He kept his head turned, and he dared not face his father.

"I hate to tell you this, but I cannot bring you with me," Soren said. His breathing was heavy, and it was no surprise to hear the chair groan as he took a seat. "And I won't leave you for the dragon-sired to find. The chances may be incredibly slim, but I won't risk them freeing you, or attempting to hold you as a hostage. You're going to die by my hand, son. You'll be my final sacrifice to this city and its people that never deserved our dedication."

Dierk raised his head, and he coughed twice, great shuddering heaves. The blood-soaked gag slipped free, the knot straining against his lower lip.

"Anwyn of the Moon," he whispered. "Hear me."

His father heard but didn't realize the significance, not at first. That moment's hesitation was all Dierk needed.

"Before me stands a man disgracing the light of his soul. His mind rejects peace. His heart rejects love."

Soren dashed from his chair, but he couldn't make those final few steps in time. Dierk didn't even look at him. He kept his eyes closed, his exhausted mind focused on the words he dared not misspeak.

"Break his pride. Split his stubbornness. Give me, in my superior wisdom, *control*."

The halt in Soren's movements was immediate. Silence filled the cellar. Dierk drank it in like life-giving water. All he could hear was his father's calm, steady breathing. Patient. Obedient.

"Untie me," he ordered.

His father obeyed. Once freed, Dierk crawled over to the chair, sank into it, and then sobbed. He sobbed for what felt like hours. At first it was from the immediate pain, which was still tremendous. After that came the hopelessly mixed feelings of relief and despair. He'd fully believed he'd die in that cellar, and knowing he was free was almost more than his broken spirit could believe. Dierk cried, and laughed, and endured in that chair until he finally felt his mind clear of the haze that fallen over it.

Then, and only then, did he stand to address his father.

"Do you have a blade?" he asked him. Soren pulled a slender dagger from his pocket to show it in answer. It was little better than a letter opener. "Good. Kill yourself."

His father pulled the tight leather sheath off the dagger, flipped its handle, and then jammed the dagger straight into his throat. Blood spurted in a long jet across the cellar floor. Dierk crossed his arms and grinned. The light was dim, but the faint glow coming in through the cracked cellar door was enough to see his father's face. His features were calm, but his eyes, oh his eyes, they were afraid. They were furious. Dierk met their gaze, and he made sure his joy was visible as the lifeblood spilled out across the cold stone floor that had been his bed for the past four days.

Once Soren's body was still, he pulled the dagger from his father's rigid grasp and plunged it a few more times into his neck and face for good measure. The last thing he wanted was to make a mistake in the exact same way his father just had.

"Good fucking riddance," Dierk said, and he cast the dagger aside.

His mind turned to his immediate fate. Properly playing this was going to be tricky. His father had told him he'd been removed from any will or inheritance, but he'd also been telling people he'd been killed. Perhaps Dierk could use that confusion to his benefit. Of course he'd be removed from a will after his death. That made sense, didn't it? But how might he steal his father's title as Mayor? Nothing in Londheim's founding articles was set up for a family transfer of the mayoral position upon death. He'd need to establish himself as a person of authority. Earning a blessing from the High Excellence would be a huge step as well. But all that was putting the cart before the horse. He needed control over his own household first.

Once he'd collected himself, Dierk calmly strode up the stairs of his cellar. A curse was already on his lips the moment a servant came around the corner.

"Anwyn of the Moon, hear me."

In the end, it wasn't too difficult. Once four or five members of the serving staff and guard staff were under his control, the rest accepted his apparent return without any audible grumbling. Several even breathlessly assured him how thrilled they were to discover him alive and well. They were the enthralled ones, but he liked to pretend they said it of their own volition.

Dierk's room was still the same as it'd always been. A blessing in disguise, he supposed. Many of his father's clothes and belongings were packed and stored in a boat docked alongside the Septen River. Dierk changed out of his sweat-and-blood-soaked clothes, and he shed them like he would a second skin before calling for a bath. The warm water and lye soap stung his cuts and bruises, but he had to make himself presentable. He even asked a servant to help with the washing of his hair, something he'd not done since he was seven. The polite young man combed and brushed his matted locks, occasionally dipping Dierk's head back into the water to rinse away the filth he loosened with his comb.

Sliding on clean clothes after his bath felt divine. He donned a gray suit, spent ten minutes adjusting its various buttons and bands so it fit perfectly, and then exited his room. One of his enthralled guards stood patiently waiting, and Dierk leaned in close so he might whisper his order.

"Soren's body is in the cellar," he said. "It would be problematic if anyone found it. Dispose of it discreetly."

"Understood," the burly man said.

Dierk had settled on a plan during his bath, and though it might have once left him flooded with nerves, now he felt only elation. After such suffering at the hands of his father, what could he possibly fear from the people of Londheim? The household was under his thumb. Most importantly, Soren, his father, the ogre of his entire life, lay in a pool of blood on the cellar floor. There was nothing left for him to fear.

Dierk stood in the center of an angry, impatient crowd an hour later, the hundreds of them gathered at the heart of the nearby marketplace. He'd paid runner boys to announce an impending speech by the Mayor's replacement, relying on intrigue to bring him his audience. A few of his house guards had gone about the city as well, to the lower, seedier places they knew well, and told their fellows of potential riots to come. Dierk had no dais to stand on, but one of his servants brought him a ladder, and he figured he'd make do with what he had.

"People of Londheim," he shouted from the top steps. He cried it out thrice more, until the noise of the market quieted down to a deep murmur.

"My father, Soren Becher, is dead," he said. "Killed by my hand."

That set the crowd back to a rumble. A brief, nervous shiver shot up and down Dierk's spine, but he suppressed it with memories of a hundred boot kicks to his stomach and groin. How many times had his father told him confidence before the masses would lead to results? It was time to put the bastard's advice into practice.

"Why would I do such a thing, you might ask?" he continued. "Why would I come here to inform you all of my supposed crime? Because it was no crime. My father was a traitor to this city, and a traitor to his position. Hear me, people of Londheim! Your leaders plan to abandon you! Even now, they load their belongings onto the city's boats. Come tonight, they hope to flee under the cover of darkness. The wealthy and the powerful of this city shall sacrifice you to the armies outside our gates! They will let the dragon-sired destroy everything you know and love while they sail to safety. This was my father's plan, and I ask you, was I wrong to call him a traitor? Was I wrong to take his life?"

Asking such questions was pointless given the rising din. He doubted anyone beyond the second row could even hear him, but Dierk shouted it out nonetheless. Excitement pounded through his veins. A victorious smile stretched his lips. He felt like Logarius before his faithful. He spoke, and people listened. There wasn't even need of a control curse.

"You may ask for proof," he continued, the last bit of flame on a well-oiled fire. "To the docks, then! To the boats! Find the wealth of cowards, and take it for yourselves!"

The furious crowd would have done so on their own without his permission, but to have the son of the former Mayor shouting such an order only gave them that much bigger a push. The people flowed east, toward the nearby docks district, and it seemed every few seconds they gained another ten people. Dierk walked at the head of the mob, and he had to remind himself again and again to keep his face determined and angry. There would be a time for joy, but not now. Not amid this populist rage.

Just as he'd promised, the docks were cluttered with boats. Just as he'd promised, their cargo holds were stockpiled with unimaginable wealth. Dierk stayed at the district entrance and watched, two house guards at his elbows to keep him safe. Only now, upon witnessing the fruits of his labors, did he allow himself to smile. Sailors dove off the sides of boats upon seeing the mob, but a few were not so lucky. The crowd strung them up by their heels from the high lantern posts. Hundreds and hundreds dashed across the docks, and more came by the second. The wood vibrated underneath Dierk's feet. The air sang with rage.

Men and women emerged from cargo holds carrying gold chains, paintings, and wine bottles. They dripped with jewelry. Others took the more practical supplies—stacks of salted beef, pork, and jars of vegetables sealed in brine. A few fought among themselves, but not many. There was a feral understanding afoot, something Dierk could vaguely sense but not partake within. There was no struggle, no theft among thieves. Perhaps it was because there was just so much to share. They took, they looted, and then when the boats were stripped clean, a few eager men set a handful aflame. Just a few, and the boats were quickly cut loose from the dock to float down the Septen, the light of their fires sending a signal seen throughout all of Londheim.

Dierk followed their passage with his gaze until the flow took them around a turn at the isolated district of Belvua and its empty docks and its protective ring of strange, colorful trees. His smile grew. The rage here was but a taste of what was to come. Deep down in his ecstatic heart, Dierk knew that Belvua was next. When those riots began, he would be at their forefront, torch in hand and a cry of murder on his lips.

A true leader.

The leader Londheim needed.

"What have you done?"

Dierk slowly turned from the spectacle to find Adria Eveson before him. Her face might be hidden behind a mask, but her eyes were visible, and they were wide with fury. Tamerlane was beside her, and Dierk struggled to hold back a sour face at the sight of the smug bastard.

"I have done what was needed to be done," Dierk said. "What should have been done, if my father were not a coward."

Adria stepped closer, and when his house guards moved to interfere, she ripped their souls out and set them to floating just above their heads.

"I have labored to keep this city peaceful," she seethed. "And now I find a riot at our docks and our boats aflame. What is the meaning of this?"

"Soren sought to flee with his wealthy friends," Dierk said. "Everything else happened as one would expect once the people were informed."

"You mean as you intended," said Tamerlane.

"They can be one and the same," Dierk snapped, hating how young and snotty he suddenly sounded when confronted by the older man. But unlike Tamerlane, Adria suddenly seemed worried and unsure. She stepped closer, and she lowered her voice despite the din. Closer, so she might whisper in his ear. Goddesses and dragons, she was so close, he could smell her rose water perfume and a hint of sweat. Parts of her dress pressed against his hands and legs. Brightest of all was the light of her soul, a blinding beacon to his nisse-blessed eyes.

"What of the High Excellence?" she asked. "Vikar Forrest? Vikar Caria? Did they plan to flee the city they are meant to protect?"

Dierk would have lied if he thought she'd have believed him, but she could see his soul, and sense any lie before it ever left his tongue.

"I don't know," he said. "My father never mentioned their names, and whatever proof we might have found was long since taken by the crowd."

Adria stepped away. A snap of her fingers sent the souls back into his guards.

"I presume you believe yourself the new Mayor?" she asked.

"Acting Mayor," he said. "Just like you are acting Vikar."

It came across bolder than he meant, but he couldn't allow any challenge to his position to go unmatched. Dierk pulled back his shoulders, and he stood to his full height.

"I understand the dragon-sired in a way these people never can," he said. "Therefore I am ready to lead the masses as I must."

"And how is that?" Adria asked. "To riots? To fires and destruction?"

Again his eyes flicked to Belvua. Part of him wanted to thank his father. After such torture and cruelty, all the challenges of the world felt like a gentle breeze.

"A cleansing," he said as a whorl of wind carried smoke from the charred boats across the both of them. "And whatever else must follow."

CHAPTER 20

This is stupid and pointless and I won't do it," Wren said as she and Jacaranda stood before the entrance to the Wise tower.

"It's too late now," Jacaranda insisted.

"It is not. He's not even at the door yet."

"If you don't want this, then turn around and walk away."

But of course she wanted it. Whether she thought it possible was a different matter entirely. Still, the door cracked open, and she decided to swallow her potential embarrassment and just roll with things.

"Hey, Jac!" Tommy said as he flung the door wide. The young man wore a loose bed robe that hung all the way down to his ankles and a long, puffy cap. "Oh, and hello . . . ?"

"Wren," she said. "I've heard much about you, Tomas."

"Tommy's fine," he said, and he shivered as the wind swirled into his tower. "Sheesh, it's colder than Anwyn's nethers out here. Come in, come in, I'll get the fire roaring."

Wren knew she shouldn't doubt her friend after all she'd seen, but it still surprised her when Tommy flicked his fingers at the meager fire burning in the stone fireplace and an orb of flame shot from his palm. It struck the center of the logs, bursting it to life with a *whoosh*. He clapped his hands, pleased with the results, and then set about tidying up cushions and blankets that lay strewn about the various chairs and couches.

"I'll stand," Wren said, refusing his offer. She lingered near the fireplace, glad she could use its presence as an excuse to remain on her feet. Try as she might, she felt her hopes starting to rise, and her fingers drummed against her palms as she held her hands behind her back. Sweat started to seep into her thick white scarf, but she dared not remove it.

"Sure, sure," Tommy said, and he plopped down on a couch that, based on the blankets and pillows, he'd likely been sleeping on when they came knocking that morning. "So, what brings you two lovely women to my door? Hopefully nothing bad?"

"Not at all," Jacaranda said. She cast a knowing glance at Wren, and words passed unspoken between them. Wren answered them with a go-ahead shrug. "We need your help for something that is on a more . . . personal level."

"Sure, of course, always happy to help," Tommy said. He clapped his hands together and rubbed them eagerly. "So what is it you're needing? Something magical, right? I'm always looking for a good excuse to try something new. Do we need to blow something up? Tell me you need something blown up."

"No, Tommy. I need something—someone—changed."

His excited smile never left his lips, even as he glanced between them with obvious confusion.

"I'm not sure I follow."

"Me, Tomas," Wren said. "She's talking about me."

Understanding still did not reach his eyes. Tommy looked so eager, like a boisterous puppy dog waiting for his master to throw a readied stick. It would have been adorable if not for how awkward and embarrassed Wren felt by the request in the first place.

"I feel like I'm missing something," Tommy said. "Do you need healing? Because that's more my sister-in-law's expertise."

Wren crossed her arms over her chest and locked her gaze with the young man.

"I'm a recast, Tommy."

He blinked.

"Still confused."

Goddesses help me, he's going to make me spell it out for him, isn't he?

Thankfully Jacaranda leapt in for her rescue.

"Tommy, since you know lots of magic, we were wondering if you could help Wren . . . change. Physically."

"Oh." His neck turned red, followed by his cheeks and nose. "*Oh!* Sorry, I didn't think about, you know, down-there stuff."

"It's fine," Wren said, though she had to grind her teeth together to keep calm. Jacaranda had warned her that Tomas was a bit different than most people, and that she might need to be patient. Despite his embarrassment, the young man seemed thrilled to finally know what was asked of him, and he clapped his hands excitedly as he started to ramble.

"I actually have been studying some spells from the Viciss school of magic—that's magic that focuses on the aspect of change, by the way. Now I'd been focusing mostly on the really weird stuff, changing people into birds and sheep and frogs, but yes, I've very much read a spell or two that focuses on altering biological attributes like that. They didn't seem too difficult to cast, either."

Despite all her guards and protections, Wren felt a bit of hope slip through the mental cracks.

"So you could make these changes permanent? I wouldn't need the wig or the padding?"

Tommy shook his head.

"Oh, the spells aren't permanent. I guess you'd want them to last a bit longer than a few hours, wouldn't you?"

Wren's meager hope shivered and died as if skewered through the breast.

"Yes," she said. "I would."

He wiped at his brow as if suddenly caked in sweat, and if she thought he'd rambled before, she discovered he was only getting started.

"Polymorphic magic is incredibly finicky from what I've read. Changing nonliving matter is far easier, but when it comes to living beings, the changes tend to last only a few hours at most. That doesn't mean it isn't possible. Far more likely, it means the spells I've read never meant for them to last, and if expanded upon by some anchoring rituals, maybe more lengthy and careful incantations, they could be made permanent on living matter. I'm sorry, I'm really sorry, I didn't mean to inappropriately raise your hopes."

"No, it's fine. You're only saying it'd be easier if I were dead."

"That is not, but I didn't, I might still... help..."

His blushing, which had begun to lessen, reignited in earnest. Wren smiled at him, more of a mercy than anything she personally felt.

"Like I said, it's fine. Now if you'll excuse me..."

She exited the tower, Jacaranda quickly at her heels.

"That was my fault," her friend and teacher said. "I should have better explained things, and given him time to research."

"How many times do I have to say 'it's fine'?" she asked as she walked the snow-covered street.

"Say it as many times as you'd like, Wren, but that doesn't mean I'll believe it."

Wren halted. The hour was young, the secluded street unnaturally empty. It felt like the two of them were alone in all of Londheim, and it allowed Wren to risk a moment of naked honestly.

"I'm hurt, I'm frustrated, and I'm embarrassed with myself for allowing my hopes to rise," she said. "Which means I need some time alone to shove all those feelings down. Can I have that, Jac?"

"Of course," Jacaranda said. "Whatever you need. And for what it's worth, I didn't mean to hurt you. I only wished to help."

"I know," Wren said, as if that meant anything. "I'll meet you later at Devin's house, all right?"

A quick check of her cloak to ensure the clasp was tight and covering her tattoos, and then Wren left to wander the early morning streets of Londheim. She had little money, and not the quickness to steal from the few vendors who still braved the streets after all the chaos that had befallen the city. Perhaps she'd have Jacaranda teach her a thing or two about that in between combat lessons. She had a feeling Jacaranda had been trained to do innumerable tricks and trades. Not like her. She'd been taught to smile and laugh and play like a little boy for her delusional grandfather. A childlike attitude and a soft voice, that's all she'd needed.

Wren forced the memory away to focus on her path. She'd shifted to the Aberdeen District, where the population was still relatively healthy. She browsed through some of the smaller stalls, most of them occupied by elderly workers who had been hired by their younger, wealthier owners. She stopped at one for a particularly long time, that of a stall selling beautiful painted stones expertly linked together with wire to form wristlets.

"Your master have you running errands?" the shopkeeper asked after a long delay.

"Pardon?" she asked.

It was such a simple mistake, and she realized it a half-second too late. Her clasp, it'd slipped, and the shopkeeper's eyes were on her chain tattoos.

"I'm here on my own," she said, turning away and pulling the thick wrapping back up to her chin.

Just go away, just go away, I don't mean shit to you . . .

"Hey, stop. I asked you a question."

Soulless would always answer questions when asked of them, and always follow an order when given. She could still perform the act. The temptation was there. Just turn around, stare back with a passive face, and make up a lie so the hairy man would leave her be.

"Have a good day, sir," she called over her shoulder as she continued. Still not good enough. His hand grabbed at her shoulder. His fingers tightened.

"Who taught a soulless to be so rude?" he asked as he spun her about.

"Do I look like a soulless to you?" she asked, glaring at him. Her contempt was a challenge. No soulless would act like this. Maybe she could make him doubt himself. The shopkeeper took a step back, and he lifted his hands in a meager apology.

"Sorry," he said. "My mistake."

Wren didn't stay to find out if he believed her or not. She hurried along, her heart pounding and her hand checking her cloak every thirty seconds. She felt eyes upon her, and no matter how many times she told herself it was merely her paranoia, she couldn't shake the feeling that they were all whispering among themselves after she passed.

Stubborn pride slowed her steps. She belonged here. She was like everyone else in that market. One little slipup meant nothing. After a minute or two she settled into a walk, and she even forced herself to make small talk with several of the vendors. Her mind calmed, and she started to put the nosy shopkeeper out of mind. A stall full of porcelain dolls caught her attention, and she slid to it and beamed a smile at the elderly woman running the stall.

"They're beautiful," she said, scanning their expertly painted faces and miniature clothing sewn and stitched to perfection.

"Thank you, m'lady," the old woman said.

Wren perused them over, her soft smile genuine, her muscles finally starting to relax. An image from the corner of her eye betrayed all that. A city guard. Wren's heart tripled in speed, and she felt a burning sensation across her throat. Part of her wanted to rip her cloak off and flee. Part of her wanted to slink into some little alleyway and cower while waiting for him to pass. Her rational mind rebelled. She didn't know he was looking for her. It was all in her imagination. So what if the guard was asking questions to those he passed. It didn't mean anything. It didn't mean *anything*...

But he kept coming closer. She lifted one of the dolls and

pretended to be interested. Nothing said the guard was looking for her...but what if he was? What if he knew of her tattoos and wanted answers for her strange behavior? What would she tell the man? The tattoo was fake? A joke? Could she make up a real owner? Her stomach twisted as she thought of pretending Devin or Jacaranda were her master. Sweat rolled down her neck. She glanced over her shoulder, and her gaze locked with the guard's green eyes.

Wren ran. No thought propelled it. A gust instinct pushed her forward, her fear fueled by paranoia and the burn across her throat. She didn't look to see if he chased. She didn't dare slow. Wren weaved through the sparse crowd, her eyes searching for somewhere, anywhere to hide. More watched, more called out in confusion. A lone word thumped between her ears, magnified by the pounding of her heart.

Hide. Hide. Hide.

Wren cut down an alley, expecting it to lead her out of the district, but at its sharp right turn she skidded to a halt. Bricks, their red color discordant with the other nearby homes, sealed off the passage. She spun, that word getting louder, angrier.

Hide. Hide. Hide.

She scanned the walls and ground for a window, a ledge, something. Her eyes settled on a strange uneven lump in the cobblestone, and she felt her stomach suddenly loop as her vision momentarily blurred. Wren dug her fingernails into her palm to focus herself, and when her vision returned, she saw that it wasn't lump in the street, but a rectangular trap door on hinges.

"A...door?" she asked, bewildered.

It wasn't locked, either, so she grabbed the weather-worn iron handle and pulled. It lifted with a heavy creak, revealing a ladder leading down into some dark passage. She cast one last look to the corner, imagining the chasing city guard, and descended the stairs. One hard pull closed the door above her, but it did not envelop her in darkness like she initially believed. Instead it better revealed the strange, wondrous nature of her surroundings.

Wren hid within an enormous tunnel with walkways on either side of a veritable river flowing underneath Londheim's streets. The ceiling was lit with a wondrous lichen that glowed a soft blue color to light up the dark. Even the walls were decorated with faint carvings, seemingly representing no singular image but instead conveying a flowing motion with long, waving lines. Wren had no idea such a thing existed below the city, and she wondered how many besides herself had traversed its walkways.

"You're safe here," she told herself as she sat beside the ladder. The tunnel continued far to either side of her, and she feared getting lost if she wandered. This wasn't a place for humans. Whatever was down here, she felt it belonged to the various dragon-sired creatures that had returned to Londheim. "They'll stop looking in time."

Assuming they're looking at all.

Was that even better? To know she'd merely been paranoid and not actually hunted for her soulless tattoo? But what if the guard did know, and the shopkeeper had him looking? The attacks on Belvua had left everyone in the city on edge. They might investigate. Her hand drifted to the wig upon her head. Of course, the guard was looking for a certain someone. She could abandon the dress and wig, and wash away her cosmetics in the nearby flowing river. The temptation was there, sickly and cowardly as it may be. Thinking of it put a ball of fire into her gut and set it to burning.

The covering above rattled with wood and iron. Wren staggered to her feet. Her hands fell to the slender dagger she kept hidden in the folds of her dress. Her progress with Jacaranda had been slow but steady, but could she handle an armed guard? Daylight spilled into the tunnel, and in dropped the soldier who had followed her. Wren readied her dagger, a few scrambled lies to explain her tattoos jumbling through her mind, but then the soldier's features began to change. His face melted as if made of clay. His clothes warped, armor and metal shifting into a long black coat and dark pants that left his chest exposed. His skin was smooth like marble. His hair altered so that it was half black, half green. His opal smile was that of a hunter.

"Why, hello there," this changing monster said. "I believe you're trespassing."

Wren lunged at him with her dagger, hoping that surprise would grant her victory. Instead he caught her wrist, hammered his other hand into her stomach, and then smashed his head into hers. Wren dropped to her knees, retching and gasping for air. Still he held on to her wrist, preventing her from collapsing completely. This strange man even twirled her once, as if she were his partner in a dance.

"My, my, my, how rude," he said. "First you trespass, then you attempt to stab me? Soulless truly are the most incorrigible of humanity. Kindly put that down before you hurt yourself."

Wren dropped the dagger. It clattered upon the wet stone.

"How did you know?" she asked, trying to hold back her deeply felt fright from her voice.

"That you're soulless?" The strange man grinned at her as his black coat became a brownish leather tunic. His shoulders hardened and stretched, growing a pair of pauldrons. The shift lasted but a moment before he once again abandoned the form of a soldier. "Sometimes boredom leads me to interesting disguises, and you humans are so very ready to spill your secrets to a man of law."

He released her hand, and she scurried away while still keeping her eyes locked on him.

"Who are you?" she asked. "*What* are you?"

"My name is Janus," he said. "As for what I am, well, could you even understand it? I am the avatar of change, the most hated creation of our wondrous maker, Viciss."

Viciss. Wren knew that name. It was the school of magic Tomas had referenced earlier. The idea of this man representing change certainly fit the abilities he'd showcased. But what did he want from her?

"Are you going to kill me?" she asked, figuring to get the most important matter out of the way first.

Janus knelt at the edge of the pathway and dipped his hand into the flowing river.

"A very good question," he said. "Have I a reason to kill you?"

"If what I sense of you is true, that isn't the right question."

"And what is?"

"Have you a reason to let me live?"

The strange man glanced over his shoulder as the water making contact with his bare hand began to freeze.

"You're a sharp one, aren't you, girl?" he asked. "I must confess that I have seen you before. You were with the Chainbreaker, whom you call Adria Eveson."

"Are you spying on her?"

"Indeed I am," he said. "I like to keep an eye on everyone in that particular woman's orbit. Consider it professional curiosity. I witnessed your foolhardy attempt to restore souls to the soulless. Admittedly I watched from afar, and could not hear all the conversation, but I doubt you appreciated that final outcome."

"Of course not," Wren snapped. "Adria turned dozens of soulless to ash, and for what? To throw a tantrum against her own Goddess?"

To her surprise, Janus laughed, a deep, full-bellied laugh that left him shaking his head and wiping away a tear.

"A tantrum," he said. "Oh yes, that is quite a vivid way to describe what transpired. The power of a Goddess, and the mentality of a toddler. I can think of nothing more humorous, nor more terrifying."

He clenched his fist within the water and then rose to his feet.

The water rose with him, hardening into ice that cracked and shifted. It spread for dozens of feet in all directions, a long, singular sheet obeying the whims of a madman. The ice rose higher, crunching inward with a near deafening roar. Within seconds he withdrew his hand, his work complete. Atop the river and built of ice stood three figures. One was of Adria, her face hidden behind her emotionless mask but her posture conveying anger and denial. The second figure was of the Goddess Lyra, come to deny Adria's attempt to restore souls to the soulless. And there, not far away, lurked the frozen Wren.

"It's beautiful," she whispered. She stepped closer to the edge, her eyes locked on her re-creation. He'd mimicked her so perfectly in the ice, her naked fury frightening to witness now from the outside. Despite living through it, she'd not realized just how brutal her rage, nor how deep her hurt at the Goddess's betrayal.

"A beautiful re-creation of an ugly moment," Janus said. His grin faded as he stared at his work of art. "You were fools to think the Sisters would allow you to change the world. They want things mired in stasis, their little children forever helpless and ignorant. To control the fate of your own souls? That's a privilege too far. That's a power and maturity reserved only for dragons and Goddesses."

"Then we were fools," Wren snapped. "Does that mean we were wrong to try?"

"Perhaps. Perhaps not. Foolish, stubborn pride has led you to climb mountains that should have defeated you. Maybe I am wrong to belittle your race's stupidity. That stupidity might be what allows you to conquer what we ourselves struggle to surpass."

Wren's eyes could not leave the icy version of herself. There was one single change he'd made along her neck. Had it been an oversight? A correction? She didn't know, but she knew that it felt more right to her than anything else.

"Can you change anything you touch, manipulate it no matter the clay?"

"Indeed I can," he said. The enigmatic man turned away from his art, and he towered over her. His presence was overwhelming, like fire and rot. "Pray tell me you aren't thinking of asking me for a favor?"

"Would you rather I cower in fear of you? You represent change. You just formed sculptures out of water. Surely you can fix my skin."

"Consider me not bored enough to manipulate human genitals."

But the strange man had it all wrong. She knew what truly bothered her, what caused her to feel joy and what caused her to cower in an alley from angry shopkeepers and curious city guards.

"Not that," she said, and she pulled the cloak from her neck. "This. Fix *this*."

Janus stared at her chain tattoos, and for a brief moment he fell silent. That pause gave her hope. He was thinking, debating. There was a chance.

"You would have me banish the proof of your soulless existence," he said. His voice had fallen soft. Thoughtful.

"I am soulless no longer."

"But that existence remains," he said. His jade eyes bored into hers. "Whether you like it or not, that tattoo defines you. It reveals you as different, for you *are* different, Wren, are you not? Was your childhood like that of other children? Before the Sisters rectified their mistake, did you live and grow and decide as any other human might? No. You may hate it all you want, but your disgust does not undo the past."

His pale hand touched the soft skin of her neck. His fingertips traced the interlocking line of the chains.

"There is usefulness in this mark. There is purpose in this memory."

"Fuck its purpose," she said. "I hate it more than anything else in this world."

Another flash of those opal teeth.

"Such fire," he said. "Maybe Adria will benefit from its heat. But do not think me unsympathetic. To regain your life and become a recast is a path I admire, as much as I can allow myself to admire your sad little race. How can I not appreciate change in all things? How do I not feel fondness for those who would yearn for the power I possess?"

Janus ran his fingers through her hair, and she struggled to hold back her revulsion.

"Few carry the strength of such conviction," he whispered. "Humanity possesses the power to change all the world, yet so often their hearts and minds are as malleable as stone. Consider this a gift for frightening you, Wren. Perhaps we shall meet again, and if you have fully accepted who you are, I might bless you with greater change."

Janus pulled away, and he scurried up the ladder and out of the tunnel with the speed of a spider. Wren stared at the circle of sunlight streaming down through the trap door, her stomach heaving and her legs turning weak. That man. That monster. He terrified her beyond belief. To stand before him was to drown in the presence of the unnatural.

And yet...

She slowly lifted her shaking hand to her hair where Janus had lovingly stroked it. Her fingers passed through the tightly woven locks. Touched the roots. Tugged, and felt resistance. She laughed at the absurdity even as she nearly cried from confusion. There would be no abandoning her truth for a disguise. She looked to her reflection in the water and saw her braids, now interlocking with an intricate looping pattern far beyond what they first possessed when Kye bought it for her.

The wig was a wig no longer, but her own hair, crafted by an artist, gifted by a madman.

CHAPTER 21

Brittany halted just inside Devin's living room and pointed at the sheep standing beside the fire, looking as bored as a sheep was capable of looking. Cold air swirled into the home from the frigid outside.

"There's... a sheep," Brittany said, feeling dumb as she said it but unsure of how else to properly convey her surprise. Jacaranda sat nearby on the couch, and she covered her face with her hand to hide her laughter.

"Yeah, there is," Devin said as he plopped into his rocking chair, lifted his feet, and set them atop the sheep's back like a footrest. "Don't worry. I haven't gotten a new pet. It's just Tommy."

This did not clarify things as Devin had intended.

"Tommy?" she asked, finally remembering to close the door. "My brother... is... a sheep?"

The beast glanced at her and let out a sharp "*Baaa.*"

"It's only temporary," Devin said, and he pulled a note out of his pocket and offered it to her. "And before you blame me, I assure you it was his idea."

Brittany quickly skimmed the tight, looping script. The note was short and to the point, an impressive feat for her brother.

Devin,

You were right. We should not use a polymorph spell without properly testing it first, and it would be improper to test on anyone who does not fully understand the risks. I should revert within half an hour. If I do not, return me to Malik so he might work on a cure. Thanks!

Tommy

"I believe he knocked on our door and then cast the spell before we answered," Jacaranda said as Brittany lowered the note. "Imagine our surprise stepping outside to find a sheep with a letter pinned underneath its hoof."

"Quite surprised indeed," Brittany said, her mind still struggling to make sense of it all. She'd come with important news, news that had very quickly been sidetracked. She approached the sheep and knelt so she and he might look eye to eye. "So is he in there still? Does he understand what's going on, or is he . . . full sheep?"

"Full sheep from what we can tell," Devin said. "I tried having him stomp a hoof once or twice for yes and no, but he seemed pretty oblivious."

The animal stared at her with his big black eyes. She pet Sheep-Tommy across his dark forehead, then rustled his woolly backside.

"You floofy idiot," she said, then stood to compose herself. "I don't mean to distract from the excitement, but did you hear of the riots at the docks?"

Devin bolted upright in his chair, accidentally startling Sheep-Tommy.

"No," he said. "What riots?"

"I arrived late with most of the church's Soulkeepers," Brittany said. She crossed her arms and leaned against the wall, her mind falling back into memory. "It was awful. Half the boats were burned, perhaps more. Several dozen men and women were hung by their feet from the lantern posts, and others were drowned and left floating."

"How awful," Jacaranda said. "What caused it?"

"The Mayor's son did. He claimed his father was a traitor, and Londheim's wealthy were planning to flee with all their worldly possessions. Needless to say, most people here didn't react too kindly to the idea of being abandoned with a dragon-sired army outside our gates. They stole everything from the boats, assaulted the wealthy and their servants, and burned what they couldn't take."

"Damn it, so this is what I miss out on while babysitting Sheep-Tommy," he said. His tone darkened. "High Excellence Albert... was he to be on those boats?"

"I don't know," Brittany said. "But everyone believes so. I'd say he isn't planning on turning himself over to Shinnoc, that much is certain. We'll have a war on our hands."

No sound or impressive effect marked the sudden and startling ending of Tommy's spell. Before Brittany could finish her sentence, the sheep was gone, and her brother was on his hands and knees, Devin's legs still resting on his back. It took him a half-second to realize where he was, and then he bolted to a stand.

"Oh, good," he said as he brushed errand strands of wool from his robe. "My clothes reverted with me. I was worried I'd be naked when I returned to being human."

"The heavens spare us from such a fate," Brittany said, and she grinned wide. "Hey, brother, how about you not do something that stupid without consulting us first?"

"I knew for a fact you'd tell me not to do it," Tommy said, and he laughed as he embraced her. When he pulled away, he clapped excitedly, but his smile did not last long. "Sorry, I know it was a risk, but I feel like I should push my knowledge of polymorphic magic if I'm to help Wren with... uh, why is everyone so glum? Did something happen while I was out?"

"Just some riots by people afraid of a siege," Jacaranda said. "They're convinced Albert won't turn himself over to Shinnoc to spare the city."

"I don't understand. Why is Shinnoc mad at Albert?"

"Shinnoc's army demanded Albert's head as payment for killing Cannac, otherwise he'll destroy all of Londheim," Brittany said. "Have you really not heard anything about this? It's all everyone can talk about."

"No, no, that's not what I meant," Tommy said. "I knew the army had arrived. I just didn't know the terms! Shinnoc has no reason to be mad at Albert, at least, not for Cannac's death. Gan killed Cannac, and he was a faery working for the Forgotten Children. As best as I can figure, they viewed Cannac as a traitor since he was working toward peace."

Devin and Brittany shared a look of shock and confusion.

"Who is Gan?" Devin asked. "And since when are the Forgotten Children responsible? Everyone knows Cannac was killed by a mob of humans who cut his head from his shoulders."

"But that was after," Tommy insisted. "An onyx faery, Gan, he was the one who killed Cannac. He flew so fast, he resembled little more than a flash of light. I guess Malik and I are the only ones that would have known what it meant. The mutilation happened after, I assure you. Cannac's death was not our fault. No human's fault anyway."

"Tommy, this is incredibly important," Devin said, and there was no hiding his frustration. "Why didn't you tell us this?"

Her brother grimaced and looked a mixture of embarrassment and helplessness.

"Why didn't I talk about one of the worst, most frightening moments of my life? I don't know, Devin, I just... I didn't think it would matter! And Tesmarie defeated Gan before she died. That meant... I thought that... I'm sorry, all right?"

Her poor brother looked ready to cry. Brittany took his wrist and pulled him close, embracing him as he sniffled and gathered himself. Devin grabbed his boots from by the fire and began strapping them on, while Jacaranda left the couch to don her coat and sword belt.

"We have to show Shinnoc the truth," Devin said. "Albert might not do the right thing, but we can. If Shinnoc knows the people of Londheim aren't responsible for his father's death, then we might prevent an attack from ever starting."

"Will it be enough?" Jacaranda asked, quietly voicing her deep fear. "The people paraded through the streets with Cannac's head on a pike. Will it matter who drew the first drop of blood?"

"I don't know," Devin said. "But we have to pray it does. It's better we try than sit here and do nothing."

"Indeed, it is," Brittany said. She withdrew from her brother. "And I'm going with all of you."

"Are you sure?" Devin asked, and she noticed, whether he even realized it or not, that he looked to Jacaranda first before asking.

"I'm still a Soulkeeper," she said. "I might not be as good as I was, but I can still swing this axe on my back. I won't stay out of something this important. What I don't understand is why they'll believe Tommy's story."

"You never met Cannac," Tommy said. "Trust me, there's no lying to a dyrandar."

Puffy popped its head up from the fireplace and waved one of its little arms as everyone prepared.

"Sure, you can come, too," Devin said, and he reached for a candle. "Let's just bring everybody, one massive party to the heart of an invading army."

The western gate had been ordered shut ever since the cloud dragon's arrival, and demanding the guards reopen it would only attract attention. Instead the group, due to having two Soulkeepers among them, was able to procure a rope ladder to drop from the wall so they might descend.

"I hope you know what you're doing," one of the soldiers said as Brittany prepared to follow Jacaranda down the ladder.

"You're not the only one," Brittany said, and she shot the soldier a wink.

The four (or five, if one counted Puffy on his candle) crossed the brief stretch of green grass before they reached the long, blackened field ruined by the black water from Viciss's mouth. Only the well-worn road west was free of the deadly grass, and the group made sure to walk single file in the wagon ruts lest they brush the grass and release a burst of its horrid dust. Brittany had not suffered from it personally, but she'd heard stories from the other Soulkeepers and held no desire to experience it firsthand.

Brittany broke the formation to slide in beside her brother as a trio of lapinkin slammed down from the sky, the butts of their spears leaving deep grooves in the earth as they slid to a halt.

"Are you nervous?" she asked him as the three lapinkin ordered them to halt.

"Terrified," he responded.

"I don't blame you. You'll be fine, though, I promise. I'm right here."

"We wish to speak with Shinnoc," Devin said from the front of their group. "It concerns his father."

This seemed enough to convince the lapinkin.

"Remove your weapons first," they said, their spears still aimed their way. "And then follow us."

They piled their swords and pistols onto the barren ground. Brittany prayed no thief came to take them as they continued. After the lapinkin side-eyed the candle Devin held, he shrugged and told Puffy to hop off. The lapinkin seemed confused by the firekin's presence, but after a quick debate, they allowed the little one to travel alongside the rest. It hopped happily along the ground, occasionally dipping off to the side to lick the black grass for a quick burst of heat and size.

Brittany did her best not to stare at the lapinkin as they traveled. She'd heard of them, of course, for Adria had done her best to keep her informed of all that had transpired while she was dead. Seeing them up close was an entirely different matter compared to hearing stories. The idea of bunny humans had put a smile on her face, but nothing about these lanky, muscular warriors made her want to smile. Their spears in particular elicited a shiver, for they were wickedly sharp and bore an additional jagged edge along the bottom to dig into the earth when they landed from the sky. She knew the furred beings could control the wind, and she wondered what it'd be like to harness such a power so she might hover hundreds of feet in the air. Exhilarating, she wagered.

Brittany's own nervousness grew as they neared the gap between the two dragons where the army had positioned their camp. The black grass had been cleared out entirely, leaving a massive expanse of barren brown earth for them to build their fires and set up their tents. All eyes were upon them as they walked to the enormous center tent. Brittany saw foxkin among their number, as well as the grasslike viridi, scattered waterkin, and even a collection of giant owls huddled around roaring bonfires. The dyrandar were by far the most intimidating. All of them were seven to eight feet tall, and that didn't count their antlers. They looked as if they were made purely of horn and muscle, and the thought of facing a single one of them in battle was chilling. Imagining the entire army attacking in unison was horrifying.

"Wait here," the leader of their escort said. "Keep silent, and stand still. Anything else will make us nervous. Humans are not above the use of assassins, so give us no reason to skewer your throats."

"We understand," Devin said.

Brittany grabbed Tommy's hand and squeezed it. Her poor brother had gone deathly pale.

It will be all right, she mouthed to him. He squeezed her hand back in response, his bulging eyes showing he did not entirely believe her.

The sun steadily approached the horizon. Brittany shifted her weight from foot to foot, well acquainted with boredom due to her profession but still not pleased with how it seemed like the dragon-sired were purposefully wasting their time. It was meant to demean them, to make them feel insignificant compared to their leaders. Brittany wanted to grab one of their lapinkin guards by the ears and shout into it about how important their matters were, but doing so would only get her stabbed by their spears.

The flap to the tent opened, and a dyrandar woman stepped out. She wore a lovely red robe tied with a flower-covered sash. Lavender ribbons hung by the dozens from her antlers.

"Our King is ready to meet you," she said. "Since you are human, consider this a courtesy. Do not lie. Do not bluster. Speak truthfully, and we will treat you with respect. Attempt to deceive or belittle, and your safety cannot be guaranteed."

Tommy looked ready to faint, but Devin meanwhile cracked a grin like he was used to such death threats.

"We wouldn't think of it," he said.

On the outside, the tent appeared fifteen feet in diameter, perhaps twenty at the most. The moment she passed through the tent flap, Brittany felt her stomach heave and her mind momentarily spin. The interior was at least five times that somehow. There were wood-carved tables and chairs positioned about two separate stone-ringed campfires, each with their own smoke holes in the fabric above them. Dozens of dragon-sired lingered about, their quiet conversations halting when they noticed the humans' entrance. Green rugs formed little pathways between the tables, all of which led to a raised dais somehow built of three slabs of stone that had to weigh tons and require wagons to move about. Upon that dais, sitting in a chair that looked like a warped tree, awaited Shinnoc, the Dyrandar King.

Brittany had never met Shinnoc's father, but if they had shared a resemblance, then Cannac must have been one imposing monstrosity. Shinnoc, despite currently sitting, was still taller than anyone present. His antlers grew several feet above his head, and they grew wide to either side before curling inward so that the sharpened points directly faced one another. Bones wrapped in leather were tied as decorations to the points, and they rattled as he stood. His dark brown robe was loosely tied at his waist, exposing his thick neck and broad, oak-colored chest. The dyrandar looked like he could rip trees up from the ground with his bare hands. His arms bulged with muscle. His neck was thicker than Brittany's waist.

"Greetings, diplomats of Londheim," Shinnoc said. His voice was surprisingly gentle, given his size. "I am Shinnoc, and I welcome you, and promise you greater courtesy than what was given to my father during his visit to your people."

"And I am Soulkeeper Devin Eveson," Devin said after a quick glance about to ensure he would be the only one speaking. "Though I must confess we are not diplomats of Londheim, at least not in any official capacity."

Shinnoc's round eyes narrowed.

"Then why have you come, Soulkeeper Devin?"

"It concerns the death of your father, Cannac, and the blame you have cast upon us. It isn't true, and we bring proof of the real culprit."

Shinnoc rose from his chair, and Brittany felt a quiver in her abdomen. It wasn't just that the dyrandar was nearly nine feet tall. There was a presence to him, a strength that effortlessly flowed through his every movement. The other dragon-sired fell silent, and a few reached for their weapons.

"I will listen with open heart and mind," Shinnoc said slowly. "But if you come with lies on your tongues, you will not leave my camp alive."

She hadn't thought Tommy could get any paler, but he turned white as freshly fallen snow. Brittany grabbed her little brother's hand and pulled him close.

"You'll do fine," she whispered. "I'm here. Devin's here. We're all here with you, so stand tall, Tomas."

Devin glanced to the group, and when Tommy nodded his head in the affirmative, he stepped aside. Tommy shuffled to the front, his head craned upward so he might meet Shinnoc's gaze.

"I knew your father for only a short time while he stayed with me and my friend," Tommy said, stammering out the first few words. "And I'd give anything to have spent longer. He was a kind dyrandar. Kind, and wise, and just…magical. Before I say anything, I want to say I am sorry for your loss. The entire Cradle suffers from his passing."

Reading expressions on a deer's face was not exactly something Brittany considered herself skilled in, but by the way the giant tilted his head, it seemed he was intrigued by Tommy's heartfelt proclamation.

"My dreams cannot reach the heights of the reality he forged," Shinnoc said. "Speak, young one. I am listening."

Tommy coughed and wiped sweat off his neck.

"I was there when Cannac was killed. I saw it all. No human hands did it, Shinnoc, I swear it. Your father was murdered by an onyx faery named Gan, who I presume was following orders of an avenria known as Logarius. Logarius, he, he's—"

"The leader of the Forgotten Children," Shinnoc interrupted. "I know of him. You make bold claims…"

"Tomas Moore," Tommy quickly answered. "And I know what I speak. I also know that if you possess powers similar to your father's, you need not question whether I lie or speak honorably.

You can witness it for yourself. Isn't that true?" Another swipe across his forehead with his hand. "That is true, right?"

Shinnoc descended the three steps of his dais. It seemed the ground shook with his hoof beats.

"It is true," he said. "Will you open your mind to me?"

Tommy stood to his full height, and Brittany felt immense pride in her little brother.

"I will," he said.

The dyrandar closed the space between them. The ground lifted beneath Tommy's feet, the dirt rising as if it were a wave in the ocean. Tommy struggled to keep his balance before catching himself, and then he quickly straightened as if nothing were amiss. Shinnoc lowered his head and closed his eyes. His antlers passed to either side of Tommy's head, placing him directly in the center of their curved formation. A hum grew in the dyrandar's throat. It rolled across all present like the deep bells of a watch tower.

"Think of the moment, little human," Shinnoc said. At least, it seemed like he said it, but the deep hum never paused, and the dyrandar never opened his mouth. "Let me witness the end to my father's time on this land."

A rainbow of colors swam across the antlers. Little rays of light crisscrossed from opposite sides, building a wondrous spiderweb, the center of which was Tommy's frightened, shaking head.

"I'll... I'll try," he said softly, and closed his eyes. The colors grew. The hum deepened. Brittany felt the hairs on her arms stick up, felt a strange, phantom touch of fingers across her scalp. Distant noises reached her ears, like the roar of a faraway crowd. It grew louder, closer, and then she cried out as the rainbow of light leapt in all directions like uncoiled snakes to strike at the foreheads of those present.

The distant roar became all too near. Men and women surrounded them on all sides, held at bay by a thin line of frightened soldiers. They were angry and shouting, but their words were a meaningless blob of sound. Malik was beside her. A dyrandar stood with her, commanding the crowd. Cannac, she knew somehow, and a similar array of lights built within his antlers. She saw through her brother's eyes. She lived through her brother's memories.

"We are one upon the Cradle," Cannac said. "So live as one. Share your emotions as one. This contention must end peaceably, for the only other fate is war."

The crowd quieted. Brittany could not quite sense how or why, but she knew something magical transpired. She felt a bewildering mixture of emotions overcome her, beginning as rage and ending with calm, quiet understanding. A deep sense of love for the noble Dyrandar King filled her chest, and she almost started to cry. Those in the crowd dropped their weapons. They let go of their hatred.

And then a blur of darkness whisked across Cannac's throat, echoed by a deep blue streak she somehow knew was a moonlight blade. Cannac stood still for a moment, quiet and confused. Blood seeped from his throat. His throat, which had been cut open from ear to ear by the near-imperceptible passage of an onyx faery moving at speeds only they and their time-manipulating race could achieve.

"No!" Tommy screamed, and Brittany screamed along with him. "No, no, no no no no!"

The memory broke. The colors retreated. Still Brittany screamed.

"No, no, no!"

It took a minute for her to fully return to the present and her own body. Tears flowed down her face, and at some point she'd fallen to her knees. She stood, keenly aware that all present had shed similar tears. Only Shinnoc remained stone-faced. He lowered Tommy back to the ground, then gently put his hands atop the smaller man's shoulders. His hands dwarfed her little brother, and made him seem like but a child.

"Your love was true, and your heart kind," he said. "I am sorry you suffered so from Logarius's great betrayal."

No, he wasn't stone-faced, Brittany realized. He was overwhelmed with such rage, he struggled to maintain stillness. His voice could not hide it. It quivered and broke with nearly every syllable as he lifted his hands and tilted his face to the heavens. The enormous tent collapsed about them, reality breaking with it so that the tables vanished and all present stood cramped together in a much smaller gathering.

"Humans and dragon-sired of Londheim, hear me!" Shinnoc cried to the suddenly exposed stars. His every word rolled across the horizon, magnified a hundredfold and then beyond despite seeming but a deep chant to Brittany's ears. She knew without a doubt every single being alive inside Londheim would hear the furious words of the Dyrandar King. "I have seen the truth of my father's murder. It was no human who cut his throat. It was no human who ended his life. The Forgotten Children bear this responsibility, and it is they who must suffer the consequences."

Brittany didn't understand just what Shinnoc meant, but Devin did, and he cried out despite the reverent awe that kept all others silent.

"No, don't do this!" Devin screamed. Shinnoc paid him no attention.

"Belvua is no longer under my protection. Consider the dragon-sired who reside within exiled. Do with them as you wish."

The spell ended and, with it, the reverence. Tommy staggered, still trying to collect himself from the memory. Brittany pulled him into her arms and held him as he sobbed.

"What's going on?" she asked as Devin and Jacaranda looked about in panicked confusion.

"Belvua," Devin said. "The riots. It's all been building, but Shinnoc was the only thing holding it back." He spun to face the dyrandar. "And you just gave them a death sentence."

"The Forgotten Children spilled blood to take Belvua as their own," Shinnoc said. "And they slew my father to ensure peace would be settled on their terms. Let them have their war, only I will not wage it for them."

"Thousands will die!" Devin screamed. "This isn't what your father would have wanted!"

"And I am not my father," Shinnoc said. He gestured to the city. "I promised to render the city of Cannac's murderers to ashes. It seems Londheim did not deserve my rage, but Belvua instead. So let their deception be repaid in blood, and let it be done with my words alone. If humanity is what I believe them to be . . . I have already fulfilled my vow."

CHAPTER 22

The hive-trees surrounding Belvua burned, the line between human and dragon-sired marked for miles by a raging fire.

"So how bad is it?" Evelyn asked as she joined the guards stationed at the barricaded western entrance to Belvua. She made sure to keep her head covered with her hood to hide her identity. Other races found avenria difficult to distinguish between one another, which worked in her favor. If they knew her true identity, and how she had fought against their own kind at the Cathedral of the Sacred Mother, then the foxkin leader might not have answered the question.

"I don't know, avenria," the foxkin said. She clicked her teeth together nervously. "We took this district with our own claws and steel. Does Shinnoc's condemnation truly matter?"

Evelyn patted the hilts of Whisper-Song buckled to her hips.

"I suppose we shall soon find out," she said. "Keep faith. A few angry humans are nothing to our kind."

"This is so far from a few."

The noise certainly implied so, but Evelyn refused to believe things could be so dire. The humans had largely left the conquered Low Dock district alone since their failed attempt to retake it. Another attempt, even if successful, would invite hundreds of deaths. Yet it seemed such risks meant nothing to the gathering crowd beyond the piled-up desks, chairs, and furniture blocking off the district entrance. The sheer light of their torches, numbering already in the hundreds, continued to grow like a citywide beacon. The angry chorus of their shouted conversations rambled unceasingly.

Evelyn dashed to the wall and used her sharp claws to vault herself to the top. She settled into a crouch and overlooked the long road leading to the blocked entrance. Whatever hope she'd held died instantly. This wasn't a singular group. The line of torches flowing their direction spread for over a mile. It was as if a call had gone out to the city, and the city had answered. Thousands of men and women armed with knives, clubs, swords, and torches came Belvua's way. All the dragon-sired had to hold them off were a mere fifty warriors and a haphazard barricade. Foxkin and lapinkin could cleave through humans by the dozens, but the disparity between their numbers was obscene.

Evelyn spread her wings and leapt back down. The foxkin leader crossed her arms and nodded toward the barricade.

"Is it as bad as it seems?" she asked.

"Worse."

The screech of an owl turned their attention skyward. The majestic bird dove with such speed and urgency, Evelyn momentarily feared he'd come to attack. At the last moment he flared his wings and curled upward for a landing. His white-and-brown feathers rustled, and his yellow eyes pulsed wide with fear.

"The skies show no hope," the owl said. "The entire city moves against you. You must flee, all of you, before it is too late!"

A communal roar turned their attention west. Torches soared across the barricade. Wood rattled and broke as those on the other side hacked at it with axes and pulled loose pieces with a thousand hands.

"What do we do?" the foxkin leader asked. There was no hiding the fear in her voice. In answer, Evelyn removed her hood and flared her wings wide. Soft gasps spread through the crowd as they realized her identity.

"I am no member of your Forgotten Children, nor am I your leader," Evelyn said. "But if I were, I would order you to run."

The barricade shook as if enduring an earthquake, then broke completely. A flood of humanity poured through like waters surging through a collapsed dam. They were pure mass without face or identity, mere carriers of torches and clubs seeking destruction. She saw no soldiers or guards among them. This wasn't an attack. This wasn't an ordered assault like the previous attempts to retake Belvua. It was something more primal, and far more terrifying.

"Run!" she screamed at the Forgotten Children. "Run, damn you all, run!"

The screech of the owl marked the end of the paralyzing fear that had overcome the lot. Foxkin dashed every which way. Three of the lapinkin stood side by side, and they raised their hands and summoned wind with the gifts granted to them by their maker. It blasted against the front line of humans, smashing them with the force of a stone wall. It didn't matter. The humans behind them pushed onward, and themselves were pushed by the next in line. Those leading the way were mutilated by the wind, and when they stumbled, they were crushed underfoot by the tide of humans, but the rest did not stop. They did not slow. The killings only furthered their rage.

"Flee!" the owl screeched as he soared across the skies. "Flee one, flee all!"

Two of the lapinkin leapt heavenward before the human mob reached them, but a third halted his gusts of wind a half-second too late. Hands latched on to his ankles when he jumped, and even with the aid of the wind, he could not clear their reach. Evelyn did not stay to see what they did to him, but she heard his screams. They mercifully did not last long.

Evelyn sprinted down the street, panic ablaze in her veins.

Logarius was still chained to his bed, helpless to the coming tide of hate. She shifted her sprint, all the while screaming at any Forgotten Children she encountered to flee east. The only hope for escape was to cross the waters of the Septen River. With the enraged humans at her heels, she had no time to explain this, no time to form a plan, but there wasn't much need. The mob had begun setting fire to every single building they passed. The night sky lit yellow, the stars hidden behind a sheer wall of rising smoke.

"Avenria!" she heard someone shout, and she reluctantly slowed. Forces had gathered around a bend, a collection of foxkin, lapinkin, waterkin, and avenria. They had their weapons drawn and magic at ready. For a brief moment she debated ignoring them, but she would not turn her back to so many dragon-sired simply for the sake of her troublesome son. Evelyn skidded to a halt and then dashed their way.

"There's no stopping it," she said as she gasped for breath. Dragons help her, this old body of hers was not meant to handle a night like this. "We need to run."

"This is our home," an older avenria named Kolash said. She'd met him a few times during her southern campaigns. Proud and stubborn, Kolash was the absolute worst person to take charge in such a hopeless situation, so of course he was the one helming the defense.

"Not any longer," Evelyn said. "If you stay here, it's your grave."

"Then let them bury us with their dead," said a grizzled black-furred lapinkin beside him. "We killed to take these streets, and we'll kill to defend them."

The lapinkin was using bravado to counter his fear. Evelyn wanted to scream that the conquering of Belvua had always been a broken dream relying on luck and subterfuge. They'd evacuated people while disguised as human soldiers. They'd ambushed a well-trained but still small collection of human forces sent to retake the district, with the advantage of favorable terrain as well as foxkin infiltrating their numbers. Drunk on victory, they'd assaulted the Cathedral of the Sacred Mother, and they'd paid dearly for it. Their numbers were few, their defenses now spread thin across the entire district. They could kill hundreds, perhaps thousands, of humans, and it would make not a dent in the overwhelming tide that approached.

"Don't you get it?" she shouted at them. "The entire damn city is terrified, but now they have a chance to strike back. Not at the army outside, but here, right here. You can't slaughter an entire city. You can't even hold this one single street. Don't do this. Don't commit suicide."

Of the hundred or so there, only a handful were willing to look her in the eye. Kolash was one of them.

"Death in battle is not suicide," he said. He put a hand on her shoulder. "You of all people should know that, Evelyn. We're tired of running. If it must come to pass, then let this be our end."

She clicked her beak together, then glanced over her shoulder. The light of raised torches turned the corner.

"Damn it," Evelyn shouted, ripping Whisper and Song from her belt and jamming their handles together. They merged, sealed, and extended. She twirled the dual-sided sickle as blue flame gifted by firekin shimmered across its sharpened edges. She braced her legs, took in a breath, and waited until she could see the fearful rage in the humans' eyes and smell the blood and sweat upon their clothes.

"Damn it all to the void!"

Kolash cried out, and the lapinkin gusted the charging mob with gale-force winds. It wasn't enough to topple them, only momentarily slow them down, but Evelyn would not waste such a gift. She dashed into the humans, her wings spread wide and ethereal. She made herself appear large and frightening, a pure monster of death. There would be no blocking and parrying, no dance like when she fought with her son. These foes relied solely on overwhelming numbers, which meant cutting down those numbers as quickly as possible.

Whisper-Song whirled in her grasp. Her legs twirled. Her body spun. The burning edges of her sickles ripped through flesh without pause. She was a reaper, and their limbs the wheat. Higher, faster, she carved through their numbers. The tiniest gap became her new destination, lest she be overwhelmed. Whisper cleaved off a man's head, then she cut a woman's leg at the knee with Song, spun a full circle to rip gashes into three men who suddenly surrounded her, and then ripped Whisper-Song apart to individually wield the sickles. She blocked a swing with a torch, kicked the woman who wielded it, and then reversed direction so her path took her back toward the defending Forgotten Children. This was no dance, but she was still a dancer, her feet barely touching the stone as she leapt and turned, the heat of her sickles and the sharpness of the blades cutting flesh and severing bone with such perfection, the weapons never slowed.

Evelyn emerged from the crowd bathed in the blood of humans. In mere seconds, she'd killed dozens.

It still didn't matter.

"Hold fast!" Kolash screamed, his voice barely perceptible above the din. The mob smashed into their ranks. The foxkin stabbed and cut with expertise, but they were smaller than the humans, weaker, and had to retreat with every move they made. The waterkin swirled into one another, growing in size until they were a tremendous golem thrice the height of a human. It waded into the crowd, sometimes swinging a single, clobbering fist, other times splitting into four arms to beat and smash its foes to pulp. The humans batted their torches at it, trying and failing to do anything more than sizzle a bit of steam into the air before being crushed. The lapinkin eagerly supported the golem with their long, jagged spears. Gusts of wind strengthened their every leap and thrust, and they used the long reach of their spears to avoid being overwhelmed.

Evelyn dared hope the waterkin might be the key to an impossible victory. If the humans couldn't destroy its form, merely inconvenience it with their torches at best, then perhaps they might win through sheer attrition. The rest of the Forgotten Children rallied around the golem, letting it be the linchpin to their defense. Lapinkin consistently took to the air, flipped their spears, and dove amid the ranks of the attackers, skewering several at once before leaping away. The few avenria there used their superior skill to cut down any rioters who tried to bypass the golem for easier prey. Evelyn joined them, her focus on preventing the golem from ever being completely surrounded. The battle raged, minutes passing, but it seemed they had finally formed a defense that could not be broken by sheer numbers.

The humans seemed to understand this, as well. After another minute they retreated, leaving a veritable wall of dead in their wake. Evelyn gladly accepted the reprieve as a chance to regain her breath. Her limbs ached, and her lungs burned. Bruises from dozens of hits, most of which she didn't even notice at the time while cutting through the human ranks, pulsed with pain across her entire body.

Cheerful shouts broke through the frightened murmurs of the crowd. The men and women parted to grant their newly arrived saviors a path. Whisper and Song twirled in Evelyn's fingertips, and she clucked a soft laugh at the sight of three Soulkeepers approaching with swords drawn and guns at ready.

"Haven't thought this through, have you?" Evelyn mocked them as they raised their pistols, not at the soft bodies of the avenria, foxkin, or lapinkin, but instead the waterkin golem. "What good will lead shot do to—"

The Soulkeepers fired in unison. It was not lead in those chambers, but spellstones. Faint blue orbs crossed the distance, two hitting directly within the golem's chest, a third at its feet. Ice exploded in all directions. Two nearby foxkin screamed as shards tore through their faces and chests, and an avenria standing beside the golem broke in half as the ice sealed across his legs and waist. The golem suffered far worse. It let out a strange, guttural groan as thick sheets sealed across its form, jagged shards spreading and growing from the center of its being. One arm froze completely, and it broke from the body with a smash. Little rivulets flowed from the larger body, waterkin attempted to separate from the main, but they were sluggish and dazed with bits of frost clinging to their forms.

Burning an enormous, angry golem was one thing, but a shattered, dazed mess was another. The mob surged forward with renewed numbers, and they let their torches lead the way. Evelyn dashed toward Kolash, and she screamed at him to give the order to retreat. He refused. Sword in hand, he dashed straight into the mob overwhelming the injured waterkin.

The roar of flamestones marked the sudden end to Kolash's valiant defense. There was no need for spellstones, not for him. The Soulkeepers shot him dead, and they reloaded their pistols as more rioters swarmed forth, batting aside foxkin blades and grabbing on to lapinkin spears. Hundreds of humans lay dead all about them, but it didn't matter. None of it mattered. The sight of the frenzy chilled Evelyn to her core, and it pulled her back hundreds of years to her long wars against humanity. The dragon-sired had never been able to fight and die with such recklessness. Humanity, with souls that lasted for eternities, were paradoxically all too eager to end their short, meager lives that filled the memories of those eternal souls.

Evelyn vaulted to the rooftops and fled. Lead shot pinged off the shingles at her feet, several shots within inches of taking her life. She dashed rooftop to rooftop, her black wings billowing to add distance to her jumps. She ran until the docks were in sight, but there was no relief for her there.

A second tidal wave of humanity had broken through the

northern entrance of Belvua, a squad of Soulkeepers at their helm. They swept alongside the river, blocking off any access. The dragon-sired were being herded like rats off a burning ship, with the northern and western exits blocked and now the river being steadily cordoned off. They were being shoved south to the wall, to be trapped. To be murdered.

The scope of it all smothered her like a thorned blanket. There was so little she could do, that anyone could do, against such an overwhelming force. The hive-trees that formed the outer perimeter were all aflame, each and every one, and they formed a nightmarish backdrop to the skyline. Based on the location of the fires, her son was safe, but not for long. Evelyn dashed across the rooftops, avoiding the occasional squad of humans run amok. Only once did someone with a pistol fire at her, but she didn't believe them to be a Soulkeeper given how terrible their aim proved to be. She ran until the dark spire that was her home was in sight and then leapt at the side wall, her wings curling before her so she might pass straight through the stone. She emerged into her son's room, which was filling with smoke from fires a mere block over.

The bed was empty. Her son was gone.

"Did you not trust me to return?" she asked aloud as her hand settled upon vacant sheets. "Or have you no choice but to partake in this violence?"

She crossed her wings and exited her home. There would be no more fighting, not for her. Without her son, Belvua meant nothing. *Let the humans have it*, she thought wearily, her convictions broken by a hundred similar battles throughout her lifetime. *Let the whole city burn. I have nothing left to give.*

CHAPTER 23

By the time Devin and his friends arrived, the hive-trees surrounding Belvua were already aflame like a fiery wall. It sealed the victims of Belvua in with towering branches awash with fire, the air deafened by the buzzing deaths of their leaves. Devin had once watched the leaves light up the sky with wondrous colors on a cold morning, but now they zipped about in frantic panic as their host bodies crackled and burned.

"I fear we're too late to accomplish anything useful," Brittany said, her mood glum.

"We must still help where we can," Devin said as they rushed the entrance to the district. "We caused this, so we'll help fix it."

"Fix it?" Brittany shook her head. "Look around, Devin. It's a wasteland."

While the hive-trees bordering the district had been easy prey for the rioters, the inside of Belvua fared no better. Smoke billowed from scattered fires, and screams of pain and fear were the midnight chorus sung to the hidden stars. Though the street was mostly vacant at the entrance, a familiar face waited there, and his grim expression softened considerably seeing their approach.

"Thank the heavens," Malik said, and he buried Tomas in a hug. "I feared you were already within."

"We will be soon enough," Devin said, and he gestured for

them to keep moving. "What's happening inside? Why are there no soldiers trying to stop this?"

"Because Londheim's soldiers are likely in there helping," Malik said. "As for what's happening, I believe it is painfully obvious."

"I was hoping for more information than that," Devin said as they passed through the archway into Belvua. Setting foot within felt like entering a new world, one bathed in red light and drowning in ash.

"I'll scout," Jacaranda said. She easily vaulted to the rooftop of a strange, obsidian-colored home with seven twisting doors at weird heights. She gazed north to south, pausing a moment to consider, and then dropped back down.

"Most fires are in the northern section," she said.

"That's where the other district entrance is," Devin said. "What about the docks?"

"Fires there, too."

If the mob was crashing in from the northern and western entrances, and already they'd burned the docks along the eastern edge, then only one direction remained.

"The survivors will be pushed to the southern wall," he said. "Follow me."

They took the southernmost street, and though it was mostly empty, the signs of damage were catastrophic. If it was glass, the mob had broken it. If it was a door, they'd smashed it in. Most of all, if it could burn, they'd set it aflame with their torches. It wouldn't be long until the entire district was a singular sprawling inferno, yet the people cared not. The single-mindedness of it terrified Devin to no end.

The few groups they encountered were wide-eyed teens, their faces marked with soot and illuminated by half-flaming torches.

"Out!" Devin screamed at them. "Leave, damn you!"

Any other time they might have scoffed or mocked his authority, but not tonight. Their eyes were wide, their pupils enormous despite the nearby fires. Shocked by the violence, Devin presumed. They'd come with the crowd, moved like water within a river, refusing to accept the inevitable violence at its end. Now they saw it, the blood, the flame, the bodies lying curled and twisted in windowsills and beaten in the ditches. They saw, and they wished for any reason to escape it.

The stunned, not-quite-there expressions were on nearly all faces they encountered as they pushed into Belvua. The group ordered their exit, but the deeper they went, the more insistent the rioters. Worse was when they turned a corner to find nearly a hundred gathered with weapons raised and fire at ready.

"Is this road needed to exit Belvua?" Tommy asked. Devin did his best to visualize the main roads of the district from his visits to Adria at her church when the place was still called Low Dock.

"I don't think so?"

"Good enough for me."

Tommy's spell sent ice flowing from his hands to form a solid wall from side to side, isolating them from the rest of the crowd.

"A good start," Devin muttered, though he wondered how the ice would fare against the steadily growing fires. "Keep going."

They pushed onward, so late into the madness that most of the crowds had scattered into more isolated groups. Devin and Brittany used their authority as Soulkeepers as best they could, shouting orders that the blood-drunk civilians still tended to obey out of fear of authority. Those that refused met swords, axes, and a pistol, all of which were more than enough to force them to back down.

"Get out," Devin shouted to any who would listen. "Get out now, before the fires take you!"

They scattered farther apart, the smoke thickening so much, it was easy to become disorientated. A scream guided Devin to one side of the road, and he squinted in the uneven light. Sometimes the surroundings were bright yellow and red from the flames;

other times it was horridly dark as patches of smoke wrapped around Devin's body like a funeral shroud.

If only there had been smoke thick enough to blot out the sight in that dead-end alley. Four men formed a wall of hate blocking in two crying foxkin children, their long sleeves and tight trousers like those of the dockworkers farther to the north.

"You know how they used to kill foxes in South Orismund?" the biggest of the four laughed. He patted the long, bloodstained piece of wood in his meaty palm. "Fucking clubs to the head."

"Yeah, while on horseback," said another with him. "We ain't got no horses for that."

"Got a dog? We can improvise."

Devin lifted his sword. If the trapped foxkin had been human, he'd have guessed them to be ten years old at most.

The red-furred body lying at the feet of the men was younger, maybe six.

"Horses," Devin said, startling them. The first to turn around received the tip of his sword straight through the throat and out his neck. Devin pivoted, ripped the blade out the side and into the face of the second. The sharp edge broke teeth and sliced cheeks on the way to the spine. The big man swung his club. Devin shifted again, his sword rotating downward so that the bulk of the blow was absorbed by the upper half of his sword.

"Horses."

He head-butted the big man, closed the distance so his elbow could follow up with a hit to the nose, and then separated. Dazed and bloodied, the man offered a pathetic block with his club that Devin easily avoided. His cut opened the man at the belly. His death scream echoed in the alley.

"Goddess-damned horses."

Did the last man fight back? Did he protest? Devin didn't know. He didn't see a man anymore. He saw a monster far more terrifying than anything he'd encountered while fleeing the black water back at Durham. As with all monsters, he slew it. Let it bleed. Let it die.

"Devin Eveson?" asked a stunned voice at the alley entrance. "What madness has taken you?"

The two foxkin children were crying, little yelps that broke Devin's heart. He put them out of mind and turned. A Soulkeeper stood at the entrance, his sword drawn and his pistol raised. Devin had seen him several times about the city since returning to Londheim. A cool bastard named Moore. His long hair was tied in a ponytail, his face half hidden beneath a foppish tricorn hat decorated with unusually long feathers. Owl feathers, Devin realized.

"No madness," Devin said. He lifted his sword and eyed the pistol. "I pray you're not threatening me with an unloaded weapon."

"I assure you, it's loaded," Moore said. His lips curled into a sneer. "And I pray you're not murdering humans to defend these monsters."

"Monsters?" Devin asked. "I only slay monsters. Didn't you know that?"

The two foxkin suddenly dashed for the exit, clearly hoping amid their panic that the two Soulkeepers were distracted. Devin let them pass, and he stared Moore straight in the eye, challenging him. Daring him.

Moore slashed at the second foxkin child, and in that brief moment when his eyes turned, Devin lunged. The pistol shot wide. The same could not be said for his sword. The steel buried into flesh, so deep the hilt pressed against Moore's thick brown coat. The other man gasped, blood drawing into torn lungs. Devin dropped him beside the body of the first foxkin, who'd been cleaved from neck to shoulder and convulsed in agony. A single, pitying strike took out both their throats, ending their mutual suffering.

The lone surviving foxkin child alternated stares at Devin, and then the corpse, with his three tearful eyes. Devin saw hurt in them, deep hurt mixed with confusion and rage.

"Run," he said. "You can't stay to cry. You have to run."

One last glare. One last unspoken promise of vengeance in a future life, when the foxkin was grown and able to wield weapons like those of the Soulkeepers. Devin wished to tell the child he was sorry, that not all humans were like this. They were ashen words, and they died unspoken on his tongue.

Devin emerged from the alley, the foxkin child having long run ahead of him.

"Hey, are you all right?" Jacaranda asked. Blood stained large portions of her coat, and even lined the rim of her wide-brimmed hat.

"Yeah," he lied. "You?"

"Eventually."

Together they passed a trio of human corpses lying in the middle of the street. Devin didn't need to ask why Jacaranda had assaulted them. A foxkin woman, most likely the mother of the three in the alley, lay cold and still amid the bodies.

"The wall is near," he said, as if he could end the night by sheer force of will. "We're almost done."

Though some of the dragon-sired creatures could vault over the wall, that wasn't true for several of the races, nor of the injured that remained with them. Foxkin were the most numerous among them, but there were also creatures made of grass, several elderly lapinkin, even some panicked waterkin that were trying in vain to keep back the encroaching flames.

And mere hundreds of feet away was the front line of the looters and rioters, come seeking blood.

"I got it, I got it, I swear!" Tommy shouted as he pushed Devin aside. He jammed his wrists together and cupped his fingers into a dome. Words of magic shrieked off his lips as the furious mob approached.

"Aethos creare, Aethos creare, Aethos creare . . ."

The magic built, and built, a shimmering flame that swirled like a miniature sun between his palms. Devin glanced over his shoulder, timing the distance. Not long, mere moments left. Whatever spell his brother-in-law planned, it better be good.

Tomas's words reached a fevered pitch. He thrust his hands toward the wall and finished his spell.

"Parvos fulgur!"

For all his time and effort, it was strangely anticlimactic at first to see a tiny red marble of light shoot from his grasp. It crossed the space between them and a bare stretch of wall in the blink of an eye, and then whatever disappointment Devin felt vanished in an explosion of stone and mortar. The district's outer wall collapsed in a roaring, belching mess of dust and noise. Devin had but a half-second to realize some of that debris was coming their direction and dove. His arms wrapped around Tomas, and together they rolled along the ground.

Chunks of the wall fell like murderous rain. Some cracked upon landing; others smashed grooves into Belvua's well-worn street. The oncoming mob pulled back at the chaos, and that turned into a full-blown retreat as the debris choking the air billowed in their direction. Devin came up from his roll, and he dared sigh with relief that none of the enormous stones had crushed the two like rotten fruit.

"I...I think I broke something," Tommy said, and he lifted his left arm. Blood drenched his entire side. A long gash cut from his wrist to his elbow, capped at one end by the decidedly wrong direction of ring and pinkie fingers.

"You're fine," Devin said, even as his heart quickened and he frantically hacked a long strip of cloth from Tommy's robe to use as a bandage. "Just a few strips of this and you'll be good as new."

"You...you're a liar," his brother-in-law said, and then he let out a long, low moan. The pain was only just now starting to hit him, and it would rapidly worsen as his excitement from battle wore off. Devin looped and tied the bandages, then gently lifted Tommy to his feet.

"I'll get him safely out of here," Malik said as slid an arm underneath Tommy's shoulder to support his weight. "Meet us at our tower should you survive."

"Thanks," Devin said, unable to decide how much, if any, of Malik's statement was sarcasm. He holstered his pistol and looked to the others. Brittany and Jacaranda were caked with dirt and blood. The light of a dozen fires danced in their eyes, and he wondered how much of tonight would scar them forever.

"What now?" Jacaranda asked.

The last of the dragon-sired poured through the hole in the wall, and to the relative safety of the field beyond. He noted they did not curl west, toward Shinnoc's army, but instead sprinted southward, following the river.

"We let no one give chase," Devin said.

"The three of us against a mob?" Brittany asked. "Four," she corrected, when Puffy hopped up and down before her.

"We only need a moment," Devin said as he loaded a blue spellstone into his pistol. "And I know how to give it."

He waited until the last of the dragon-sired were safely beyond the wall and then aimed with his pistol. A glowing blue orb, remarkably similar to the orb Tommy had just released, flew from his pistol upon pulling the trigger. The orb struck the boulder in the center of the rubble and detonated. Jagged shards of ice spread in all directions, not stopping until they hit the intact side of the remaining wall.

"There," he said, as if he'd actually done anything other than shoot his pistol. "That'll do."

With no victims left to exact their vengeance upon, the people turned to the dragon-sired buildings, with their weird architecture and distinctly inhuman design, and did as humanity often did when confronted with the unique and the strange: They destroyed it. Fires burned across all of Belvua, the pace of their spread rapidly increasing compared to the start of the massacre. Not a blip of the sky was visible beneath the waves of smoke that billowed heavenward.

"No bucket crew will fix this," Jacaranda said darkly.

"This inferno will spread beyond Belvua," Brittany said. "Perhaps it is for the best that it take all of Londheim with it."

Devin wasn't willing to abandon hope just yet. Bucket crews and well water might not stop the blaze, but what about a creature made of living flame?

"Can you put the fires out?" he asked Puffy. The firekin tilted its head to one side. Its foot elongated so it might draw a message on the ground as if the foot were a pen and flame its ink.

YESBUTDANGRUS.

Could fire be dangerous to a firekin? It didn't make sense to Devin, but he was hardly an expert on their physiology. He knelt before the creature and dipped his head in respect.

"I won't ask you to risk your life," he said. "It's likely too late as it is. Do as you wish, little one. I will not blame you for your choice."

Those beady eyes glanced about at the raging infernos on either side of the street. It stood up straighter, its tiny shoulders pulling back.

ICANDOIT.

Puffy sprinted to the nearest fire and dove right into its heart. Devin stood, and he leaned his weight against Jacaranda as she slid to his side.

"Half the district's aflame," she said. "Can Puffy really stop it?"

"We're about to find out."

A shudder ran through the existing flame, as if a heavy wind had blown along its core. At first it seemed nothing happened, but then the light dimmed. The fire coating the blackened building shriveled inward like a receding tide. Its roar abated. Its heat faded. In mere seconds the entire blaze had ceased, and then from the building's wreckage Puffy re-emerged. The little one had doubled in size, its color brightening from a somber red to a much more vibrant yellow.

"Lead on," Devin cheered the firekin. "We'll follow."

It dove into the next house, and the next. With each one the process quickened, the firekin's authority over the blaze growing. With each one, the firekin's body grew. Soon its head towered over the collapsing rooftops, and its arms and legs elongated with unnerving length. Within minutes the entire block was extinguished, and with the heavy smoke blotting out the stars, it was Puffy's light that gave them sight, and what a sight it was. The firekin started extinguishing multiple buildings simultaneously with its outstretched hands. Torrents of flame would billow up from the homes like upside-down tornadoes, funneling directly into the firekin's body as it rumbled down the street, leaving enormous circular grooves of flame as its footprints.

By the next street, Puffy was as large as the homes it saved. By the next, it was twice their height, and visible from all corners of Belvua.

"I'd have never guessed it wielded such power," Brittany said as the trio followed in the firekin's wake. Neither dragon-sired nor rioters dared approach the creature. It was a walking sun. It was an emblazoned god.

"Not to this extent," Devin said, thinking of when Puffy had saved his life multiple times as he fled the black water's wrath. "But can it take on too much?"

Another street. Another collection of homes ripped of their fire and left a smoldering ruin. They had to sprint to follow, for not only had Puffy's strides grown dozens of feet in length, but it was absorbing fires from nearly a dozen buildings at a time. Fire and heat flowed into it, growing it, feeding it. The ground rumbled with its every step. Now ten times the height of a human. Now twenty. Even the dragons beyond the walls might think twice before challenging such a creature.

"Puffy?" Devin whispered as the firekin suddenly halted. It grew an additional pair of arms, so that all four could reach in a different cardinal direction. "Puffy, no, stop, it's too much. It's too much!"

It no longer needed to travel, so great was its reach. Fire soared through the air in hundreds of streams, collecting together like tributaries merging into rivers. The firekin was the grand ocean all inevitably flowed to at their end. Its beady little eyes had become tremendous obsidian boulders. Its light was blinding. The warmth of its body was an inferno painful to approach. Jacaranda and Brittany fell back, but Devin pressed onward with his coat held up as a meager defense against the blistering heat.

The last bit of flame melded into a being simmering with power, and with it, Puffy reared back its head and opened its mouth. Devin had never heard the creature speak. He had no idea it could even utter a sound. From its opened mouth came a roar composed of a hundred bonfires crackling. It was a roar of consumption, of destruction, and it shook the ground with its depth. Devin's eyes widened as Puffy raised two arms heavenward. The ends hardened into clenched fists.

"Oh, fuck me sideways," Devin muttered and then turned to run. Puffy's fist slammed the ground, the impact smashing the stone to leave a jagged crater. There was no awareness in those eyes, no hint of the friendly creature that had sneaked into his campfire at night to feed. Whatever Puffy had become, it was wild, reckless, and Sisters save his sorry hide, it was *chasing him.* Devin loaded a spellstone into his pistol as its goliath footsteps thundered behind him. He feared he'd wither away like a charred leaf before it even caught him, but he had to try something, anything. He spun as he pulled the hammer back and drew his pistol up to bear. Puffy towered over him, a god of flame, a potential destroyer of all of Londheim.

"Sorry, buddy," he said as he pulled the trigger. The hammer fell, smashing the blue orb in half and releasing one of Tommy's prepared spells. A faint blue star shot across the distance, hit the firekin in the chest, and then detonated. Ice exploded in a sphere, eliciting another roar from the chasm that was Puffy's throat. The ice melted instantly, bathing the enormous creature in steam. Devin had only one more ice spellstone, and he loaded it into the pistol and fired it straight into Puffy's chest. This detonation rocked the firekin harder, and its form visibly shrank as it lost heat from turning the ice to water and the water to steam.

"Devin, run!" Jacaranda screamed from afar, but Devin holstered his pistol and did the exact opposite. He approached his friend with his hands held wide. With the firekin's reduced size, he had to believe it had regained some measure of control. He had to, because if the firekin broke through the wall surrounding Belvua and set other parts of Londheim ablaze, nothing would stop it from destroying the entire city.

"You in there, buddy?" Devin shouted to the burning monstrosity. "I need you back, Puffy! I'm your friend, remember? Your friend!"

Puffy shook off the remainder of the steam and fixed its gargantuan obsidian eyes in Devin's direction. Was there recognition within them, or did he see what he wished to see? The firekin stepped closer. The ground rumbled.

"Friend, Puffy!" Devin screamed as the creature raised an enormous fist to smash him to dust. "Friend!"

The fist hesitated. The firekin stared at him intently. Was it thinking? Debating? Devin dared not lose that chance. He turned to the nearest building, which was charred black from flame, and he used the hilt of his sword to scrawl a message into its surface. Ash easily shifted from his movements, contrasting with the darker interior that had not fully burned. Puffy watched him the entire time, seemingly curious. Its light shone upon the message, which Devin wrote large enough to cover the entire wall.

YUWELCOMFREND.

"Remember Crynn?" Devin shouted at the firekin. "Remember the spider-wolves? We are friends, Puffy. Friends, damn it, now remember!"

Puffy's body shuddered. It stood to its full height, lifted its arms up above its head, and suddenly cast its weight aside in great, molten blobs. Chunks collapsed off its legs and waist, splashing across the cobblestone and simmering with heat. Puffy twisted and shook, flinging more blobs of heat through the air to the river, where they splashed into the Septen with hissing bursts audible for miles. It took him nearly a minute, but at last Puffy had shrunk its size down to the tiny little friend no larger than Devin's fist.

"Thank the Goddesses," Devin said, and he let out a breath he hadn't known he'd been holding. "I was convinced you were going to roast me, little buddy."

Puffy sheepishly lowered its head and drew letters with its finger in the air.

SORRYIBAD.

"You only *tried* to kill me," Devin said with a tired grin. "It's not like you succeeded. I think that means I can forgive you."

He pulled out the candle he'd pocketed when they first arrived in Belvua and held it out in offering. The firekin hopped on and settled in, looking so tiny and harmless. Nothing at all like the towering inferno it had been mere minutes ago. Jacaranda and Brittany rejoined him, and Puffy offered each a flickering bow to show its sorrow.

"That's one problem solved," Brittany said. She clipped her enormous axe onto her back. "So what now?"

It was a fair question, but it seemed that night's conflict had come to its end. The fires had chased away most of the crowds. The dragon-sired lucky enough to escape had done so through the newly created hole in the southern wall, and all that remained of the rioters were scattered looters making their way through the wreckage. If some were still looking for trouble, they wouldn't be for long. A familiar voice echoed through the sudden quiet.

"Disperse!" His sister's every word reverberated throughout Belvua with the power of thunder. "Disperse, and return home! Disperse! Disperse!"

"About damn time," Devin muttered. He turned to the two women. "I'm going to wait for Adria. Feel free to leave if you wish, either of you."

Jacaranda slid beside him to show without words she'd be staying.

"I'll make sure Tommy is all right," Brittany said. If she was hurt by the action, she kept it well hidden.

"Take Puffy with you then," he said. She accepted the candle, then tipped her hat with her free hand.

"See you at Tommy's."

Devin found a wall to lean against and sat, too exhausted to move and too tired to care. Jacaranda settled in beside him, and he held her close with an arm around her waist. Dawn was still hours away, and without Puffy's light, they were afforded a dark moment of solitude.

"We caused this," Devin said, and he gestured to the destruction with his free hand. "When we went to Shinnoc, I thought we'd be saving lives. Maybe we did, but..."

What else was there to say? Jacaranda leaned her head on his shoulder, and he kissed her forehead. So much violence. So many dead on either side, and for what? An ashen heap?

"You did what you thought was best," she said. "You always do. It's what makes you... you."

Adria's voice echoed not with magic but actual proximity.

"Disperse!"

Devin slowly rose to his feet at his sister's approach. She marched with a contingent of Mindkeepers, twenty or so men and women in monochrome robes and faces hidden behind masks.

Half held torches so they might see as they traveled. That the other half wielded swords and clubs did not go unnoticed. Adria held up a hand, ordering the others to halt, so she might embrace her brother with some measure of privacy. Devin accepted her arms about his chest, and after a moment, he hugged her back.

"I'm glad you're all right," she said.

"I might be," he said. "Thousands more aren't. Tommy isn't, either. He'll need healing, if you can spare a moment."

Adria glanced about and nodded in agreement.

"I will hold a pyre ceremony for all of Belvua just before dawn," she said. "I still cannot believe Shinnoc would be so reckless. I thought we had a chance at peace. I thought wrong."

"There might have been peace," Jacaranda said. "If you hadn't aided the rioters."

Adria slowly withdrew from Devin's arms and cast a glare Jacaranda's way.

"I did no such thing," she said.

"Then where were you when the slaughter began?" she asked. "Where were you when the fires burned?"

Jacaranda left without giving her a chance to answer. Adria stammered momentarily, and though her mask covered her face, it did not hide the red splotches growing in her neck.

"That is completely unfair," Adria seethed. "I was caught off guard by Shinnoc's message, the same as everyone else. What would you have had me do? Force our people to leave under the threat of death?"

"It's what I did," Devin said softly. The words impacted Adria enough to shock her into silence. She glanced about, her frustration simmering.

"I didn't know what to do," she finally admitted. "Whichever side I chose felt like the wrong choice, and so I chose neither, and stayed out of it until the bloodshed had run its course."

Devin kissed the center of her mask.

"But you did choose," he said. "Inaction isn't neutral. It never is."

He left Low Dock to join Jacaranda, left the Mindkeepers and the looters and the dead. Low Dock, or Belvua, it no longer mattered the name, for it was ash now, exactly as Shinnoc had promised.

CHAPTER 24

Brittany had never fought in a full-scale battle before, and certainly nothing like the chaos they'd all endured within Belvua. The Three-Year Secession had ended long before her appointment as a Soulkeeper, and even if it hadn't, Soulkeepers were banned from participating in military conflict. Yet there had been plenty of times she'd fought alongside villagers dealing with pesky raiders, particularly along the western reaches of Orismund, where soldiers were few and the eye of the church rarely turned their way. Each of those various instances fluttered through Brit's mind as she sat on the floor beside the fireplace of the Wise tower, her back braced against the wall and the heat washing over her. Not memories of the fights themselves, but the moments afterward. The checking of wounds. The lighthearted banter and smiles to wipe away the trauma of the blood and murder.

"Consider yourself lucky," Devin said as he elbowed Tommy in the side. "You had an excuse to get your ass out of Belvua. We had to keep doing all the hard work, and this time without our wizard."

"Lucky?" Tommy asked. He and Malik sat practically cradling each other on the couch, and he had to untangle himself to lift his heavily bandaged right arm. "That spell nearly took my damn arm off at the bone!"

"And Adria fixed it right up with a prayer. See? Lucky."

Brittany closed her eyes and softly smiled. Those times after a battle, they were so similar, and so familiar to her. Whatever collective trauma they'd endured, they'd bury it down deep beneath layers of laughter, jokes, and alcohol. There was a rawness to the bonding, a reminder of how fragile their connections truly were. Even though she understood it, she felt it all the same. The attack on Belvua was mere hours behind them, yet already it was beginning to feel like a dream.

"You can't deny it, Tommy," she told her brother as she snapped her fingers at Devin. Her husband—(ex-husband, damn it)—stood so she might have room on the couch. She flung an arm around Tommy's shoulder, stealing him away from Malik. "You're one of the luckiest little bastards alive."

"It is empirically true," Malik added, and he refused to crack a grin at Tommy's betrayed expression. "You did win me over, after all, and in spite of my rather well-thought-out refusals why it shouldn't happen."

A deep crimson blossomed along Tommy's neckline and spread all the way up his throat to his cheeks.

"All right, so I might be somewhat lucky," he muttered. "But my arm still really hurts."

Brit laughed and kissed Tommy's cheek. He flinched a moment beforehand, nothing much, but it was a subtle reminder that he was unfamiliar with her current form. Her mood, already precarious, dipped back down toward the somber. Across the room, she caught Devin whispering quietly with Jacaranda for a moment, accept a modest kiss, and then step outside. Her somberness threatened to turn into depression.

"I need some fresh air," she said, pushing herself up and away from Tommy and Malik. "Being near you two lovebirds is like suffocating on rose petals."

"Are you referring to my cologne?" Malik asked, and he sounded honestly hurt.

"I more meant you're all cuddles and romance. Your cologne smells just fine."

Brittany grabbed her large axe from its resting spot beside the door and then exited the tower. Jacaranda's eyes trailed her all the while, but Brittany pretended not to notice for both their sakes.

"Mind if I join you?" she asked Devin as she shut the door behind her. He had his back to the gentle wind and his hat lowered over his face, but his jaw was visible, as was his smirk.

"Would you go back inside if I told you no?"

"Probably not."

"Then sure, you're welcome to join me. We might even make a habit of this, you and me. Why talk while basking in the warm glow of a fire when we can freeze our asses off outside?"

Brittany rested her axe against the tower and then flicked the edge of his hat so it lifted slightly.

"Is it so wrong for a wife to seek a conversation with her husband without others prying?" she asked.

"Am I still your husband?" he asked. "The law is a bit muddy regarding deceased spouses returning from the dead."

"I see you still make terrible jokes when you're nervous."

"I like to think it's part of my charming personality."

Brit elbowed him in the side, but she was smiling now, smiling in spite of her nervousness and worry. Devin could always bring the best out of her like that. It was what had made her fall in love with him in the first place. The levity, the fondness he still clearly felt for her, almost made her abandon her plan. The secret could die with her. It had once before.

"Devin," she said, refusing to take the easy way out. "There's something you should know."

"And what's that?" he asked, his tone hardening ever so slightly. His demeanor stayed relaxed, but she recognized the way he crossed his arms and shifted his weight. Many times in their relationship she'd had to break hard news to him. He recognized that tone in her voice, just as she recognized his defensive response. The secret burned in her chest. *Damn it. Damn it, damn it, damn it.*

"I died fucking another man," she said, practically shoving the words off her tongue before she lost her nerve.

Devin cocked his head to one side. For once, she struggled to read him.

"Did you now?" he asked.

Brit stomped her feet and looked away.

"Yeah," she said. "Forrest kept it quiet for my sake, and for yours. My heart was never right, we both knew that. I could hone my body fit as a fiddle but my heart hammered in my chest with every jog or fight as if I were a first-year novice. Well, it finally gave out, and given the timing, I'd say it was because our beloved Anwyn has a sick sense of humor. I don't remember most of it at the very end, but I remember lying on the bed struggling to breathe. All I could think about was putting on my trousers. I didn't want to die naked. How stupid is that? How stupid. How incredibly stupid."

She'd begun crying. Of course she had. Not much, just a trickle of tears that fought against the cold. Her training kicked in, and she forced steady breaths in and out of her lungs to gather herself. Now the secret was exposed, she craved his response. This had hung over her head every single moment of her new life like an executioner's axe. Finally, goddess-damned finally, the axe would fall.

And when Devin spoke, its blade was sharp as a feather.

"So who was the lucky bastard?"

Brit smiled despite the quiver of her lower lip.

"Soulkeeper Havelock," she said. "And I'm not sure I'd call him lucky. He got to fuck me twice, then watch me die. I'd wager it traumatized him."

That forced a chuckle. Brit kept waiting for the explosion, the hurt, the betrayal. It never came.

"Why the affair?" he asked. "Was it me? Us? Did we go wrong, or was this a passing thing?"

A small but fierce spark of flame inside Brittany's breast fluttered and died. There had been a time when this knowledge would have broken Devin. He'd have been furious with her, and himself, and looked for someone to blame. He'd have felt guilty for his anger almost immediately, for that was how their fights had always gone. Then he'd look to fix it, to find the error and make it right.

Since awakening in this new body, in this new future, she'd held on to the slightest hope something remained between her and her husband. Seeing his calm reaction, his almost clinical examination of their relationship, ended it once and for all. He'd matured, of that there was no doubt. He'd grown. And in the most heart-wrenching irony possible, he'd grown because of her death. She felt the wind drain from her body. Brit sat upon the stone steps leading to the tower door and wrapped the long folds of her coat over her legs to fight a chill that grew stronger by the second. After a moment, Devin sat beside her.

"I don't know," she said. "And believe me, I've given it some thought. Distance? Boredom? The long months of separation when our travels took us to opposite corners of West Orismund? Maybe I'm just a shitty person, because that wasn't the first time I cheated, either. I was always the wild one before we married. Perhaps monogamy wasn't meant for me. The Goddesses know most Soulkeepers aren't good at it, either. Except you. I bet you remained faithful every second of our marriage. Shit, I bet you were faithful to me years *after* I was dead. Am I wrong?"

A half smile cracked his face.

"You're not wrong, but you're still a bit of a bitch for saying it."

Brittany leaned her weight against him, her eyes closed and a fresh wave of tears falling down her nose and cheeks. She felt his arm wrap about her. Goddesses above, she did not deserve him. She never had.

"I'm sorry," she whispered. "You know that, right?"

"Why Havelock?" he asked, pointedly ignoring her question.

"He was nearby, he was handsome, and he was just enough of a scoundrel to not care that you and I were married."

"Yeah, that sounds like Havelock, all right. Forrest transferred him east not long after your funeral pyre. I never gave it much thought. He'd acted cold to me the moment I came back for the pyre, but I assumed it was because I botched the reaping ritual."

"You botched my reaping ritual?"

Suddenly it was Devin's turn to act embarrassed.

"Yeah," he said, glancing away. "I never finished the chant. Instead I reached out to touch your soul, but before I could, it descended back into your body."

"Oh, Devin," she said, and she reached out for his hand. Their gloves intertwined, and she noted the lack of spark between them. "You blamed yourself for that, didn't you? Of course you did. Fuck me. I died cheating on you, and yet you're the one who suffered the guilt."

He gently squeezed her hand.

"Brit, if you don't stop blaming and hating yourself, I will, despite all risks to my own safety, have to slap you."

That got a laugh out of her. She sniffled and cleaned her face with the sleeve of her coat, then leaned her head on his shoulder.

"You needn't worry. This body is such a lightweight. I'm shorter, too, with less reach and less muscle."

"I'm sorry Adria wasn't able to find a soulless woman who was six foot tall and made of pure muscle. I bet your heart is healthier, at least."

"Always looking at the bright side of things, I see."

"It helps balance out the sarcasm."

Brit felt herself mostly collected, and she released Devin's hand so she might stand. Having the truth out helped, even if it came with the sting of seeing how little it truly hurt her former husband. Her shoulders felt lighter, her chest loosened, and her jaw unclenched. This is what it took to move on, she understood now. For *her* to move on. This closure had always been for her, and never him. She could tell herself a hundred times her husband had moved on after six years, but she'd still needed to see and feel it to make it real.

None of this made it pleasant, or eased the pain in her heart, but fuck it. Devin had taken six years to grieve her death. If it took her a few months to grieve over what she herself had lost, it was only fair.

"I'm going to go for a walk," she said, and she grabbed her axe. "I'll understand if you and Jacaranda are gone by the time I get back."

"Brit, wait."

He wrapped his arms about her, and she allowed herself a moment of weakness. Her eyes closed, and she melted against his chest, the scent of his body awakening a thousand memories within her tired soul.

"I love you, Brittany," he said. "I always have. I always will."

"I know," she said, and she pulled away. "Even if it has to be from afar."

Brittany walked streets that should have been familiar to her. Was it the passage of time that made them seem foreign, or had the city truly changed so much with the awakening of the old forgotten world of magic and monsters? She abandoned any specific destination and merely wandered, annoyed by the rapid pace she had to move her arms and legs to pass through the city at her preferred speed. Anwyn bless her, what she'd give to have her old long legs back. The air was thick with smoke, a burning layer adding to the city's newfound mystery. She walked the dark, wishing to be alone. She wasn't.

"This body's muscles may be weak, but my eyes still work fine," she said, halting before an elaborate collection of tents crowding an alleyway that had cropped up to house refugees. The tents were empty, their canvases torn. "Care to come down from there?"

Her trailing shadow hesitated a moment before descending from one of the nearby rooftops. Brit wasn't surprised by her identity in the slightest. Though her clothes were dark, and much of her face hidden with a cloak, the bright scarf about Jacaranda's mouth and neck might as well have her name written upon it.

"I was trained well to shadow a person," Jacaranda said as she pulled the scarf down to speak. "Yet you spotted me with ease."

Brit jammed the long handle of her axe to the stone and leaned her weight upon it with her arms crossed over her chest. She took in Jacaranda's demeanor as an awkward silence fell over them both. She observed the way she stood, the practiced stance so her weight remained balanced at all times. How her hands were never far from her weapons. How her eyes never quite focused on Brit's, as if enemies might lurk in every unseen corner of Londheim. Those lovely, soft violet eyes and her pale skin crowned with a shock of red hair...

"You're prettier than my old body was," Brit said, and she cracked a smile.

The tension broke between them, and an embarrassed blush filled Jacaranda's face.

"I'm sorry to have followed you," she said. "I'm still learning to resist my curiosity."

"It kills cats, you know."

"I'm sorry?"

Brit pulled her axe free and slung it over one of her shoulders.

"Don't worry about it. So you found me, Jacaranda. Is your curiosity sated? Or would you like to play a few games of ten questions to learn more about yours truly?"

"It seems odd to play such a game standing in the middle of the street," she said, gesturing to the houses on either side of them.

"You're right. So let's walk."

Brit resumed her aimless walking. After a moment's hesitation, Jacaranda slid in beside her. For long moments they said nothing, merely walked. It felt strangely good to Brittany, having her there. Seeing this woman, this replacement, equally confused and nervous validated her own jumbled tempest of feelings. Most importantly of all, she sensed no animosity or resentment, which impressed her. Most people would consider Brittany's return a threat, and rightly so. Even if she had no intention of rekindling a romance with Devin, her very presence meant a dozen additional layers of confusion and complication to their relationship.

"Devin loved you so much," Jacaranda suddenly blurted out. "That… that sounds stupid and obvious, I know, but he loved you so much, it… it scares me. Even after we met, he wept over your grave. So I feel like you're what I have to live up to. It's intimidating."

It was wrong to respond with any sort of levity to those deep-seated worries, but Brittany couldn't help it. She chuckled and shook her head as if she'd heard the most absurd of jokes.

"Devin's a sweetheart, but I assure you, his opinion of me is tinted heavily by nostalgia. I'm a colossal failure, Jacaranda. Always have been, and I suspect always will be. You don't have much to live up to, and with how badly Devin is enamored of you, I'd suspect you have already done the job. Just try not to break the poor sap's heart."

Jacaranda removed the hood covering her face, and she ran her fingers through her hair in an obvious nervous tic.

"Thank you," Jacaranda said. "I was worried you would… you know…" She blushed again. "Try to take him back."

It'd been a thought she'd had, of course, when first awakening. Pretending that Devin's loving arms were around her had allowed Brittany to push through the initial few days of confusion and torment inside that tiny room of Adria's as her soul slowly erased the former memories of her new soulless body. But Brittany had always considered herself a practical woman. Flights of fancy were Devin's domain.

Brittany put a hand on Jacaranda's shoulder and leaned close so there might be no confusion between them.

"It may have only been a day for me, but it has been years for him. He's moved on. In time, I will, too. In some ways, I think I already have. I have no intention of trying to form a wedge between you. And if it's my blessing you want, well, you have it."

"I have no need of your blessing," Jacaranda said, and her face hardened for just long enough to make Brittany wonder if she'd misjudged. "I only want to ensure you won't cut my head off with that giant axe of yours."

Laughter burst from Brittany's chest, and she smiled with a sincerity she had not known since Adria Eveson ripped her soul from the dark ground of the Cradle and thrust it into a soulless body. She embraced Jacaranda, and after an initial moment of shock, Jacaranda returned the embrace.

"Devin is beyond lucky to have you," Brittany said, newly released tears falling upon Jacaranda's red hair. "Assuming we live through all this madness, I think you two will do just fine. And if it makes you feel any better, I hereby solemnly vow there will be no decapitations."

CHAPTER 25

"If you're looking for Adria, she's not in there," the lurking woman said as Faithkeeper Sena hesitated before the entrance to the Wise tower. Sena turned from the door to see a woman leaning against a wall in the slender space between two homes on the opposite side of the street, her dark skin and clothes nearly invisible in the deep night.

"Excuse me?" Sena asked, her voice perfectly pleasant, as if she'd not spent an exhausted night tending over wounded and praying for the dying after the Belvua attack.

"That's why you're here, isn't it?" the stranger asked. "They've already turned away three other groups tonight. Are you not number four?"

"I suppose I am," Sena said. She had indeed come searching for Adria, and having not found her at her allocated home nor at Devin's house, she'd come next to check with her brother-in-law. "But who are you, my friend? Did you come here seeking the Sacred Mother reborn?"

Even her practiced Faithkeeper tone could not keep away a bit of venom at the title. She blamed her exhaustion and the late hour.

"Adria?" this unknown woman said. "No, Faithkeeper, I believe I am done with her. I would not have entered if she were home, truth be told."

The bitterness, the familiarity, piqued Sena's interest. Her legs ached from spending so much time both earlier in the day, and then that night, rushing about to offer aid. She crossed the street and took a seat with her back leaning on the shuttered home. A pleased groan slipped from her throat as she stretched her legs. She noticed the other woman tensed as if she were prey in proximity to a predator. The reaction was familiar to Sena, and sadly shared with far too many people throughout Londheim. It was a fear of the church, of its members, and its beliefs. Someone had hurt this recast, hurt her deeply.

"I am Faithkeeper Sena Meisen," she said.

"Wren."

Sena stared at the Wise tower. A fire burned inside, as well as several lit candles. Shadows danced across the open window along the front, and from within she saw blurry figures move and talk.

"Well, Wren, you know why I am here," she said. "But why do you lurk outside?"

"I'm friends with someone inside," Wren said. "At least, I like to think we are friends. It's hard to know sometimes."

Sena thought of the countless hours she and Adria had worked together to serve the people of Low Dock, all seemingly powerless against a single moment of Adria dismissing her concerns in a quiet graveyard before bringing life back to Brittany Eveson.

"The sum of our decisions, beliefs, and memories cannot be stacked on a scale to be weighed," Sena said. "Who we are shifts like a river. Sometimes we change little, and sometimes we carve canyons and flood valleys to become something new. Whoever this friend is, if they care for you, and you care for them, try not to obsess on the particulars."

Wren softly laughed.

"Did you read that from a book, Sena? Or was it taught to you in some school of the church?"

"I've been a Faithkeeper for more than ten years, Wren. Sometimes you pick things up along the way."

"Like a river?"

It was Sena's turn to laugh.

"If you wish to push the analogy that far, then sure. Like a river."

Silence fell over them, not entirely uncomfortable. Sena let her mind drift as she watched the golden light flickering against the window. How long ago was it that Adria had been assigned to her church? Six years? Seven? Sena had often joked that together they would change the world, and every time Adria would remark that she was fine with merely changing Low Dock for the better. Meager goals, for a meager corner of their weary city. Had power changed her friend so thoroughly that she would consider herself above the Goddesses they both faithfully served? Or did Adria always desire something more, and merely never believed it within her capabilities?

"It didn't feel right," Wren said, pulling Sena from her thoughts.

"What didn't?" she asked.

"Going inside." Wren gestured to the tower. "You asked why I stayed out here. It's... I heard about the attack on Belvua, and I knew my friends would help. That's how they are. So after things calmed down, I came here, but before I could knock, I heard them through the door. You can still hear them. Talking. Laughing. And it hit me that... I'm not like that with them. I barely know them. Even my friend Jacaranda, we've known each other for but a few days. Do I really belong in there? Am I a member of their family in that way? Of course not. I watched those shadows on the glass and felt so separate, so... alone. So why bother them? Why butt in like that, unwanted and unasked for?" She wiped growing tears from her face. "Shit. Here I go rambling whether you want to hear it or not."

"I'm a Faithkeeper," Sena said, and she smiled at the younger woman. "I'm used to unexpected confessions."

That small comfort seemed to help, and Wren looked away

while she cleaned her face. Sena let the quiet fall back over them. She knew how these conversations went, for she'd lived through them hundreds of times. Once the words began, nothing would stop them. People so wounded, so broken inside, might take years before they opened up, but once they did, they were like a flood bursting through a dam. Sena need not press further. The silence would be enough.

"Do the Goddesses love us unconditionally?" Wren suddenly blurted.

"Why do you ask? Do you seek comfort on a dark night? Or have you committed actions you seek atonement and forgiveness for?"

"Do you ever answer a question without asking five of your own?"

Sena suppressed a chuckle.

"I've been told that," she said. "Yes, Wren, the Goddesses love us unconditionally. We are their beloved children. They have given us life, and a world to support us so we may thrive and grow."

"They made a pretty dark and shitty world."

"Whatever darkness you find within it, I assure you it is of our own creation."

"Is it?" Wren asked. A fire awoke within her tired voice. "Is it really? Bullshit."

Sena furrowed her brow. She'd offered her response without much thought, for it was a common question and she gave it her common answer, yet now she knew she touched on a nerve. For this woman to be so distrusting of the church, to doubt the Goddesses' love, and be so certain of the Goddesses' failures in creating the world…

"You clutch a painful secret to your breast," Sena said as she shifted her legs into another stretch. "You need not tell me, Wren, but know that I would pray over it with you if you would trust me."

Their eyes met, and she did not anticipate the depth of pain she saw in them. How lonely was this woman? How abandoned?

Then Wren pulled low the scarf she wore about her neck, revealing a set of chain tattoos, and Sena knew.

"You're an awakened soulless," she said. Wren's mention of a friend inside suddenly made perfect sense. Hadn't Devin claimed the woman living with him was also the same? "Just like Jacaranda."

"So does that change your answer, Sena? Still care to feed me that lie that the Goddesses love us all equally?"

The existence of soulless had challenged church doctrine since their first appearance some eighty years ago. Sena had often felt it a symptom of their world, of a steady fading of people's faith. Such an answer felt weak when faced with an awakened soulless. How satisfying was it to tell a person their own suffering was from the lack of others' believing? How was that fair? How did that fit with the neat stories of perfect Goddesses cherishing all living beings as their beloved children?

"I am not perfect," Sena said. "Neither is my understanding of the Goddesses. I can only answer by what I know, and what I have felt. I have seen the light of souls amid the reaping ritual. I have felt Lyra's touch in the cold of night, and seen the lives that have been saved by her unconditional love. I do not know if the Goddesses are perfect like we once thought. I don't know if they are as powerful as we believed. But they love us, Wren. I know that. I *know* it."

"I don't!" Wren seethed amid the quiet street. "How do I believe the Goddesses love me when they spent so long ignoring me? How do I believe them all-knowing and all-powerful when I passed unnoticed beneath their gaze? Would you have me believe them cruel, and unwilling to grant me the life I deserved? Or would you have me believe I am so wretched, so pitiful, I should not have this life I now live? That I should have remained soulless, obedient, a fucking little mindless slave for my owner, doing as he said, behaving as he ordered? Pretending, lying, my entire life just lying..."

Wren slammed her fist against the wall, and she bit her lip to halt any tears. Her sorrow was overwhelming, and she fought it back with an equal amount of naked rage. Sena tried to imagine herself in this woman's place, and she could not. Her parents had prayed with her every night, asking for Lyra's blessing during her sleep. Her childhood had been spent convinced of the Goddess's love and protection. To awaken to much of your life already spent, to know without a shadow of a doubt that the Goddesses had not granted you the gift they granted all others...

"Have you no words?" Wren asked. "No rehearsed speeches or bits of wisdom?"

Sena rose to her feet. She grabbed the woman's hands, the sudden action surprising her into silence.

"No words?" Sena said. "No, Wren, you are so very wrong. I have a million words, so many I wish to say that they tie my tongue and clog my throat. I want to tell you that you are loved. I want to tell you that you are worthy. I want to spend hours soothing your hurt and banishing your loneliness so that you never again believe you are undeserving of happiness. We were not made to suffer. We were not born for sorrow. I would speak a thousand hours of joy, if only you would believe me as I spoke them."

Wren's lower lip trembled. Her body shivered, but not from the cold. For a brief moment, Sena saw hope blossom in those umber eyes. She pulled her close for an embrace. Wren buried her small face into Sena's neck and shuddered.

"I want to believe you," Wren whispered. "I just...I don't know if I ever could."

The tower door opened, the rattle of wood and metal pulling Wren away like a startled rabbit. The two sank into the dark space, going unnoticed as Devin Eveson emerged from within.

When Sena turned back, Wren was gone. A long, tired sigh vacated her lungs. Exhaustion clawed at her every limb. Her every desire was to find a bed, climb into it, and not leave for a week.

"Not yet," the Faithkeeper whispered as Brittany exited the tower to join Devin in quiet, hushed discussion. "Lyra help me, not yet."

If Adria was not home, or at her brother's, there was one place left for her to be, and she feared the reason. Soul heavily burdened, Sena trekked to the empty, ashen district of Belvua.

No apprentices and no keepers waited with Adria in the dead of night. She stood alone among the bodies, which were positioned around her as if she were the heart of a flower and they the outwardly spiraling petals. *How long had it taken to gather them?* Sena wondered. No doubt guards and church members helped her drag the hundreds to the southernmost portion of the district, where they lay in the shadow of the broken wall.

"No one should be alone tonight," Sena said as she approached. She held a cloth to her nose in a vain attempt to block out the stench. "Least of all you."

"Sena?" Adria said, turning to face her. "I haven't seen you since the graveyard. I pray you are well?"

It was enough to make Sena laugh. Adria stood amid a field of corpses, and she greeted her as if all were well, and Belvua not a burned-out husk about them.

"How goes Brittany Eveson?" Sena asked, pretending she had not just seen the woman talking with her former husband the previous hour. "Did she endure the resurrection as you hoped?"

"Better, even, but that's not why you've come here, is it?"

"No, Adria. I come because I love the stench of burned corpses."

The humor died on the both of them. Adria cast her eyes to the bodies. No doubt hundreds more had died throughout the district, but either they were lost to fire, or there had not been time to gather them. Time for what, Sena feared she knew. Careful not to step on any limbs, she wove to Adria at the center, and despite the smell, she removed her cloth from her face. Adria's face remained covered by her porcelain mask, but it was meager protection. Sena could read the slightest twitch and flicker of Adria's eyes, she knew her so well. At least... she believed she did.

"Why are you here?" Adria asked, all pleasantness gone. She sounded tired, defeated. "Why, really? Have you come to stop me?"

"How can I stop what I do not yet know?" Sena asked. "Why are *you* here, Adria? What is it you would do to these corpses? The midnight hour is passed, but with your gifts, I suppose it is not yet too late to perform a reaping ritual."

"I could send them to the heavens, yes," Adria said. "But that's not what I'm debating."

"You're thinking of resurrecting them like you did those at the cathedral," Sena said.

"I am."

"Do you have the power to do so? Or would you need to steal power from my soul to do it like you did when protecting our church?"

She hadn't meant her words to be so biting, but the hurt from that earlier betrayal had never quite healed. Adria winced as if pricked by a knife.

"There would be no need. I'm learning, Sena. I'm learning, and I pray, I'm growing with it."

"That doesn't mean it would be the right path to take, Adria. You already dabbled in the forbidden with Brittany. Would this be any better, this making a mockery of life and death? These souls belong in Anwyn's hands, not your own."

Adria tilted her head and looked to the stars.

"Earlier tonight my friends condemned me for inaction, for not stopping the riots, or for letting the soulless remain soulless. And now you come, and you condemn me for the actions I might take. No matter my course, I am condemned. So why should I bother fearing the condemnation of others? Why let it guide me?"

Sena's heart started to race, and she felt panic start to scrape its way along her neck and back. Power was growing in the air about her, so overwhelming, it was as if she could reach out and touch its presence.

"Adria, wait," she said, but her friend did not. Adria lifted her arms, and with them lifted the souls from those hundreds of bodies. They lit the wide street with a brilliant glow, like blue fires, or twinkling stars so large and near. They were so many, and they moved and hovered about one another in a mesmerizing dance. The display overwhelmed Sena with awe, but it was not awe that moved her friend.

"I'm frightened, Sena," Adria said. "Perhaps more frightened than I have ever been in my life."

"Of doing what is wrong?"

"No, not that." Adria looked to the heavens. "I'm frightened of finally doing everything I know is within my reach. Of discovering I have no true limits. I can feel the power of these souls. It draws into me. It strengthens me. I've started to learn how to use it, to truly harness it like I was meant to. Not just as a Chainbreaker." The souls swirled higher, dancing above them in a sparkling dance. "Like a Goddess."

"You speak blasphemy," Sena said. "You are powerful, Adria, but you are no Goddess."

"I speak the truth that terrifies me," Adria said. Her fingers danced in the air above her head. "And I don't think you understand. Not yet. But I shall show you."

Sena felt a rush of wind wash over her as Adria slammed her hands together. The souls shot higher into the air, and they numbered far more than a mere hundred. Thousands of souls joined them, a brand-new starscape hovering a mere few hundred feet above the city of Londheim. It was every single human life lost during the attack on Belvua. The gathered bodies, they didn't need to be near her. The realization shook Sena with fear, and she stared at her friend with dawning horror. Thousands of souls, burning with power, and they all obeyed Adria's slightest whim.

"I could resurrect them," Adria said, her soft voice easily heard despite the sudden roar of wind that seemed to shake the heavens. "These here, these dead at my feet? I could give them back their lives. Life? Death? If neither mean a thing to me, then *what am I*, Sena? What else could I be, if not a Goddess?"

Do you ever answer a question without asking five of your own?

"Is that what you want to be?" Sena asked. The sudden thought was dark and humorous, yet it somehow kept her sane as she pressed on in the face of a display that shook her to her core. "A Goddess? Would you have me bow in worship?"

"I don't want worship. I want to make this world a better place."

"But you can't remake the world, Adria."

"Can't I?"

At last, Adria removed her mask. It broke Sena's heart seeing the confusion raging in her brown eyes. They were so similar, Wren and Adria, both so confused and abandoned in their own way by the Goddesses. The only difference between them was that when Adria raged against the Goddesses, she did so with power beyond human understanding.

"Then what would you have me do?" she asked. "Tell me, dear friend. Tell me, and I will do it."

Sena hardened her jaw and straightened her spine. No weakness, not here, not now. Let her will and faith be iron.

"I would have you trust the Goddesses as you always have, and respect the balance they created. These men and women lived their lives, and they died lost in rage and fear. Death has taken them. Send their souls to the heavens, and let eternity be their judge."

The souls danced closer and closer, swirling together like a tremendous tornado of light and memory. Adria commanded them with such ease, Sena finally believed her every word. Perhaps her friend truly had no limits. Perhaps she could even remake the world, but what world would it be, one made by human hands instead of a Goddess or a dragon?

"So be it," Adria whispered. "Take them, Anwyn. They are yours."

She gestured to the stars, and the souls raced to them in a sudden, spontaneous barrage. They faded away, the thousands becoming distant stars that within moments flickered away into nothing. It should have made Sena feel better, but instead it deepened her worry. Anwyn's holy task was to take souls into her bosom deep in the heavens, yet Adria performed the same task with a mere flick of her wrist. The overwhelming sensation of power faded as the light dimmed and the ruins of Belvua darkened. Sena wiped sweat from her shaved head. The world seemed cold and empty, and it felt like she could finally breathe again.

Adria watched them until they faded, then abruptly turned and stepped over the corpses toward the broken gap in the city wall.

"Where are you going?" Sena asked.

"I need answers, so I go to those who have them."

"You would seek the Goddesses in the fields beyond?"

"Not the Goddesses," Adria said as she replaced her porcelain mask. "The dragons."

CHAPTER 26

Finding the Chainbreaker was no great difficulty, not when her presence was a blinding star. What surprised Janus was *where* he found her. It seemed the woman had fled the walls of Londheim, which was just fine with him. Smoke still billowed from Belvua's destruction. Janus held no desire to be anywhere near the damned city.

"Do you come here for solitude, or for silence?" Janus asked as he stepped into the light of her campfire.

"Are they not the same?" Adria asked without glancing up. Her gaze was locked on the center of her small fire, her knees pulled up to her chest and her chin resting on her folded arms. Despite the late hour and a sky full of stars, she still wore her mask over her face.

"One can have solitude even within a giant city such as Londheim," Janus said. "Peace and quiet, however, is a rarity."

"Peace, quiet, solitude...whatever it is I seek, you deny me it with your presence."

He laughed as he sat opposite her at the fire. Laughed, because it kept his fury in check.

"I would ask your forgiveness, but you would never grant it. I suppose I've sinned against you enough to deserve that."

"Don't say it like that. You never sinned against me. I'm no

Goddess for you to sin against, no matter how many times you scrawl it in gold on the city walls."

Janus held his hand out to the fire. His skin turned to marble so its heat would not burn. Then, with but a touch of his fingertips, he pulled the grass about the fire higher, shifting it to logs, to stone. What had been a meager campfire became twice its size and with a decorative ring of stones and an abundance of kindling.

"A blunt message, for an often blind and dullard species. Was I wrong? Are you human? Chainbreaker? Goddess? Perhaps you are all three, Adria, but I come not to question what you are." He turned his attention to her black-and-white mask, which was bathed in the yellow hue of the fire. "I want to know where you were when Belvua burned."

Adria pulled her legs closer to her chest. There was a time when she'd have shown fear at his presence. No longer. Had she grown accustomed to him? Or had her confidence in her own power grown so much that she was unafraid of what he might do to her?

"I prayed over the souls of thousands who charged into Belvua only to die," she said. "I sent them to the heavens, beyond the void to the eternal flow of Aether beyond, to dwell for an eternity. I sent them despite them dying in fits of rage and fear. I sent them despite the dragon-sired they murdered and the fires they set. I am out here for a reason, Janus, and it is because I want nothing of Londheim's love and adoration. Not tonight. If you need to hear it for yourself, then no, I wasn't there. I was not part of the mob that burned Belvua to the ground."

"You could have stopped it."

"How? By slaughtering my fellow humans? Bloodshed marked Belvua's creation, and bloodshed marked its end. What would you have had me do?"

"*Anything*," Janus said, and it took all his effort not to scream. "Is this the fruit of our labors? Ash and bone surrounded by a ring of dead trees? Belvua was meant to be proof that humanity and dragon-sired could coexist. Was that not worth your effort? But I suppose I shouldn't be surprised. This truth has been etched into the very stars that protect us from the void. We will never get along. We will never coexist."

Janus clenched his fists, changing them from marble to steel to flesh. He hated feeling this naked. It was foreign to him. It was wrong.

"Why come to me if that is what you believe?" Adria asked softly. "Why blame me for failing to prevent what you consider inevitable?"

Could he admit what he feared? Janus stared into the fire. He let its light overwhelm his sight, for it was better to think on it than the two looming dragons to their north.

"Because I have to believe that peace is possible," he said. "Otherwise I will have accomplished nothing in my entire existence."

He almost choked on those bitter words, but he forced them out. Perhaps here in the barren hills beyond Londheim's walls, just him and the Chainbreaker, he might admit what frightened him most.

"From the moment I met you, you have hated our kind," Adria said. "Why now do you hope for peace? Why does our coexistence trump your own art?"

Janus thought of Nihil and Viciss bickering over humanity's fate, and the fate of their sired children. It was all plans and curiosities to them, he knew. The lives were inconsequential. When Belvua burned, neither dragon had stirred. The games they played overruled all.

"You humans have no idea how lucky you are to have not met your creators," he said. "You don't know your purpose. You don't know your reason for existing, the Goddesses' intentions; none of it. All you humans live your lives in a haze of uncertainty, and from that uncertainty you gain the belief that what you do carries meaning. It carries purpose. The Sisters gifted you with souls over us, and that imbalance has broken any chance of peace the Cradle has ever held."

Adria stared at him thoughtfully. He wished he could read the emotions in her eyes. Most humans were simple, but not this one. Not the divinely gifted Chainbreaker.

"There is something I fail to understand," she asked. "You say you have no soul, and neither do all other dragon-sired. Then why do you not act like our own human soulless? Why are you capable of choice and free will?"

Janus's bitterness grew like a cancer, and he laughed out his sickness.

"You circle around the truth, so close to touching it yet still oblivious. It was the dragons who crafted this world. They molded their children with the power given to them, but the mastery over souls was not one of those gifts. The Sisters reserved that only for themselves, and their precious human children. Don't you see? You were *created flawed*, your shells meaningless without a soul. It was their way of ensuring your eternal worship. We call you Chainbreaker, Adria. Did you never think on the nature of those chains we would have you break?"

He'd shaken her, he could tell. Her understanding of the world, and humanity's place within it, was steadily crumbling on its unsteady foundations.

"How does it not break you?" she asked softly.

"Whoever said it didn't?" he asked. "Other dragon-sired believe they will be remembered by their dragon makers, cherished within their memories to be one day lifted to the heavens at the end of all life upon the Cradle. No such fate awaits me, I assure you, even if it were true. I am no beloved human. I am no cherished child."

Janus rose to his feet. Fire sparked like embers from his teeth when he grinned, for his molars were now flint. His skin was iron. His rage was a furnace. His body was a joke.

"Unlike humans, I have met my maker. I know my purpose. I was made to kill in a moment of weakness and fury by my dragon creator. When the Sisters demanded my death, Viciss kept me alive, not out of love, not out of compassion, but out of *spite*."

He slammed his foot into the fire, scattering its burning logs. His body became flesh once more. The weakness of it, the blood and skin, had always been most appropriate to the cowardice he felt living within him.

"You humans go about your lives convinced of a holy purpose. Do you know what I have, Adria? The knowledge that there is nothing awaiting me when my time ends. No soul lives within me. No eternity shall bear my memories. Even my creator will spurn my essence, for I was made in a moment of weakness and pride. You live with possibility, with purpose, yet I live knowing my sole reason to exist is to cause misery in others by the mere beating of my heart."

He didn't remember doing so, but his jacket had turned to dust by an errant thought. His clothes were gone. He stood naked before Adria, naked as the day Viciss made him.

"You will exist forever," he whispered into the starlit silence. "While I will cease the moment I stop breathing. But through you, I might finally scrawl a mark on eternity. If you replace the Sisters, if you become their better, a true arbiter of peace in a world that has known only hatred, then perhaps my contributions will mean something. I will have a legacy that Viciss cannot ignore or deny, no matter how much he may loathe my existence. Is it possible, Adria? Are you capable of becoming that? Of replacing the Sisters? Or do I hope in vain?"

Adria stood, and she matched Janus nakedness for nakedness with the removal of her mask. Tears stained her face, and they reflected the starlight like diamonds.

"What you call luck, I call curse," she said. "You seethe at the knowledge of your making, but I would give everything to hear a reason for mine. After Belvua burned, I went to the crawling mountain. I screamed for the dragon to come and tell me why I was made. Tell me, I begged, why I was given this power. And your demigod's response? Nothing, Janus. He told me nothing. Yet even that was better than what Lyra gave me."

She lifted a clenched fist, and it seemed all of reality shook with a silent rumble.

"You're wrong, Janus. I *have* spoken with my maker. And do you know what she asked of me? To take my own life. The Goddess I served, the Goddess I have spent my whole life praying to in times of need, to whom I entrusted my fears and hopes...she seeks my death. She fears I will become what your dragons would have me become. Yet why should I embrace their vision? They offer no alternative, no replacement. I cannot be that replacement, Janus. I cannot bear such a weight. I'm confused, and torn, and I stand here looking upon a city destroying itself and I feel nothing but helplessness. I cannot give guidance to humanity. I cannot lead us to the peace you think is within my grasp. I can't...I can't even let them look upon my true face anymore. I can't endure their love. I don't want it. I don't want any of this, I never did, yet you chose me. *You* chose *me*, Janus. How dare you place such burdens and hopes on my shoulders?"

Janus stared at this collection of bone, organs, and tissue. He stared at this weeping thing that called itself "woman." She was more than that, so much more, for she bore a power of startling light within her mind that her mask could never hide. From his very first breath, he had hated beings like her. He had been pulled from the dirt and molded by Viciss, given sentience, a sliver of power, and declared his avatar of change. Knowledge of the infinitesimally small atoms that built every block of matter was granted to him. He could shape them. Change them. Yet with all that, he'd been made to murder. He'd hated Viciss equally for that cruel fate, but at least humanity was within his reach. Humanity, he could slaughter and paint canvases with their blood. They were wretched beings, pathetic and shallow. Yet no matter what they did with their limited number of heartbeats, they would continue on into eternity, forever remembered, forever a part of the great Aether stream beyond the stars, beyond the void, in the realm of the gods and Goddesses.

Yet for the first time, he looked upon one such creature, and he did not feel hate. What it was, he could not say, but of all his emotions, hatred was his most well-known and well-defined, and that was not what crept about his heart when he saw the tears running down the frightened Chainbreaker's cheeks. He was not so foolish as to think it love. He was not so optimistic as to think it hope. But it was something. It was meaningful. And it terrified him.

"The dragons and Goddesses will not give us peace," he said. "But I think, together, you and I can. Is that something you even want, Adria?"

"Peace, or to work alongside you?"

The naked Janus laughed.

"Both?"

She cracked a weary smile.

"What happened at Belvua cannot happen again. Such destruction will ruin us both, and I fear whatever eternity that would accept our memories of hatred and murder."

Janus knelt to the grass, and he rearranged the molecules of the dirt to become a loose pair of brown pants and a long black coat. Once he was dressed, he glanced at the fire he'd banished and remembered that humans could not withstand cold as he could. A brief scrape of his fingertips turned stone to wood, and he set it alight with a scrape of his fingernails.

"The dragons hoped that Chainbreakers could replace the Sisters," he said. "If humanity itself possessed the power to draw down souls from the Aether for newborns, and then return them to the heavens upon their funeral pyres, then what purpose did the Sisters serve humanity? Oh, they've provided their morals and screeds, but what *functional* purpose do they fulfill? I see now that the dragons underestimated the danger humanity becomes when in possession of such power. You may not have helped burn Belvua, but I remember your fury at the cathedral. I remember the slaughter at the square. It cost the fae, Tesmarie, her little life, and that was accidental. I shudder at the thought of the purposeful slaughter an army of Chainbreakers might unleash.

"But things cannot remain as they are, even if the Sisters are vital to humanity's existence. So long as the dragons fear a second imprisonment, they will plot for the Goddesses' downfall. I say we seek a compromise. Birth and death, Alma and Anwyn, are vital. But during life? Unnecessary. Together, we slay Lyra. The three struggled to imprison the dragons with their combined strength. With Lyra's death, they could never hope to do so again. Free of that fear, the dragons will abandon any attempts at making more Chainbreakers. You'll no longer be necessary, for that was your true reason, Adria. You were there to replace the Sisters so the Sisters might be slain. I say we just jump a few steps and call the matter settled."

Adria stepped away, and she slid her mask back over her face.

"You would have me slay my own Goddess," she said.

"It's only fair," Janus said, and he grinned in spite of himself. "After all, she ordered your death. Why not you order hers?"

"Would the dragons accept such a peace? Or would they, now unafraid of the Goddesses, seek to wipe us out completely?"

"Truth be told, I don't know," Janus admitted. "Nihil will help us, I am sure, though Viciss may try to interfere. He has always held on to a hope that the dragons might reconcile their grievances with the Sisters once the matter of souls was put to rest."

"And if he does interfere, could you do what you ask of me? Could you kill your own maker?"

Janus offered his hand to Adria, as if they were friends, and he offering a simple dance.

"It is an act I have dreamed of since my first breath," he said. "Both our makers would see us dead, and together, we plot the death of our makers. Would you care to be my partner in this dance of the damned?"

She stared at it, pondering, and after an interminable length of thought, she shook her head.

"I need to dwell on this, though I fear my soul deserves condemnation for even entertaining such thoughts. Give me time."

"Time we may not have," Janus said, and he gestured toward Londheim. "Belvua is just the start. The city shall follow, and then the Cradle. Try not to delay."

Janus returned to Londheim, leaving the most powerful human woman alive to ponder her course. Could she lead humanity to peace? He didn't know. Could he slay Viciss, even with her help? Again, he did not know. But there was a path before him now, one of their own choosing, and as he passed through the southern gate of the city in the guise of an elderly woman, he dared hope that his finest work of art would be a world of peace neither the Goddesses nor dragons were able to attain.

CHAPTER 27

For a brief few weeks before the fires, Belvua's morning sky had been a wondrous flurry of color as the leaves of the hive-trees took flight. The district had been surrounded by the sentient trees, the tens of thousands of leaves overwhelming the dreary blue sky with shimmering oranges and reds as they soared heavenward before splitting in all directions. It'd been the most beautiful sight, a reminder of the days that were lost, and it had warmed Logarius's heart every time he watched it from his window.

There would be no such displays of color anymore. Humans had burned the hive-trees down to the last. The surviving leaves had fled the ashen husks that ringed Belvua like a corpse crown.

"The destruction of humanity," Logarius muttered as he walked alongside the western wall. "Never has it been so complete."

Fire had claimed all. Windows were shattered. Smoke stained walls and rooftops. Every home, every store, every decoration: If it could burn, it did. The black stench lingered in the air, and though Logarius covered his nostrils as he walked, the smell would not be denied. Try as he might, he could not prevent the memories such odors resurfaced. This was not the first wreckage of war he had walked through. Though it was the most extensive, it did not hurt the worst. It was close, perhaps, but nothing would compare to the overwhelming inferno that had taken the life of his daughter with its thick pall of smoke. Meager comfort, that. Belvua may not have been his own feathers and blood, but it had been his child nonetheless.

Like all things he cherished, humanity had murdered it.

"Logarius? Is it really you?"

He halted before a heap that had been a foxkin den, its unique intermix of mud, brick, and twig having collapsed in on itself and burned down to resemble a grotesquely large campfire.

"Sometimes I wonder," he said as he turned, and he dipped his head in respect to Aerreth Crimshield. "Greetings, phantom. I'm happy you survived the chaos."

"Happy?" the foxkin woman said. She leaned against the blackened bricks of what might have been a restaurant of some kind. How he'd not seen Aerreth as he walked past was a mystery. "I'm far from happy, avenria. Where were you? When we needed you most, you abandoned us. We thought death claimed you, but I see we thought wrong. What then, Logarius? What took you from your Forgotten Children?"

He glanced to the drawn daggers in her hands. She held them casually, with such second nature, they might have been her own fingers. He had a lone dagger on him, one he'd taken from his old home prior to his escape. A paltry defense against the phantom death of Nicus.

"Will you slay me if you do not appreciate my answer?" he asked.

"It depends how terrible the answer."

He raised his arm and shifted his shirt to reveal the gap in his soft feathers along his side. The scar his mother had left him, while healing, was still angry and red.

"I did not die, but I came close," he said. He felt himself sliding back into the role he'd occupied over the past month. He had his Forgotten Children to command, and by the dragons, he would not let such atrocities go unanswered. "Forgive my absence, but I am here now, and I am ready to act. Where are the survivors? We must rally them into strike forces, and quickly, while the humans are still reveling in their victory. If we hit them hard enough, we might..."

He stopped as Aerreth pushed off from the wall and approached while shaking her head.

"What?" he asked.

"You fool," she said. "You damn fool, but that's always been you, hasn't it? Only a fool would think we could accomplish something here in Londheim. You were the fool we needed, but we underestimated the cruelty of humanity. We, the killers who should have known better. There's enough blood in our past to teach a thousand lessons, yet we heeded not a one. I'm sorry, Logarius, I really am. But it's time you wake up."

Logarius felt blood rush to his beak and neck.

"What are you talking about?" he asked.

"There are no dragon-sired to rally to your cause. Those who survived last night have fled the city, and they will not be returning. I'm here looking for the wounded and the unconfirmed dead, that is all. Belvua is ash. Let the humans take it. It's ours no more."

Logarius glanced up and down the street, as if he might find a better argument nearby. Yet the section of the city was so ghastly quiet. No children, no families, no trade or travelers or wildlife.

"No," he said, nearly choking on the word. "We can't give up yet."

"We can," Aerreth said. "And we have. Shinnoc may have cast us aside for our role in his father's death, but his army remains outside the city gates. The humans will grant us no kingdom. They will honor no lands or treaties. Who would ever believe it possible after Belvua's destruction? Our races march toward the same war we were fighting when the great slumber came for us, and it is a war we have already lost." She shook her head. "Damn it all, we could have still fled west, to the mountains, and the coastal lands beyond where humanity has not yet spread. They'd find us eventually, what with humanity spreading like the disease that it is, but we might have known a few centuries of peace. I could have watched my son raise his pups, and we could have built quaint homes and thatch-wood towns outside the reach of the waves."

The defeat in the old foxkin's voice hurt him worse than the ache in his side. Aerreth had been one of his most trusted advisors when they infiltrated Londheim. She'd tried to pass responsibilities to her son, but her years of experience, experience her son lacked, had often thrust her back into the leadership role. For her to be so broken instilled a fear into Logarius's chest even worse than the fiery devastation had accomplished.

"It's not over yet," he said. "I'm back, and I'm willing to fight. Would you let these wretched humans win?"

Aerreth sheathed one of her daggers and used the free hand to take him by the wrist.

"I thank you for all you have done, and all you have sacrificed, avenria," she said. Her pale yellow eyes watered. "But it is time to accept that war is upon us. When I finish here, I will go to Shinnoc, beg for his forgiveness, and offer him my blades. That short, bloody path is the only one left before my feet. No more ideals. No more hopes for coexistence. I am too old and too tired to keep lying to myself. Look around you, Logarius. Breathe in the ash. Take a long, hard look at the rage the humans possess against that which they do not understand. Was it ever this terrible? Was it ever this grand? I don't know anymore. Perhaps it was, but I am no longer young enough to endure it. Let Shinnoc burn Londheim to the ground, and let us slaughter human men and women until the Goddesses put us back into our prison. That is the only future I am certain of. It is the only fate worth my daggers."

Logarius wished to argue, but he could see the certainty in the foxkin's eyes. His words had a better chance of moving mountains than her heart.

"Shinnoc would be a fool to deny you," he said, and he clucked in muted laughter. "Go on then, Aerreth, and I wish you well. I shall remain, for now. I have much to dwell on."

Aerreth patted his arm, then continued on. Her footfalls skirted about the indention where water had once flowed to all the houses of Belvua. It was dry now, yet another barren reminder of the damage humanity would inflict upon the world in its ignorant rage. Logarius waited until she was gone, then resumed his walk. Four hours later, he had observed every destroyed building of Belvua, and not once did he encounter another living member of the dragon-sired.

At least the privacy gave him time to think, and to weep. Belvua, his greatest creation, destroyed in a single night. He'd watched the fires spread from his window as he spent hours violently thrashing his ankle against the chain, steadily cutting a bleeding groove deep enough to slip his wings through so he might enact their magic. By the time he escaped, the battle was nearly over, and much of Belvua aflame. Could he have prevented this if his mother had not imprisoned him? His pride said yes. The blasted ruins said otherwise.

Ever since Belvua's creation, human guards had patrolled the two entrances to the district, yet when Logarius approached the southern exit, he saw it unguarded. Were the humans so confident in the destruction they had wrought? Logarius strode through with his beak held high. Damn them. Damn them all.

A fluttering scrap of paper gave him pause. It wasn't much, hardly bigger than his thumb, but it was pinned underneath a stone just shy of the district entrance and his keen eyes spotted it immediately. Logarius usually had to send in a disguised foxkin or one of the smaller dragon-sired to sneak over to the spot, but the district entrance was quiet and empty, with hardly a human soul in sight. He retrieved the piece of paper and glanced it over.

Just a few numbers in a rushed script, but the meaning was clear.

The human Ravencallers were requesting a meeting, and they'd signified when and where with those numbers. Logarius crumpled the scrap of paper in his fist. An hour before midnight, at a posh mansion owned by some human diplomat in the nearby Church District.

"Why not?" he muttered. "What else have I to do with my time?"

When Logarius had spread his Ravencaller faith, he'd done so with careful consideration to his every action. When he arrived at meetings, he did so with dramatic entrances through ceilings and floors. He cloaked his body in shadow and smoke, and he relied on his intimidating presence to unnerve and frighten the human populace. It made him seem like an ancient monster of old, which was not far from the truth. But he conveyed power, and certainty, so that when he questioned their Goddesses, they were willing to listen and believe.

Now, though, as he lay across the rafters of the attic and listened to the murmurs, he cared not for any such considerations. He felt too tired and weak. His wings flattened below him, granting him passage, and he landed with a flutter in the center of the grand hall. Two dozen men and women quickly halted their scattered conversations and turned his way. They were affluent, most of them, drinking from sparkling glasses and wearing expensive suits and dresses underneath their dark robes. He'd targeted the wealthy and powerful when forming his little cult, and he'd found them all too eager to betray their fellow humans for even more wealth and power. Humans were gluttons, Logarius decided. It didn't matter if it was food, or influence, or lust. They wanted it all, and more, no matter how disgusting it made them in the end.

"Logarius!" a woman called out, and several others quickly

joined in. They used to call his name with such reverence, but not this time. They were afraid, all of them. The stench of it sickened his already weak stomach. He had landed atop a long dining table, and he kicked a little tray of sandwiches aside.

"Where were you?" shouted others.

"Betrayal cut my flesh deep," he told them. "And it took time to heal from such wounds. I am here now. I saw your message, and so I have come."

"I knew he would," a man told his husband. "Didn't I say he would?"

A chubby man beside him tried, and failed, to hush him. Logarius turned their way, and he pulled his hood back from his face.

"I am here," the avenria said. "Though reason dictates otherwise. You should have come to me. You should have seen the riots and the fires of Belvua and put a stop to it. Do you think I am ignorant of your names? Your identities? With your wealth, your power, you could have intervened. Yet Belvua still burned. Why, my children? Why did you fail to live up to the promise of the Ravencallers?"

The aura of the room shifted instantly. Whatever relief these humans had felt at his arrival quickly turned to dread.

"Logarius, please, you must understand," an older woman in her sixties or seventies said. Absurdly, she wore a bird mask over her face, as if it would hide her identity from anyone there. "Once the desire for rioting gets in the common folk's blood, there's naught anyone can do to stop it. It's best to let it play out until it is out of their system."

"Play out?" Logarius asked. The words slid off his break with the scraping of a whetstone on steel. "Do you hear yourselves, Ravencallers? Belvua is ash. My people are dead or gone. There is no recovering from this. There is no overcoming. You left the dragon-sired for dead, and so they died, and now you seek comfort from me?"

It seemed all their tongues were tied. Logarius swept his wings to his left, shoving a tray of twenty wineglasses shattering to the floor.

"Everything I built is in ruins!" he screamed at them. His wings swept the other way, flinging peeled apple slices and the accompanying caramel bowl into the thick of the crowd. "Everything I have done has achieved nothing!"

Horrid pain spiked from the wound in his side. Logarius ground his break together and fought against the debilitating waves. Silence followed. The Ravencallers clung to one another, fearful, uncertain. It sickened him.

"Please, forgive us our inaction," a much younger woman said. She wore a blue dress and a necklace of raven feathers. The dark color of the feathers matched her short, cropped hair. "We're ready to do our part, but for that, we need your wisdom. The army of dragon-sired remains at our gates. This is what you prepared us for, isn't it? What you preached about?"

"Will we be safe?" someone shouted over her.

"Will they leave us be?" a third person echoed in agreement.

Logarius closed his eyes. He felt keenly aware of the beat of his heart, and the steady pulse of blood through his veins. With each beat, a little jolt of pain would radiate outward from his healing wound. The same for his every inhalation and exhalation. Constant reminders of his mother's betrayal, but he at least understood her decisions. He had crossed lines she could never forgive, and dabbled with the presence of the void. But these wretched humans?

"I have lost friends," he whispered. He didn't even know if they could hear him. Did it even matter if they could? "I have lost family. I have seen the home of my people destroyed, and yet when I come here, do you weep for them? Do you feel sorrow for the loss? No, you don't. You care not for others. You care not for the death you could have stopped, nor the lives you could have improved."

His wings flared wide to either side of him. He drew the long, curved dagger he'd stolen from his mother's home.

"And so I care not," he seethed. "Belvua's fate shall be your own."

He tore through them in seconds, unafraid of their curses, their whimpering shouts, and their frantic hand movements. They were not soldiers. Most had never taken a life, at least, not with their own hands. Logarius cut open their bodies. He slashed his hardened claws across their throats. His wings flapped, propelling him from wall to wall, and he took a life with each and every beat. The screams gave him no joy. The blood sated no appetite within him.

When they were all dead or dying, Logarius knelt amid the bodies, his wings curled about his shoulders and his claws carving grooves into the wood floor. Tears flowed down the sides of his beak to drip, drip, drip upon the blood-covered wood.

"Did you know it would come to this, Mother?" he asked the quiet hall, whose silence was broken only by the gagging and sobbing of the dying. "Did you know all my efforts would be for naught?"

If only she had stabbed his heart instead, and done it the moment he first set foot and wing into this wretched city of Londheim, and all its worthless riches and glory. His tears mixed with the blood of his victims. He looked at the bodies and saw the only future left for him.

"Will you grant me a place in your army, Shinnoc?" he wondered aloud. "The slaughter of humans is all I have left to offer, but I will do so with such joy and excess the Cradle has never seen."

CHAPTER 28

Logarius's black wings granted him passage through the outer wall, and under cover of night he made his way to the army encamped before the city of Londheim. At first he feared patrols, but it seemed the humans held no desire to step outside the safety of their walls now that an army awaited them. Still, he kept his head down and his wings spread wide about his body like a cape to darken his form. Just because no humans kept watch didn't mean the same could be said for the various factions of dragon-sired.

Twice Logarius caught sight of a lurking lapinkin hovering high in the sky with his or her spear at the ready. If they noticed his approach, they did not fear it, for he arrived at the outer edges of the camp undeterred. Once within the lights of their campfires, he walked with his head held high, careful to hide his limp with his gait. The last thing he wanted was to appear weak.

"My name is Logarius," he told the first guard to stop him, a deep green viridi holding a spear in her grasslike arms. "I come to speak with King Shinnoc."

After a bit of debate with additional guards who came running, the viridi agreed to lead the way. The guards whispered heavily among themselves, and multiple times he caught them stealing glances. He caught more stares as he walked through their neat rows of tents. So it seemed his reputation preceded him. No avenria appeared to be among their number, which surprised him. He'd thought that after the destruction of Belvua, most of the Forgotten Children would flee outside the city to join Shinnoc in seeking revenge. Hadn't Aerreth professed a similar plan?

The center of the camp housed the deceptively simple tent that was Shinnoc's command. Deceptive, for he could sense the dream-magic sparkling throughout its every fold. Two towering dyrandar stood watch, great axes held comfortably in their mighty grips. They glared at Logarius but said nothing, only parted so he might enter.

When I finish here, I will go to Shinnoc, beg for his forgiveness, and offer him my blades, Aerreth had told him. Logarius planned a similar approach. Shinnoc might still bear resentment for his father's death, but he was also a King for his people, and the chosen leader for the united dragon-sired army. He would have to think beyond his feelings. He would have to accept the potential benefits of having an avenria with his skills at his side. Besides, it wasn't as if Logarius had held the killing blade himself. He'd merely given the order, and had it not been the right choice? Who could look at Belvua's ruins and believe any peace Cannac achieved would have lasted?

All that logic and belief faded the moment Logarius stepped into that tent and the Dyrandar King rose from his stone dais.

"You would dare show your face here?" Shinnoc roared. He lifted the tremendous two-handed sword that leaned against his throne and flung its leather sheath aside. "If you come to beg for your life, then do so with dignity. Drop to your knees, and offer me your head."

"I come to offer my services, not my head," Logarius said, though he did drop to one knee to show the Dyrandar King respect. "Last night humanity committed a greater crime against us than ever before in their wretched history. They must pay."

"You would murder my father, then come to me offering your services, as if I would ever accept them?"

Two dyrandar behind him at the entrance, a collection of viridi, foxkin, and lapinkin inside, and then of course the King himself with his enormous two-handed sword—all of them looked ready to rip open his stomach and force-feed him his innards. The magnitude of Logarius's misjudgment settled over him like a dragon's claw.

"Everything I did, I did to grant us a home," he said as the dyrandar closed the distance between them.

"Your home is in ruins," Shinnoc seethed. "And your ruins cost me my father."

Logarius's dagger would mean nothing compared to the power and weight of the dyrandar's sword, but he drew it anyway and crouched low. His wings wrapped about his body, hiding his positioning. He needed whatever advantage he could get. Others readied their weapons, but they kept back, granting the King his space. They all knew that Logarius's death must be at Shinnoc's hands. To steal the pleasure would risk invoking his wrath.

"Your father would have betrayed us all," Logarius said. There was no point in holding his tongue. He could not make Shinnoc any angrier than he already was. "The peace he sought was nothing but appeasement. Londheim, *all* of Londheim, should have been ours. And if your army hadn't abandoned us, we'd have had it. Who are you to condemn me for ordering the death of one dyrandar, after your pronouncement last night led to the deaths of hundreds?"

"You and your Forgotten Children plotted and schemed for war, and so I demanded your honorless wretches to fight it with your own strength, and with your own blood. Do you think I am unaware of your machinations? That I was oblivious to your reliance on my united forces to keep Belvua safe? You sought to use me, then when I refuse to play along, you lash out for your own misjudgment and failures."

Shinnoc slammed his sword to the ground, and it seemed like all the world shook with its impact.

"You fools bleed and die for a city while I seek a nation!" his deep voice rumbled. "As did my father, you damn fool avenria. Cannac *was* willing to wage war. It was not a betrayal that he sought peace first. It was kindness. In return, you had his throat slit and his body tossed to the barbaric humans. I give you nothing, Logarius. Whatever legacy you sought, let it be ash. Whatever home you carved, may it be rubble and bone. Your avenria are dead to me, as are all your misbegotten 'children.' Fall to your knees and present me your head. Die with honor, the first and last you shall ever know."

Even now, Shinnoc was trying to be noble and honorable. There was so much of his father in him. Far too fucking much.

"Piss on your honor," Logarius said. "I will live instead."

The two dyrandar guarding the entrance grabbed for his arms, having attempted and failed to sneak up on him while their King ranted. Logarius pretended not to have noticed until the moment they made their move. He twisted while dropping to his knees. Shinnoc's wide, overhead swing halted for fear of hitting his own men, and in that half-second reprieve, Logarius flooded his wings beneath his feet so that he sank into the very soil itself. The sword resumed its fall, but it hit only air before crashing into the barren dirt an inch to the side of his head.

The moment the sword hit, Logarius forced every muscle of his body to act in concert. He kicked with his legs, flapped with his wings, and shoved himself upward with his hands, which emerged from the soil. In one smooth motion he shot into the air while rotating his body like a dancer. His dagger carved a slanted line from hip to shoulder across the Dyrandar King's flesh. Blood flowed, the mighty King bellowed in pain, and in that chaos Logarius slipped between the two guards and out of the tent.

Chaos was his only friend now. Logarius sprinted toward Londheim while weaving between tents and campfires. Blood spilled across his waist as his wounds reopened from his sprint, but he dared not slow down. Shouts trailed behind him, but so far the soldiers of the army were unaware of what transpired. None yet moved to stop him, but that would change soon. He could outrun most, but not the owls and the lapinkin once they took to the air. He needed distance. He need space so he might hide.

Once in the field beyond the army, he spread his wings and fell into the earth. He passed through the rock and dirt as if it were water, and he a swimmer holding his breath. Everything above became dark and irrelevant. The avenria pushed onward until his lungs ached and his body felt loose and strange. Only then would he emerge aboveground, gasp fresh air into his lungs, and then drop below once more. Twice he was spotted, but from afar, and his wings had already pulled him back underground before the chasing lapinkin could make their dive.

Logarius had never considered Londheim safe, but compared to the outside, its walls were a blessing.

Logarius's limp was more pronounced than ever as he aimlessly wandered the broken streets of Belvua. It was quiet now, so very quiet. Only the occasional rat or roach called the district home. The fires had consumed all. Logarius limped and stared, lost in his imagination. He saw the homes as they had once been, pristine and unique, a collection of styles and architecture belonging to the many races that had formed Belvua. He saw the district as he wished it to be, so similar to what it had been in his younger days. Homes filled with families and friends of all races. It never would have happened through peace and negotiation; he firmly believed that. The humans never would have given up their land, their buildings, their homes. It had to be taken by force. It had to be taken through violence.

Because otherwise he was the monster Shinnoc claimed him to be.

"You've reopened your wounds."

Logarius paused in the center of the ash-buried street. He did not turn to look at his mother perched upon a half-collapsed ruin of wood and stone.

"They never healed."

"Not from a lack of trying."

Evelyn landed before him with a flutter of her dark wings. Whisper and Song shimmered in her grasp. Her hood was up and over her face, hiding much of her expression, but he could hear the frustration in her voice clear as a spring day.

"I've been tracking you since you escaped," she said. "It didn't take you long to fall back into old habits, did it?"

"I'm not returning to your care," Logarius said. He readied his own dagger and lowered into a stance. "I won't be your prisoner, nor will I be your caged little pet."

"Oh, I know," Evelyn said. "I found that gathering of your Ravencallers, what was left of them anyway. Why murder them? They worshipped you. They did everything you asked of them, betrayed their own kind for the power you offered, and in return you butchered them down to a man. Why, my son? Why do you know only cruelty and betrayal?"

"I won't listen to this," he said, and he lifted his dagger. "Is this what you want? A continuation of the beating I gave you at the cathedral?"

"How little you know me, my son. None of this is what I want."

Logarius had heard enough. He dashed at her, his dagger cutting toward her neck. He might be injured, but his blood was pumping through his every limb, and his mind was lit with rage. He hacked and stabbed at his mother, who defended with the weapons that should rightfully be his. Whisper-Song, the symbols of leadership of the avenria. But were there even avenria left to lead? How many of his brethren had survived the slaughter of Belvua? How many had lived through that damned dark night of fire and ash?

Evelyn parried his next set of thrusts, and she surprised him by closing the distance between them instead of falling back to take better advantage of her weapons' longer reach. Her elbow caught his beak. In return he kneed her in the groin. Their weapons interlocked, blades and hilts trapped so their sharpened edges could only press against feather but could not cut. Logarius tried to pour his strength into the clash. She was old. She was broken. He was stronger, his convictions hotter, but he watched with detached horror as his dagger was slowly pushed aside.

"Damn, stubborn fool," said his mother.

Her boot slammed into his stomach. Whisper's hilt cracked across his beak. When he stumbled, she kicked directly into the wound she'd opened two weeks before. What had been a minor tear became a horrid spike of pain as the stitches broke and the skin ripped open. Logarius screamed, and despite his determined attempts, he could not force his body to obey.

"I don't want to fight you," she said. The swift crack of her boot into his mouth seemed to contradict that. "I'm not here to take you home. Don't you get it, Logarius? I'm *done* with you."

Another kick to the stomach rolled him onto his back. He gasped for air as he lay atop his wings. Evelyn stood over him, blue flame roaring to life across the edges of Whisper and Song. He thought to sink into the earth to hide, but his mother would just chase him, so instead he glared up at her and fought for breath. So long as he had his dagger, there was a chance—

Whisper hacked off his left hand at the wrist. Song took his right.

Logarius howled as he clutched his arms to his chest. No blood flowed from them, for the heat of the enchanted weapons had sealed the flesh the moment of the cut. Shock blanked his mind. He didn't understand. How could she do this to him? How could she?

Evelyn buckled her weapons, crouched to her knees, and

grabbed his beak in her gloved hand. Her firm grasp forced him to look her way, and he fought to keep his glare strong despite the tears swelling in his eyes.

"You'd betray everyone," she said. "You betrayed the humans who swore you their lives. You betrayed the Forgotten Children who looked to you for leadership. You even betrayed your fellow dragon-sired by taking the life of Cannac, the Dyrandar King, perhaps the wisest and kindest to ever walk the Cradle. Death should have taken you a hundred times over, and yet you learn nothing. Your hatred only grows."

She released him and rose to her full height. A shudder ran through her wings.

"I wash my hands of you, my son. I have tried to heal you in both mind and body, but it is beyond my meager abilities. My heart cannot continue. You're on your own. Perhaps without your ability to kill, you will find another reason to live in this wretched world our Goddesses and dragons created."

"Don't do this," he groaned. With a flex of his wings he pushed himself up to his knees and glared at his mother. "Don't you dare leave me! Put a sickle through my skull. Tear my throat out with Whisper-Song. Anything but this!"

Tears flowed down his mother's beak, but none of that sorrow or sadness dared touch the cold iron that was her voice.

"Find a life, Logarius. One without me."

Logarius staggered to his feet, his stumps clutched to his stomach.

"I have nothing!" he screamed at her. "Where shall I find a home? Human, dragon-sired, even my own flesh and feathers; I bear all their hate. End this, damn it. End it!"

He'd thought his pride greater than this, but he was wrong. Here he was, pleading for his own execution, but he could not bear any other fate. How could she subject him to such cruelty? How could she abandon him so? Yet she did not turn when she sprinted several hundred feet and then vaulted to the top of a half-collapsed home made of stone. Her wings spread, she jumped again, and then the wind and her wings carried her beyond his sight. He did not chase. He did not have the strength to walk, let alone run. Instead he trembled, and watched, and let his tears fall.

"This is how you would have my life end," he whispered. Here, in the wreckage of Belvua. The ashen reminder of how pitiful his legacy would be. Alone, abandoned, forgotten.

This need not be your legacy, a cold voice whispered into his mind. *If you still bear the rage to fight.*

That voice. That icy, hollow speech. He recognized it, even as he feared it. How could it speak to him here, in the light of the stars meant to keep it at bay?

"My rage burns unceasing," he said aloud, his tear-streaked eyes focused on the charred stumps of his wrists.

Then come to me and prove it.

The voice did not tell him where or how, but he knew. Logarius closed his eyes and focused his mind on the realms beyond the physical. It was hard, at first, given his pain and anguish. Detecting the void's presence required calm concentration. After a time his troubled mind settled, and he felt its presence as clearly as he might hear a distant ringing bell. It was the presence of discordant wrongness, of a thing never meant to touch the surface of the Cradle. Below him, and not far. His wings sank to the ground as if becoming liquid, granting him passage.

Before he led the attack on the cathedral, Logarius had mapped out the entire infrastructure of the machinery the dragons had painstakingly built to deliver the power of the Sisters into the frail flesh of a mortal human. Nine smaller chambers formed a star about the central chamber. These smaller segments contained wells that collected the funneled power of the stars drawn out from untold miles away with magic beyond even his understanding. The power flowed to the center like blood through veins to the heart. From that enormous cavern of steel and bone, the laws of all reality were bent to suit the dragons' purpose. Doing so carried a tremendous risk, however, for by draining power from the stars, they weakened their protection and left the walls of their world thin and brittle.

And with the stars weakened, and the walls thinned, the void could pierce through.

Logarius's body emerged from the black chasm opened by his wings and fell the few feet from the ceiling into one of the nine smaller chambers, this the one located directly beneath Belvua. The wrongness of it all was immediately apparent. The stars lining the curving wall were dramatically dimmed, with half having burned out altogether. Light pooled into the well, and a singular crystal hovered just inside its three-triangle construction, but it, too, felt askew, as if the world were underwater. The reason was the thin, wriggling tear in reality just to the side of the well. It was almost like having a hair lodged in your eye, just barely perceptible, and it seemed neither large nor deep. Appearances were deceiving. From within that tear lurked the infinite void, always churning, always hungry.

You come, said a voice from within that tear. *Crippled and broken, you come. In pain and despair, you come. Perhaps you are worthy.*

"Worthy of what?" he asked. The rational part of his mind knew speaking with the void was madness. The reason for the avenria's existence was to destroy all hints of its presence from the Cradle. He betrayed his maker, his very purpose, in conversing with it. Yet he had already betrayed human and dragon-sired alike. What did it matter if he blasphemed the dragons and Goddesses?

Of my gift.

Such a simple statement, but it sent a shiver through Logarius's tired body.

"Why should I want your gift?" he asked that wriggling scar on reality. "And what gift could you even offer? You would destroy all of creation if allowed."

We do not seek destruction. We seek correction. *We seek to unmake a terrible wrong.*

Logarius stepped closer. He could feel emotions leaking out of the tear, feel them as tangible as water upon his feathers. One emotion dominated all others: hatred.

"Why do you hate us so?" he asked. "What crime did we commit? What terrible wrong would you correct?"

Six tendrils ripped through the tear to latch on to his face, neck, and beak. They lacked all texture, surface, or weight. They were the absence of matter, of purpose, of existence itself. He felt the shockingly cold tendrils burn through his feathers to sink into his flesh. Hooks of it prodded at his eyes, locking them open. Little creeping pieces wormed into his ears.

Empty your mind, and you will see.

Logarius knew emptiness. He need not close his eyes to bathe in its darkness, for there was no light for his eyelids to protect against. Perhaps he did not possess eyes at all. These were not things Logarius pondered over, more like distant observations made a frightening many years later. In that present, in that locked memory and space of time, there was only contentedness. He felt no other emotion. No joy, no anger, no sorrow or fear or curiosity. Content. Infinite, warm, smothering content.

And then the Sisters came. Their light split the infinite expanse of dark. The perfect order of emptiness was broken, and oh, how badly did they break it. They descended upon a barren rock and sprouted it with what they declared "life." They gave it a sun to warm it and bathe it with light, and they gave it a moon to reflect that sunlight even in their darkest of hours so they might never be truly alone. These Sisters, they were but a little puddle flung off from the great river that was the Aether. The Aether, and its cosmic flow of power and light, had existed in a place the void never knew. It was, in so many ways, the exact opposite of the void. From that Aether, and that realm never meant to touch the void, these Sisters tore free a piece, declared it the First Soul, and brought it down to the wretched, chaotic creatures they called their children.

It was with dawning horror that Logarius realized the greatest crime committed by the Sisters' trespassing. The Goddesses did not create the void, for the void always was. They did not harm it, for it could not be harmed, only kept at bay. But they gave it the one thing it never wanted. The void was emptiness. It was always meant to be emptiness. Yet by being everything the void was not, by forcing the void to become the antithesis of their light, the Sisters had inflicted upon it a gaping wound that had forced its hatred for untold centuries.

Sentience.

The tendrils withdrew. Logarius dropped to his knees and vomited. The emptying of his stomach did little to ease away the horrid presence of the void. Neither did it extinguish the lingering emotions he'd felt. The rage. The agony. The inescapable need to return to nothing, to bring about an end to awareness and sentience within a being that knew no other need, no other desire, a being that felt not the touch of time nor possessed the ability to create.

Do you now understand? asked the voice within the scar. *The reason for our hatred is not hollow. It is not unreasonable. Within our very bosom beats a heart of light that tears into us with every pulse. The Cradle is a wound that cannot heal. Not until its souls are gone. Not until its light is extinguished. Not until its Goddesses are dead.*

Logarius felt his strength slowly returning. He staggered unevenly to his feet and glared at the wriggling tear.

"What do you want of me?" he asked.

Be our champion. End the Goddesses. Extinguish the light.

Logarius closed his eyes, and he let the last of his tears fall. Human. Dragon-sired. They had all turned against him. They had denied him his legacy. They'd choked the life from his daughter and stolen the love of his mother. Now he stood crippled, unwanted, denied even the ability to kill. No future awaited him. No moments of happiness or joy. Only hatred. Only anger.

"Do it," he whispered.

Six more tendrils emerged, followed by another six, linking and merging together to withstand the pale light of the stars that ringed the chamber. They stabbed into his flesh. They wrapped about the stumps of his wrists, punched into his eyes, and seeped into his every feather. A distant scream sounded in his ears, filled with indescribable agony and abandonment, and it lasted so very long before he realized the scream was his, the horror and pain, all his, forever his.

The void gave of itself to shift and mold its champion, and all the while his only act of gratitude for the power pouring into him, power so vast it could break the world, was to scream, and scream, and scream.

CHAPTER 29

"I will be gone for only a little while," Adria said, and she lifted her porcelain mask halfway up her face so she might gently kiss Tamerlane's broad cheek. "Remain here until my return."

Tamerlane bowed low, then crossed his arms and leaned against the broken rubble of the wall that had surrounded Belvua. The hole in the defenses was a terrible risk given the army of dragon-sired camped outside, yet no city guards or Westreach soldiers were stationed there. The High Elected had instead chosen to seal off the district's two entrances farther inside the city. Not that it mattered either way. Should war come, the walls would mean little to the magical gifts of the dragon-sired.

Adria passed through the collapsed segment of the wall, carefully judging each step before putting her weight down. Once safely over the collection of stone, brick, and mortar, she settled into a calm gait alongside the Septen River and followed its travel southward. Her destination was clear despite not once being told of Janus's location. As much as it frightened her, she knew her power was growing. With her every prayer, she drew in strength from nearby souls, much gentler and more expertly done than when she first healed the sick and weary. Tiny sips, causing little harm or notice. And with her increasing awareness to the world of souls, so, too, did her awareness grow of those who stood out among it like black shadows cast upon white canvases.

Janus sat with his back to her beside the river, his legs tucked underneath him and his hands held out to either side with his palms upward to catch the falling snow.

"I see hiding from you would be pointless," he said without turning.

"For what reason would you hide?"

The avatar of change lowered his hands, and he grinned at her when she sat opposite of him in the snow.

"Sometimes we all need solitude. I would expect you of all humans to understand."

"Why not cross the river then?" she asked.

"I do cross it sometimes, but those flood lands are dull and empty during winter. The merfolk used to build sprawling compounds among them out of mud and rock, but it seems they chose to flee downstream rather than stay here. Not that I blame them. If there is one place humanity cannot chase, it is the deep waters of the ocean."

"Merfolk?" Adria asked, and she looked to the river. "As in mermaids, like our stories?"

"I'd wager most of your stories are of us in some shape or form," Janus said, and he shared with her an honest smile. "Tell me, these 'mermaids' as you call them, what do they look like?"

"Humans, mostly, but with fish tails instead of legs. Supposedly they could sing wondrous songs to entrance mortal minds. Some tales have them mating with pirates, others devouring them with their sharp teeth."

Janus laughed. The sound of it warmed Adria's insides.

"Ah, humanity, so reliably simple," he said. "A creature different than you? Then surely it seeks to either eat you or fuck you. Did the Sisters strip you of all concepts of subtlety? Or is the moralization they drill into your skills so painfully simple, you cannot comprehend any shade of gray between black and white?"

"I did not come here to listen to you insult my people."

"When one meets with me, it should always be assumed."

Adria couldn't help herself. She laughed at his wolfish smile, and his twinkling emerald eyes.

"Very well," she said. "I'll keep that in mind."

Janus reached to the pale grass between them and stirred it with his fingers like he would a bubbling pot. The grass and dirt formed into perfectly matching sticks in a cross-stacked pattern. When finished, he snapped his fingers, setting the fire alight. Adria leaned closer, thankful for the warmth.

"So tell me, Chainbreaker, why have you come? It surely wasn't to listen to my sparkling wit. And you come in the daytime, no less. This must be important."

"Important indeed," she said. Her gaze settled on the fire. It was easy to fall into those flames. So much easier than to look Janus in the eye as she spoke. "I've made my decision. I will embrace who and what I am. Now I must learn if the Sisters will *allow* me to become what the dragons are hoping I would become."

"The Sisters, embrace a Chainbreaker?" Janus laughed. "Why would they ever allow you to supplant them?"

"Not supplant them," she corrected. "Merely coexist alongside them. I will perform miracles, and I will accomplish what they refuse to fix. Tonight, I will draw down souls for the soulless from the cosmic Aether and deliver them to their intended vessels."

"You did this once before, and Lyra stopped you. What would be different this time?"

"She ordered me to stop, and I listened. This time I won't. Either she accepts my abilities, or she uses her power to intervene. Either way, her actions will speak far louder than any words."

"I suppose, but perhaps she decides a few soulless gaining souls isn't worth the risk?"

Adria grinned at him.

"You misunderstand me. I don't mean only a few soulless, or even those who live in Londheim. All soulless, Janus. I will pull from the heavens the proper soul for every single soulless across the entire Cradle."

It was not often she saw Janus surprised, and the sight of his pleasure at her boldness again put a bit of warmth in her belly that she very much disliked.

"You wonderful madwoman," he said, his smile showing off his opal teeth. "Do you think you can pull off such a feat?"

"Now is not the time for doubt," she said, and she pointed a finger his way. "If the Sisters let me correct their failure, then it means they accept me as a new force upon the Cradle. If this happens, I will not betray my Goddesses. They will still have my love, and my faith. But if Lyra appears to stop me, then I will rely on you to keep your promise."

She stared deeper into that geometrically perfect fire.

"Can you truly do it, Janus? Can you kill a Goddess?"

A loud clap brought her attention up from the flame. Janus's hands, one of metal, one of deep brown bark, clasped together excitedly. His grin was practically ear to ear.

"I don't know, Adria, but I'm eager to find out. When will you do this?"

"Tonight," she said as she rose to her feet and brushed off snow that clung to the thick wool leggings underneath her coat and dress. "I have other matters to settle first involving both family and church that will take up my time today. Besides, is there any proper time for a miracle than during the reaping hour?"

"Perhaps not. And where will you perform this miracle?"

Adria grinned behind her mask.

"I found you," she said. "And I suspect no matter where I go, you shall always find me."

Another flash of opal teeth.

"You are a blinding beacon within Londheim," he said. "Do as you must. I will be ready."

Adria returned to the city, and to Tamerlane waiting impatiently at the wall.

"To the church now?" he asked her as she carefully climbed over the rubble.

"Not yet," she said. "We have one other stop first."

Adria knocked twice on the door to her brother's home, then announced her presence with raised voice.

"It's unlocked," came the muffled reply from within. Adria squeezed Tamerlane's hand and then entered. Tamerlane remained outside, for this conversation was likely to be highly charged, and however little it might help, she would keep the discussion solely between family.

The atmosphere within that home was colder than it'd ever been. Veritable waves of ice wafted off Jacaranda. No need to touch her soul to sense that. Adria tried her best not to feel offended. Janus had shared similar frustrations. Everyone expected so much of her, and until she accepted that responsibility, they would all resent her. That was part of why she wanted to tell Devin and Jacaranda her plan. However slowly, she was finally taking up the mantle forced upon her.

"I'm glad you're both here," she said as she shook a bit of snow off her coat. "Might I ask where Wren is?"

"I don't know," Jacaranda said after exchanging a glance with Devin. "I haven't seen her since Belvua burned."

"Such a shame. I believe she'd appreciate what I have to say."

Adria removed her porcelain mask, which was like a sheet of ice across her face, and slowly turned it in her gloved hands.

"Tonight, I will make right a terrible wrong," she said. "Despite the Sisters' protestations, I will bring down souls for the soulless of the Cradle, and not just here in Londheim, or even Westreach. Every soulless in all the Cradle. This shameful scourge will be erased, no matter the chaos and trauma that will follow. Let the east and its factories crumble if they must. If I am to possess this power, then I shall use it for humanity's betterment, and this is the most obvious wrong that I might correct."

The two of them stared at her in subdued shock. Adria bit her lower lip and glanced at her mask, unable to meet their gazes. If she kept her focus upon them, she'd see the emotions swirling through their souls like bright mist, and already it was too much. They disbelieved she could do it. They feared for her. They were afraid *of* her.

"The entire Cradle," Jacaranda said. "Is that within your power?"

"I believe it is," she said, annoyed that Jacaranda echoed a similar sentiment to Janus.

"I'm not worried if you can," Devin said, and he stood from his chair. "I'm worried if you should. Remember what Lyra told me? She feared you would tear the boundaries of this world and release the void upon the Cradle. What if this plan of yours is how that happens? What if it's too much, and it's not just souls you summon?"

"I can do this," Adria said through clenched teeth. "I'm strong enough to do anything my mind desires, and this is what I desire. It's the one course before me I know is just. The soulless were never meant to be denied their souls. Tonight I fix that error."

"Even over Lyra's objection?" asked her brother.

Can you truly do it, Janus? Can you kill a Goddess?

"The Goddesses have my love, and they have my faith," she said. "But they do not have my enslavement. The paths we walk are still our own. If the Sisters wanted slavering obedience, then they shouldn't have given us souls in the first place."

Another worried glance between the two. Did they not realize she could see their wordless communications?

"Is that why you wanted to speak with Wren?" Jacaranda asked. "To tell her this?"

"After my previous failure, it seemed right that she know and be there."

"It wasn't a failure," Devin insisted. His hands clenched into fists. He was so frightened. So nervous. Did he truly hold so little faith in her? "Adria, you didn't fail. Lyra stopped you. Stopped all of it. What will you do if she comes to stop you again, sis? What then?"

I don't know, Adria, but I'm eager to find out.

"I won't be stopped," Adria said softly.

"But if Lyra—"

"I won't be stopped." She slid her porcelain mask back on and pulled her coat tighter about her body to prepare for the winter storm outside. "Not by man. Not by dragon. Not by Goddess. I shall summon the power of the stars in the chamber that made me what I am. Attend if you wish, but this is the future I shall make, even if I must do it alone. Once the deed is done, I shall proclaim all former soulless as true citizens of Westreach. The church will take in those who find themselves without home or occupation, just as the Deakon before me should have done."

"The Deakon before you was a monster," Jacaranda said. "Would you become the same?"

"You would compare me to Deakon Sevold?" Adria asked. She put a hand to her breast, honestly wounded. "Tamerlane cursed him for a reason. I would think you would understand that, Jacaranda. In what way am I like that vile man?"

"He did what gave him pleasure, and he used the church to justify it," she said. "You're not there, not yet, but you're close. Do you really care for the soulless, Adria, or are you proving you know better than the Goddesses?"

Of all the people to disagree, Jacaranda had been the one she'd least expected. How could a former soulless be angry that she was to give souls to other soulless? What logic was there in that? What misguided reason? Was she still bitter because of Belvua, or did she share in Devin's trepidation?

"Then it is a good thing Tamerlane will be my Vikar of the

Day," she said. "If he sees me become akin to Sevold, then may he curse me to a similar fate."

Adria stormed out the door to cold white Londheim, and to a surprised Tamerlane.

"Did it not go well?" he asked as she pulled her hood over her head.

"It went as it did," she said, leaving it at that. "It is time for the church to declare me Deakon, and you Vikar."

"Neither Forrest nor Caria seemed eager to allow it," Tamerlane said as he walked beside her. "What will you do if they refuse?"

Goddesses help her, everyone was so frightened of what would happen should she be refused. Why did no one fear the future awaiting them if she did nothing?

"They won't refuse," she said. "They can't."

"They may also believe they can't accept. What then?"

Adria glanced over her shoulder, to the pale-skinned man in a dark coat following her along the rooftops, his half-black, half-green hair dusted with snow.

"Then it comes to bloodshed," she said, and turned away. "Pray they accept."

CHAPTER 30

With every step, it felt like Wren's feet melded with the broad, flat stones. The small space of poorly tended grass and weeds that grew in a secluded corner of Windswept District seemed to stretch on as if for miles. The door was as distant as the sunrise.

Get your act together, she told herself upon pausing halfway there. *You're better now. You're stronger. It's not the same.*

She crossed the remainder of the steps with a sprint, and when she knocked on the door to her former home, it sounded less like a greeting and more as if she were an invading army battering a drawbridge. Her heart danced a crazed beat inside her chest as she heard the floor groan on the other side. An old, creaking voice shouted as door locks rattled.

"I'm coming, I'm coming, Sisters have mercy, you need not break my door down."

Wren crossed her arms over her chest, uncrossed them, put them at her sides, and then slid them completely behind her back. It was ridiculous, how nervous she felt. She was the one in control. She was the one with a long dirk hidden within the folds of her dress.

"Yes?" asked Kennet Sommers as the elderly man thrust open the door and leaned out of it with a nasty crook in his back. His hair was stark white, even his bushy eyebrows and neatly trimmed mustache. Milky blue eyes peered at Wren, and for a brief moment she feared recognition in them. That fear dimmed, but didn't leave completely, when he pursed his lips and looked ready to spit. "Do I know you?"

"Not me, no," she said. Though she didn't try often, she made sure to adjust her voice to a higher pitch. Her voice was most likely to identify her, to betray her. "But I am a friend of your grandson. I was hoping I could speak with you about him?"

Kennet squinted at her, and he chewed on nothing as he thought.

"All right, come on in," he said. "You better not be teasing an old man, though. Getting his hopes up for nothing, it'd be a cruel jest, I tell you."

The man Wren had called grandfather for the past seven years of her soulless life turned about and entered his home, not even bothering to hold the door open for her. She caught it just before it slammed shut. Her fingers clutched the wood hard enough to whiten her knuckles. She had to resist the memories. They might belong to her, but they didn't define her. The split, the dichotomy, had to be maintained if she was to remain strong.

"What do you mean by getting your hopes up?" she asked, trying her best to put on an innocent air.

Kennet limped along the narrow hallway, then paused at the first open doorway. The home was small but finely furnished, the lifelong reward of his years as one of the sharpest and most ruthless fur traders west of the Septen River. He was leading her to the living room, to where he'd have a fire absolutely roaring regardless of how hot the home might be. Wren lingered as she followed. Paintings covered the hall, some of them stunning in their detail. Many were of Kennet and his deceased wife, Corella. Others were of his only son, Samuel, a charming-looking chubby fellow with a smile that lit up his paintings. Even the fading of age and a covering of dust could not dim that smile.

Wren paused before the largest painting of Samuel. This was

the man she had grown up being told was her father. She'd never met him, of course, only known this idealized, frozen version of him. Beneath the rows of Samuel paintings were a handful of similar portraits of a young, twelve-year-old Warren. Wren stared at the picture and felt an overwhelming sensation of vertigo wash over her. That painting wasn't even of her, but of the boy she'd been molded to resemble during her soulless state. Yet it unleashed an uncomfortable attachment so awkward, she nearly ripped the painting from the wall so she might tear it to pieces.

"Miss?" Kennet called from the doorway.

"I'm sorry," Wren said, and she tried her best to hide her shiver of revulsion. "I was admiring your paintings."

She smoothed out her dress before sitting in Kennet's offered chair, then checked her newly purchased scarf to ensure it hadn't fallen. Revealing her chain tattoos was another scenario she didn't want to imagine playing out.

"So what is it about my grandson?" Kennet asked, impatient and to the point as ever. "If you're looking for him, you won't find him anywhere, so you can leave if that's why you came."

"You said you didn't want me to get your hopes up," she asked. "What do you mean by that?"

"I mean that the owls got him," he said, and he cast his gaze about as if his eyes were incapable of remaining still. "I mean that's got to be it, right? The whole world goes mad, and my poor little Warren, the last flesh and blood of my son, he goes and vanishes. I've heard the rumors. My eyes may not be the best, but my ears work fine, and I hear the rumors, I hear them. The owls took my grandson. He always liked going out at night, he did, even when I warned him it wouldn't lead to no good. The owls got him. Poor Warren. Poor little man."

Wren clasped her hands together to keep them from shaking. That was decidedly *not* how she had departed this household upon her soul's return. She hadn't left quietly, like a thief in the night.

She'd left screaming, and that'd been after two days of imprisonment in her bedroom. Those long two days and nights, relearning how to walk, to breathe, to eat and dress and make decisions, still haunted her sleep. In those nightmares, she was naked and beating against the door, begging to be let out. From the other side, her grandfather would berate her incessantly.

"Where's my grandson?" he'd screamed. "What'd you do with my grandson!"

When her soul had returned, she had abandoned all her training, her mannerisms, her polite smiles and cute little tics to imitate a twelve-year-old boy despite being nearly nineteen. Kennet's sickly mind no longer saw his deceased grandson but a stranger, and his frightened anger and confusion were terrifying despite his frail body.

"Are you certain the owls took him?" she asked. "What if he ran away?"

"Ran away? Course not. My little Warren was a good boy, a real good boy. He'd never hurt his grandfather like that."

Was he lying? She truly didn't know. Kennet's mind had broken with age. From what she'd pieced together through half-remembered conversations, training sessions with Belford, and talks with Gerag, Kennet's son Samuel and his grandson Warren had died in a bandit raid while riding a raft north from Wardhus to Watne. Kennet had turned reclusive, and angrily insisted to anyone who would listen that Warren wasn't dead, but missing. The idea of using soulless as a replacement grandson had been a plan of his daughter-in-law, who had been busy taking over the fur trade that Kennet could no longer manage due to his deteriorating mind.

Some people bought a kitten or puppy to cheer up their depressed relative. Kennet's daughter-in-law bought a soulless remade into Warren. Equally disturbing was knowing Wren had not been the first replacement, but the second. She'd been delivered when the first soulless had grown too old to maintain the illusion even for Kennet's fading eyes and rotting mind. Wren dreaded the fate of that soulless, who had returned to Gerag Ellington's care. The wealthy of Londheim had sick, perverted tastes. Gerag had most certainly found a use for a twenty-year-old soulless man trained to behave like a twelve-year-old.

"Forgive me," Wren said, and she put on her best smile. "I didn't mean to offend."

She crossed her hands in her lap, her fingers settling over the hidden dirk.

Remember why you're here, Wren. Don't lose your nerve now.

"Well, you're doing your damnedest to offend anyway," Kennet said. He scratched at his ear. "Why are you here again?"

"Because I saw your grandson," she said. "And I—I thought you'd like to know that he's alive and well."

She thought he'd be happy hearing this. Instead he lunged to his feet so swiftly, he had to grab the side of his chair to prevent himself from toppling over.

"You get out of here," he snarled. A bit of saliva clung to his lips. "Get out of here now, you hear me? I won't listen to lies. My grandson ain't out there alive. He'd come home if he were. He wouldn't leave me like this. He needs me. He's a good boy. My good boy. My last, wonderful piece of Samuel on this goddess-forsaken land."

His milky blue eyes were starting to tear up. His free hand pointed a violently shaking finger at her. Yes, this was what she remembered. A volatile old man without a single grasp on reality. Did he remember when Wren had cursed him and fled his home, or had he dismissed it as a particularly dreadful dream? Did it even matter? She drew the dirk free of its hidden pocket and clutched it between her fingers. Kennet's finger wagged in front of her. His hunched form drew nearer.

"You listen here, miss," he said. "You're telling lies, and I won't hear them. I won't!"

He had no idea she held a weapon. It would be easy. So easy. One quick cut across his wrinkled throat and it'd all be over. He deserved it, didn't he? He'd used her, just like all the other people Gerag sold his illegal soulless to for comfort and pleasure. There hadn't been anything sexual in nature, but did it matter? She'd still been used. She'd still been forced to imitate a life that wasn't hers, to play a role for this sick man's happiness.

"Are you even listening to me?" Kennet asked. He stepped closer. His presence filled Wren's entire vision. All she saw was his snow-white hair, his quivering lips, and his glazed-over eyes. She told herself to hate him. She told herself she was justified.

"I said, are you listening... to..." He froze. His head tilted to one side. "Warren? Is that you?"

The question jammed a spike right into Wren's gut. She froze, suddenly uncertain. The dirk felt cold and heavy in her grasp. His milky blue eyes became her whole world.

"My name is Wren," she said with parched tongue and dry throat. The old man's hands flitted about her with a touch as light as a butterfly's landing. He brushed her dress, her scarf, and her hair.

"But you... what did... why are you wearing a dress, my boy?" His shaking fingers slid across her forehead to the roots of her hair, most certainly searching for proof of a wig. But it wasn't a wig, not since her brief encounter with the strange being named Janus. "Your hair, it's so long. You need a trim." He laughed with such relief and joy, it was like a knife to her gut. "A damn big trim, but we'll get you fixed up, yes, we will."

And then he embraced her, still clueless to the dirk. Wren stood there, her feet nailed to the floor. Her mind reeled with waves of emotions she couldn't begin to understand. He'd used her, she told herself, but he'd also loved her. But he'd not loved *her.* He'd loved the boy she pretended to be, the boy she was trained to be, yet he'd loved her nonetheless. And here he was ready to love her again.

"I'm sorry," Wren said. "I can't. I can't. You're just a confused old man."

She didn't even know what she refused. Killing him? Loving him? Both? No matter the reason, she could not endure his presence. This house, this overwhelming reminder of her soulless past, weighed on her in a way she had not anticipated when coming to kill the old man. She'd arrived furious at the world and with a yearning for freedom crawling inside her heart. Ending this figure from her past was meant to free her future, but it would never work. Nothing would come that easy, not to those the Sisters had failed so deeply.

"What are you talking about, my boy?" Kennet asked, and he reached for her hand. It was then, only then, that he saw the dirk.

She didn't wait to see his reaction. Wren shoved the old man aside and ran. His howl of pain and betrayal echoed after her like that of a wild animal. Its sound rattled inside her skull. Its hate bit at her heels as she burst out the door to her home and dashed along the worn cobblestones. It followed, and followed, reminding her of the pain she'd caused, of the damage she'd done to a sick man with a broken mind. Guilt ripped at her, empowered by a thousand memories of his gentle embraces and bedtime stories.

Buildings passed by her unseen. Men and women walking the street gawked at her, but she refused to acknowledge them beyond a check to the scarf hiding her chain tattoos. Those damn tattoos, forever marking her, forever reminding her of what she'd been robbed. At last she could run no more, and she could not stand the leering eyes and questioning frowns. One of the nearby homes had an elevated porch, and she stumbled toward it.

It was a tight fit, but Wren managed to slide underneath. She curled her legs into her chest. She buried her face into her arms. Curses flowed off her tongue in a never-ending torrent. Damn this world. Damn the Sisters. Damn whoever had cursed her to being born soulless. Damn Gerag and Kennet and Adria and every other person in the whole wretched Cradle who was born as they were meant to be born. Not her. Never her. She'd described it best to Jacaranda as she looked upon the mighty dragon's arrival to Londheim. They were born to suffer. The world offered them nothing more lest they take it with blood and broken bones.

"Then take it."

The voice slid over her like melting ice. She'd been certain she was alone. That someone, anyone, could be underneath that porch with her and yet go unnoticed was impossible, yet when she lifted her head, she saw a small child on his hands and knees. Revulsion immediately filled her stomach. The boy's face was perfectly smooth, without eyes, nostrils, or a mouth. His skin was pale like smoke. His clothes were a single black shift made of an impossible dark fabric.

"Who—no, *what* are you?" she asked.

"Am I not what you see before you?" the boy asked. He had no mouth, yet somehow he spoke with a voice that echoed in her ears. It was deep, far too deep for one so young.

"Whatever I see before me is monstrous."

"Then I am a monster. Will you speak with a monster, or must I present you a less monstrous form?"

A face emerged upon that smooth, blank canvas. She recognized it at once, and she thrust her dirk between her and whatever occupied that childlike body. That face. It was Warren's face.

"Will this suffice?" he asked.

"Get away from me before I kill you," she said.

"You cannot kill me as you are." The voice changed with the face, becoming like an actual young boy. Not her own voice, thankfully. Her mind may have broken completely hearing that. "Perhaps you could with the power I offer you, Wren. I merely wonder, are you willing to take it?"

Something was wrong. The porch above her was too high, much too high. It wasn't that the ground was sinking, either, more like the porch was rising. The world was darkening. Whatever this child-thing was, it wielded incredible power over reality itself.

"What do you want with me?" she asked. Despite the creature's mockery, she kept the dirk raised and its point aimed directly at its chest. "Speak plainly."

The face of Warren twisted back into smooth emptiness. The voice that spoke shifted and transitioned between a man's and a woman's, nearly every word like that of a different human being trapped within that childlike body.

"I am Nihil, one of the five dragons of creation, and I come offering you power unimaginable. Is that plain enough, meager human?"

One of the dragons? Not the crawling mountain. Jacaranda had named that one Viciss. Did that mean...

"The cloud dragon," she said. "That's you?"

"That is my physical body, yes."

"How do you know of me, dragon? Why come to me with this, this... unimaginable power?"

The body stepped closer, and it seemed the world darkened by his proximity. No, not "his," she realized. It was wrong to assign a gender to this thing before her. This little body was a mere shell hiding absolute chaos. Every word revealed a new existence trapped within the physical constraints.

"I was there when you met with the avatar you call Janus. I witnessed your hatred of the Sisters and their Keeping Church. My first choice refused me, and so I come to you with the same offer. Power, Wren. Power over souls, of their delivery to the Cradle, and their expulsion to the distant river of Aether."

What it described, she recognized it. Fear deepened inside her gut, but within her despair she felt the first spark of hope in ages.

"Adria," she whispered. "You would make me like Adria."

There was no face to show a reaction, but the way the childlike body tilted its head seemed to convey surprise. Every word shifted in sound, some not even human, but she still understood their meaning.

"The Chainbreaker has failed. A new human must walk the path she rejected. A future without the Sisters. A humanity that lives by their own creed, that fights their own battles, and delivers the essence of eternity by their own hand. Can you walk that path, Wren? Can you tear down the old and build something wondrous and new?"

Could she bear such a burden? Wren thought of the worship Adria received, of the responsibilities laid upon her shoulders. Her first instinct was to refuse, but it did not last long. The memory of the Chainbreaker bowing to the will of the damned Sisters, of returning the souls to the starry sky while charring the soulless bodies to ash, wiped away any shred of her resistance.

"If I have this power, can I fix the failure of the Sisters?" she asked. "Can I deliver to the soulless the souls they were always meant to receive?"

"You can," Nihil said. "You will."

Wren lowered her dirk. She held her head high in a space that defied logic and reason.

"Then tell me what I must do."

CHAPTER 31

Sena read the words of the 5th Devotion again and again despite having them memorized since she was a nine-year-old novice living in the Cathedral of the Sacred Mother.

"Help me, Lyra," she whispered in prayer. "I need your strength now more than ever."

The Faithkeeper sat on the steps of a shuttered tavern, calmly waiting between Adria's home and the mansion that was the newly assigned headquarters of the church leadership. Rumors had reached her ears, rumors she didn't want to believe, but all the city knew them, so what choice did she have? The friend she had worked alongside for years was gone. Whatever Adria had become, be it a Goddess, an abomination, or the Sacred Mother reborn, it was no longer the quiet, humble woman who had buried her face in books when she wasn't administering herbs and bandages to Low Dock's sick and injured.

Sena closed her copy of Lyra's Devotions. Adria approached, traveling alongside a tanned and handsome Mindkeeper she did not recognize, but she could guess. Tamerlane, a relatively unknown man who had somehow wormed his way to Adria's side. Rumors placed him as the next Vikar of the Day, should Adria complete her mad desire to anoint herself as Deakon. Sena brushed snow off her dress and stood.

"Adria!" she called, and she lifted a hand to wave.

Her once-friend turned her way, and though she wore her two-toned mask, Sena could tell she smiled behind it by the light that reached her brown eyes.

"Sena," Adria said, and she hurried her way. "It's good to see you."

They embraced, and there was nothing false about her joy, nothing cold about her greeting. Sena dared hope there was a chance she could still reach her friend.

"I was hoping we might have a moment to speak with one another," Sena said. She had to resist a temptation to glare at Tamerlane, who lurked mere feet away. There was something off-putting about his aura, like he was a sickly man pretending to be a surgeon.

"I'm on my way to speak with Vikar Forest and Vikar Caria," Adria said. The lines about her eyes deepened for a half-second. "But you already know that, don't you?"

Sena nodded. Adria glanced at Tamerlane, who dipped his head and retreated back a few steps.

"Pray tell me you aren't here to change my mind," Adria said softly.

"And if I am?"

"Then I would tell you that you waste your time. In my heart, I know this must be done."

Sena flashed her brightest smile. It was a smile she normally reserved for troublesome patrons of their church who thought themselves much too big for their trousers.

"Do you remember what I said to you when you were first appointed to my church all those years ago?"

"'Welcome to Low Dock,'" Adria repeated. "'Everyone is poor and miserable and never meant to leave. Are you here to help me change that?'"

"And you did help," Sena said. She stepped closer, her voice simultaneously dropping in volume and rising in intensity. "You helped because you were dedicated to every single unfortunate soul born without a silver spoon in their mouth. You bled for the lowest of the low. You worked your fingers to the bone stitching and mending the wounded. In a very dark place, you were a light for those who needed it most. Everything you said and did was the finest example of the work the Sisters call for us to perform."

Sena grabbed her friend by the shoulder. Adria's eyes widened behind her mask but she did not pull away.

"Who do you bleed and die for now, Adria? To who or what have you dedicated your heart? Because it's not the desperate and the destitute. It's not the Sisters and their mercy. You lust for power. You crave authority. It isn't you. It isn't the Adria I know."

Finally the other woman batted her hand aside and stepped away.

"You would have me remain humble?" she asked. "You would cut a giant at the knees to pretend at meekness? I don't lust for power, Sena. I *am* power. And I cannot let fear and doubt prevent me from using it to make the Cradle a better place."

"Even if it means taking the lives of others?"

"This world is cruel. We both know that. There is a reason our Soulkeepers carry pistols and swords."

She could feel her friend slipping away from her. Whatever progress her argument had made, it was faltering.

"If you do this, there will be no going back," Sena insisted. "If you begin your rule with a shower of blood, it will forever stain your name and legacy."

"How many Vikars have blood on their hands?" Adria asked. "How many of them killed rivals or stole from the cities they ruled? History erases the ugliness of our heroes. Our sermons elevate the righteous while diminishing their failures. Let people talk. Let them judge. I care only for the legacy I leave behind from the power I have been given. This is a chance for deep, structural change, of the kind that happens only once a century. Without it, in this world of awakened magic, I fear we cannot survive."

"And to do so, you will become a murderer."

Adria clasped her hands before her, and she let out a long sigh.

"I am already a murderer," she said. "But consider this my promise to you. I will not kill the Vikars, not even if they refuse me. I will bring them low, and force them to acknowledge my authority, but I will not take their lives. My rule as Deakon will not begin with blood. Will that ease your spirit?"

Sena thought of that night Adria had brought life back to the dead, transposing a long-deceased soul into the body of a soulless. It was more than just a thirst for power. There was a fearlessness to her actions, a willingness to walk the realm of the Goddesses themselves. No human should possess that power, yet Adria Eveson did. Could there even be a kind ending to such a blasphemous existence?

"It is a small comfort," she admitted, "but a comfort nonetheless. Keep the Sisters in your heart, Adria. Walk in their footsteps, for their path shall lead us to paradise, while our own leads to ruin and misery."

"Walking the path of the Sisters has never guaranteed paradise," Adria said. "The ruined and miserable filled our church, old men and women who walked faithfully their whole lives and received naught but disrespect from those beyond the confines of Low Dock. I am tired of waiting for eternity for the meek to be made great, and the faithful to be pulled from the wasteland. Great change is coming, my friend, and comes for all."

Tamerlane returned to her side, and together they resumed their walk. Sena watched them go, their conversation repeating itself again and again in her mind. Was there something she could have done or said better? Had she truly reached her friend, or was it all an act? Even being so familiar with the woman, it was still hard to read Adria behind that porcelain mask.

She had to trust her, Sena decided. Trust her to do the right thing, no matter how much she feared otherwise. The Mindkeeper turned to leave, but she managed a single step before she froze in place. A horrifyingly familiar man leaned against the pillar of the front porch beside her, his arms crossed over his bare chest and his black coat fluttering in the soft wind.

"Such delicious irony," Janus said. "You appear more frightened of Adria now than you ever were of me."

"What do you want, monster?" she asked. Had he been there this whole time, listening to their conversation? "Must I blind you with another prayer?"

"I'd rather you not," he said, his grin spreading literally ear to ear, the flesh and bones of his cheeks giving way to allow its growth. "What you did was quite rude, if you ask me."

"I'm sorry I didn't let you kill me," she said. "Perhaps I'll be kinder to you next time."

"There will be no next time. I grew bored of killing meek little Mindkeepers and Faithkeepers. The Chainbreaker has inspired me to aim much, much higher. Why slaughter keepers when one can slay dragons and Goddesses?"

"You jest."

Janus winked at her.

"Time will tell."

Sena turned and ran. The mere sight of that monster shivered her soul. Whatever anxieties she had about this coming meeting amplified tenfold. It wasn't far, but despite the cold, she was still sweating underneath her white suit by the time she reached the steps of the mansion the Vikars had begun using as a replacement headquarters while the cathedral was rebuilt. Two novices armed with clubs moved to block her, but she flashed them her palm while whispering the words of the 17th Devotion.

"I mean no harm," she said as they staggered backward while clutching their blinded eyes. "But I must bear witness to this changing of power with my own eyes."

Sena flung the doors open and dashed down the carpet to the

grand dining room, which had been converted into a meeting hall. The double doors were open, allowing her to see Adria and Tamerlane standing before the two Vikars on the opposite side of a large oak table. They were not alone. Eight other Mindkeepers joined them, four to each side of the room. Flanking the front table with pistols drawn were two additional Soulkeepers. A few glanced her way upon entering, but most kept their eyes firmly locked on the greater threat.

"You waste our time with pathetic tantrums," Adria said. She faced the two Vikars, but her words clearly addressed the entire crowd. "With but a thought I can tear your souls from your skulls and burn your bodies to ash. Whatever plan you have, it will not work. Step down, now, while you still live."

"You're a far cry from the meek little girl who requested a position in Low Dock," Vikar Caria said. The woman looked unusually regal in her finely tailored black suit. A pistol lay before her on the table, and Sena held no doubt it was loaded. "But you have overstepped every boundary imaginable. You are not superior to the Sisters. You do not walk equal to our beloved Goddesses. And when you die, we may at last expunge your blasphemous name from the tongues of the foolish and easily swayed."

Sena's feet rooted to the floor. A wordless protest died on her lips. What were they doing? Did they truly believe they could challenge Adria? The eight Mindkeepers began a soft prayer, the droning words filling the entire room. Adria lifted her hands, and faint light shone across her fingertips.

"Enough," she said, and power flared outward like an erupting beacon... only no souls obeyed her commands. The air shimmered like the disturbed surface of a pond. The praying Mindkeepers shuddered as if they had been struck by invisible fists, but their prayers did not halt. Sena felt the prayer wash over her, and it was as if a great weight settled upon her mind. When Adria had stolen her soul to use during their church's defense, it'd felt like being pulled from within herself, and losing total control and feeling. This was the opposite. She felt heavy. Burdened.

Vikar Caria lifted her pistol off the table.

"The Goddesses answer our prayers, too, Adria," she said. "And you're not the only one to research the old magic our civilization has forgotten."

Tamerlane slammed his body into Adria's as the pistol fired. Smoke billowed into the air. His lanky body spun from the impact. Blood splayed across the marble tile as he fell.

And then Adria screamed.

The shock wave rocked the foundations of the mansion. The pistol shattered in Caria's grip, its metal shards cutting across her face and hand. The chanting Mindkeepers dropped to their knees, but their prayers rose in volume so that Sena could make out their words.

"Grant us permanence, O Goddess, to this world and flesh. May our souls be one with our mind and body, so we may serve. Grant us permanence, O Goddess…"

Tamerlane landed on his knees beside Adria, who knelt over him. Still alive, from what Sena could tell, the bullet hitting somewhere in his chest, but he'd need healing soon to prevent bleeding out. Healing she could do. Healing she would most certainly not be allowed to give.

"Your power is incredible," Forrest said as he circumvented the table, his giant axe swinging in his hand. "But it's of a single source, and that source alone. Without souls to steal, you're nothing. You're not a Goddess. You're not the Sacred Mother reborn. You're just a charlatan with one neat trick."

He swung his axe, forcing Adria to scramble away. The sharp edge ripped a thin line across her dress. Blood stained the dark cloth from a long but shallow cut. With her retreat, the way to Tamerlane was clear, and the giant man stood over the gasping, bleeding Mindkeeper while shaking his head.

"You deserve as much blame for this as anyone," the Vikar said. He raised his axe. Adria lifted her hand, seeking her magic, demanding the miracles that had been hers since the crawling mountain arrived, but it would not come to her.

"Grant us permanence, O Goddess..." droned the Mindkeepers.

"Do not weep," Tamerlane said, craning his neck to look at Adria. "Do not weep, for I—"

The axe slammed down across Tamerlane's forehead, cracking his skull open like an egg.

Adria's scream rattled the walls and split the marble tiles, but the prayers of the Mindkeepers would not break.

"You brought this one on yourself," Caria said, still behind the table. Her face was as impassive as any mask Adria might wear. "You were a lock for Vikar of the Day. After time, and paying your dues, you might have been Deakon of Londheim. But you couldn't wait. You wanted everything, and you wanted it now."

"The church is dying under your leadership," Adria seethed as she rose to her feet. "I have only done what I must."

"As have we," Forrest said as he approached, his bloody axe swaying.

Sena thought to interfere. She wielded her own prayers, but what might she do against so many? And was it even right of her to do so? Whatever Adria had become was beyond her understanding. This outcome was easier. It was safer. Let the terrifying prospect of change die on a white marble floor and be forgotten with the passage of time.

Adria rose to her full height, and she tilted her chin to grant Vikar Forrest a clean shot at her neck. A faint hint of the emotion wracking the woman's heart leaked into her voice when she spoke, but not much. Even facing death, her control was incredible.

"Do it," she said. "But at least honor me with a clean kill."

The right wall shifted, wood and plaster becoming smoke. From its center burst Janus, his form a monster of steel and wood.

His bladed right hand slashed Mindkeepers in twain, his thorned left sprouting vines that curled into their eyes and penetrated their throats to choke out their lungs. The imprisoning chant, once overpowering the room with light, faded in both volume and power.

Forrest swung his axe. Adria lifted her right fist. Light burst from between the gaps of her clenched fingers, halting the axe as if it had connected with a stone wall. The impact traveled up its handle, and then the entire weapon exploded into splinters. Adria lowered her head, and in the ensuing chaos, the woman's words echoed like thunder.

"I promised not to begin my rule with blood and death," she said. "Damn you, Forrest. Damn all of you for this."

Forrest's soul ripped free of his forehead. The shimmering ball of light hovered as the Vikar's body went slack. The light about it grew brighter, fiercer, as if it burned from contact with the very air. It lasted only a moment, and then Adria plunged it back into his chest. The flesh caught fire. The bone withered like ash. The now soulless body screamed from the pain, but it did not move, and it did not resist. His own soul consumed Forrest's mortal flesh, charring it into a collapsing heap. A flick of her fingers sent the soul skyward, to become part of whatever eternity awaited those who passed on from the Cradle.

The next moments passed like a nightmare. Janus dashed across the room, his mouth elongating into that of a wolf so he could sink his teeth into the throats of the Mindkeepers on the opposite side. Adria rushed the table blocking her path to Vikar Caria. It broke in half with a mere movement of her hand. The two Soulkeepers protecting the Vikar lifted their pistols, but Adria whipped their souls out from their bodies and spun them in a protective circle. Their searing flame tore holes through the surviving Mindkeepers. A whispered prayer, and the Soulkeepers' soulless bodies erupted as if their chests were filled with flamestones.

"Blessed Sisters, I seek your protection," Caria said, the Devotion flowing expertly off her tongue. "Bind the darkness so it may not touch my flesh. Show mercy so I may stand in the light."

Adria reached out to touch the shimmering shield of light that emerged to protect the Vikar.

"Your faith is not stronger than mine," she said as the Vikar repeated the prayer on a loop. "It is only more desperate. More afraid."

Her fingers pressed. The light shimmered, cracked. A single fingertip slipped through, and that was all Adria needed. Vikar Caria stood perfectly erect as if chains had lashed about her body and pulled her tight. Her face shook as if she were shivering in the cold. Her eyes blackened. Her mouth dropped open, and ash spilled out. Sena gasped in horror at the sight. Adria was burning Caria alive from the inside, torching her mind with her own soul. Her skin shriveled, peeling back to reveal bone. Somehow she screamed, but only ever so briefly.

When the body collapsed, her soul remained hovering in place. Adria stared at it for a long, long time, and Sena feared what sort of blasphemy the woman might perform upon it. Would she corrupt it? Destroy it? Had it come to this, that Adria believed herself a better judge for the fates of the eternal than the Sisters themselves?

At last Adria sent the soul heavenward. The rest of the Mindkeepers were dead, allowing Janus to join her side. Blood slid off him as he turned his limbs back to familiar human arms. His skin, which had been steel and bark, softened and regained its thick black coat for covering.

"That was fun," he said, flashing a grin of his opal teeth.

Adria ignored him. Her attention was locked upon Tamerlane's mutilated corpse. She knelt over his body and removed her mask. Her tears fell upon the dead man's face.

"I'm sorry," she whispered. "I should have been smarter. I should have known better than this. And now I must endure without you."

She lifted the man's soul from his corpse, the shining light bathing the bloodstained room. Janus squinted as he drew closer.

"Your affection makes you weak," the avatar said. "Cast him aside. You have work to do."

"You heartless bastard," Adria said in response.

"The title of Deakon was a boon sought solely out of pride. You're the Chainbreaker. It's the only title you've ever needed, yet you still wanted the respect and adoration of your former peers."

"You call it foolish to rule the Keeping Church in Westreach?" she asked, whirling to face him.

"I want the Keeping Church buried in the ground and something better to grow from its soil," Janus said, not backing down. "In short, yes."

Adria pulled Tamerlane's soul close enough for her to embrace. It did not burn her like it did others.

"Some of us still had hope for reform. Damn us for that hope." She cast the soul to the heavens. "Come then. Let us prepare for tonight. We shall remake this world, starting with the soulless."

Adria replaced her mask, and it was only when she turned to leave that she realized Sena was there, and had witnessed the entire travesty. Sena felt a chill travel down her spine at the look she received. It wasn't angry or heartless. It was a look of tired, defeated apathy. Her longtime friend approached her, and she hesitated briefly at the door. Whatever words Adria meant to say, they never came. She continued walking.

Later, mouthed Janus, and he tossed her a wink before following Adria out.

Sena felt her throat tighten, and her hands clenched into fists as she watched the two leave. Dark thoughts followed. Adria's back was to her. Her defenses were down. The words of a prayer came to mind, and it was no Devotion.

"Anwyn of the Moon, hear me," she whispered, the long forgotten words of the mutilation curse coming to mind, the only curse she'd ever read when helping Adria with her research. She made it no further before a hand settled upon her shoulder, and a soothing voice whispered in her ear.

"Let her go, my daughter. Do not mar your soul with such ugliness."

Sena turned, and her eyes widened at the sight of the Goddess Lyra standing amid the carnage. Her long black hair spooled about the room, covering the bodies and sweeping away the blood.

"Forgive me, my Goddess," Sena said as she dropped to her knees and bowed her head. "I only seek to do what is right."

"As does Adria." Lyra cast her gaze to the retreating woman and her monstrous friend. "The world changes, my child. Know that I have cherished you always, and make not this decision lightly. Before you waits a harsh, lonely road. Your burdens will be tremendous, but that road leads to peace if you possess the strength to walk it."

Lyra's hand left her shoulder. When Sena lifted her eyes, the Goddess was gone, as were the bodies, their weapons, and their souls.

In that quiet loneliness, Sena finally allowed herself to weep for all she had lost.

CHAPTER 32

Devin crouched upon the rooftop of his home, his favorite place to go when confused and frightened. It was up there he had lamented Brittany's death. It was upon those shingles he had screamed to the Sisters his furious challenge, demanding they strike him down if they hated him so. Only this time he wasn't alone.

"You could confront her directly," Jacaranda said. She sat beside him, her legs folded underneath her and her weight gently leaning against his right arm. "Maybe there's more to it that we don't know."

"What more could there possibly be?" He shook his head. "Excuses, Jac. Reasons and lies. Nothing changes the undeniable truth. Nothing changes the dead."

It had seemed too cruel a joke to be true when Devin first heard the rumors spreading like wildfire throughout the city. Vikar Forrest and Vikar Caria were dead, slain by the hand of the Chainbreaker. Murdered by the Sacred Mother reborn. Based on the exuberance of those spreading the stories, much of the populace was *excited* by the prospect.

"It could have been self-defense," Jacaranda said. The Sisters bless her, she was trying so hard to keep his spirits high. "The Vikars no doubt viewed her as a threat to the Keeping Church. They might have thought it best to eliminate her."

"Self-defense," Devin said. He laughed bitterly as he shook his head. "I've seen what Adria can do. With but a thought she can rip the souls out from a person's body. She can tear down buildings with her sheer will. For her to claim anything in self-defense is ridiculous. She is the one with the power. She is the one who bears the responsibility. For whatever reason, she chose to execute our Vikars. This isn't about her being Deakon anymore. This is about her becoming the lone voice of the church to all of Londheim."

Jacaranda intertwined her fingers into his, and he accepted her touch with gratitude. He looked at the cloudy sky and tried to work through the future left before them.

"Anyone who accepts a post from Adria now does so in full knowledge of the blood spilled to grant them their position. Goddesses help me, I'm worried she's going to offer me the position of Vikar of the Dusk. What a joke, a sick joke."

"What about the rest of the church?" she asked. "What of the Soulkeepers and the Mindkeepers? Will they accept her rule? Or will they try to bring her down?"

That was his greatest fear, and he saw no potential future that wasn't filled with betrayal and death.

"They're going to kill her," he said softly. "Or they're going to die trying. I can't stay neutral in this, either. So what do I do, Jac? Do I watch my friends and comrades die? Or do I join them in an attempt to kill my own sister?"

"Is there no other way?"

"I wish there was," he said. His mind was so dark, his choices so grim, he could not help but laugh. "Fuck me, Jac, I haven't a clue what is right and what is wrong. Given my past history, I'm pretty confident that whatever decision I make is going to be the completely wrong one."

Jacaranda kissed his cheek.

"Have a little faith in yourself," she said. "You stuck with me. That's at least one smart choice you made."

"It helps that you're absurdly sexy with more fire in your hair than the sun."

He squeezed her hand, and she melted into him. Silence followed, and Devin did his best to relish it. No, he wasn't alone in his preferred place of solitude, but it was nice to have someone there to pull him back from the cliff of despair. He leaned his cheek against the top of her hair. The scent of lilacs hit his nostrils, and he closed his eyes to enjoy it better. He remembered being with her when she chose that particular small glass vial of perfume. It'd taken her ten minutes to decide between the various scents the merchant had bottled, yet instead of being frustrated, it seemed she enjoyed every second of the choosing.

"I spoke with Brittany," she said.

Devin's eyes fluttered back open.

"Did you now?"

She nodded, the movement sliding her hair across his cheek.

"After the fires in Belvua. I had to know, what was she like? What did she want? I guess I . . . I feared she'd try to take you from me. And after seeing you crying over her grave not so long ago, I thought, I thought you still . . ."

Devin clenched his jaw so tightly shut, his teeth ached. He hadn't a clue how to respond to the difficulties caused by his sister. To explain his emotions dealing with a return of his deceased wife after he'd finally accepted in his heart it was time to move on? How did one even begin?

"It's been six years," he said, and he pulled her closer to him. "She may be back, but it doesn't erase what has already been. No amount of magic ever will. My loneliness over those years remains. My grief, my acceptance, it all stays with me. I have changed, as all things can and must change. But one thing I know will absolutely never change, no matter who or what returns to my life."

He pulled back from her and gently tilted her face with his fingers so she might look him in the eye.

"How my heart goes crazy when you smile at me."

Jacaranda laughed, and when he leaned in, she kissed him eagerly.

"You're so sappy, Devin," she said after a minute. "Please never change."

"Were you not paying attention to the very deep speech I just gave about the nature of change?"

"I tried not to for both our sakes."

Jacaranda kissed him again to erase his indignation. Devin cherished the moment, the tremble of her lips, the gentle touch of her fingers along his jaw and neck. He'd have given anything to let it last forever, but Londheim was a cruel and baffling place.

"Devin?" cried a familiar voice from the street. "Are you up there, Soulkeeper?"

"It can't be," he said as he disentangled from Jacaranda and pushed to his feet. It seemed that day was to be one of morbid surprises, for when he walked to the rooftop's edge and leaned over the side, there waiting for him at his door with her arms crossed over her bright white chest was the araloro, Lavender.

"Can I help you?" he asked, feeling dumb even as he said it.

"Don't humans tend to live inside their homes, not atop them?" she asked, ignoring his question.

"We're adaptable."

He crouched low enough so he might grab the edge with both hands and then swung himself off. He landed upon the cobblestone with a grunt, the ache in his knees a reminder he wasn't a spry man in his twenties anymore. He noted that Jacaranda had not followed, nor made her presence known. If Lavender came with ill intentions, Jacaranda would be able to leap unsuspected to his aid.

"I'm surprised you were able to find me," he said. A quick glance up and down the street revealed no gawkers or followers. "And that you arrived without stirring a crowd."

"I am capable of hiding myself when I wish," Lavender said. She tapped her nose with her long blue fingers. "And your scent is one I am intimately familiar with, Soulkeeper. Tracking you to your home was no significant task."

"Fair enough," he said, and he crossed his arms. His sword and pistol were inside. If she attacked, there'd be no reaching them in time, but he didn't feel particularly threatened. It made no sense for her to track him down just to assault him before his front door.

"So why are you here?" he asked. "Not that I don't appreciate your visit, but I wasn't aware we considered ourselves on friendly enough terms for the occasional unscheduled visit."

"Such dry wit," she said, flashing him a predator's smile. "And I come as Shinnoc's representative, of course. Even with the matter of Cannac's death resolved, there is still much we must discuss. If there is to be a future without violence, our nation's borders must be established."

"Sure, of course," Devin said, and he raised an eyebrow her direction. "But why are you telling *me* this?"

"Because I am uncertain of whom I should speak with regarding these decisions, so I thought that, given your connection to your sister, you might aid me in navigating human politics."

"You shouldn't be speaking with me or my sister," he said. "You should meet with the High Excellence." A deep sense of unease bubbled to life inside his stomach. "You should know that. You've met with him once before."

That perfectly white smile of hers grew ever so slightly.

"You don't know?" she said. "How adorable. High Excellence Albert Downing is dead, Soulkeeper. His entire household was murdered."

Shock locked Devin's limbs in place, and his mind blanked, stumbled for words, and then blurted out the only thing he could manage.

"Albert is *what?*"

CHAPTER 33

Dierk walked the blood-soaked halls of Albert's former mansion with a gigantic smile on his face and the lingering magic of a curse swirling about his fingertips. The carnage, the slaughter, it had been so beautiful. So easy.

"Keep all the gates locked," he told one of his house guards. "You open them for only one person, Deakon Eveson, is that clear?"

"Yes sir," the guard said.

Dierk grabbed the man by the wrist and pulled. The guard froze in place, his eyes widening slightly out of fear.

"Yes, High Excellence," Dierk corrected.

"Of course," the guard said. "As you wish, High Excellence."

The man looked all too happy to be gone from Dierk's presence. Fine with him. He didn't need anyone, didn't want anyone, not when he could bask in the joy of his ascension. He slipped around bodies that would need to be removed in time. Some were armed, some were mere servants. It didn't matter. Dierk had given a simple order for the crowd he had gathered on his way to the mansion. Kill everyone inside. No survivors. The rule of Londheim needed to be wiped clean and started anew.

Dierk passed one body that lay mangled and twisted in a most unnatural way, with his bones protruding out of his skin at every joint. He knelt beside the body and admired his handiwork. The Book of Ravens contained many curses, and this poor fellow had been his first attempt at the mutilation curse. Sadly Dierk had been forced to rush the curse, what with the battle and all. If only he'd had time to practice, to perfect.

"Well, there's always next time," he said, and that thought returned the smile to his face.

Dierk wound his way back to the makeshift throne room Albert had constructed upon declaring himself High Excellence. It'd been a painfully obvious attempt to mimic the royalty still enjoyed by Queen Woadthyn in East Orismund, but sometimes one needed the obvious things to convince the masses. Dierk crossed the bare tiles of the converted ballroom to his throne, which still bore its former occupant.

"So unlike you, I thought," he told the slumped-over corpse. Such a pitiful "throne," little more than a chair with some added gold and plumped red cushions to imitate the royal style employed in Oris. He'd need a true throne constructed for his rule. This just wouldn't do.

"I thought," he continued as he tugged at Albert's sleeve, "that you'd face me at the doors instead of cowering here on your throne. I thought you were a good man, Albert. A smart man. And yet you'd have abandoned us all. You'd have clung to power over principle. In the end, you were just like my father."

Dierk grabbed Albert's shirt with both hands and pulled. The pale corpse crumpled on the three steps of the wood dais. Albert's face, forever locked in a frightened cry of pain, smashed into the tiles. Dierk had burst his heart in his chest with a curse from the Book of Ravens. That singular kindness was for the respect Albert had shown him even when he hadn't controlled his father's estate.

"Good riddance to the both of you."

He peered at the throne's cushions and frowned. Damn it. Albert had shit himself when he died. Of course he had.

"Need these replaced, too," he muttered, his frustration mounting. Pitiful as the throne might be, he wanted to be seated upon it when Adria arrived. Even among the most powerful, image and context were necessary weapons.

"High Excellence?" asked a guard from the room's entrance. "Deakon Adria has arrived."

"Bring her here," he said. When the guard was gone, he pulled Albert's jacket off and rubbed away as much of the cushion's stain as he could. It wasn't working. A quick glance about, and he settled for the curtains. He'd barely ripped one off the rungs and folded it atop the throne before Adria arrived. Dierk took his seat, his heart racing, his grin ear to ear.

At least until he saw she wasn't alone. A strange man was with her. He wore a long black coat that matched his trousers and vest. His hair, while it seemed normal at first glance, Dierk could swear it carried a hint of green when the light shone off it just right.

"They call you High Excellence now?" Adria asked, looking prim and proper in her elegant dress. She'd forsaken the white suit traditionally worn by the Deakon, though he supposed she might don it once she had time to get it tailored. To his surprise, her eyes were red and puffy, as if she'd been crying. "This answers many of my questions, but one important one remains—why?"

Dierk adjusted his rear atop the uneven curtains, already second-guessing his decision. The folded material was so thick, it made him feel like a child sitting on a stack of pillows to join the grown-ups at a table.

"Why?" he asked. "Isn't it obvious? You of all people should understand the reasons for this necessary act. Just this morning you destroyed the old church leadership and set yourself up as Deakon. I have done the same with Londheim's secular structure."

"Adria acted in self-defense," the man with her said. "Can you say the same?"

"What does it matter?" Dierk asked, not bothering to hide his dismissive sneer. "The act needed to be done, and now it's done. And who are you to question my decisions?"

"I question everyone's decisions," the stranger said, and he flashed an unnerving grin. No human teeth should be that shiny...

"Enough, Janus," Adria snapped. "There is so much that must be done today, but I could not ignore the mess you have created in killing the High Excellence."

Dierk could not see Adria's face due to her porcelain mask, but he could see the brilliant light of her soul behind that mask. The emotions leaking out of it surprised him. Anger. Frustration. Doubt. He couldn't help but feel wounded. Did she truly think so little of him? Most overwhelming, though, was a feeling of sorrow and loss. It wasn't directed at him, either, so then who?

"I don't understand why you judge me so harshly," he said. "How is what I've done different than what you did this morning?"

"The Keeping Church abandoned Westreach," Adria said carefully, her every word measured. "When faced with the greatest upheaval to our spiritual understanding of this world, the Ecclesiast and the Queen together cast us aside. Vikar Forrest and Vikar Caria, despite that betrayal, would have remained faithful to the Keeping Church and its doctrine. They wanted to re-create the rules that had bound us for centuries. What they wanted, *High Excellence*, was to maintain their power despite a shift in everything that granted that power in the first place."

Dierk pulled his shoulders back and thrust out his chin. He would not cower, he would not cower, he would *not*, no matter how damn terrifying her disgust and rage.

"So tell me, Dierk, what grants you the power you feel you deserve?" she asked. "What right places you upon that throne?"

"You said the church and Queen abandoned us," he said with a tongue that felt as dry as sand. "Albert sought the same. He and the rest of the elite wanted to take their wealth and their belongings, pack them on boats, and leave us here to die. Well, I'm not leaving.

I'm here, and I have the Book of Ravens at my disposal. Londheim is my city to rule, which means I'm going to protect it at all costs. That's more than can be said for the previous High Excellence. And unlike Albert or my father, I'm not frightened by the dragon-sired outside our walls."

"You're not frightened?" Janus asked. He crossed his arms over his bare chest and laughed. "If you aren't, then you are a fool, *High Excellence.* Do you think your walls mean anything to the lapinkin who command the wind? Or the owls who fly overhead? What shall you do when the dyrandar march toward your gates? Do you think your soldiers and their little swords and rifles will bring low those who reshape reality to fit their dreams? Declare war, and watch everything you pretend to rule come crashing down into ruin."

Dierk stared at this bizarre man, desperately trying to figure out who he was or why his name sounded familiar. That he traveled with Adria meant he was important, but why?

"One more word from you and I shall have you hanged," Dierk said, attempting to regain control of the conversation. Janus's smile deepened. No, his teeth weren't just shiny. They were a rainbow of colors, glinting as if made of opals, and the sight of them made Dierk's stomach churn.

"You have no idea how badly I would love for you to try," said Janus.

"Enough!" Adria shouted. Her words staggered them both with physical force. Janus retreated several steps while Dierk plopped into the cushions of his throne. She cast her gaze between the both of them, her eyes wide behind her mask.

"Dierk, your rule here is tenuous at best," she said. "Albert was beloved by the populace. You are not. I can subdue their anger if I give you my blessing, but I am not convinced you're worth it. So convince me, Dierk. Tell me the real reason you assaulted this mansion and slaughtered Londheim's ruler. No lies this time. No delusions, not to me, and not to yourself."

Dierk's neck flushed. His next few words stammered and fell into nonsense. What delusions? What lies? He meant every word he spoke, damn it... didn't he? He glared at Janus, who looked absolutely disgusted. Oh, to use the mutilation curse on that cocky bastard...

"The truth?" Dierk finally said. "The full truth, that's what you want, right? Fine. If you want me naked before you, then I'll strip. I'll bleed. I don't care. It's what you asked for."

Dierk stood from his throne and ripped the shirt off his back. Light poured in from massive floor-to-ceiling windows along the western wall, casting a golden hue across the purple and black of his innumerable bruises and cuts. Cold, uncaring passivity washed over his mind as he let them witness the results of the beatings his father had laid upon him while imprisoned.

"My father... Soren was a bastard, a cruel, heartless bastard," he said. "And your beloved High Excellence Albert trusted him. No matter how good or kind Albert appeared to others, he relied on the most ruthless man to guide his actions so he might maintain his power. They worked together. They plotted together. And now they're dead together. If I could have, I'd have made them die in each other's arms while choking on each other's blood. Is that *honest* enough for you, Adria? Is it? *IS IT?*"

He stepped closer, and he offered her his hand. His eyes had begun to water, but he pushed onward.

"Don't you see? The two halves of Londheim, its heart and its mind, are now unified within our grasp. We can rule in tandem, me in charge of the law, you in charge of faith and spirit. We'll wipe out the old traditions and build something new. It's so perfect, Adria. You see it, don't you? How perfect we'll be together? Call it destiny. Call it logic. It doesn't matter. It makes sense, you and I, such perfect sense. So will you finally accept what I have to offer? Will you finally accept me as I am, and the couple we were meant to be?"

Even her soul closed off to him. Her face betrayed nothing. The silence weighed like a millstone.

"No."

Dierk had dreamed of a moment like this, of his innate power manifested, his enemies crushed, and Londheim's rule firmly gripped between his fingers. This was it, the final culmination of those dreams. Yet instead of feeling powerful, he felt more helpless than he had in his entire life. This was worse than lying on the floor feeling the fists of his father rain down upon him. He stood naked, exposed, his bruises cast in daylight. All that he was, laid at beautiful, stunning, divine Adria's feet.

And she rejected him.

"No?" he asked, his voice quivering.

"No, Dierk," she repeated. She stepped close enough to wipe tears off his cheek with her black-gloved hand.

"There is the heart of a sweet child buried somewhere deep within you," she said. "But it is not my burden to unearth it. And no matter how adamantly you believe otherwise, you have never seen *me* for who *I* truly am."

How could she believe that? Had he not seen the divine nature of her being when she was still a meager Mindkeeper passing out bread to the hungry?

"But I did this for you," he said. "Doesn't that count for something?"

Adria stepped away. Back to the foot of the dais. To Janus's side.

"It does," she said. "That's why I will smooth over your transition to power. Keep within these walls, and travel only with an armed escort. That should buy me the time necessary to spread word throughout the city of my approval. Provided, of course," she added, "that you will be true to your word and aid me in tearing down the old rotting bones of Londheim to build something wondrous and new. We shall work together as friends, understood? For peace between us and the dragon-sired. For the future of Londheim."

"Sure," Dierk said. The next word charred a hole from one side of his tongue to the other. "Friends."

"Enough wasting time here," Janus said. "We have soulless to save, and if luck is with us, a Goddess to slay."

Neither of them bowed or gave him his proper respect before they left. Dierk stood, eyes locked on the door, his emotions a tumultuous storm of anger and hopelessness. He wanted to rage, but he had no strength left for it. Adria's words haunted him. Her dismissal condemned him. He collapsed upon the throne and buried his face into his hands. He cried as he stared through the gaps in his fingers. It was then, and only then, that he realized a long smear of shit stained his right leg from knee to shin.

"Damn it," he screamed, ripping at his belt with flailing hands. "Damn it, damn it, damn it all, all of you, I'll curse all of you, I'll—I'll—"

He couldn't get the stupid belt undone, and when it suddenly did, he tripped, his lanky body was rolling, the throne room spinning. His trousers bunched at his ankles. His stomach heaved. He beat his fists against the tiles and wordlessly screamed. This was his moment of triumph, and it'd been stolen from him. Half-naked, he curled into a ball and wished he could be a thousand miles away.

Pathetic, broken child, the voice of Vaesalaum whispered in his ear, but the nisse wasn't there, no one was there, he was alone, now and forever.

"Um, your, uh..."

Dierk scrambled to his feet, and he wiped his face with one arm while he vainly tried to hide his nakedness with the other. A very confused and nervous soldier stood at the entrance to the throne room, his gaze pointedly staring at the floor.

"What?" Dierk shouted.

"A representative of the dragon-sired army comes to speak with you," the soldier said. "A creature by the name of Lavender. She says it's important. She, uh, is also escorted by Devin Eveson, the Deakon's older brother."

"I know who he is. Give me five minutes, then let them in."

When the soldier was gone, Dierk grabbed his shirt and pulled it back over his bruised body. Next came the trousers. He used a knife to hack them off at the knee, then tossed the shit-covered part beside Albert's dead body. Last he readjusted the curtains atop the throne to ensure proper protection, kicking himself for not having checked before sitting down. He had just enough time to situate himself before the door opened, and three new visitors arrived into his throne room.

"Greetings," Dierk said. He wiped his eyes and hoped they weren't too red. This was his life now, one of endless meetings and diplomacies. Fuck Adria. He didn't need her. Londheim, and all the rest of Westreach, was his to rule, and that meant making the hard political decisions even when he wanted to crawl into a hole and die. At least his father had beaten that useful lesson into him amid all the rest of the horribleness he'd inflicted.

"Greetings, High Excellence of Westreach," the alluring dragon-sired woman said, stepping ahead of Devin and a red-haired woman he did not recognize. Dierk recognized Lavender from her unforgettable meeting with Albert, when she'd unleashed Shinnoc's memory upon all present. To his sick amusement, she wove about Albert's body as if it were a mere inconvenience so she might bow before him. "I congratulate you on such a—recent appointment."

"Birth is often messy and bloody," Dierk said, trying to sound noble and wise. "And this is a birth for Westreach. I would welcome you better, if I could."

"Indeed." She smiled, and a soft scent washed over him. It was a mixture of flowers, coupled with the scent of autumn leaves and fresh morning dew, but true to her name, lavender was the strongest of them all. "All the Cradle is discovering how bloody a birth can be since our return."

Dierk forced a smile to his face. Of course Lavender was equally witty. She was the chosen representative of the dragon-sired lurking outside the city walls. Her tongue was silver and her scent flowers and honey. He could feel an innate desire to please her building in his chest and he countered it with what he knew best: disgusted anger.

"So why have you come?" he asked. "I doubt it is to congratulate me on my new appointment."

"It is not," Lavender said after a guarded glance back at Devin. "We must discuss matters of peace, High Excellence, so we might avoid an unneeded war."

"I thought we had settled all that nonsense," Dierk asked, thinking of the proclamation Shinnoc had magically blasted across the entire city. "Isn't that why Belvua burned?"

Lavender's smile seemed to grow that much more pleasant, but Dierk saw it for the illusion that it was. Disgust hid behind those blood-red lips.

"Just because King Cannac's murder has been addressed does not mean all our differences have been settled," she said. "We seek assurances from humanity regarding the formation and sanctity of our borders. If we are to coexist without bloodshed, we must have lands of our own, and our authority acknowledged and respected."

"A fair enough request," Dierk said. "What is it you want?"

"We want to renew the original agreement we had reached with humanity before your Goddesses imprisoned us. All lands west of Londheim and north of the Triona River belong to us, to be divided among ourselves as we see fit. Humans will not encroach upon them, and all humans who still live there will immediately vacate their homes lest they be forced out by claw and blade."

Dierk's jaw nearly hit the floor.

"Are you fucking insane?" he said. "You'd have us carve Westreach in half and then just... hand it over?"

Devin cleared his throat and stepped forward in an attempt to intervene.

"High Excellence, might I remind you that there is a damn army outside our walls?"

Declare war, and watch everything you pretend to rule come crashing down into ruin.

"Be quiet!" Dierk screamed as he stood from the throne. His anger toward Adria bubbled back to life, and it spilled over at everyone around him. His meager body felt too small to contain it. His hands shook, and he sneered down at the dragon-sired woman.

"Things are changing here in Londheim," he said. "I'm not afraid of your army, or your dragons. We have magic now, too. The keepers of the church have their prayers and spellstones. I have my curses. If you want peace, then march your rabbits and birds and foxes away from our walls and stop threatening us with war. Have I made my position clear?"

Lavender looped her arms and then offered a most extravagant bow.

"Your position is most clear," she said, her smile unchanged. "I had hoped with new leadership we would see wisdom and mercy prevail over ignorance and fear. I see my hopes are wrong. Will the men and women who die by our hands share your sense of bravado, I wonder?"

"Are you threatening me?"

"If you do not accept our demands, we shall burn all of Londheim to the ground like your people burned Belvua," she said with a smile. "Yes. I am threatening you."

Shadows gathered around Dierk's fingers as the words of a curse slipped across his tongue. The Soulkeeper stepped between him and Lavender, one hand on his pistol, the other pointing a finger Dierk's way.

"It is incredibly bad form to strike the diplomat of a foreign nation," he said. "Surely your father taught you that?"

Dierk clenched his fists together and bit his tongue to halt the curse. He would fail no comparison to his father, not even when it was so clearly made to manipulate him. Dierk would be a far better ruler of Westreach than Albert, than Soren, than the whole damn lot of cowards that had tried to abandon Londheim on their boats when the city needed them most.

"So be it," he said. "Leave. Now. You're no longer welcome in our city. Take your army and your dragons and go. Once you do, then maybe I'll be willing to entertain talks of lands and treaties."

"As you wish, High Excellence."

The three bowed again, but he wasn't done yet.

"No, you two stay," he ordered Devin and his companion.

Lavender blew the other two a kiss and then sauntered away. Her confidence unnerved him, and he felt his temper growing unchecked.

"You need to speak with your sister," Dierk told the Soulkeeper once Lavender had left. His feet moved of their own accord, and he found himself pacing back and forth before the throne. His path took him around Albert's dead body like a circle, and for some reason this amused him darkly.

"About anything in particular?"

"She is too confident in her power!" he snapped. "Though her role is strictly as a leader and teacher of the church, she has begun to meddle in politics. This could lead to difficulties in our relationship that perhaps you, as her brother, might help convince her to avoid."

Devin cocked an eyebrow in his direction.

"Forgive me, High Excellence, but if you believe I can convince my sister to change anything once her mind is set, then you do not know her very well."

. . . you have never seen me *for who* I *truly am . . .*

The door creaked before he could respond, and in stepped the same guard yet again, looking just as nervous and worried as before.

"Your Excellence," he said. "You have more guests."

"Not now," Dierk said. "I'm busy."

"You don't understand, I couldn't stop—"

The door slammed all the way open. Dierk's eyes widened as a group of armed Soulkeepers marched into the throne room. His first instinct was that it'd been coordinated with Devin's help, but he seemed equally alarmed by their arrival. He and the red-haired woman with him stepped aside as the twelve Soulkeepers gathered in the center of the room.

"What is the meaning of this?" Dierk asked, his pulse quickening. Was this a coup? Had Adria commanded them to come and dispose of him after his outburst?

An auburn-haired woman sporting a small tricorn hat with five raven feathers stepped forward, and she bowed to one knee.

"I hear you're High Excellence now," she said. "My name is Soulkeeper Lyssa. Consider me currently in charge of what's left of my sacred division. We've come looking for Adria Eveson."

"What do you want my sister for?" Devin asked softly before Dierk might answer.

"Don't play stupid," Lyssa snapped at him before returning her attention to Dierk. "Adria murdered Vikar Forrest and Vikar Caria in cold blood so she might declare herself Deakon. We cannot allow the church to be conquered through bloodshed. We hoped to find her here and put an end to her madness."

"She left not long ago," Dierk said, relief washing over him. So they weren't here to kill him. Still, what to do about this situation? Half of him recoiled at the thought of Adria's death. Half relished it with unequaled pleasure. Devin's reaction was far less complicated. He stood with his hands at his sides, his entire body so stiff he might have been nailed to the floor.

"You would murder my sister?" he asked.

"What other choice do we have?" Lyssa asked him. "This power Adria possesses has warped her into something inhuman. If she's murdering our Vikars, what shall stop her from killing any of us? Or the people of Londheim?"

"She wouldn't."

Lyssa approached Devin, and she lovingly put a hand upon his cheek.

"She would, and you know it. The time for talk is over. Which side are you on, Devin?"

Dierk watched with mild curiosity. Could Adria's own brother turn against her? And if so, then maybe...maybe he should rethink his own understanding of her? Adria insisted he did not know her true self. When he looked upon her, he saw shining, divine light and beauty. Maybe he was wrong. Maybe everyone else saw the truth. A killer. A murderer claiming power at all costs.

"I will help bring her to justice," Devin said. "But I will not help murder her. Is that clear?"

"And when she refuses to surrender for trial? When then? What prison could even hold her?"

Devin shook his head.

"I have to hope, Lyssa. I have to believe she's not the monster you think she's become."

Lyssa withdrew her hand and let out a loud sigh that filled the entire room.

"Hopeless and foolish as always," she said. "High Excellence, you said she recently left. Did she say where she was going?"

"No, but the man with her did," Dierk said. "Some nonsense about restoring souls and killing a Goddess."

"Killing a Goddess?" Lyssa asked, and she looked pale at the thought of it. "She wouldn't...she couldn't...can she?"

"I pray we never find out," Devin said. He grimaced as if speaking pained him. "And I believe I know where they went. Beneath the city, in a chamber built by the dragons."

The growing excitement within the room was palpable. Dierk stood to his full height and did his best to sound in charge.

"Go with my blessing," he told them. They filed out, their weapons rattling and their guns clicking as they loaded them with flamestone. Lyssa tossed one last barb, a reminder of how little respect he commanded.

"Thanks," she said, and she turned to leave along with the rest of the Soulkeepers. "Not that we needed it."

CHAPTER 34

Logarius crossed the rooftops out of habit more than need, the void's gift clutched tightly between his newly formed hands. He did not fear the humans and their guards, soldiers, and keepers. Not with the power flowing through his body. Even his footsteps left dark shimmery indents upon the shingles. The void had become him. It was insatiable. It was unstoppable. Logarius halted his run only when arriving at his destination: the slaughtered hive-tree at the center of the city.

"Let it be here," he whispered. "Let it be now."

He spread his wings and floated to the ground. While the city was a barren shell of what it'd been mere months ago, here in Londheim's heart there were still plenty of travelers, and they shrieked and fled at his appearance. A cluck of amusement escaped his beak.

"Nowhere is safe within these walls," he said. "Not while I hunt."

Logarius lifted the gift of the void high above his head. It was a most wondrous scythe, its handle perfectly smooth and straight. It was made not of wood or metal, but pure black obsidian. Such weight should have made the weapon untenable, but he wielded it with hands made of shadow, a manifestation of the void that obeyed his commands as perfectly as his former bone and blood.

Merely holding the obsidian handle flooded his muscles with energy. The blade itself was the true power, though, a long, curling piece of the void granted to Logarius to wield as his scythe. It robbed the air of light. It showed no depth or edge, merely existed as if it had for all eternity.

"Swallow this city," Logarius said as he sliced the air with his scythe. "Swallow this whole damn world."

For a brief moment, strength flowed not to him but out of him and into the obsidian handle with such intensity, it stole his breath away. Momentarily empowered, the scythe blade cut through the walls of the very world, ripping a slender tear to the void beyond. Air pulled into it, adding a strange, otherworldly roar. Logarius slashed a second time, deepening the tear, granting passage to the tendrils and claws worming their way into the daylight before he felt the void's gifted strength return to his body.

"Come feed," he told the monstrosity that emerged. It resembled a flea, only its size was that of a horse, and instead of an insectoid head, it bore the face of three humans pressed together to form a circle. Londheim's people might have feared him before, but when that monster leapt dozens of feet into the air, their screams traveled all the way to the other districts, so great was their panic. Logarius let it fuel his rage. He gazed upon wretched humans with the fires of Belvua burning across his vision. They had destroyed his home and left him with nothing. It was only fair, it was only just, that he do the same.

His wings carried him with speed their human legs could not match. His scythe cut through their bodies with a blade that would not be dulled. Logarius dashed, and hunted, and killed for the sheer pleasure of it. He ricocheted to a rooftop only to dive back down upon a man and woman running hand in hand. His scythe cut through their fingers. His second strike took their heads. Screams guided him. The flea-creature slammed upon victims with such weight, the ground shook with every landing. Whatever its prey, it quickly ceased to resemble anything human with how quickly and viciously it ripped their bodies apart. Bone and sinew scattered upon the cobblestones.

Soldiers came to stop him. Logarius laughed in their faces. There were five of them, quaking as they stood in the center of the street with their swords held high. One even possessed a rifle. Logarius spread his arms in mockery.

"Fire," he told the man with the rifle. "Shoot me dead."

The bullet struck Logarius in the chest with the impact of a kiss. A soft ringing sound filled his ears. The void-scythe protected him. Its strength perfected him. All so he might fulfill his grand purpose.

"I admire your dedication," he said when they refused to retreat. "Come die. I shall make it quick."

They charged into the range of his scythe, trusting numbers and the strength of their steel. Logarius cut the first in half with a single swing, pivoted closer into their group, and tripped the next with a sweep of his obsidian handle. A quick twirl of the scythe severed his legs at the knees. They didn't bleed. Instead little pieces of the void flaked off the blade and crawled along their flesh, swallowing them, consuming them. Logarius blocked a sword strike with his arm, noting how its edge could not pierce even the black cloth of his outfit, and then sliced the man open from crotch to nose. His body collapsed like a grotesque tower of gore no longer held aloft by its foundation.

Now the others tried to retreat, but it was too late. The flea-monster arrived with a horrific shriek, its six spindly legs catching two of them as it landed from its leap. Logarius twirled his scythe and clucked with laughter as the thing sank the teeth of its three heads into the final survivor, ripping out massive chunks of the soldier's face and neck as it ate.

"Dragons save us, Logarius. What have you become?"

Logarius spun, his void-scythe vibrating in the grasp of his shadow hands. Excitement and dread rose within his breast in equal measure.

"You arrived sooner than I thought," he told Evelyn, who knelt atop a nearby roof with Whisper and Song clutched tightly between her gloved fingers. "Have you been tracking me?"

"I thought I tracked the void," she said. "Is that what you've become, my son? A tooth in the mouth of the insatiable?"

"I'm the final nail in this world's coffin," Logarius said. "Have you come to plead for the lives of this miserable city?"

His mother shook her head.

"I've come to kill you. Nothing more. Nothing less."

Logarius felt the blood in his veins quicken, and his senses heighten in a way no other battle could manage. His legs braced for the attack, but Evelyn leapt instead for the void-monster busy feasting. Whisper and Song slashed across its scaled side with their sickles, the blue-flame about the metal flaring at the contact. The void-beast howled with pain, only to have those three heads lopped off with a powerful upward chop. The thing melted into a puddle of shadow and emptiness, smoke wafting off its surface as the sunlight slowly ate away the power of the void.

"Sorry about that," Evelyn said as she turned his way, her two sickles twirling in her loose grip. "I'd hate to have anything interfere with our mother-son time."

"I wouldn't dream of fighting unfair," he said, though a bit of his bravado was bluster. She'd defeated him the last time they dueled, and it was only with surprise that he'd taken her down with a cheap shot. She'd let him live, a sign of weakness deep inside her heart. That weakness was gone. He saw that now. There would be no hesitation to her strikes, no pity in her eyes. His mother wanted him dead.

Logarius twirled his scythe. Then it was a good thing he wanted the same.

The two circled one another, eyeing each other's movements,

gauging each other's reach. Logarius's expertise with such a long scythe was relatively untested, given his preference to dual-wielding long, slender daggers, but the strength the scythe poured into his body made up for that lack. What mattered now was matching the speed of Whisper-Song. The two sickles steadily shifted back and forth in his mother's grasp, their steel bathed in blue flame. They were blessed with ancient magics, one of the few weapons upon the Cradle that could directly resist the power of the void. He'd have to be careful. He'd have to be quick.

Evelyn twisted her right foot a half-inch, her heel scraping against the street as she subtly shifted her weight. There.

His mother leapt with speed unmatched, her two sickles a flash of blue cutting across the air, but Logarius had already begun repositioning his scythe. He blocked the dual downward slash, felt the impact down to his elbows as the curved blades hooked the obsidian handle. He kicked her knee, rotated his weapon to the right, and flapped his wings. Their bodies collided, her beak hitting his upper chest, his elbow cracking across her forehead. They rolled once and then separated in a clang of metal on metal. Evelyn jammed Whisper and Song together into a singular staff as she came up from the roll, and the weapon danced a circle as she batted aside his first two strikes.

Instead of following it up with a third, he hopped several feet backward, aided by a flap of his wings, then crouched low. His entire body flexed, and then he released all of that energy in one single swing. His wings billowed, his legs extended, and his arms swung his scythe with unnatural strength. The void-blade cut through reality itself, for Evelyn was not his target. The rift opened, and Logarius instinctively collided with it. Pure darkness flowed out of it like a liquid, and it wrapped itself about his body, bathing him, sealing him within. He saw nothing, felt nothing, but his mother was before him, and he continued onward with his scythe looping up and about to strike again.

He felt sharp pain in his chest as Whisper-Song tore at the void protecting him, but it could only scratch a thin line across his feathers. That small spray of blood was nothing, nothing at all, compared to the impact of his void-bathed body slamming into his mother. The liquid darkness flowed off, finding a new host. Unlike Logarius, his mother did not bear the void's blessing. Her body would not be spared its hunger.

Logarius skidded to a halt and turned, the obsidian handle twirling in his shadow grasp. His mother lay on the ground, gasping for air. Her left arm, side, and wing were gone, swallowed by the void. Blue blood spilled across the cobblestone. Whisper-Song had separated, with Whisper dropping free of her grasp with the destruction of her arm. Song lay underneath the limp fingers of her right hand.

"I warned you," Logarius said as he closed the distance between them, clutching the obsidian handle tightly. "No one made you come here. No one made you fight."

"Bullshit," Evelyn said. Her voice was wet and raspy. She tried to stand but could not manage to rise off the ground. The void was eating at her, he realized. Thin layers of impenetrable darkness chewed at her exposed ribs, and at the featherless, bleeding lumps where her wings had once connected to her spine.

"You could have left Londheim," Logarius insisted. "You could have run. What does it matter if I destroy this city? What does it matter if I tear apart every last human to ever walk this damn world that the Sisters stole from us?"

"This won't... stop with... humans," Evelyn said. She lifted Song and held it before her battered body. Wisps of blue flame curled around its impossibly sharp edge. "Not too late... my son. Can still stop it. Die to me, before you... before you... die to *it*."

Logarius smacked Song out of her grasp with the butt of his scythe. The weapon clattered across the stone. Evelyn didn't flinch. She stared at him, challenging him even in her final moments.

Logarius met that gaze. He tried to remember the good times when they'd been a family. Those memories were all too thin and distant. They had faded like smoke to the fire that had been the war with humanity.

"Dragons," Logarius said as he lifted his scythe. "Goddesses. Kings. Vikars. They're all rotten. They've all failed. I don't know what awaits us when the void consumes the light of this world, but it must be better than this."

Evelyn lowered her beak to her chest.

"You believe that?" she asked. Several deep hitches prevented her from speaking, but at last she forced out the words. "Then I failed."

The deep black of the void swelled across his blade as he held the scythe aloft. His heart hammered in his chest. His throat constricted. Tears ran down the soft feathers of his mother's face. None fell from his.

"Do it," she hissed. "Do it, damn you."

Logarius brought the scythe crashing down. It cut straight through her body, through the meager flesh and feather and bone, to carve a deep groove into the streets of Londheim. He cut and dragged so the gash in the street grew like a canyon. He cut until he found the strength to turn and face the body of his mother, but no body remained. The void had swallowed it all, like it swallowed the cobblestone and the street and the buildings on either side. The ruins tumbled into a pit so deep, its bottom shimmered with the distant red glow of magma.

"I will not weep," Logarius said. The words burned across his tongue. They were the words of the Book of Ravens, the tome of wisdom his mother had spent the last days of her life fighting to destroy. "For I have wept what tears this body has to shed. All that is left is anger, and so I will not weep. I will rage."

Logarius turned his gaze to the side. This mindless slaughter was beneath him. Only one threat to his power truly remained in

Londheim, and he need not search for her. His body had changed with the void's blessing, as had his eyes. Adria's presence was a blinding sphere of light as clearly visible as the moon was against the midnight sky. Focusing upon it revealed her location, and he felt a shiver run through his body.

"You return to where it all began," he said, and he cradled his scythe to his chest to grant himself the strength to continue. To his disbelief, a similar beacon of power and brilliance shone beside her, twin stars visible through stone and corridor to his altered eyes. His initial shock turned to maniacal glee, and he clicked his beak together with excitement.

"And you're not alone..."

CHAPTER 35

"And to think you were my prisoner the last time I brought you down here," Janus said as they walked the long dark tunnel connecting the smaller outer chambers to the center of the cosmic machinery.

"Do you regret choosing me as your host?" Adria asked. Despite the excitement of her pending task, she felt mired in melancholy after witnessing Tamerlane's death. He had been a needed friend, a trustworthy voice for truth, and now he was yet another victim of a church that seemed intent on destroying everything good. She'd spent the day solidifying her position as Deakon, meeting with Mindkeepers, and preaching before churches. None of it had removed her melancholy. The meeting with Dierk had only worsened her mood, and left her tired and ready to be done with the whole damn city.

"Regret?" Janus said. "No, not me. I do think the dragons have had second thoughts."

"I weep for failing to live up to their expectations."

"Do I detect a rare moment of sarcasm from the ever-dour Chainbreaker?"

Adria chuckled bitterly.

"My brother's wit does rub off on me sometimes."

Adria had not mentioned it to Janus, but something was different about the machinery since her last visit. The pulsing veins connecting the outer wells to the central chamber were swollen with light. The very ground beneath her hummed at a tone so deep, it felt like it vibrated her bones. The air was thick, pregnant with potential.

"Janus," she whispered as they neared the heart of the complex. "The magic, it's preparing to enact."

"That isn't possible," Janus said, but the worry was evident in his voice. "Who else even knows the machinery is here, let alone how to activate it? Not unless..."

The enigmatic avatar refused to finish the thought.

"Hurry, Adria," he told her. "And prepare your magic. I fear the worst."

The two emerged into the grand, cavernous chamber of flesh and steel, and they were not alone. Two others stood in the center, their figures bathed in the soft blue light of the multitude of veins that lined the walls and ceiling. The first was a bizarre apparition given human form. It was a living distortion, a humanoid misshapen in the darkness that turned the blue light falling upon it into a schizophrenic rainbow mixture. That light ran down its form as if turned to liquid, and the mere sight of it made Adria's stomach uneasy.

Beside it, trapped inside the rebuilt mechanical heart that had imprisoned her a lifetime ago, stood a proud but frightened Wren.

"Who is that?" Adria whispered. "*What* is that?"

"Nihil, the Dragon of Conflict," Janus said. "Or the Dragon of Chaos, as your kind believed. Tread lightly, Adria. You have never faced so fearsome an adversary."

The dragon turned. Its body solidified slightly, as if an oily water were transforming its substance into skin, but the innards remained transparent.

"I did not think you would come, but it is appropriate that you are here," Nihil said. Its voice was deep and rumbling, like the bowels of the Cradle granted a voice. "Let the death of the first Chainbreaker herald the arrival of the second."

"Let her out of there," Adria commanded.

"No."

Nihil slammed his fist against the heart-like shell. Light poured through the tubes in a liquid form akin to souls, but not quite the same. It was the raw essence of the Aether, not yet tainted and shaped with the memories and emotions of a life. This was the energy that shimmered within the stars and held the void at bay. A smoke-like substance poured into the heart chamber, slowly filling from the bottom as if it were a liquid.

"You refused to do what must be done," Wren shouted from inside the heart. "But I won't."

"This is a mistake, Nihil," Janus insisted. "I thought you of all the dragons most loathed the concept of a Chainbreaker."

"I work within the confines forced upon me," Nihil said, its voice shifting so it sounded like two bickering, elderly men. Its oily skin warped so it resembled blood. "If we cannot slay the Goddesses, then we must replace them. Only then will our children be treated as equal."

"We're *not* equal," Janus said. "We're better. But you're going to butcher our chance to prove it."

Not a sentiment Adria agreed with, but now was no time to debate philosophy. The veins pulsed harder. Aether poured into the chamber through the veins of a false heart. A sound like thunder rolled unending.

"Wren understands what Adria does not," Nihil continued. Every syllable marked a slight shift, from masculine to feminine, young to old, sometimes not even human but with the sing-song voice of a bird or the bark of a dog. "The Sisters have not just failed. The Sisters have poisoned the very foundations humanity was built upon. The Goddesses' weakness and pride brought about the soulless. Their favoritism forced us to watch our own children suffer. The Keeping Church must not be conquered and reformed. It must be—"

The dragon suddenly halted in mid-speech. Its eyes stared into nowhere, as if seeing something across a great distance.

"Damn it, Viciss, you fool."

The ground shook. Nihil cast one last look at the heart full of Aether and shriveled into itself, vanishing completely. Adria had but a moment to stare in shock before she thought to act.

"The machinery," she said, sprinting toward Wren. "We have to stop it."

"It's too late," Janus said, chasing after her.

"Don't fight this," Wren shouted from inside the heart. "You can't. I'm ready, Adria. I'm—"

Light blasted into the heart with the force of a sundered star. Unlike before, when she was a frightened, confused human, Adria's eyes could witness the cosmic forces being thrust into Wren, reshaping her body and ripping unseen chains off her soul. The magic required stole Adria's breath away. This was the power to build worlds. This was the essence in which the five dragons had covered the Cradle with life. The glass-like surface of the imprisoning heart shattered, and within this blue-white beam of change, Wren rose skyward, her arms pulled wide and her head flung back. She screamed a familiar scream.

At last, Adria turned away and covered her eyes. She could watch no more.

As suddenly as it began, the flow of Aether ceased. Wren floated to the ground and gently landed on her knees. Her head bowed, and her palms opened. Faint smoke wafted off her fingertips. Without a word spoken between them, Adria could already feel a connection. It felt as if they were melded together at the hip, their blood flowing through one another. She could even hear bits and pieces of Wren's thoughts, little soft whispers from a distant room in the dead of night.

"Wren?" Adria asked. Deafening silence replaced the roar of the machinery. "Wren, you must listen to me."

"Listen?" Wren asked. Her head lolled back. Her eyes struggled to focus. The way her speech slurred, she could pass for being intoxicated. "I can hear you already. You're so loud, Adria. So very loud."

Wren clenched her fists. The pull hit Adria's forehead like a physical blow. The other woman was grabbing at her soul, trying to rip it free of her skull. It took only a moment for Adria to gather her breath and smooth the impulse away, but that momentary disorientation frightened her. Wren was equal to her in every way, but she was new to this, still flailing to understand the powers she logically knew she had inherited.

"Cease this at once," Adria snapped. "I'm not here to fight you. I came here to help soulless like you!"

"Like me?" Wren asked, and she laughed amid her delirium. Her hands lifted above her head. "Who else is like me? Just you, Adria. Just you."

Power was everywhere, floating in the air, billowing across the floor, permeating the stone, and shimmering in the weary veins. Adria could see Wren drawing it into herself, as if she were the heart of a grand maelstrom. It swelled across her soul. It arced to her fingertips. Adria's eyes widened upon realizing exactly what her counterpart planned, and she began pulling equal Aether into her own breast.

A keening sound marked Wren's completion, and from her extended hands blasted a tremendous beam of pure, raw Aether. Adria crossed her arms and formed a barrier of the same magic, and when the beam hit, she drew further strength from her own soul to endure the impact. A gasp escaped her lips. For one brief moment she thought she would falter against the beam that continued on and on, blinding in its whiteness, untouchable in its fury. Adria's gasp turned to a scream. She poured more of herself into her shield. Her crossed arms shook. Her breath vanished.

The beam ended, and Wren collapsed, her energy spent. She lay on her stomach, her breathing raspy and weak. Janus's heavy footsteps thudded upon the weirdly flesh-like ground. His right hand extended, fingers merging together and sharpening to become an axe.

"Wait," Adria said. Her words were weak, her breath equally raspy as Wren's. "Don't kill her."

"You'd let her live?" Janus asked. "After what you just saw? There will be no better time than now. The longer she lives, the more she learns how to control the gifts granted to her..."

"No. She lives. She must."

Janus stepped aside as Adria crossed the space between them. She knelt before Wren and softly put a hand upon her sweating face. Her fingers cupped her cheek. Amid the fire and fury, she felt love for this newborn Chainbreaker, the only person upon the entire Cradle who could appreciate the burdens which lay upon her shoulders. Wren glared back up at her, and there was no love in her returned gaze.

"I see it," Adria said softly. "No. I *feel* it. You hate me, Wren. Why? Why this fire?"

Tears trickled down the exhausted woman's face.

"I feel it, too," Wren said. "This tremendous power you were given. And you didn't think to help us. None of us. The first soul you gave to a soulless body was a gift to your brother. People like me, like Jacaranda...we were so far beneath you, we never even entered your mind. Instead you took your tremendous power and helped yourself and those you love."

Wren grabbed Adria by the wrist. Her eyes widened as her strength rapidly returned.

"You rule the church now," Wren said. "The church that made us slaves. The church that declared us inhuman. The church who serves Goddesses that refuse to heal the wounds they made, and who threaten you with death for attempting to do what they deny. That is who you serve. That is who you rule. But it shouldn't be ruled. It shouldn't even exist. The church should be burned to the ground, every last rotten corner, so that something better may grow from its ashen soil. The Sisters don't deserve my love. They don't deserve my obedience. If you are to become the church, then neither do you."

That was it then. As with Jacaranda, it came down to those chain tattoos upon her throat. Adria clasped the other woman's hands in hers, and she laid her soul naked before someone who wielded the power to see that very soul.

"Do you know why I came down here?" Adria asked. "I planned to use the same power that crafted you into a Chainbreaker to call souls for the soulless. Not just the ones here in Londheim, not even Westreach, but the entire Cradle. Yes, I seek to reform the church, but I'll make it something better, I swear. The Sisters will see that. They must. Their responsibility to their children goes beyond granting us souls and then hiding away like absent gardeners waiting for a harvest."

That connection between them allowed Adria to feel Wren's hope flickering to life like an ember amid a thunderstorm.

"And if they try to stop you?" she asked.

Adria lifted her arms and gestured to the vastly empty chamber.

"They have not yet," she said. "And if they do? This time it will take more than words. I will put an end to all soulless. I will rectify the weakness of our Goddesses. Let them call it blasphemy if they must, but I will not stand idly by when I have the power to make things right."

Wren's hope blossomed. For the first time since her transformation into a Chainbreaker, she looked upon Adria and saw something more than an enemy.

"Can you stand against a Goddess?" she asked. "Can you refuse their divine will?"

"With Janus at my side?" Adria asked. "With *you* at my side? I think I can, Wren. I think we three can."

Wren was so close to believing her. Her experiences after awakening from her soulless life had taught her to distrust others. She viewed the world through a lens of hurt and betrayal. But hope still lurked within her, soft and fragile. Adria offered the woman her hand.

"Will you help me?"

Before Wren might answer, mocking applause stole their attention to one of the side tunnels.

"Such a touching moment," Lyssa said as she led a group of Soulkeepers into the grand chamber. "Bonding through heresy. What a beautiful sight."

Adria spun to face them, words of a prayer already leaping to mind to protect herself. Janus crossed his arms, hardening his face and chest into steel in case they fired their pistols.

"How did you find this place?" she asked.

In answer, Devin stepped to the forefront. He was yet to draw his pistol, but his hand rested on its wooden handle. Adria looked past his grim stare to his soul beyond, and she sensed his apprehension and fear intermixed with disappointment.

"You killed Vikar Forrest and Vikar Caria," Devin said. "And now you openly promise to defy our Goddesses."

Adria rose to her full height and pulled back her shoulders. Her fingers tensed. She could rip the souls from their bodies, but they were so many, and all it'd take was one single shot through her forehead to end it all. Most worrisome, Wren was watching with rapt attention. If the other Chainbreaker chose to help the Soulkeepers in battle, things could turn dire fast.

"I do not defy them," Adria said. "I fulfill their responsibilities. A soul upon our births, to be reaped upon our deaths. Is that not the promise given to every life born upon the Cradle?"

"Every human life," Janus said, unable to stop himself.

"And how does murdering our church leaders fit into that promise, pray tell?" her brother asked.

Adria set her jaw and glared.

"They made the attempt on my life first," she said. "You should know that, or is your faith in me so very little?"

She had no need to see his soul to know her brother felt ashamed for such an accusation. The Vikars had tried to kill her to keep their titles instead of forfeiting them over to her, the Chainbreaker, the clear heir to the Deakon position. He knew that. They all knew that. Some of them just didn't care.

"Self-defense," Lyssa spat. "What of the ultimatum you gave them? You can't demand complete surrender and then whine about self-defense when those you threaten fight back."

Adria glared. There'd be no reasoning with that one. Deep down, she found herself shockingly numb to their threats. Killing the Soulkeepers meant nothing to her. It was only her brother who mattered, her brother and Wren, who quietly watched, revealing nothing of her own opinion on the matter.

"Devin, don't do this," she said. "You've been with me every step of this path. You know my heart is in the right place. I gave everything to this city. I healed their sick and I tended their wounded. I prayed until my body collapsed. Have you no faith in me? No trust? Or will you point a gun to my head and demand my surrender?"

Her brother looked at the floor, and she sensed him gathering his thoughts.

"You wield more power than any other human alive," he said. "Which means you bear the greatest of responsibilities for its use. You murdered those who challenged you. How do I trust you now, Adria? How do I believe you are right in this, and disbelieve the warnings given to me by my own Goddess? Lyra says you will bathe the world in void. What if this is how you do it? What if this single act is what breaks the dam? It doesn't matter your intentions then, only the death that follows."

Janus's arms elongated into twin, jagged-edged cleavers. Despite his now fully steel face and jaw, he spoke with ease.

"This is your last chance to escape with your lives," he told the Soulkeepers. "Your dead Vikars aren't worth this."

Lyssa lifted her pistol, and when Devin refused to address their gathered members, she did so instead.

"Hold faith," she said. "Adria cannot kill us all."

"I very much can," Adria whispered, and her fingers tensed, preparing to defend herself from the barrage of lead shot.

The barrage did not come, not yet, for the ground suddenly heaved beneath them. All present but Janus collapsed to their hands and knees. The ceiling shook, long cracks splitting across its surface. This was no rumbling of the unseen machinery that powered the chamber, but something much greater, and much more frightening. Janus cackled like a madman, his arms held wide at his sides and his coat slipping to expose his bare chest. His feet and ankles melded with the flesh-like floor to grant him stability.

"Don't you hear them?" he shouted. "Don't you hear the world ending?"

"What are you blathering about?" asked a frightened Lyssa.

"The dragons," Janus cried, his voice a cross between mania and laughter. "The dragons! *They're fighting!*"

CHAPTER 36

Adria had told Dierk that the wisest course of action was to hide inside his mansion and wait for her to soothe the tensions of Londheim's people. It was that reason alone he marched with a small escort of guards to the outer wall of the city. He felt a desire, no, an undeniable *need*, to defy her, to be anywhere but inside that blood-soaked mansion. So he found himself a spot on the wall and looked out upon the sprawling army of the dragon-sired.

"Have our soldiers gather along the walls," Dierk ordered.

"Most are already here," said the bearded man with him. General Kaelyn had fled the city upon learning of Albert's death, so he was the newest man in charge of defending Londheim. Dierk tried to remember his name but couldn't. What even was his rank? Things he should be paying attention to, he realized, but wasn't. Damn all the distractions and confusions. The soldiers were under his authority, but he needed an official liaison he could trust. Hopefully the bearded man, based on the few medals pinned to his breast pocket, counted as one.

"Then get the rest of them," he said.

Dierk stared at the camp, flanked on either side by the two dragons. They seemed such opposites of one another, yet from what Dierk had learned of them, they should be like brothers. First there was Viciss, the crawling mountain, a gargantuan construction whose weight and girth appeared immeasurable. This was the Dragon of Change, so had said Vaesalaum before Dierk killed the bothersome nisse. Carried on those twelve legs, it was slow and inevitable. Should it wish to breach the walls of the city, nothing would stop it.

Opposite Viciss was what he believed to be the Dragon of Conflict, Nihil. Its form was of clouds and smoke, intangible and fleeting but no less dangerous. Compared to Viciss, it could be quick and nimble. Why would they oppose one another? Was conflict not an inevitable aspect of change? Surely they had worked together in tandem to shape the Cradle.

And yet, so far, neither had made a move against Londheim, not even to aid the dragon-sired army. Dierk smirked at the thousands of tents between them. The bothersome creatures. They thought themselves so mighty. Had they not seen what happened in Belvua to those who tried to oppose humanity's rule? Dierk's disgust mixed with his frustration and anger at the world steadily conspiring against him. What did he need Adria for? Londheim had lasted for hundreds of years, never once falling to a siege. Under no circumstances would he allow his newfound rule to begin under a stain of cowardice.

"Fetch me a messenger, too," he told one of the other guards with him. "And some ink and paper."

Not long after, a soldier rode out on a horse bearing a short, simple letter Dierk had written: *Send me Lavender.*

Twenty minutes later, Lavender approached the walls of the city. Dierk crossed his arms and tried to look smug. At such a distance, the strange dragon-sired creature appeared far less frightening and beautiful. Just a green and red bug standing amid the dying grass. It seemed shouting up at him was beneath her, however, and so she extended the long blue spinnerets on each of her hands. Webs spun from grass to wall, forming her a bridge with which to meet him.

"Greetings, newly anointed High Excellence of Westreach," Lavender said, her hips swaying as if she walked the sturdiest of pathways instead of a thin strip of webbing. "Have you given any thought to your position? I must confess, Shinnoc was not impressed with the message you asked I deliver to him."

"I have indeed changed my position," Dierk said. "You, and your army, occupy my lands. Leave them at once, or we shall have you slaughtered."

Lavender tilted her head to one side. Her scaly rainbow hair tinkled like crystal as its locks clinked against one another.

"I beg your pardon, High Excellence, but I fear I misheard."

"You misheard nothing," he snapped. His voice rose in pitch as he shouted, and but he dared not stop to clear his throat lest he seem uncertain. "Flee west, and keep fleeing west, until you're so far beyond the mountains we never see you again. Westreach belongs to us. These are my lands, *human* lands."

"Human lands." Lavender crossed her arms as she halted several feet from the edge of the wall. "There are no humans left upon those lands, Dierk. They have fled, either from our armies or the black water the crawling mountain unleashed amid his waking rage. This is your last chance. Will you not honor the treaties we signed with your predecessors? There is still a chance for peace."

"I don't give a shit about your old treaties!" he screamed. "Are you deaf? Get. Fucking. Lost."

Goddesses above, it felt so good to see that frustration on the woman's face. Her disgust was like fuel to a fire burning deep within his stomach. Lavender bowed low, her clawed hands looping in an intricate figure-eight pattern.

"As you wish," she said. "I shall relay your—message—to Shinnoc. I expect you will not like his reply."

A swipe of her sharp claws cut the webbing so it lost much of its support. The remaining strands sank from her weight, carrying her gently back down to the barren ground. Dierk made a rude gesture with his fingers as she descended, then clapped his hands together excitedly.

"They're going to attack," said the bearded soldier in charge.

"Of course they're going to attack," Dierk snapped. "Why do you think I asked you to bring all our soldiers to the wall?"

"But we're not prepared," the man insisted. "You should have warned us this was your plan."

"I am High Excellence. I need not explain a damn thing to you, you hear me? Their army's coming. Do your job."

Chaos erupted about him as men and women started running every which way, relaying confused and often contradictory orders. Dierk stayed upon the wall, his hands clasped behind his back and his weight shifting from foot to foot. He felt like a child on the night before his birthday. This whole city had been cowering in fear of the dragon-sired army, but now they'd see how toothless they truly were. They had their walls, their swords, and their riflemen, and he had his curses. What were a few oversized rabbits and deer going to do against that?

Minutes passed, interminably slow. Dierk's impatience grew with each tedious second. He'd hoped Lavender's spreading of his message would have the various races charging the walls in a frenzy, but it seemed they were carefully dismantling their tents instead.

"Are they...are they actually leaving?" he asked in disbelief, but he received no answer from those around him other than shrugged shoulders and grim smiles.

"We could only be so lucky," said the bearded soldier.

"That sounds like the talk of a frightened boy," Dierk said, puffing out his chest.

"It's the talk of someone who doesn't want to see his men and women die." He pointed. "But don't worry, High Excellence. You will be getting your fight."

The army had their supplies packed, their weapons gathered, and their various units set up in formation. The distance made it difficult, but it seemed they grouped by their races, with the rabbit-like lapinkin leading the way.

"All right, all right," Dierk said, and he scrambled through the various curses of the Book of Ravens in his mind, trying to decide which if any were best suited to a field of battle. "We, uh, we're safe here on this wall, right?"

"The lapinkin take to the skies as well as birds," the bearded man said. "No. I don't think we are."

Dierk hadn't actually seen the battle at the Cathedral of the Sacred Mother, only its aftermath. What had stuck with him was how the dragon-sired had died in equal numbers to the humans, despite being the ones with the advantage of surprise...but of course, Adria had ended the battle with her tremendous power. Adria, who was somewhere underneath the city doing whatever involving the soulless of the Cradle.

We don't need her, he thought as the army approached, first at a walk, and then a sprint. *We have this. We're strong.*

The distance closed. Riflemen, their numbers barely in the fifties, readied their weapons. Soulkeepers should have been among them with their pistols, but Lyssa had led their survivors underground to confront Adria. Dierk tried to tell himself he didn't need their numbers as the riflemen fired. Smoke billowed into the air, and though their shots were true, their kills were but a pitiful drop of the advancing horde. Dierk rehearsed the words of the mutilation curse in his head as his pulse quickened. They were close now, close enough for him to realize just how gigantic the dyrandar were, their upper bodies bulging with muscle and their hooves pounding indents into the grass. He saw the sharpness of the lapinkin spears, and in a sudden chorus he heard the keening of owls high above, lurking unseen behind the clouds.

"Oh, shit," Dierk said.

The army was nearly to the wall when the crawling mountain turned. Black water roared from deep within its belly like a sideways waterfall. The otherworldly liquid rolled across the field, directly blocking the path of the approaching army. The liquid, dark like oil yet deep like the night sky and full of stars, sank into the grass and became fire. It burned higher, and higher, a wall of purple flame that showed no sign of dwindling. Most eerie of all, it burned without smoke or sound, just a curling, consuming violet wrath.

The crawling mountain lumbered forward a single step, and for the first time ever, Dierk heard it speak.

"No war. Not when peace lies within reach."

Dierk glared at the gigantic beast. What nonsense was this? It would scar the west with its black water, then settle itself on Londheim's doorstep with the perverse claim it was fostering *peace*?

"This is bullshit," he grumbled, trying to hide the relief sweeping through him with a vulgar facade.

But there was one who sought war, and it was not the one Dierk had ever expected. The cloud dragon lifted its head. Its body shimmered with a sudden ripple of twilight. Pale smoke blasted from its throat in equal measure to the black water. It bathed the purple flame, smothering it down to faint embers that withered and died, leaving a long, barren stretch of ashen earth between Londheim and the army. The ground trembled as the crawling mountain braced its legs.

"*We shall not interfere,*" said the cloud dragon with a voice like a windstorm sweeping through a forest. "*Let this world play out as it must.*"

"*This world is of our own making,*" argued Viciss, a cacophonous avalanche to counter the windstorm. "*We must interfere. We must partake.*"

In response, the cloud dragon reared back its head and let loose a tremendous roar that shook the walls of the city. Dierk grabbed the stone balustrade to steady himself, and his arrogance quickly dissipated into pants-pissing fear.

"Are... are they going to..."

The dragons answered his question before he could even finish.

Nihil lunged like a striking cobra, moving with speed that should have been impossible given its tremendous size. Its forearms sank marble claws into the mountainous side with an ear-splitting crack. Its mouth opened, its teeth sinking into the area just above Viciss's lizard-like head. Stone shattered, grooves the size of houses burrowed along the ground, and then with a collision that sounded for miles, the crawling mountain tumbled to its side.

The ensuing earthquake was the greatest Dierk had experienced in his life. He collapsed to his knees and clung to the wall until a sudden lurch cracked his teeth against its hard stone. Blood spilled across his tongue, and he yelped as he fell onto his back. The shock waves hit a moment later. Stones cracked, and all across the city, walls and rooftops collapsed in on themselves as their foundations failed to endure the rolling blast. As the shaking softened to steady rumbles, Dierk pulled himself up to the edge of the battlement, his curiosity overcoming his fear.

The dragons tore into one another with power beyond what any living thing should possess. Their every swipe or bite shook the ground. Boulders collapsed from the mountain's sides, pounding the cloud dragon on their fall. Viciss's every shudder slammed them together, shattering deep cracks into both their bodies as Nihil struggled to hold on. Deep claws ripped free pieces larger than buildings. The clack of their teeth colliding sent shivers down Dierk's spine. Their roars threatened to loose his bowels. Nihil cut and carved, ripping into Viciss like an eagle trying to split a tortoise. Viciss belched black water across the cloud dragon in return, but whatever power it possessed could not change its foe, only char deep grooves as if its breath were fire.

Nihil bellowed out in victory as the crawling mountain finally split down the middle. Star-filled black water exploded in all directions, yet it washed clean off the sides of the cloud dragon without finding purchase. Its lower two legs joined the upper two in sinking claws into the edges of the torn opening, strengthening its pull. The split widened to an enormous gap, and the sound of shrieking metal joined that of breaking stone. The heart of the mountain lay exposed, a hovering prism of purest night, its dimensions perfectly smooth, its magic overwhelming to Dierk's nisse-blessed eyes. He saw the power of creation condensed into a crystalline structure twice the size of his father's mansion. Flesh-like tendrils fell from its sides, severing its connection to the physical body of the dragon, Viciss.

"The death of a dragon," Dierk whispered. What would it mean to its creations? What sort of eruption might follow the destruction of that eternity prism? He watched the cloud dragon rear back its head with excitement and dread in equal measure. The outer body was meaningless. This was the heart, this crystal, and Nihil would shatter it with one final clench of its jaws.

Its face slammed into a shield of light. Its teeth cracked and splintered. The front of its face broke like a statue struck by a maul. Dierk's dread amplified tenfold as the furious form of a Goddess materialized in the air between the two dragons. By her midnight skin and seemingly endless dark hair, there was only one who it could be. Lyra, Goddess of the Day. Her voice echoed throughout the land as she raged against her creations.

"I will have peace!"

Lyra turned to Nihil, and the full display of her fury brought tears to Dierk's eyes. Her physical form might be that of a dark-skinned woman of size and stature equal to a human, but to his nisse-blessed vision, she was a supernova of light. Enormous tendrils of pure white essence, like rivers of souls, stretched from her fingers and sides to strike the cloud dragon. They formed fingers and sank into its smokey exterior. Thunderstorm winds billowed across the city as they ripped the dragon apart. The shriek of metal and rip of flesh threatened to shatter eardrums. The shock of such a sight stole Dierk's breath, and he sobbed despite having no attachment to either dragon. His senses felt overwhelmed. Beings more ancient than humanity were breaking before him, and he felt far too young and ignorant to fully comprehend what transpired.

Lyra's rage subsided. She hovered in the air above the ruin, slowly fading away from view. Beneath her lay the bodies of two of her dragons; twisted shambles of flesh, stone, and steel forming gargantuan monuments to their former glory. The dragon-sired army slowly approached their wreckage in solemn awe. Dierk did not watch them, for his eyes were locked on the two prisms.

The substance of the soul, whatever otherworldly Aether that made up its shimmering existence, was the same substance that filled the prisms that defined the power of the dragons. And when he looked to Lyra's vanishing form, he saw her as an even greater sentient collection of that power. The dragons were her children, for she had granted them a shard of her own being. Dragons, Goddesses: They were the same. The same power. The same Aether.

"There's no difference between us," Dierk whispered. The soul in his own skull, it was the same power, just infinitesimally smaller. They were all shades of the same essence. If he could wield it as they did, as *Adria* did, then he could be equivalent to a dragon. He could even be a god.

Hundreds of dragon-sired knelt before the physical corpses of the dragons. Did they know their dragons still lived on, that these shells meant nothing compared to the near-infinite power contained within those prisms? He doubted it. They didn't see with the eyes he possessed. They likely could not see the prisms, only sense their power. Shinnoc's ensuing proclamation confirmed this. Magic strengthened his voice so it joined Lyra's in echoing across the land, though who it was meant for, humans or dragon-sired, Dierk could only guess.

"We have lost our brethren. We have lost a king. And now we lose our creators. What else may you take from us, children of the Goddesses? We have nothing left to give."

A great distance separated them, but Dierk swore he could see every twitch of the Dyrandar King's muscles, every subtle shift in stance and tone as his voice hardened and he lifted his tremendous axe to the heavens.

"Ashes, wretched humans. I vowed for ashes, and I shall uphold my vow."

The dragon-sired army charged the walls of Londheim, but there was something different about this charge. There were no exuberant shouts. There were no cries of eagles, no pounding of drums. This was the cold fury of the hopeless and abandoned. They were not there for victory, pride, or conquest.

Only slaughter.

"Ready your weapons," Dierk screamed as scores of lapinkin took to the air, the fading sunlight glinting off their jagged spears. "Ready everything, damn it, or they'll kill us all!"

CHAPTER 37

Brittany charged across the battlements, engaging the dragon-sired only when she must. Her fury gave her strength where her meager muscles failed. The battle was a nonsense of spells and magic, of a kind no human architect would have considered when building walls for defense. Lapinkin and giant owls slammed down upon the ramparts, devastating groups of soldiers before pulling away. One lapinkin nearly impaled Brittany through the chest, and was halted only by the misfortune of another soldier taking her place.

"You brought me back for this?" she wondered aloud as the wall shook from the hit of a battering ram. It wasn't a physical battering ram, either, but one conjured by the collective thoughts or prayers or whatever it was the dyrandár were doing as they chanted near the gates of the city. It faded in and out of view between each hit, but the blows it rained upon the fracturing gate were very much real.

A screech sent Brittany diving back to her stomach. An owl scraped his claws along the stone, carving a long groove that ended with the claws hooked into a luckless soldier. Blood splashed beyond the ramparts. His dying scream ended when the owl's beak ripped the man in half.

"Thanks, Adria. Just... thanks."

Brittany lurched back to her feet, her axe feeling useless in her hands. Another lapinkin landed, his spear punching through the chest of a rifleman. Brittany swung her axe, hitting nothing. He had already leapt away to the safety of the air. If only she could do the same. The only reason she stayed was for Tommy. He'd joined in the defense of the city, and she would not abandon him no matter how nightmarish the surroundings.

Finding her brother was no difficult task, but as she feared, he was right in the thick of the battle. The viridi were collecting their focus on a singular area of the wall. They laid their bodies flat against the stone and caressed it with their hands. A wave of grass, at least one hundred feet wide, flowed up the wall like a green river. Dyrandar used it as a ladder, and they climbed with terrifying speed. Tommy stood at the top of the flow, fire leaping from his hands as he unleashed his magic. Yet with every chunk he burned, more would take its place. Malik stood with him, and though he clearly cast his magic as well, she could only guess at its results. From what she understood, he dealt with illusions of the mind compared to her brother's more obvious elemental destruction.

"Tommy!" Brittany screamed, then skidded to a halt as a lapinkin slammed to a landing between them, her spear clacking off the stone. Brittany lifted her axe, having long ago used the last of her flamestones. Their eyes met. A half-second pause enveloped them both, a heartbeat to gauge reach and anticipate reactions. The lapinkin moved first, a puff of air billowing about her frame to quicken her charge. Her spear led the way, a lethal thrust for Brittany's heart. The Soulkeeper relied on gut instinct instead of her training, which would have suggested she parry the weapon harmlessly aside. Instead she leapt forward, her body twisting sideways to avoid being impaled. The movement put her axe out of position, but she had other weapons. Her elbow slammed into the lapinkin's flat nose.

Brittany screamed from the pain traveling up her arm to her

shoulder. The lapinkin suffered far worse. She staggered unevenly, her spear's next swing frantic and wild. Brittany easily ducked underneath, grasped her axe with both hands, and then swiped upward in a wide arc. She cleaved the lapinkin's left leg off from hip to thigh, dropping her in a shower of blood and gore. Brittany's muscles tightened as she continued the weapon's arc, curling it up and around to slam the edge back down into the lapinkin's face, ending her pained cries.

An explosion of sound spun her about. Tommy lay on his rear, an expression of shock on his face. Whatever spell he'd just cast, it had been enormous. An inferno consumed the grass along the wall, charring it from the edge completely. Black smoke billowed into the air, thick enough that the owls veered aside lest they be rendered blind. Dozens of viridi and dyrandar lay lifeless at the base of the wall. The sight was enough to make Brittany sick to her stomach.

"Brit?" Tommy asked, finally noticing her presence. She couldn't hear him from where she stood, but she could easily read that single word on his lips.

"Are you all right?" she asked as she sprinted the distance to him. Malik helped her brother to his feet and wiped a bit of ash and char from his robe.

"What are you doing out here?" he asked.

"I'm a Soulkeeper," she said. "I'm where I should be."

"Then where are the other Soulkeepers?"

Brittany grimaced.

"That's the point, Tommy. From what I gathered, they're off somewhere trying to avenge Adria for killing our Vikars. And Devin..." She hesitated, unable to believe it herself. "Devin is with them."

Her brother's jaw dropped.

"That can't be true."

"He's not home. He's not here. Where else could he be?"

"Tomas, this matter must wait," Malik said, putting a hand on her brother's shoulder. "The battle rages in earnest. It won't be long until the viridi try again. We must be ready."

"No," Tommy said, and he pushed the older man back. "Devin, try to kill Adria? That's insane. I—I—I must talk to them. I can fix this. Where did they go? Where is Adria?"

"I don't know," Brittany said. She'd pieced together what she knew from rumors spread by soldiers who had been with Dierk Becher during his coup to overthrow Albert. "Devin knew where Adria was somehow, but I don't."

"Then I'll just have to find him," Tommy said. He patted himself down, then pulled a scrap of paper from a random pocket. "Been meaning to try this one for a while now."

"Tomas," Malik said, his expression as stern as the stone wall they stood upon. "If that is the spell I think it is, this is not the time nor place for experimentation. The city needs us!"

"Devin and Adria need us!" Tommy shouted back. He flailed his arms about at the fires along the wall, the dying soldiers, and the horrifying carcasses of the two dragons. "All—this—is beyond me, but damn it, Adria could make it better. She could help fix this. Now shut up and let me concentrate."

He read the words on the paper twice, then stuffed it back into his pocket and began to chant.

"Gloam ieiun ambul, ieiun ambul Devin Eveson."

A circle opened in the air before them, its swirling blue as pure as the ocean. Fractured images shifted within the circle, like reflections across water, only foggy and uneven. Air billowed into it, and feeling its pull set Brittany's stomach into a knot.

"What in Lyra's name is that?" she asked.

"Think of it like a door to Devin," Tommy said.

"Is it safe?"

"There's a slight chance we could reappear horribly mangled, very slight, now jump in. We only have ten seconds!"

Brittany hoisted her axe and stared at the heart of that swirling blue "door."

"Tommy, if this is how I die a second time..."

"Five seconds!" her brother shouted. "Go!"

Brittany leapt into the circle. As soon as her skin touched its surface, her vision blanked. Her stomach churned. Her sensation of gravity spun wildly. A sound like the winds of a storm filled her ears, and though it lasted but a moment, the sensation of both time and distance stretched like a tearing muscle. The instant her feet touched ground, her vision returned, though it was murky and akin to intense intoxication.

"Oh, fuck," Brittany said before immediately collapsing to her knees and vomiting. It was in this undignified state, her stomach heaving, her ears ringing, and bits of drool hanging from her lips, that she observed her wondrous new surroundings. The room was enormous, with walls deep as the night and pulsing with faint blue rivers that were disturbingly similar to veins. The ground was soft, gray, and felt akin to flesh. Tommy and Malik exited the blue circle behind her, and they collapsed beside her in similar manner.

"Never... again," Malik said before emptying the contents of his stomach.

Brittany pushed to her feet, her senses rapidly returning to her, and she almost wished she'd stayed at the wall. Another battle raged before her, only this one was far more one-sided than the siege of the dragon-sired.

"Who, no, *what* is that?" she asked.

A monster ripped through the ranks of the Soulkeepers who had made the journey below ground. His form was a bizarre dichotomy, his left half shimmering steel, his right the deep brown of a forest oak. His arms were weapons, one a sword, the other a thorned branch he wielded like a whip. He dashed through the Soulkeepers, lashing their faces, cutting apart their limbs, and howling with the pleasure.

"Janus," Tommy said as he staggered to his feet. "A sick piece of shit, that one."

Selfish it might be, but Brittany searched for her former husband first, not caring for the others. She felt relief sweep through her upon spotting him and his lover, Jacaranda, both locked in battle. They appeared unharmed, though that would not last long given their foe's animosity.

And as much as she wished to disbelieve it, there was her sister-in-law, Adria, aiding this monster. Three souls swirled before her in a protective arc, and they burst with light every time one of the Soulkeepers fired their pistol in her direction. The Soulkeepers wielded her brother's spellstones, and it was likely that power that kept Adria on the defensive. Fire, ice, and lightning erupted about the woman, massive blasts that could level buildings yet could not seem to break the shimmering white shield that surrounded her form.

Even then, Brittany wondered why Adria did not end the fight immediately. She certainly had the ability to do so, but instead she merely batted aside anyone foolish enough to attack her, the raw power of the souls burning flesh to bone and melting weapons to liquid. Was she hoping the Soulkeepers would leave voluntarily? Or did she merely prefer to let the monster with her do the killing?

"Stop it!" Tommy shouted, his fists clenched and his skin pale. "All of you, stop!"

He dropped back to his knees and slammed his hands upon the ground. A wall of ice spread in a perfectly straight line, dividing Adria from the Soulkeepers. Janus reacted instantly, his legs elongating and bending backward so he leapt like a lapinkin to the top of the wall. There he sat, his grin ear to ear.

"Interlopers?" he asked. "Oh, it's the little runt who burned me the last time we fought here. I've been meaning to have a word with you."

"Enough," Adria snapped. Light shimmered across her fingertips, the tremendous power of her soul gathered and ready. "Tomas, what are you doing here? And you, too, Brittany? Have you come to kill me as well?"

"No killing!" Tommy shouted. "I don't—I don't want any killing. I'm here to stop it, you understand?"

"Noble," Janus laughed. "Stupid, but noble."

"We do this for the Cradle," Lyssa shouted from the other side of the ice wall. "Adria will burn our church to the ground so she can appoint herself God-Queen."

"God-Queen?" Adria scoffed. "I want no such thing."

"Not yet, but it's coming. Our dead Vikars prove it."

Brittany readied her axe. This delay would not last long, and she had no intention of remaining neutral. A hand gently touched her shoulder as Malik slowly leaned over to whisper in her ear.

"Attack quickly. I will delay her long enough for a killing blow."

"Please, let's just all calm down and figure this out," Tommy said, approaching Adria with no clue as to Malik's plan. Adria gave her brother-in-law a look of love, and pity.

"I'm sorry," she said. "This must be done."

"*Gloam tavrum insecar,*" whispered Malik, activating his spell. The change was subtle. Adria tilted her head slightly as if she'd heard something that confused her. Brittany broke into a sprint, easily surpassing Tommy to close the distance. Adria remained where she stood, her eyes glazed, her mouth locked in a slight frown, as if her mind were confused and not present. Janus realized what was happening and screamed out wordless fury, but he was far too distant from his perch atop the ice wall.

Brittany hoisted her axe above her head, and she begged the Goddesses to forgive her for what she must do.

The Goddesses might have forgiven her, but her brother would not.

"Brit, no!"

Lightning tore through her hip and out her shoulder. The

impact lifted her off her feet, and she felt the grip to her axe slip from her suddenly weak fingers. Both she and her weapon hit the ground and rolled with a loud clatter. With Tommy's concentration broken, the ice wall crumbled to water, which evaporated as if beneath a summer sun.

"Finish her while you can!" Brittany shouted to the surviving Soulkeepers. Both Janus and Tomas realized the danger and acted immediately.

"Please... please stop, all of you!" her brother screamed as fire burst about his fingers. "Don't do this, any of this, please stop, please, just stop, just stop..."

Whereas Tommy proved frightened and locked with indecision, Janus erupted like a rabid animal. The remaining Soulkeepers fell in a display of gore bewildering in its speed. Only Devin, Jacaranda, and Lyssa remained when he leapt out of their center and tore into the sky like a bird. Skin connected the gaps between his sides and arms, and a second pair of black wings sprouted from his back. He crossed the distance between him and Malik in the blink of an eye. His legs curled forward like those of a diving hawk, and his feet split in the center of his soles to become gaping mouths with gnashing teeth. Tommy screamed. Magic sparked on his hands, but he would not react in time.

This freakish bird of prey slammed into Malik, feet-mouths clamping on to each of his wrists and biting down hard enough to shower blood across the ground. Malik screamed, his spell ended. The two tangled together as they collapsed, their roll ending with Janus crouched atop him with his human face elongating into that of a raven. His beak opened to reveal dozens of jagged shark teeth.

"Bothersome, aren't you?" asked the monster.

Brit slammed her axe into his spine as an answer. The steel sank several inches into his skin, and she felt sick pleasure hearing his cry of pain. Blood spilled, but his skin hardened around her axe. If she'd cut his spine, it didn't seem to have affected him. The blood became fire. The flesh she cut turned to stone. He rammed his beak into Malik's forehead to daze the older man, then spun to face her.

"You'll suffer ages," Janus said as he ripped the axe free. "Your blood will cover my tongue. Your innards will be my feast."

She tried to roll away but he proved faster. His hand latched around her throat and hardened into iron as he held her aloft. His other hand elongated while sharpening, becoming a perfectly smooth and shining blade to press against the vulnerable skin of her neck.

"No!" Adria shouted, finally having regained her bearings. Light rolled out from her body in a seismic wave. "Let her live."

The pitifully few survivors gathered around as Janus contemplated Adria's command. The sharp tip of his sword-hand softly rubbed up and down Brittany's throat. His jade eyes hungered for blood. His other hand holding her neck tightened.

"But of course," Janus said. "You resurrected her, didn't you? Very selfish of you, Adria, but you've always been selfish with your power. Mercy for those you know and love, but death for the rest? I'm beginning to understand little Wren's anger with you."

Brittany assumed Wren was the name of the other woman who stood near Adria. She'd not participated at all in the battle, merely watched quietly from afar. Something was special about her, for there was definitely worry in Adria's eyes when she glanced back to see how Wren reacted.

"Perhaps it is selfish," Adria said. "But I did not bring these men and women here. I did not ask for them to die. Let them go, all of them."

"Such a pity," Janus said. The grip about Brittany's throat loosened. "I was having such fun, too, but it would be hypocritical of me to object." He spun to grin at Devin and Jacaranda. "After all, I left you two alive for last. I'd hoped to have a bit of fun in return for our final meeting, but it seems the Chainbreaker shall protect those she still loves." His hand extended so the steel fingers became a spear. "But there's at least one person left no one here loves."

Janus's arm extended as if it were a rope. The spear's edge shot outward to pierce Lyssa's throat and then puncture out the back of her neck.

"Lyssa!" Devin screamed. He lashed out at Janus with his sword, only to have it easily deflected by Janus's other hand. Janus twisted the spear, then withdrew it with a chuckle. Lyssa dropped to her knees, the life leaving her eyes as her blood poured from the wicked gash.

"You bastard," Devin said as he slid to Lyssa's side. His hands cradled her face, but she was already gone.

"Am I a bastard?" Janus asked as he stalked the space between them and Adria. "I have no mother, and I am hated by my father. I suppose there are similarities."

Brittany's fingers yearned for her axe. She'd give anything to bury its edge deep within that monster's skull. The pleasure he received from seeing Devin suffer was inhuman.

"Enough," Adria said. "This was meant to be an exultant moment, not one of bloodshed. I will not mark a new age for the Cradle with the execution of the last members of my friends and family. Leave them be, Janus, or I shall have you join the ranks of the dead."

Janus's hands molded back into pale flesh.

"If you insist," he said, and he flashed them all a grin of his opal teeth.

The survivors gathered together at Janus's prodding. Devin remained with Lyssa's body, Jacaranda hovering at his shoulder. Tommy and Malik stood together, Tommy doing his best to staunch the bleeding from the weird bite marks Janus left on Malik's wrists. Brittany lurked at the edge, wishing there were something more she could do. On the other end of the massive room, Janus, Wren, and Adria gathered together like points on a triangle.

"Do not interfere," Adria told the others. "The power required will be tremendous, and I fear what would happen if I am interrupted." She offered her hands to Wren. "Will you aid me, Chainbreaker? Will you help me change the world?"

Wren hesitated. The air thickened. Brittany could only guess at this woman's purpose, but if Adria was calling her a Chainbreaker, then she might even possess power to rival Adria's. What could it mean? Or did it even matter if the two were working together?

Whatever hesitance Wren felt, she shook it away and smiled.

"Yes," she said. "I will."

Their fingers touched.

A familiar circle ripped open in the air high above them all, only its surface was black instead of blue. Its arrival was marked by a clap of thunder with such brightness and intensity, Brittany had no choice but to cower and look away. When her vision returned, her mouth hung open, and her mind struggled to believe the undeniable truth before her.

"No," said the Goddess Lyra. She hovered several dozen feet in the air, her skin darker than the false night that made up the ceiling of the magical chamber. Her hair reached the floor, and it pooled together in a soft pile. She pointed to Adria, and her crystalline voice shook with naked rage. "At last, we bring this to its end."

CHAPTER 38

Jacaranda felt the strength in her legs give out and her breath come in thin little wisps down her throat. Her eyes dared not leave the presence hovering over the false starfield high above their heads.

"Lyra," she whispered, as if naming the entity would make her more real to her mind. This was a being of unspeakable power, one who made even the dragons seem meager by comparison. One of the three Sisters who had built the world, who had crafted humanity from the dust and given it the light of a soul. To look upon her, and to hear her speak, was surreal beyond measure.

Even stranger, her heart felt nothing but rage toward the divine being addressing those gathered.

"Adria Eveson," said the Goddess. "Wren Sommers. You bear stolen power, granted by dragons seeking to upend the natural order of the eternal. You are children walking a land of fire and frost. It is time to put this danger to an end. It is time the Cradle is made right."

Adria approached the Goddess with her fists balled at her sides.

"We seek to correct your mistakes," she shouted through her mask. "You grew weak, and in your weakness you failed to send souls to all who were born. I would do what you did not. That is all I seek, yet you would accuse me of destroying the proper order that you failed to maintain? You would cry out against this as if I commit some grave sin?"

"We were weak because we gave everything for you," Lyra's voice boomed within the cavern. "The children of the dragons would have slaughtered you if not for our interference, and when they were not sated with killing you, they sought to kill your faith in us as well. Chainbreakers were not meant to elevate humanity. They were meant to free you from us. As if gifting you souls was a slavery. As if you never needed our guidance, and we deserve nothing in return for granting you life and a world to live upon."

"Then let us make up for what was lost while you suffered in our name," Adria said. "Why do you fear what we may do? Why does pulling down souls for the soulless ignite such fury within you?"

Lyra lifted her hands before her and stared into her palms. Little tendrils of light swirled about them, as if the burning light of a million souls were trapped within her meager human form. Jacaranda feared the Goddess would strike Adria down where she stood for such a challenge, but it seemed something held her back.

"The future is unknown even to myself," said Lyra. "But I see glimpses like shadows upon water. Your meddling threatens all that my Sisters and I have built. Life is precious, Adria, and it is rarer than you can fathom. Beyond the boundary of the stars lurks the void, and it is hateful, and it is always, always hungry. Your actions risk destroying the delicate balance we have constructed. You risk tearing a hole through the veil and allowing the void entrance into this world. I see that dark future. I see it so plainly. Whatever certainty you feel, whatever belief in your own self-righteousness you possess, it is not worth such a risk. The entire world destroyed, all to grant souls to a few thousand soulless? What madness is that? What foolishness?"

Adria refused to back down. She shouted up at the Goddess, the divine light reflecting off her mask so that it seemed she herself bore a heavenly face.

"You're afraid," she said. "And you doubt me. You doubt Wren.

But we can do this. Every single day Alma brings the seeds of a soul down from the Aether to our world. The void does not take us then, and it will not take us now."

"That is because we are the divine," Lyra said. "You are children smashing about in a world of glass. To compare us Sisters to you is to diminish us. There is no comparison. There is no risk in our aiding of humanity. But you... you would disobey? You would commit such blasphemous acts despite our commandment? Who are you, Adria, to consider yourself wiser than the eternal?"

Jacaranda could feel the frustration and anger radiating off Lyra like a physical force. She burned like a sun in the sky.

"I'm not wiser," Adria said. "But I will not be persuaded. This is the right thing to do, and I will do it."

"Your mind may be set," Lyra said, and she turned to Wren, "but yours is still awakening to the newly gifted magic inside you. The world rests in your hands now, Wren. Strike down Adria. Put an end to this madness."

"Yes, strike her down," Janus said in mockery. "Do the dirty work the Goddesses cannot do."

The Goddess waved a hand toward the avatar and then clenched her dark fingers into a fist. Janus cried out as invisible hands gripped his body and lifted it a foot off the ground.

"I cannot kill," she said. "But I can change. I can alter. How greatly do you cherish the abilities gifted to you by Viciss, avatar? Would you weep if I stole them from you?"

His skin rippled as if it were water instead of flesh.

"I'd rather die," he said.

"Then cease your prattle."

Her fist opened, and he dropped to the ground with a gasp. For several long moments his rattling breath was the only sound in the chamber as all others stared, fearful to speak or incur the Goddess's wrath. Only Wren found the courage, and she threw back her shoulders and did her best to stand at her full height.

"Is what we seek so great a crime?" she asked her maker. "We just want to make everything better for the soulless. Awakening like I did, like Jacaranda did, it was a good thing. I believe that, I have to believe that, because...because what else am I to do? What does this life mean otherwise?"

"The soulless bear no concept of their differences," the Goddess said. "They have lived every second of their entire lives never making a decision for themselves. They have lived a vacuous existence, of meaning and purpose less than that of the animals of the forest or the birds of the sky. There is peace in that, yes, and a simplicity that breaks my heart to look upon, but think on what you are doing, for you have experienced it yourself. Remember your first moments of your awakened life. Is that what you want thousands of soulless all across the Cradle to experience?"

Lyra shook her head, the movement sending ripples down her star-studded hair.

"These soulless have taken no actions, and made no choices, but they will feel the guilt of their past nonetheless. They will bear the burden of the lives they lived despite owning no true responsibility for it. You do not meddle in simple affairs, Chainbreakers. You dabble in the realms of eternity. Would you have every single soulless enter into the Aether flow forever linked to decisions they never made? Would you have them granted eternal permanence to choices that were never theirs? It is not your place to take such a risk, neither of you, no matter what power the dragons have given your frail human flesh."

Lyra rose higher, her body itself seeming to expand as her beauty grew. Jacaranda felt her arms shake and her knees tremble. Words died on her tongue as her mind tried to accept what she heard, yet no wisdom, no divine power, could fully make her believe. A Goddess of humanity was decrying Jacaranda's very existence. Nothing could wound her worse. Nothing could so inspire her rage.

"A few souls made their way to the Cradle upon our awakening, but this was done by accident, and in confusion," Lyra said. "We have witnessed this changed world, and we have decided there shall be no more. You have heard our wisdom. There is no value in granting souls to the soulless who have lost so much of their lives already. This is the hard choice. This is the greater mercy."

"Bullshit!" Jacaranda screamed at the Goddess. She turned her attention to Wren. "Don't you dare listen to her. It doesn't matter what life we have left, fifty years or fifty seconds, it is still *our* lives, and lived as we would live it. Don't you dare believe that *we* are unworthy of eternity. Don't let her deny our own existence."

"I deny nothing," Lyra said. She pointed a slender finger her way. "Think on the horrors you endured, Jacaranda. Remember them, as you will in the Aether flow."

Jacaranda's spine snapped rigid, and her eyes widened as memories overwhelmed her mind with terrifying ease. This went beyond remembering. Her senses lived through every single detail, fully re-experiencing the sight, sounds, and touch of a moment of her past. That chosen moment, however, was a cruel one. She was on her knees, Gerag above her. His trousers were at his ankles. Her hands were tied behind her back, her body stained with fluids and bruises. Her master had been at it for hours, yet still he was not done. Jacaranda tried to scream, to resist, but she remained perfectly obedient and still, just as she had in the past.

Lyra's words pierced the memory, guiding her through memory after memory.

"Remember the abuse."

Needles pierced her skin. A whip lashed her back. She cried out, just as she'd been trained to cry out in emulation of actual horror. Her past self may have merely acted, but Jacaranda's awakened mind silently protested, and it was real anguish, real horror.

"The degradation."

Every time he called her his plaything. Every act that showed her she was little more than a tool for her master's pleasure. Jacaranda relived it with clarity that horrified her. Though mere seconds passed, she felt as if she lived another lifetime before Lyra finally released her from the memories of her own soul. She collapsed to her knees and gasped in shuddering breaths as she wept.

"You knew none of it as your soulless self," Lyra said as the others watched in silence. "You did not feel its sting. All that pain and suffering you experienced would have ended in dust, harming no one, haunting nothing. Can you tell me, truthfully, that you would endure it willingly?"

Jacaranda looked to Devin with tears in her eyes. He'd remained silent, knowing this fight, this argument, was not his to make, but hers. The Goddess's words echoed in her mind as a grim smile crossed her face. Lyra had called this a hard choice, but this was no hard choice. It was the easiest one of all.

"For those I love?" she said. "I would endure it a thousand times over. You are wrong, Lyra. You may be our Goddess, our maker, but you are *wrong*."

Jacaranda pushed to her feet. She was so frightened, she felt ready to break at any moment, but she would not be silent. Not even before a Goddess.

"I know it, and deep down, Wren knows it, too. We are worthy of life, of love, of making our choices and experiencing their consequences. No one is promised an easy life, nor a long one. That same promise goes to the soulless who will awaken. We stand before you, two awakened soulless, telling you we would never regret what we have become, and yet you refuse to listen. You aren't just wrong. You are deaf. You are blind. You are prideful, and you would have us suffer in silence rather than fix the errors you made. Fuck that, and fuck you."

Jacaranda did not know what the Goddess might do to her. Lyra's fury overwhelmed the chamber, so deep she felt it like a heat on her skin. Could Jacaranda be unmade? Her soul ripped from her skull and obliterated? Whatever the punishment, she stood tall. Of all the errors and trials of her awakened life, this was the one thing she believed beyond any doubt. Her time with Devin, and meeting her new group of friends, was worth every last awful second she had spent amid her soulless existence. Nothing would deny her that. Not even a Goddess.

"Do not listen to them, Wren," Lyra said, turning to the other Chainbreaker. "Do not believe seductive whispers assuring you of your own power. There is still time to do the right thing."

Wren and Adria exchanged a look. The recast woman closed her eyes, and she slowly shook her head.

"This is the right thing," she said. "I will help Adria correct your failure. No matter what, today is the end of the soulless."

Lyra's voice grew tenfold as she admonished them like disobedient children. Her arms spread wide, deep blue light gathering about her fingers as dark shadows pooled above her head.

"You would usurp my role as guider of humanity?" she cried. Wind tore wildly through the chamber. The ground shook with her rage. "You would cast aside the three Sisters, we who built your world? We who brought you souls to elevate you from the worm and the ape? You would endanger all the Cradle with your dabbling in the realm of souls, stars, and the void? I have tried reason. I have pleaded for sanity. But if your faith is so weak, so brittle…"

The shadows became wings. A monstrous form pierced the ceiling of the chamber, his hood and cloak billowing as he spun his entire body to add power to the swing of his void-kissed scythe.

One swing, that was all it took.

One swing, and Logarius's scythe cleaved the Goddess Lyra in half.

CHAPTER 39

No scripture, no teaching, and no story from Devin's childhood, nor his years studying to be a Soulkeeper, granted him a way to fathom the body of a Goddess collapsing to the floor of the enormous chamber. She did not bleed, not as mortals did. Crystalline light floated out of her, from her shoulder, along her midsection, to her left hip. The lower half of her body and legs shattered into stardust upon hitting the ground. Her hair withered, losing its luster and light. Silence filled the chamber, the only sound that of the air rippling Logarius's wings as he lowered.

"Lyra," Devin whispered in shock. It couldn't be true. None of this could. Logarius was dead. Evelyn had killed him. A dead avenria couldn't kill a Goddess. Nothing could kill a Goddess. Lyra had existed when the world was first made. She gave it light. Gave it life.

"A second Chainbreaker," Logarius said as his wings curled around his body like a cloak. "It seems the infection spreads."

Adria lifted her arms, shimmering light sparkling about her fingertips as she stared a death glare through the eye holes of her mask.

"I thought we were free of you," she said.

"Not yet," he said. He lifted his obsidian scythe, the voidblade sparkling with energy. "We'll all be free soon, though. The darkness comes. The emptiness awaits. The stars will fall, and I will be the one pulling them from the sky."

"You'll be dead," Adria said. "And no one will mourn your loss."

Souls from the dead Soulkeepers burst from their corpses and shot like arrows toward the avenria. Shadow leapt from his obsidian staff to meet them. The light and dark swallowed one another, bursting the souls into sparkling embers that rose toward the heavens, the memories and experiences remaining but disjointed, unfocused, and unable to be of use. Logarius spread his wings and laughed. A quick swing of his scythe severed the air, ripping open a tear to the void. Air poured into it, and from within leaked darkness like liquid shadow.

"I have no soul for you to command," he said. "You mean nothing to me, Chainbreaker. For all your gifts, you are but a child compared to the powers that have existed since the dawn of time." He pointed his scythe toward the dying Lyra. "Not even the Sisters can withstand it. The Goddesses? The dragons? We, their children? We're all candles flickering amid a storm, and it's time we were snuffed out so the universe might know peace."

"Peace?" Tommy asked. Fire burst about his hands and wrists. "Peace!"

Logarius acted faster than any could react. A great torrent of flame flowed from Tommy's joined wrists, but it washed over Logarius's folded wings like harmless water. His heel struck Tommy directly in the throat, and it was only due to the flames washing over him that his scythe swung blindly, failed to connect. Tommy staggered backward, hands clutching his throat as his face turned red.

When he reopened his wings, his legs tensing for a killing lunge, Logarius halted. A new challenger positioned himself between the injured spellcaster and the avenria.

"I applaud the kill," said Janus. "But whatever you are is a mockery of all life. We need to be free of the Sisters, not free from existence."

"I'm not giving you a choice," Logarius said. He spun, two quick cuts that ripped gashes in the air and left essence of the void spilling into the chamber in the form of long, thorned tentacles. "Our hatred. Our vileness. All our sins, swallowed in shadow and forgotten."

Jacaranda positioned herself opposite Janus, so the two might flank the avenria when he attacked. Devin knew he should help, but he could not turn away from the Goddess of the Day. With every rise of the sun, he had bowed his head in prayer to her, asking for her guidance and protection. He knew her voice. He knew her presence. Anwyn's silver symbol may hang from his neck, but Lyra had been the one he truly loved, and it was she who called his name as she lay dying.

Devin knelt beside her body, his eyes watering from the brightness of the substance that flowed out from her gaping wound. It was liquid light, thick like blood yet shining as if made of stars.

"My Goddess," Devin said softly. "I don't... I don't know what to do. I don't know if I can help."

Her body shuddered as if every muscle within it were tightening beyond her control. Her skin, normally so rich and dark, was steadily draining of color so that she appeared an ashen husk.

"My child," she said. Her voice trembled, yet she spoke as if all were well, and her body were not cut from hip to shoulder. "I had hoped—but I hoped in vain. The world changes. We must change with it."

Devin bowed his head, his quiet tears making their way down his face. Behind him, he heard the clash of metal, and a roar of wind as the blade of the void-scythe continuously tore gaps in the space between worlds.

"I don't understand."

Lyra grabbed his wrist. Before he could protest, he felt a change sweep over him, the strength of it sapping his breath and jolting his head backward.

"Be hope, Soulkeeper. Be light. My world…my Sisters…it rests on you now."

The strength left her hand. The life left her eyes. A Goddess died.

"Hope," Devin whispered as he rose to his feet. He drew his sword from its sheath and clutched it between his numb fingers.

"Light."

He turned to face Logarius. Janus and Jacaranda alternated attacks, but their meager weapons could not cut through the shadow that wrapped about the avenria like a cloak. Janus's form shifted from silver, to stone, to iron, vainly trying to become a substance that could penetrate. At last his body shimmered into diamond. His hands became axes, and he braced his legs and brought his arms up to block a killing blow. It meant nothing to the impossible edge of the void-scythe. Logarius cut him down, one single strike that tore through his left arm and severed his body along the midsection. Janus shrieked in pain, and his body mutated wildly as darkness clung to the wound, swallowing him, making a mockery of his ability to change.

Light shimmered across Devin's blade as Lyra's gifted power manifested.

"A world," he said, and approached the monster of shadow and void. Unearthly wind howled from the tears in reality Adria and Wren fought to seal. "So be it, my Goddess. I shall honor your final wish."

Logarius flapped his wings to soar into the air, his scythe eager and cutting. Gash after gash opened up gaping doorways to the void. Wren and Adria lifted their arms and braced their legs, sweat pouring off them as they focused upon the wounds of reality and struggled to seal them before the ever-hungry presence of the void entered. The avenria laughed at them, amused by their struggle.

He cut the air three times to replace the two they closed, and with every stroke it seemed reality warped, and the sun high above in the sky lost a shade of its glow.

"Logarius!" Devin shouted, and he lifted his sword. Lyra's gifted strength flowed from his hands into the blade of the sword. Though its light was blistering, the sight of it was a comfort to his eyes. The darkness of the void lessened. The wings of the avenria quivered.

"Even in death, the Goddess must be a bother," Logarius said. He curled his body, folded his wings, and dove like the bird of prey he was. At the last moment he extended his weapon and spun, adding tremendous power to the void-scythe gifted to him. Devin denied his fear of the charge, braced his legs, and swung. Scythe and sword connected, but this time there was no breaking the steel. A shock wave rolled through the chamber from the impact, with such strength, Devin thought his limbs would surely break, yet he felt nothing. Logarius glared from underneath his hood. It was such a human expression, it put a grin on Devin's face.

"What's wrong?" he asked as his foe tried and failed to break him with an extra push. The two separated several feet, Logarius landing lightly with the obsidian handle swirling in his grip. "I thought I was an insignificant candle to be snuffed out?"

"You will be."

Logarius was expertly trained, there was no debating that, but he was lost in rage and drunk on power. Most importantly of all, he showed Devin no respect as a worthy foe. Devin easily read his next few attacks, and he calmly blocked swing after swing. The air crackled with every meeting of their blades, one powered by the void, the other a gleaming weapon of purest Aether. With every swing, Logarius relied on being faster, and stronger. With every swing, Devin proved him wrong. Sword and scythe struck again and again, with Devin adjusting his parries often moments before impact to account for the uniquely curved weapon of his foe. The contact traveled up his arms and numbed his fingers, but he found grim satisfaction in seeing the surprise steadily growing in Logarius's silver-blue eyes.

Devin tried to steal the initiative, but he failed to account for how quickly Logarius might react. When he leapt forward, simultaneously parrying aside a lengthwise swing while attempting to pull his sword around for a thrust, he received a face full of dark wings as the avenria battered him with a single flap. Disorientated and out of position, Devin flung his sword upward, correctly guessing at the direction. Their weapons struck off one another. He bit down a scream of pain as the hit traveled all the way up his elbows. Before Logarius could try again, Jacaranda came sliding in, aiding Devin just as she had aided him in their first battle with the avenria. Her weapons glanced off his side, the steel of her short swords seemingly incapable of penetrating the armor of shadow and darkness that swirled about the void's champion.

"No!" Logarius screamed. He whirled on Jacaranda, nearly slicing off her knees until she twisted to one side and rolled. His scythe shimmered as it cut across reality, opening another portal to the void. From within it a two-headed dog bearing a lizard's tail came bounding forth, slobbering shadow as it snarled at Jacaranda.

"I will fight Lyra's champion alone," he shouted as Jacaranda readied her swords for the monster's charge. "I am the void's champion. Let us together decide this world's fate! Let things be as they must!"

Devin thrust for Logarius's neck while lunging back to his feet, nearly scoring a kill if not for the obsidian handle batting his sword up and past the shoulder. Devin's reward was a kick to the stomach, and he gasped as he retreated several steps.

"Champions," Devin said, hoping to buy time to recover. "That's all we are, aren't we? Champions, avatars, Chainbreakers, Goddesses, dragons..."

"Would you have mere humans decide the fate of the Cradle?"

Logarius asked. He raised his scythe and spread his wings for a charge. "You have never been worthy of the responsibilities foisted upon your shoulders. You have never justified the gift of eternity that was denied to us."

Devin lifted his own sword and let its brilliant light shine across his face.

"And like a spoiled child you would tear it all to the ground? The good and the bad? Humans and dragons, together, swallowed by the void?"

Logarius hesitated for the briefest moment.

"With a world this broken? Yes, Devin. I would."

Logarius slammed into him with his scythe leading and his wings flapping to grant him power. Their weapons connected, the now-familiar sound of their conflict ringing in Devin's ears as he stood firm. He refused to let a single fearful thought enter his mind. Instinct took control. His years of training, recently honed by repeated battles against the various dragon-sired, guided his sword. He knew not a single hit could pass his defenses. No armor would shrug off that void-scythe, nor would any minor scratch heal from its touch. The battle demanded perfection, and so Devin gave it exactly that.

Logarius swept at Devin's legs with the handle. When Devin leapt over it, the avenria thrust an elbow toward his face, buying distance. Down came the blade of the scythe. Devin blocked, shifted his arms to lock the curved weapon out to the side, and then slid his own weapon free. His feet danced, drawing him closer and granting power to his swing. Logarius shifted the curved blade in the way just barely in time. The impact sent him staggering, and Devin forced himself onward, letting his rage mix with Lyra's blessing to grant him stronger and stronger attacks. Shock wave after shock wave rolled outward from their weapons' collisions, but still the avenria would not break.

My world . . . my Sisters . . . it rests on you now.

Devin couldn't see how. He tried every feint, every subtle shift and thrust, but the result was always the same. The movements of Logarius's staff grew more and more fluid, beyond just an extension of his body and becoming something more. Worse were the long, squirming tentacles reaching through the tears Logarius opened. He danced about them, ducking the occasional blind swipe, but there were so many, and more opening by the moment. Desperation fueled Devin's swings, and it gave his sword strength, but it also made him sloppy. Once, twice, three times he slammed his sword against the void-blade, and it was only upon that third hit he realized Logarius was toying with him.

Out came the hilt of the scythe's handle, striking him in the kidneys. It immediately slammed upward, cracking his chin and sending blood flying from his split lip. He staggered backward, his vision swimming. When he lifted his sword to block, Logarius immediately slammed it aside, positioning it far too wide for him to bring it back in time to defend. Logarius lifted his scythe high for the killing blow. Devin attempted blocking no matter how hopeless it seemed. He need not have worried. A jagged shard of ice slammed into Logarius's chest and pierced his shadowy armor. Logarius gasped as blue blood flowed across his feathers.

"F...fuck you," Tommy shouted from across the chamber despite the clear pain it caused his raw throat. The rapidly dissolving body of a two-headed void-monster lay bubbling at his feet. Devin used the moment to retreat as Logarius ripped the ice shard from his bleeding side and crushed the projectile in his grip. One long slice from his scythe opened an entire wall of the void between him and Tommy, sealing him off from his spells.

"You'll never beat me," Logarius said, turning his attention back to Devin. "This wound is nothing. My strength grows with every tear to the void I open. But you? I see exhaustion already taking you."

Devin planted his feet. The avenria wasn't wrong. Devin's heart pounded inside his chest. It seemed the whole room was growing dark from the portals Logarius ripped open. Avoiding the wildly thrashing tentacles was proving harder and harder. Had to end the fight, but how?

And then he knew. His body loosened, and he stood with a relaxed grin. Cocky, even. He kept his gaze locked on Logarius, refusing to look away even the slightest inch. Surprise was their only chance now.

"I could beat you," Devin said, and he pointed his sword at Logarius. Let him think it a challenge. Let him be blinded by the light blazing across his steel. "But I don't need to."

Lyra's power shimmered across the blade and then shot forward like a beam. Logarius curled his wings and readied his scythe, but the attack was not an attack at all, nor was it aimed at the avenria. Devin relinquished a portion of the gift granted to him, passing it on to other humans equally worthy. The light passed above Logarius's head and pooled into Jacaranda's swords and Brittany's axe, the two women already in mid-leap. Logarius turned, his beak dropped open, and he managed a single squawk before Jacaranda buried both her swords into the avenria's ribs. Brittany's axe smashed in his beak and sank down to the neck. The avenria's armor of shadow withered and broke.

"Some champion," Jacaranda said before Lyra's gifted power blasted outward in an explosion of light and sound that ripped Logarius to pieces. The explosion sent both of them rolling across the ground, and Devin quickly dove underneath a swipe of shadow tentacles to chase after the two women. He reached Jacaranda first, and though his love bore slight burns on her face and hands, she sported a wicked grin as well.

"I think we got him."

"I think we did." Brittany laughed beside her. Devin helped both of them to their feet, and he tried not to let his worries show.

"Him, yeah," he said, and he looked at the nearly two dozen

portals to the void tearing wider and wider despite Adria's and Wren's attempts to seal them. The tears were merging together, connecting to form a singular gigantic opening. A head emerged, and it snapped with a dozen mouths.

"But what about *that*?"

CHAPTER 40

To our side!" Adria screamed, earning a bitter laugh from Jacaranda as she tucked into a roll underneath a swiping hand of crackling shadow. As if it would be that easy. A thin tendril with its end sharpened like a spear shot toward her from one of the portals, and she sliced it into pieces with her glowing weapons. Whatever magic Devin had infused them with lingered, and it was a good thing, too, because she doubted her regular steel would make a dent.

One tendril down, but three more remained, knifing out from the slender gap in reality. Jacaranda braced for the impact, her mind scrambling for a way to block them all, but Devin dashed past her with his sword slashing. He cut all three, spun his sword so its light shone across the tear, and then beckoned for her to run.

"I'll get it," Wren said, turning her attention in their direction. Light shimmered across her hands, and her face winced with pain as she forced the small tear closed. With their pathway clear, the three sprinted to the center of the chamber. The moment they arrived, Adria lifted her arms and screamed out a wordless cry of defiance. A brilliant stream of light burst from her forehead and then curved, forming a protective shield about the group. Wren somehow picked up what Adria was doing and joined in, a similar stream of light flowing from her own forehead to strengthen the shield holding back the void.

"What the fuck is that thing?" Brittany asked as she readied her glowing axe. She pointed to the many-faced monstrosity biting at them in sick mockery.

"The void," Devin said. "At least, a piece of it."

"The void-dragon is real?" Brit asked. "I thought we made that shit up to scare children."

"It's no dragon," Adria said. Sweat trickled down her brow. "And it is very clearly real."

The hungry emptiness that was the void pooled around them, long fat tendrils that filled the enormous chamber. Only the shimmering white shield Adria and Wren projected kept it at bay. Jacaranda feared that protection would only last so long. Both the Chainbreakers appeared exhausted, having expended much of their strength attempting in vain to close the tears Logarius had ripped open prior to his death. Now the tears had shifted and coalesced into one tremendous window into a realm of pure, raw emptiness, and from within stirred something furious and hungry. It leered at them with a dozen mouths. It reached for them with one hundred hands. Unearthly winds roared about them, but to the Chainbreakers' credit, it could not breach the shield.

"The tear is getting bigger," Tommy said, carrying the wounded Malik on one shoulder.

"It will keep growing, too," Adria said, a faint glow flashing across her eyes. "Lyra's dead. The stars fall, and the sun is fading. This is what it's waited for all these years. It won't stop with Londheim. It wants the Cradle. It wants *everything*."

Jacaranda glanced upward on instinct, but she saw only the ceiling to the domed chamber, and its mixture of flesh and steel. The pulsing blue veins had faded completely. She struggled to understand the meaning. The religious nature of the world was far from her specialty. Did Adria speak literally? Was the sun itself fading in light? Could the stars truly fall from the sky?

"Then we have to close it before it gets worse," Malik said as he gently freed himself from Tommy and slumped to his rear on the weird not-quite-flesh floor. He clutched his bleeding wrists to his stomach to smother the bleeding. "Can you do it, Adria?"

"I can try," she said. "But not while maintaining this barrier at the same time."

"Can you hold it on your own?" Devin asked Wren. The other Chainbreaker clenched her jaw and nodded.

"Maybe, but things will get through."

"Then we'll cut down whatever gets through," Jacaranda said, and she looked to the rest of the group. "Won't we?"

Devin glanced at Brittany, who readied her glowing axe in response.

"We will," he said, turning his attention to the monster crawling forth. "We have no choice."

The three positioned themselves between the gigantic tear and the two Chainbreakers, Jacaranda on the left, Brittany on the right, and Devin in the center. Tommy stood behind them all, his hands shaking as he muttered random words of magic in preparation. Jacaranda twirled her short swords, her jaw set and her stomach clenched into knots. The shield of light shimmered and cracked as the tendrils pounded across its surface. It felt like they were on a small raft in the center of a raging ocean. There was no denying the energy she felt sparking within her weapons, but how could they battle such a foe?

"Ready?" Adria asked. Jacaranda and the two Soulkeepers lifted their weapons. Three of them against the unleashed power of the void. Adria told herself it was possible. She held her head high. She felt Lyra's dying light shine upon her, and for one brief moment, she truly believed they could win.

"Hold nothing back," Devin said softly. "We will get no second chances."

"Keep us safe," Adria said as she ceased the flow of light from her forehead. "The Cradle depends upon it."

The strain hit Wren like a punch to the gut. She crumpled to her knees, her breathing rapid and her hair billowing in wind that seemed to burst from the very ground. The wall of light, which had been nearly opaque, immediately turned translucent. Cracks splintered across it. Jacaranda bent into a crouch and curled her arms to her chest. Her entire body felt ready to explode.

Here we go, she thought as the first blob of shadow burst into their protected clearing like water leaking through the side of a ship's hull. Whatever calm they'd known ended in an explosion of sound and shadow. Jacaranda dashed toward the shapeless blob, which was rapidly re-forming itself into a nightmarish creature with four arms and two heads. Her short swords slashed, one for each head. The gifted light across her swords flared upon contact, and it gave it a cutting power no mere mortal blade could possess. The monster crumpled, and two more quick slashes evaporated it like a puddle on a hot summer day.

If only the rest of the battle could be so easily, she thought as she retreated several steps. Watching the void test the shield was like watching hail strike a window. It constantly pinged and hit, and she could never be certain where, nor the damage when it did. The best she could do was watch for where the cracks were at their largest and prepare.

A stinger punched through a section near the top of the dome, wielded at the end of a multi-hinged scorpion tail. Its aim was for the two Chainbreakers. Jacaranda dashed in the way, sliced the stinger off, and then crossed her short swords. Light blazed off the steel, melting the darkness. Angry roars loosed from a thousand mouths as the void raged in protest. More tendrils slammed the shield, straining Wren and her magic. Tommy charred several openings with fire before anything might slip through. Devin and Brittany held strong their positions, keeping Adria safe.

We can hold, Jacaranda told herself as she hacked down a tentacle whose sides bristled with spikes like a porcupine. *We must.*

The smaller hits paled in comparison to what followed. The amorphous creation spilling out from the tear collected its many tentacles into a singular claw that slammed into the shield. The light cracked with a glass-like shriek. The spike shoved and twisted, its form mutating wildly to add spikes and stingers until it finally forced a large enough hole for it to penetrate.

"Bring it down!" Devin ordered as void-essence poured in like a flood.

"Fucking *how?*" Jacaranda screamed. She cut with both hands, spun sideways to avoid being mauled by a clawed tiger paw at the end of an insectoid arm, and cut twice more. The tendrils retreated a few feet, sharpened their ends to points, and thrust again. A burst of fire from Tommy pushed them back, allowing her to leap into the air over the swipe of a tentacle that had reshaped itself into a giant leg covered with thorns. She landed squarely on her back, the impact stealing her breath away and locking her lungs into an ineffectual hitch.

"I got you," Devin said, suddenly above her. His sword looped, cutting down each and every grossly mutated appendage that sprouted from the large central tentacle forcing its way through the gap in the shield. Meanwhile Tommy thundered multiple shards of ice into the base, beating it backward, weakening it so it might be dislodged.

"Thanks," Jacaranda said as she rolled to her feet. Her vision was swimming with stars, and her lungs still didn't feel quite right, but there was no time to rest, no staying out of this. Brittany was holding the other side as best she could, her gigantic axe proving an effective tool to chop down tentacles and appendages like gangly tree limbs, but they were just so many. The shield was cracking. Wren was far too weak to maintain it on her own.

A flicker from the corner of Jacaranda's eye halted her movements. A thin little weed of darkness had formed itself into an arrow, and it launched straight for Adria. Jacaranda dove in its way, her swords crossing right as it tried to pass. The arrow shattered, she landed lightly on her heels, and then she dashed for Brittany's side. Her swords were a blur of light as she spun, slicing through a dozen reaching hands and severing their many fingers.

"The base," Jacaranda shouted. Her words came out rough and pained. "Cut into the base. I'll be right at your heels."

Brittany followed the order immediately, her long coat billowing as she sprinted straight at the gigantic tentacle that had lodged itself into the shield. Jacaranda cut at two more tendrils right as they broke through and before they could reshape, then turned her attention to the major weak point. Tommy, seeing his sister's charge, unleashed a massive stroke of lightning that exploded several attempted attacks of shadow into dust and air.

The way clear, Brittany leapt the final space, her entire body elongating to add strength to her swing. Her axe slammed into the base of the tendril, and its darkness could not withstand the gleaming edge. The steel buried all the way within it, Lyra's gifted power swelled, and the essence of the void roiled and melted in a violent explosion. Jacaranda cheered despite her exhaustion as Wren's shield sealed over the gaping wound, locking the essence safely outside.

Wren, however, shared no such joy. Her limbs shook, and horror twisted her features.

"I can't," she muttered, that chant all she could manage as light poured from her forehead into the shield. "I can't, I can't, I can't."

"Adria?" Jacaranda asked, turning to the other Chainbreaker. Yet she looked equally exhausted as she wrestled against the enormous tear in reality. Even worse, she appeared to make no headway in sealing it.

Devin put his free hand on Jacaranda's shoulder. Despite everything, he stood tall, somehow brave in the face of the terrors threatening to break through.

"We hold," he said. "We must."

Jacaranda knew then and there she would be with him until the end of all things. Even if this was humanity's last day upon the Cradle, she would trust him to be there for her, to keep her safe from the cold dark that followed. She kissed him once, quickly, then laughed so she might not cry.

"To the very end," she said, for it truly seemed it had come. The ceiling collapsed with a deafening roar. Its rubble twisted and fell, but instead of crushing the group underneath with its tremendous weight, the pieces flew outward in all directions. In its absence Jacaranda saw the dwindling daylight sky. The sun appeared weak and gray, and the surrounding sky had taken on an image akin to twilight, only instead of deep oranges and purples, it shone a sickly green. Stars twinkled in and out of view, as if they were mere lightning bugs. Everything about the sight of it screamed *wrongness*, and it flooded her body with a panic primal in its nature.

Two humanoid forms floated amid the opening, and they calmly descended despite the shadow tendrils and six-fingered hands hungrily reaching for them. One appeared made of the same star-filled essence as the black water that had devastated the western lands. The other was more a distortion than a being, light and sound refracting off wherever it stood. They batted aside the shadows of the void with waves of their hands, the power they unleashed strong enough to shake the ground.

"This mess is of our own doing," Viciss said as his feet touched down within Wren's faltering shield.

"And so we shall make it right," said Nihil.

The two dragons joined the Chainbreakers. Nihil offered Wren its hand, and it helped her to her feet.

"Aid Adria in closing the tear," Viciss said to her. "We shall keep us safe."

The shimmering shield that protected them, which had dwindled down to almost nothing as Wren faltered, suddenly surged back to life. The reprieve allowed Devin, Brittany, and Jacaranda to gather before the center of the void-monster and collect their breaths. Adria and Wren were not so lucky. They cried out from their exertion, but it was like they were trying to hold back the rise of the sun. Soft white light sparkled around the edges of the swirling tear in reality. Perhaps they were slowing its expanse, Jacaranda couldn't say, but they certainly weren't stopping it.

"You have to help them," she shouted to the dragons. "They can't do it on their own!"

"Then do not distract us," Nihil bellowed with a voice like the roar of a bear. The two dragons stepped forward, and the shield moved with them. They forced an approach toward the gigantic tear. Did they think to close it? Seal it off? Jacaranda didn't know, but she did her best to help them. The moment their shield cracked, she rushed it, her swords dancing, their light severing whatever piece of the void that punched through. Closer and closer to the tear, until at last it had no choice but to react.

The various tendrils, hands, and tentacles pulled backward. The collective bulge of shadow that was the void coalesced together, shaping itself, becoming a single feline face with a thousand teeth and nine rows of pointed ears. Six arms, shaped like the forelegs of a praying mantis, spread out its back like the legs of a spider whose bulbous lower belly was stuck wedged deep into the gaping wound Logarius had torn into reality.

And then it spoke with a voice that pierced their minds like cold steel.

We seek peace. We seek sleep. We seek oblivion.

"Not at the cost of our lives," Nihil said. It sounded like a tired grandfather addressing his grandchildren around a campfire. "We have denied you from the very moment of our creations. We deny you still."

Then we will take what is not freely given.

The six arms snapped forward with staggering speed. They were the size of tree trunks. They bore the strength of the infinite void. The two dragons cried out, caught off guard by the raw fury unleashed upon them. Five of the arms battered backward, but a sixth punched through the shield, its sharpened end skewering Nihil through its center. A horrific wail blasted out from the dragon, the sound of it pure madness. This was the frightened howl of a trapped hound, the screech of an angered bird, the squeal of wounded horses, and the death cries of a thousand dying children. Jacaranda clutched her fists to her ears and fell to her knees, but she could not look away.

The tendril retreated, and Nihil came with it. The demigod thrashed wildly, and it seemed the air about itself rippled and exploded from its every movement, but the void brought Nihil into its mouth without fear for the damage. The sharpened teeth closed about it, and as they ripped apart the divine, one hundred new mouths formed across the face of the monster, each and every one of them laughing.

The stars and shadow that swirled together to create Viciss dimmed, and he let loose such a wail, it brought tears to Jacaranda's eyes through the raw, aching loss.

"Remain strong," Devin said as he grabbed Jacaranda's wrist and forced her to her feet. "All of you, stay strong! The battle is not yet lost!"

But how could it not be? Despite the dragons, despite the Chainbreakers, it wasn't enough. Nihil had given its life, yet still the tear grew larger. They were holding back a flood with their bare hands. Inch by inch the swirling gap spread, consuming more of the chamber, its walls, and the surround tunnels. High above, the sky darkened, the sickly green turning to a frightening gray. What stars were visible were pale pinpricks of light hardly brighter than the dead sea they floated within. Even more terrifying were the long veins of shadows that crawled across the sky. *Was this it?* Jacaranda wondered. Was this when the entire Cradle would at last be swallowed into nothing?

Perhaps, though not without a fight. The dragons were not the only ones ready to give their lives to protect the Cradle.

The Goddesses arrived with a flash of thunder. Alma stood beside Viciss, her hand gently resting on the shoulder of her mightiest creation. Her blue eyes were the color of a healthy sky, her dress greener than any forest. Her long hair was spun gold, and with her every movement, it sparkled with transcendent beauty. Opposite her hovered Anwyn, the Goddess's feet held aloft by a small cloud of smoke and shadow. Unlike her Sister's golden skin, she was liquid shadow swirling steadily across a naked ethereal body. Her head was shaved and her face hidden behind a perfectly smooth, featureless mask. Unlike the porcelain re-creation Adria wore, this mask seemed made of no corporeal essence that existed upon the Cradle. It was an illusion, an idea, given form to hide a face no living thing should ever bear witness.

"How great is your hatred?" Alma asked the monster tearing into the Cradle. "We never acted in malice. We never meant to give birth to your existence. We shone a light upon the world in order to create beauty and life. Is it our fault you are a shadow furious at its sentience?"

We never wanted made, roared the incarnation of the void as it struggled to withstand the sudden surge of brilliance. *You denied us peace. Your creatures are chaos and failure. They must be cleansed. This must all be cleansed.*

"You are eternal," Anwyn said. "No beginning. No end. I cannot grant you the death you seek, nor will we sacrifice our lives to sate your emptiness. Be gone. The antithesis of creation shall not ruin the joy of ours."

The laughter of the void was more horrifying than any wail of death or cry of pain.

The stars fall. The sun falters. Our time has come, Sisters. For so long, we waited, but at last your sky breaks beneath our grasp.

Pure, raw Aether gathered upon the palms of both Goddesses.

"We shall see," they said in unison.

They unleashed their power, and it was enough to drop Jacaranda's jaw. Massive beams of pure white light blasted into the heart of the beast, and it bubbled and roared as if its innards were boiling. The Goddesses released volley after volley. They tore into it, evaporating the physical form of the void in massive chunks, yet the moment they ceased, more came tumbling forth, like floodwaters bursting through a broken dam.

What hope Jacaranda felt upon seeing the Goddesses' arrival quickly faltered. With every blast, every attack, it seemed the sky darkened that much further. The Sisters were focusing upon a gap in their protection of the Cradle but, in turn, weakening their protection elsewhere. The Sisters let loose twin cries of fury and pain, the emotions raw enough to break Jacaranda's heart. The power of creation, of life, pulsed out of them with such brilliance, she could not look upon it. That brilliance could reshape mountains. It could divide continents. It could not break the savage hunger of a being that represented emptiness, and silence, and eternal calm.

It was a standstill, Jacaranda realized. A knife-edge balance that neither side seemed capable of breaking, but there was no doubt in her mind that time was not on their side. Viciss shielded Wren from the occasional attack of a shapeless beast, allowing her to offer what little strength she had left to the fight. Devin and Brittany fought back to back, cutting down the tendrils and hands that reached without ever stopping. Jacaranda looked to her own two swords, and they felt so meager, so worthless compared to the humbling power of demigods and Goddesses. Who was she compared to a dragon? What might she do if the manipulator of souls like Adria could not break down the darkness?

Jacaranda froze, and she looked about the small clearing completely baffled.

Adria? Where was Adria?

The ground rumbled beneath her, but her answer came from

above. A sudden, defiant cry struck her directly in the forehead. Sights and sounds lost all meaning. Jacaranda felt herself rising, her surroundings darkening, as Adria ripped her soul free of its mortal shell and blanketed her entire consciousness in a sea of nothingness.

CHAPTER 41

The battle against the void raged all about her, but Adria could not focus upon it. Simply being in its presence scraped her mind like nails across glass. To be so near the Goddesses overwhelmed her. She felt like a match burning near a bonfire. She felt like a sparrow caught in a tornado. She couldn't breathe. She couldn't think. Something blocked her path, and she stumbled.

"Adria?" she heard a raspy voice call out to her. There, at her feet, lay the dying Janus. She brushed his two-tone hair away from his sweating forehead. His body attempted to shift and change, but no matter how short or long his arms grew or the fur and scales that covered his skin, nothing stopped the steady flow of the void swallowing him from the waist up. Color seemed to drain from him. His voice was weak, yet still he managed a bitter laugh.

"I must see," he said as he reached up for Adria's face. "I must know."

His finger brushed the center of her porcelain mask. It split perfectly in half, the two pieces gently falling into his spread palm. Adria remained strong for him, and she met his jade eyes with determination in her own.

"No tears," he said. He looked at Viciss, who waged his war against the void to protect Wren. "Neither will my maker weep for my loss. No one will. Not even you." A subtle change swept over him. "I should have known. This mask is your true face anyway."

Janus slammed both pieces against her, and it felt like fire. She screamed and tried to pull back, but his grip was iron, his magic unstoppable. At last he relented, and she staggered away while pulling on the edges of her mask. Pain was her reward, but still she pulled, yanking harder until blood trickled down her neck. The mask was melded to her face, her flesh and the porcelain now one. Janus laughed at her panic, long, wet laughs without mirth or joy, just misery.

He died laughing, the ravenous flow of the void ceasing just beneath his arms and fading away.

Get out, get out, get out, screamed Adria's mind as if taking on a life of its own. The presence of the Goddesses, the dragon, the void; it all overwhelmed her. It was like standing in the midst of a blinding fire, and she couldn't think. Couldn't speak. She looked at the broken ceiling, and the dying sky, and yearned for it on instinct. The grand chamber was awash with power, and it was child's play to tap into it and demand it move the world to obey. Light sparkled about her limbs. Her physical form rose, defying gravity as she soared higher.

No relief awaited her upon exiting. She hovered high in the air only to see smoke billowing from the western wall. Even without any magical aid, her eyes could plainly see the dragon-sired army attacking the city. Portions of the wall had collapsed, and already small groups of dragon-sired were setting fire to various districts. Most shocking of all were the two corpses of the dragons beyond the wall. They had been magnificent creations, beautiful beyond measure, and now they were broken husks hollowed out of their power and left to rot.

"But why?" she asked, baffled. The world was dying, yet the humans and dragon-sired would wage war with one another?

Immediately she sought the one responsible, sensing his soul like a blight upon a clear landscape. With but a clenching of her fist, she grabbed him from his perch upon the wall and pulled him across the city in a manner similar to how she kept her own body afloat. Lights shimmered across his skin so gravity could not take hold of his body.

"What the *fuck*?" Dierk screamed as he came to a sudden halt before her. He squirmed, but no chains held him that he could resist. All he managed was to rotate his body about in his current weightlessness.

"There was an agreement," Adria said, and she pointed to the wall. "There was to be peace. What happened?"

"What happened?" Dierk asked. "You rejected me, that's what happened! You were meant to be at my side while we ruled Londheim together. Do you think those little shits outside the wall could have done anything if you were with me? But no! I'm not good enough for you. I bet no one is good enough for you. I'm the only one who sees you for what you are, but you don't respect me. You don't listen to me. You won't acknowledge any of the sacrifices I've made for you. You left me to do as I wished, and so I did. We won't live in fear of those monsters. We'll fight them, and we'll win."

He crossed his arms and sneered at her despite literally hanging upside down.

"That is, if you'll finally help us. There's an army attacking our city. How about we deal with that instead of you throwing your tantrum at me?"

Adria looked to the thousands of dead, and the corpses of the dragons.

"You're wrong," she said. "You don't see me for who I truly am, but I see you. I see exactly what you are."

She grabbed his soul inside his skull, clutching it tightly, digging her mind's fingers into its sides and twisting. Dierk writhed before her, his mouth open and drool sliding off his lips as pain wracked his entire body.

"I'm done with you," she whispered as she drew power from his soul, allowing it to feed her rage. She turned her attention to the void below, to the hungry shadow raging against the very concept of life. "You, and every last disgusting soul like you who knows only how to destroy."

Adria arced her back and screamed her fury out in a singular demand that the Cradle seemed determined to deny to its dying days.

"THERE WILL BE PEACE!"

With that exultant cry, she ripped Dierk's soul in half. The force detonated his physical body into dust and powder. Everything that had once been the High Excellence of Londheim broke upon the wind. Adria drew in every last flickering wisp of memory and existence to give herself strength. Something inside her broke, a previously unperceived mental dam, and as her command boomed across Londheim, so, too, did a shock wave of white light. The souls of every single human within the city ripped from their physical bodies and hovered several feet above their heads. Their light sparkled in Adria's mind, and she felt wisps of their power drawing into her, fueling her.

The shock wave continued, propelled by her rage. Onward, to Stomme. Across the Septen River and beyond the Oakblack Woods to Steeth. Her mind's awareness rolled with it, expanding in a way that both exhilarated and frightened her. Farther east, to the capital in Oris. Across the tens of thousands of people living in Nicus. Even the Ecclesiast deep within Trivika in the Kept Lands. Everywhere, from sprawling city to tiny little village, the souls of humanity rose from their worldly shells.

Adria gasped in rapid breaths as a newborn field of stars flooded her vision. Hundreds of thousands of souls, each one granting her the tiniest sliver of power, but together they added into a flood. The dragon-sired within Londheim witnessed the spectacle, and they looked upon Adria hovering above the city like a shining beacon, and wisely retreated. Adria watched them go, the blistering strength of the souls pooling within her yearning to be used.

Her attention turned to the tear of the void, currently held at bay by the combined might of the dragon and Goddesses. The balance was so narrow, so close to breaking on either side. But the Cradle would not be consumed. Not while she endured. Adria lashed the nightmare creature back. She healed the wound that bled darkness into the land. Her power could not run dry, for with her blessed eyes she saw the rivers of Aether billowing from the form of the dragon, from Alma and Anwyn, and especially the slain Goddess, Lyra. All of it flowing straight into her own reservoir. She was a siphon fully opened, and nothing could resist her. With but a thought, she could absorb them completely, if doing such a thing did not break her physical body. Perhaps even that didn't matter. Her every muscle was trembling. Reality felt weak and pliable.

With an exultant cry to the heavens, Adria sealed the void, ending the last threat poised by the defeated Logarius. She tried to feel relief, or happiness. Instead she felt her mind continue to strain against her physical limitations. Viewing the grand chamber from above ignited a thought, and she looked at the wreckage of the two dragons beyond the city. She saw their twisted flesh and steel, and there was something achingly familiar about them. As the light of souls continued to swell within her breast, she looked back to the great underground construction and its connected chambers.

"I know what I am," she whispered.

The chambers that collected the power of the stars. The gigantic central chamber with a beating heart, a ground of false flesh and encased in ribs of steel. It was a body, one built by the dragons just like the ones they built for themselves. The dragons were no different than humans. They built physical bodies to house a spiritual soul that contained their power. With that understanding, Adria knew she was not merely a Chainbreaker. She was a dragon, the sixth dragon, the Dragon of Humanity, meant to embrace and convey their concepts no differently than Viciss did Change or Nihil had Conflict. Her human flesh was but a small piece of her, insignificant compared to her greater presence.

It was the dragons who crafted this world, Adria thought, remembering what Janus had claimed. Was it true for her, too? Could she do such madness? She cast a glance to Nihil and the Goddesses, who knelt in pain, unable to resist her pull. They couldn't stop her. The Goddesses had already admitted they could not kill her. She could ascend. She could become one of them. Her eyes looked at the horizon, at the hundreds of thousands of stars that were the souls of humanity. And amid them, she saw the dragon-sired retreating Londheim, leaving scores of dead humans in their wake.

The other three dragons remained scattered across the Cradle, hunkered down in the ocean, the desert, and the distant gulf far to the south. They had held out hope for her, she knew. The great Chainbreaker, meant to free humanity from the imprisonment of the Goddesses. But she could take them, too, take their power as she took Viciss's. The conflict would never cease, but she could end it. The world, its factions, its races; she could start over. She could build anew. The entire Cradle, reborn.

"Adria!"

A soft, barely perceptible voice calling in the distance. She looked down. No, not distant. Within the chamber of her dragon's body. Her brother was reaching out to her. His soul, she realized. She could not grip his soul as she had all the world's. Lyra's protection bathed over him, anchoring him even after her death. If she focused her attention, she could break it and render him helpless as she had all the rest, but she did not. Instead she wrapped him in her mind and lifted his body into the air, soft white light shimmering about his limbs.

"What are you doing?" he asked, and it was remarkable how casually he asked his question, as if they were debating daily plans over tea.

"My power," she told her brother. "It's growing inside me. I don't even know if I can stop it. I'm a dragon, Devin. I am the Dragon of Humanity, and I need to embrace it or lose myself completely."

"Embrace it how?"

Adria closed her eyes, and within her mind she sensed the entire landscape of the Cradle, every little hill, deep burrow, and towering mountain.

"I can remake the world. I can strike down every last life to dust, send their souls to the heavens, and start anew. It wouldn't be the first time this barren rock was reseeded. The Sisters failed once. The dragons have failed now. I can try again. I can learn from where they erred."

It should have sounded insane when she spoke those words, and though they frightened her to her core, they felt proper somehow. They felt inevitable.

"This can't be the right thing to do," he said. He hovered closer, as if the intensity of his words drew them together. "Killing everyone? Destroying all we've built? How could it be? Please, Adria, listen to what you're saying!"

But she *was* listening. To the entire Cradle. To the emotions leaking from the tens of thousands of souls. All their pain and suffering. The injustices of their rulers, the hunger of the destitute, the shivers of the homeless, the hatred and ugliness toward the dragon-sired and those who were strange and different. How could she make her brother understand?

"It may not be right, but what other choice do I have?" she asked. She pointed to the western wall. "Look around you. Look at the dead. Look at the ruins of Belvua. This won't stop. The killing, the bloodshed, the fear and betrayal...we can't let this go on." Tears were starting to build within her, her human mind struggling to withstand the overwhelming waves of emotions rolling across her from the collected experiences of thousands upon thousands of souls. "I feel so helpless. I am filled with such unbelievable power, and overcome with a need to do something, to help, to make things right...but I don't know what that is, Devin. I must do something, yet I know nothing that will work. Nothing that will make this better."

She gestured with her arms wide to the entire Cradle and its bloody civilizations.

"Why should I stop at fixing the soulless?" she asked. "Why not go farther? Why not scoop everything into one giant ball of souls and be done with it? The stars are fading. The void is ready to swallow us all. What path do I walk? Tell me, damn it. Tell me, before I take the wrong path and doom all I love."

Devin slowly, gently reached out to her. His hands settled over her shoulders.

"I don't know the solution," he said. "Humans? Dragon-sired? We bear different gods, and different lives. Perhaps there is no solution, Adria, but there is one thing I do know, one truth I cling to when all else turns dark."

His forehead pressed against her mask, and despite the roar of the wind and the crystalline ringing of the souls, she heard his whisper so softly, so clearly.

"No matter how confused my heart, I know the wrong path is the one that gives up all hope." His arms wrapped about her. "Stay with us, Adria. Believe in us. This world is not yet lost."

Adria's tears intensified, and it was no longer from the emotions of others. She embraced her brother and tried to believe him. Her gaze crossed the Goddesses and Viciss still crippled within her dragon body. They were surrounded by dead Soulkeepers she herself had slaughtered. Who was she to remake the Cradle? Who was she to believe she could make a world without hatred and rage? Her eyes settled on Janus's body, and his own words echoed within her mind.

You will exist forever, while I will cease the moment I stop breathing. But through you, I might finally scrawl a mark on eternity.

"Devin, I have an idea," she said. "It's insane, but I think it's what I need to do."

"Then do it," he said.

"You're so certain?" she asked. "Why? How could you possibly know it's right?"

He pulled back and grinned at her, that cocky, lopsided grin that had always brightened her life.

"Because I have faith in you, sis. I always have, and always will."

It was so simple. It was so heartfelt. It was everything she needed to hear.

"I may not survive this," she said as she gently pushed Devin away. Her brother floated toward the ground, softly guided by a shimmering field of light. "If I don't, know you've always been the world to me. You've pushed me to be my best, even now, at the end of all things and the beginning of the new."

Adria turned her gaze to the heavens. Beyond the skies, beyond the stars that surrounded the Cradle, beyond the great expanse of nothing that was the void, flowed the eternal Aether. It was a river of souls, of memories and emotions, from which the Goddesses themselves had emerged. It was from there the little spark of power that was the seed of a soul flew across the cosmos to settle into the body of a newborn human child. It was a gift Adria had long believed humanity did not deserve. Now she felt differently, and she clung to that belief to harden her resolve. The Cradle would change. She prayed the Goddesses were willing to change with it.

She lifted her arms and drew in the power eager for her to take.

Her vision turned white with the glow of souls. Her mind cracked beneath the strain. She felt herself gasp for breath as her physical shell struggled to maintain control. So much, she needed so much. Reach out to the Aether. Touch its flow. Demand a tribute from eternity. Take it, into her hands. Into her heart.

"No more favorites," she whispered. "Come to us all."

A second shock wave rolled across the Cradle, billowing outward from her chest. She felt her bones break. She felt her flesh tear. The work of a Goddess flowed through her hands, but her body was merely human. For the briefest moment she thought to reshape herself, to allow herself to endure beyond the mortal limits, but she refused. No matter her fate, no matter her task, she would remain human to the very end.

The mask that covered her face shattered. A tributary broke from the Aether and flowed across the void, crossing the vast, unknowable distance in the mere blink of an eye. Its flow spread as it approached the Cradle, dividing into a rain that showered across the continent like a million falling stars. The hovering souls returned to the bodies she had paralyzed. Seeds of new souls plunged into the bodies of the soulless that had been denied them at birth.

But that was not all.

Souls plunged into the minds and bodies of the dragon-sired. They settled into the deer and the squirrels. The insects that crawled beneath the soil. The birds that flew across the skies. Tears flowed down her cheeks as her physical shell descended toward the flesh-like floor of her dragon's body. The gift, once held sacred and given solely to humans, now lit the Cradle with light so blinding, she could not look upon it. Every creature, every life, sparkled with the divine.

The manacles that held Viciss and the Goddesses prisoner vanished. The power within her faded. She hit the ground and rolled, but her broken body was already numb to the pain. When she came to a halt, she lay perfectly still and gazed at the flickering stars. A face blurred them after a moment. Wren, the other Chainbreaker, frightened and sobbing as she touched Adria's face, and the blood that flowed from her ears and nostrils.

"We are all children of the Goddesses now," Adria said with a voice so strong, it could not be her own. "And we are all worthy of eternity."

CHAPTER 42

Wren brushed Adria's dark hair and wept. The other Chainbreaker bled from her eyes, ears, and nostrils. Her physical body was twisted and broken. How she even drew breath was beyond belief.

"You didn't have to do this for us," Wren whispered.

"I did," Adria whispered back. The woman couldn't move, but despite the pain it caused her, she could still speak. "Please, Wren, do not let this be in vain. We must have three Sisters. There must be a Goddess of the Day, and it can't be me."

"Don't ask this of me, please, I can't."

Adria gently shook her head.

"Will you watch over all creatures great and small? Will you be mother to human and dragon-sired, showing no preference, no favorites?"

Wren pressed her forehead to Adria's. Her mask was gone, she realized. Their skin touched, and she saw how beautiful, and how broken, the other Chainbreaker truly was. How could she answer such a question? What madness was this? How great a burden?

Wren stood and cast a worried look at Alma and Anwyn and their blinding light. Would they stop her? *Could* they stop her? She didn't know, and she dared not give them time to realize her plan. Wren brought her focus to the corpse of the Goddess of the Day.

Despite her death, Lyra's tremendous power remained within her body. In time it might fade, like a dying star, but Wren would not let it. Her hand extended. Her eyes widened.

It was insane. It was terrifying.

"Yes, Adria," she whispered. "I will."

Wren pulled Lyra's power into her, bonding with it as only those gifted by the dragons could accomplish. The shock hit her with such force, she feared her mind would break. In a way, her mind did, for she felt its limits crumbling and her awareness expanding. The souls upon the Cradle lit within her mind in a brand-new way, and she felt a kinship to them, a connection as if every soul were a part of her own self. Time itself seemed to slow. Pain burst throughout her chest, spread to her extremities, and lit her whole body aflame.

Her mortal shell could not endure such power, and so Wren cast it aside. Flesh and bone withered to ash, and with stunning ease, she crafted herself another, the body of a Sister, of a Goddess. It was bound not by sinew and tissue but pure, sparkling Aether. The pain faded, and it seemed her senses cooled as she plunged her massive, terrifying essence into it. Still the transformation was not complete. Lyra's lingering soul flowed into her, greater and greater, overwhelming her mind with memories and visions. The Goddess was not dead and gone, Wren realized, every part of Lyra melding within her, joining her in protection of the Day.

All life, she had promised Adria, and so she would. As her mind expanded, so, too, did her understanding of her newfound role. She looked at the sky and saw the weakened sun and the protective stars beyond the blue. They were fading, having been severely damaged by the void's relentless assault. Wren gave of herself to them, strengthening them. The life that bloomed upon the Cradle would not be swallowed by darkness and emptiness. It would endure, and it would endure by her strength and the strength granted to her by the prayers of the living. The setting sun brightened. The stars twinkled with newfound strength. It took so much of her, but it was her duty now as Goddess of the Day, and she would not fail.

Wren let out a long sigh, her mind finally easing into a comfortable state. Mere seconds had passed, but it felt like she had endured a dozen human lifetimes during the transition. She examined her hands, her body, and then as an homage to the woman who came before, she brushed her fingers through her tightly woven hair. It grew dozens of additional feet, trailing out behind her, but unlike Lyra's, she kept it within those tight, intricate braids.

That done, she faced those who gathered, human and dragon and Goddess, and smiled. Devin was the first to find the words to speak.

"Holy shit."

Alma and Anwyn seemed far less amused. They approached her, but their light was no longer blinding. Wren could see their physical forms, crafted of Aether, and infused with the same power that now dwelt within her.

"A Sister lost," said Anwyn.

"A Sister gained," added Alma. "Is that the truth?"

Wren shook her head at her new Sisters.

"Not yet," she said. "There are still wrongs to be righted."

She crossed the chamber to where Adria lay, a broken shell still valiantly struggling to breathe. Kindhearted Tomas wept over her as he cradled her battered body in his arms. Wren knelt over them both and gently cupped Adria's face with her hands.

"You did it," Adria whispered, tears mixing with the blood that covered her cheeks.

"I did," Wren said. "And it won't be alone."

The woman had given everything of herself to change the Cradle for better. So long as Wren wielded power, she would not reward such a sacrifice with death. Flesh healed. Broken bones mended. There was a time Wren might have viewed it as a miracle, but she saw the very building blocks of life, the thousands of them stacked within every speck of matter, and she made them dance to her will.

"I can free you," Wren said as Adria gasped. "If you want it."

The Chainbreaker closed her eyes, and after a long, deep breath, she nodded.

"Do it."

Wren mended, and shaped, and reconnected veins and rerouted nerves. Last of all, she touched the woman's very soul, and the changes lashed upon it by the dragons. Adria did not resist, and with that permission, Wren tore it down, remade it as it once was. When finished, she offered Adria her hand and helped her stand. She rose a Chainbreaker no more, but a Mindkeeper of the Day, servant to the Goddess she herself helped create.

"Adria!"

Devin practically slammed into his sister as he wrapped her in a hug and lifted her off her feet. He laughed as he sobbed, their embrace so joyful and heartfelt that Wren turned her back to them to give them their privacy. The other two Sisters awaited her, still impossible to read. They let no emotions escape the grasp of their souls, nor any hint of their thoughts be made visible on their perfectly still faces.

"We sense the changes she has wrought," Alma said. "Souls granted to all living things, not just humans. The animals. The dragon-sired. The balance we created is irrevocably broken."

"As if it were ever balanced," Wren said. She drew herself to her full height. If she backed down now, if she showed any weakness, then she would never be on equal terms with the other two. This was her role now, and she would fulfill it to the fullest extent. "This is a chance for something new. Will you accept it, Alma? Will you bring souls down to the Cradle for all who are birthed, not just your human creations?"

The beautiful form of a spring morning and hair of golden light shook her head.

"I will side with Anwyn's decision. I will not increase her burden without her consent."

Wren looked to the translucent shadow of death and ending.

"Will you reap all souls to eternity, Anwyn, not just those of your children?"

The masked face within the shadow slowly nodded.

"We warred with our own creations. We imprisoned our beloved dragons and sacrificed our strength to preserve a crumbling balance. It cost us the faith of our followers. It took the life of a dragon. Now it cost us a Sister. So be it, Wren of the Day. We will give this new balance a chance."

Wren smiled with relief. Without the help of the other two Sisters, what Adria had achieved would not have lasted. Still, there was one other faction needing to agree.

"And you?" she asked, turning to Viciss. The shimmering embodiment of Change laughed.

"Who am I to object to something so new?" he asked. "But this cannot be the only change. My children, and the children of my fellow dragons, must be given a place to live. And this makes no guarantee of peace. Conflicts of land, wealth, and trade are bound to follow regardless of any treaties or agreements our races reach."

"We don't need guarantees," Adria said as she pulled away from her brother. "We merely need hope of a better future. Without the interference of Goddesses and dragons, and the Sisters ensuring divine preference, I do believe we have that hope."

"More hope than before, at least," Viciss said, and there was no hiding his sneer toward the other two Sisters. "Anytime we dared fight back, you demanded our surrender and retreat. You pushed us to the edges of the world, and still it was not enough. We will never forget your orders to slaughter our own children, all to make way for your precious humans. But if you will allow us our place, then I will speak with my fellow dragons. We will accept this chance. We do not promise eternal peace, nor avoidance of bloodshed. We bear a thousand years of scars. They will not heal overnight." He chuckled. "Yet, just perhaps, they will still heal."

"Good," Adria said. "We can start with establishing official boundaries both sides will acknowledge." She blushed with mild embarrassment. "Once we determine who exactly is in charge of Londheim and Westreach, that is. I might have killed our previous High Excellence."

"You killed Dierk?" Devin asked. "Good. He was a little shit anyway. We'll need someone better if we're to rebuild from this whole mess."

Wren took a moment to collect herself. The pull of the stars above was already starting to wear upon her. As a human, she'd known little of the three Sisters, and had only the vaguest idea that the Goddess of the Day was meant to watch over humanity and protect them. Now she sensed the terrible burden of the void, always clawing at the edges of the starlight. It took so much of her to hold it at bay, and to steadily pour light back into both the stars and the sun. Could she guide the Cradle? And could she do so without making things worse?

"Someone must preach these changes," she said. "A prophet or prophetess for the human world, who will protect the lives of all awakened soulless, who will spread word of Lyra's demise, and of my ascension."

Adria crossed her arms and shook her head.

"It cannot be me," she said. "I have too much blood on my hands."

"Don't look at me," Devin said. "I'm just good at hitting things with a sword."

Wren closed her eyes and sank into the memories of a past that wasn't hers. Lyra's memories lurked within her, waiting for her. In time, she would immerse herself completely and view the vast centuries the Goddess had lived. Wren would bear witness to the creation of the dragons, and the Cradle, for her burden was so great and she must be prepared. Right now, though, she had to focus on the present. A lingering feeling tickled the back of her mind, a deep certainty that Lyra had known this possibility awaited her in the future. Wren clutched that memory and followed it to see where it led.

The world changes, my child. Know that I have cherished you always, and make not this decision lightly.

"You are right, Adria," Wren said, reopening her eyes. "It shouldn't be you, and it won't be. There is another."

It didn't even take a full thought to know where the woman resided, for the mere desire to know her location was enough to pinpoint her soul. Wren evaporated her body as if it were mist, her physical limits already shifting with her constantly growing understanding of the world around her. She floated through the air, spiraling across the winds and dashing across the clouds. Within seconds she was back in Londheim.

No sound marked her arrival, but she felt it within her body like a faint shudder. They were in a small bedroom, one of many in the church Sena Meisen now called her home.

"Rise, Faithkeeper," she told the woman who knelt beside her bed in prayer. "We must speak."

The other woman stood, her mouth dropping wide.

"Who?" she asked as she took a terrified step closer. "Lyra… but you're not Lyra. Not fully."

"No," Wren said. "The Cradle changes, and I need a voice to speak its change. Will you listen, and believe?"

Sena lowered her head, and she put a hand over her heart.

"A hard, lonely road," she said, the words igniting memories within them both. "Yes, Goddess. I am listening."

CHAPTER 43

You don't have to do this," Devin said as he and his sister embraced outside Londheim's walls. "The people here still love you."

"I know they do," Adria said as she pulled away. "That's part of the problem. Sena needs space to do her work. It's hard enough as it is, and me being around will only make it harder. Did you hear some people propose I be the new High Excellence? Me, after everything I've done? It's ridiculous."

"They just fear Sena will become Queen of Westreach as well as its Deakon," Devin said.

"She's becoming more than either title. Perhaps it is necessary, perhaps it will lead to complete destruction further down the road. All I know is that for good or ill, I won't be a part of it. I've killed and destroyed too much of the old. Let others guide the healing amid the new."

Devin wished he could argue, but this was a battle he'd been steadily losing over the past few weeks. Ever since Adria forfeited her powers, she had played the recluse, hiding away from the world while Sena solidified her control over the shambles that remained of the Keeping Church. Given the complete absence of Vikars and a Deakon, the difficulty hadn't been in rising to power, but maintaining the loyalty of the remaining keepers. Many had given up hope. Many more saw her as a heretic preaching word of a new Goddess of the Day.

Knowing all this didn't make it any easier to say good-bye to his sister. All of her belongings, packed together in a single meager rucksack, rested on her left shoulder. She had requested permission to join the nearest village of dyrandar in the newly created Kingdom of the Sired, and Shinnoc had readily accepted. They knew she was responsible for the gift of souls to all living creations, and from what Devin had gathered, the collected tribes of the dragon-sired were eager to debate the theological implications of what Adria had done.

"You can always come back if you don't like living among deer people," Devin said. "Tommy will make you a disguise if that's what you need to live here in peace. And the dyrandar better let me come visit you every few months when I can afford to sneak away."

"I'll make sure you're welcome," she said. "And don't worry about me, Devin. I'll be fine. Try to focus on your own life for a change. You deserve happiness, too."

"That's debatable," he said, and he hugged her one last time. "Stay safe out there, sis."

They pulled away, and she trudged west with a cheerful wave good-bye. She wore simple trousers, a long shirt, and a heavy coat to hold back the bite of winter. No Mindkeeper dress, no mask, just Devin's tricorn hat hanging loose atop her head.

Devin sat upon the rooftop of his home and stared at the stars. He held a simple gold band in his right hand, and he slowly twirled it between his fingers. He hadn't been up there for long, but just as he'd hoped, Jacaranda soon came out to join him.

"Everything all right?" she asked as she hoisted herself up.

Devin did not hide the band, or act like it was anything noteworthy. "This doesn't tend to be your happy place."

"I'm fine, I promise," he said. He gestured to the western horizon. The reaping hour approached, the energy of it starting to lift the hairs on his neck. "I'm not sure I'll ever get used to it."

"I know I haven't," Jacaranda said. "I stepped on a roach today and was petrified I'd see a tiny little soul rising up to the heavens when I lifted my foot."

Devin laughed and shook his head.

"I can't quite say for certain if roaches have a soul or not, but I doubt you'd be able to see it even if it existed. I've heard some stories that larger animals like dogs and cats have faintly visible souls, like tiny little lightning bugs."

"I'm not sure I like the idea of spending eternity with roaches," she said.

"What about an eternity with dogs and cats?"

Jacaranda looped her arm through his and leaned her weight against him.

"That's a little easier to stomach."

With the power of the three Sisters fully restored, there was no need for the church's reaping rituals. Devin held his breath as the moment arrived, and he smiled as he watched the upward fall of several dozen shooting stars across the western sky. They were the souls of the recently deceased in Londheim, as well as the dragon-sired villages beyond. It warmed his heart imagining everyone across the entire Cradle seeing very similar sights.

When the moment passed, Jacaranda finally addressed the ring. Her voice remained calm, almost coy, when she spoke.

"So what is that?"

Devin lifted the ring so it could better reflect the light of the stars.

"It's the wedding band I gave Brittany when I proposed."

"You kept it all these years?" She snuggled closer. "I guess I shouldn't be surprised, given how you're such a softie."

"But I didn't keep it," Devin said with a chuckle. "I buried it with her body. Brit dug it up and gave it to me."

"Isn't digging up graves incredibly forbidden by both church and state?"

"It is, but when it's your *own* grave, I think it's allowed."

He continued to roll the ring between his fingertips, his memories a mixture of joy and sorrow, as they often were when he thought of his first marriage. Brit was, in a darkly comic way, the oldest remaining Soulkeeper in Westreach, and as such had been appointed by Sena to be the new Vikar of the Dusk. She'd handed him the ring while telling him the news earlier that morning.

"Dead for six years, now about to take on a role I am painfully unqualified for," Brittany had said. "Life is damn bizarre sometimes."

"So is death, if we go by your case," he'd said as he accepted the ring. "Is this your way of officially divorcing me?"

"Marriages end at death according to the church, so a divorce isn't necessary. Think of it more as my way of... letting go."

The two had embraced, and they'd both shed their tears. There'd been something cleansing about receiving the ring, and finally voicing an understanding they'd had and kept unspoken ever since her return. Now the ring meant something very different as he twirled it between his fingers. No longer just a memory, but a token of potential. Of a future.

"So why did Brit decide to go and do that?" Jacaranda asked, pulling him from his thoughts. Still coy. Still not even looking at him while she spoke.

"She seemed to think I might have use for it."

"Was she right?"

Devin slowly offered her the ring and then gave a shrug.

"I don't know. You've liked making choices ever since awakening. Would you like to make another one?"

Jacaranda drove her elbow into his side, and he made a great show of exaggerating his pain. While he grimaced, she took the ring from him and slid it upon her finger. Her eyes sparkled as she lifted it to stare at the smooth, polished gold.

"Is that a yes?" Devin asked.

"After such an nondramatic proposal, do you think you deserve a dramatic answer?"

"I don't deserve anything from you. I don't even deserve *you*, but you're still up here with me in the cold of night. I must be doing something right."

Jacaranda shut him up with a kiss, then softly laughed as she pressed her forehead to his and let her red hair fall across them both.

"Yes," she said. "It's a yes, you big, bumbling fool of a Soulkeeper."

"Well, that's good," he said, his grin spreading ear to ear. "Because for a moment you had me worried."

She kissed him, her own smile growing as a few stubborn tears of joy trickled down her face. He returned the kiss, relief swelling inside his chest. No matter how certain he'd been she would say yes, it still felt wonderful to hear those words, and to see the happiness overcome her. He buried her in his coat as she fully climbed into his lap, her hands cradling his face, her lips and breath warming his neck.

"We should get back inside," Jacaranda said she kissed a line across his cheek.

"Why's that?"

Her tongue flicked across his jaw as her lips rose to his ear. Her hand brushed his inner thigh and traveled upward.

"Because there's things I want to do to you that won't be comfortable doing on a rooftop."

EPILOGUE

I promise we'll be perfectly safe in the east," Tommy said as he hugged Devin good-bye in front of the steps to the shuttered and locked Wise tower. "I bet most of our findings are already well known, so we won't be making any real waves."

"Except when you tell the Council of Wise about the dragons," said Devin. "And the magic schools, the void, Lyra's death, Wren taking up her mantle, and Sena's new role as prophetess."

"All right, so things might be a little controversial, but I still assure you we'll be totally safe."

It had been a month since the climactic showdown against the void monster underneath Londheim. Tommy and Malik had worked together to smooth out the political side of things, using what respect they had as the Wise to pore over old laws and supervise a quickly done vote of land owners on a new High Excellence. The winner was some minor noble who owned hundreds of acres northeast of Londheim that had been spared the damage of the black water. Given Sena's growing authority, he'd likely be a puppet leader, but at least it helped give some sense of stability to the shaken realm.

"You'll be preaching heresy when it comes to Wren," Devin said. "Just be aware of that, all right? The church isn't exactly known for its flexibility when it comes to doctrine."

"Tomas may not be worried," Malik said from his driver's seat of the wagon they had purchased for their journey eastward to the coastal city of Nelme. "But I am, and I'll keep us both safely aware of what political and spiritual factions are emerging."

"At least there will be one adult in the room then," Devin said, and he grinned and waved good-bye. "Stay safe, the both of you, and good luck with your presentation to the council. Bring some fancy Nelme wine with you on your return, so we can drink to your successes and failures."

"Failures?" Tommy huffed as he climbed into the wagon. "Nonsense! This trip will be one of complete success!"

"So do you have absolutely everything?" Malik asked.

"I'm pretty sure," he said. "Are you sure you know how to drive a cart? It's a long trip to Nelme, you know. And I doubt the roads have gotten any easier, what with all the magical creatures everywhere."

Malik did a soft flick of the reins to set their donkey moving.

"If we do encounter trouble, it is a good thing you'll be paying attention and ready to roast them with a fireball spell."

They made it a mere thirty seconds away from the tower before a shadowy blur flashed across their path. Tommy grabbed the side of the cart, his eyes wide with shock. Hovering before them was an onyx faery wearing a familiar leaf green dress. For one brief moment he thought it was Tesmarie, but her hair was much longer, reaching all the way down to her ankles, and her face was not quite so gentle and young. Malik pulled on the reins, halting their cart in the middle of the street as they stared dumbfounded at their new arrival.

"You," the onyx faery said, pointing at Tommy. "You're a wizard, right?"

"A...a wizard?" he asked.

"Yes, a wizard, a magic user, a human spellcaster. You are one, aren't you?"

Tommy glanced about, starting to seriously wonder if he was dreaming.

"Yes? I guess I am?"

The faery's eyes shimmered a rainbow of color, just like when Tesmarie had used magic to view events in the past. Her wings buzzed as she hovered in place.

"I've been looking for my…friend, Tesmarie," she said. "And I found her. What happened to her, I mean. You were friends with her, too, weren't you? I've seen you together with her when I watch the past, and the life she lived here."

Tommy stared at the faery, little pieces of memories clicking into place. Tesmarie's story of why she had been exiled, of how she'd been betrothed to Gan but instead loved another.

"Elebell," he said. "You're Elebell, aren't you?"

The little faery crossed her hands behind her back and looked away as she hovered.

"So she told you about me then? And what I did?"

When Tesmarie had been expelled from her village, it had been due to her love affair with Elebell instead of her arranged betrothal to the complete asshole that was a faery named Gan. She had expected Elebell to come with her, but instead her lover remained behind, forcing Tesmarie into exile all alone.

"Yeah, she did, a little," he said, feeling awkward and unsure. Saying this obviously hurt Elebell, but he didn't want to lie to her, either.

"It was wrong of me," Elebell said. She lowered her face, her hair cascading forward to hide her body. "I've had a lot of years to remember that awful day, and I couldn't…I couldn't take it anymore. So now I'm here, and I'm worried it's too late, but I have to try. I have to see if I can make things right. I've already done a lot of the work, the rune carvings and preparations, but now I need your help. Will you help me, human, with your magic?"

Tommy looked to his companion, who let out a long, exaggerated sigh.

"We can delay a day or two," Malik said. "If it's important."

"I think it is," Tommy said, and he turned back to Elebell. "So what is it you need me to do?"

Late the following day, Tommy and Elebell crossed the street with a wooden box in his left hand and the faery hidden in his robe pocket. Relationships between humans and dragon-sired might improve in the future, but emotions were still very raw, and he felt it best to keep her away from prying eyes while they traveled.

"Well, here we are," he said as they arrived at their destination. They stood in the center of the Tradeway Square, where the Forgotten Children had ambushed Adria. It was where his sister-in-law had first ripped apart a soul. Where Tesmarie died.

"I've come here every day for a week to carve my runes," Elebell said as she fluttered out from his pocket. "Yet it still feels so strange to me."

"That's putting it mildly."

The effect of destroying a soul had irrevocably damaged reality, altering physical landscapes to match scattered, destroyed memories. Patches of grass and mud formed little rivulets in the cobblestone. Nearby buildings leaned on warped foundations. Two buildings had trees growing from their centers as if they had been built around the bark. Even the ground rolled unevenly, like the meeting of two separate hills. Because of the damage, not to mention the slaughtered and hung children, no one had been eager to return, leaving the square unnervingly quiet as the sun began its descent.

"So what do we do now?" he asked as he shifted his weight from foot to foot while trying to hide his nervousness.

"Now we see if your doll is of significant quality."

Tommy lifted the small box and removed the lid.

"This was very difficult to make," he said. "And I don't mean physically, or magically."

Inside was an exact replica of Tesmarie, or at least, as close as he could manage from memory. Twelve straight hours of casting Viciss spells had built it. Elebell flew above the box, and she sniffled as she turned away.

"It's good," she said. "Very good. Thank you, Tomas. Please, hold on to it, and no matter what you see or hear next, remain perfectly still and quiet. Can you do that?"

"Sure," he said. He swallowed down a rock lodged in his throat. "Whatever you say."

Elebell flew about the square, inspecting over two dozen runes she had carved into cobblestones, lantern posts, and building walls. Once she'd done several revolutions, she flew to the center and bowed her head as if she were offering a prayer.

"I abandoned you once, Tes," she said. "I won't do it again."

The faery closed her hands. Her hair fluttered in the soft wind. Blue light began to sparkle across her fingertips, which were clenched tightly together before her.

"What we are about to do is very, very forbidden by my kind," she said. "It is also extremely dangerous. Are you sure you are ready?"

"Ready," Tommy lied.

Her spell began, the words of magic granted to her by her maker, Chyron. They floated across the cold dusk air, full with the promise of power. The many carved runes began to glow a soft blue light. Tommy watched quietly, knowing the plan but hardly believing it. This was insane. It couldn't possibly work.

But the space around him was running with color, like a dry painting suddenly splashed with water. The wind blew, but in opposite directions. The ground shifted. On and on the words of magic flowed from Elebell's lips, manipulating time in ways Tommy did not understand but feared he was about to learn.

The sound of the wind deepened unnaturally. His surroundings drained of vibrancy, leaving things paler, dimmer. Phantoms flickered about, flicking ghosts attempting to make their presences known. There was no need for Elebell's command; fear kept Tommy's feet firmly rooted in place.

Whatever power flowed from the onyx faery drastically heightened. Faintly visible shock waves of pink light rolled out from her in all directions. Each one washed over his skin and set it to tingling. The marketplace about him shifted again, more phantoms, and then with a singular startling *crack*, the ground rumbled beneath his feet. The carved runes cracked and shimmered away into dust.

"Elebell," Tommy whispered, his eyes widening as he bore witness to the new reality about him. "Is this..."

"The past," the faery whispered, her eyes still closed and her head still bowed. "Her past."

It was a singular frozen moment in time, one Tommy had heard the stories of but not witnessed himself. The bodies of twelve children hung from ropes tied to the nearby buildings. A motley assortment of dragon-sired lined the rooftops with crossbows in hand, all of them trained upon Adria. His sister-in-law stood with her hands lifted before her. A soul burned between her fingers, its light weirdly static and dulled. Devin and Tesmarie were beside her, Devin with his hand on his pistol, and Tesmarie hovering behind him to hide.

One second later, the soul would erupt in two. Adria's rage would wash over the entire square, blasting apart each and every dragon-sired within the vicinity. Poor Tesmarie would be caught in that blast, her body broken and left lifeless upon the cold stone.

Another pink wave of magic rolled out from Elebell as she cried out to him.

"Make the switch!"

Tommy ran to Tesmarie, and when he skidded to a halt, he nearly dropped the box and sent the false body tumbling out. He wiped sweat from his brow and muttered to himself to get a grip.

Carefully he took the real Tesmarie into his hand. Her body was perfectly stiff, as if he'd grabbed not a person but a sculpture. In her place Tommy lifted the false Tesmarie he had painstakingly created with his magic, turning clay and sticks into a lifeless facsimile. As he brought it to where Tesmarie had once been, it seemed invisible hands grabbed it from his grasp, the limbs positioning the faery doll to match how she herself had once been.

"It's done!" he shouted back to Elebell. Despite the stillness of the surroundings, it felt like a waterfall roared so loudly in the distance, it made his ears ache.

"Close your eyes," the faery said. "This won't be fun."

Tommy did as requested. The roar in his ears became overwhelming thunder. Air billowed across his body from all directions. He felt his stomach suddenly clench, and he couldn't shake the feeling he was moving across a staggering distance at mind-bending speeds. A powerful need to vomit hit him, and he had to clench his jaw to fight it off. The roar grew louder, closer, and he feared it would break him completely. Why wouldn't the sensation of moving stop? Why did his knees tremble, and why did it feel like the sky looped despite his tightly shut eyes?

A sudden return to his normal time flow hit him with the grace and subtlety of a brick wall. Tommy let out a soft gasp, and he wobbled on unsteady legs that had suddenly turned to jelly. Yet all of it, every awkward and disorientating second, was worth it the moment he felt Tesmarie stir in his hand.

"Tommy?" she asked. "Where am I? What's going on?"

Tommy opened his eyes to see Tesmarie staring up at him with complete bewilderment on her face. He lasted about one and a half seconds before uncontrollable sobs overcame him, robbing him of any hope of explaining the situation. And then Tesmarie saw Elebell flying to join her, and it was her turn to fill with tears and struggle to speak.

"Elebell?" Tesmarie forced out. "Seriously now, will someone please tell me what is happening because I'm worried I've lost my mind."

"I can explain some," Elebell said as she hovered close. "Tomas here will have to explain the rest."

They walked the darkening streets of Londheim, and this time no faery hid in Tommy's pocket. They hovered together, sometimes chatting away, sometimes listening to Tommy speak. He filled in Tesmarie as best he could over the events of the past weeks, no easy feat giving all that had happened. His sister had returned from the dead and his sister-in-law nearly became a Goddess. Keeping things simple was out of the question.

"Things really do seem hopeful, though," Tommy said as they turned onto Sermon Lane. "I mean, obviously a lot of people aren't happy about losing the lands to the west, but most of the people who would be upset about it are dead. That, uh, sounds worse than I meant it to, by the way."

"Stop being so worried," Tesmarie insisted. "Everything's going to be just fine now, I'm sure of it. And I'm back, too, so I can doubly make sure of that! Not that *I* felt like I went anywhere, but you all seemed to think I did."

"So long as you're convinced, then I'm convinced," Elebell said, and she offered Tesmarie a soft smile. Tesmarie blushed, seemingly unsure of how to respond. Tommy could tell there was an ocean of suppressed feelings between the two of them. With time, they might work things out, and perhaps Tesmarie would forgive Elebell for that distant betrayal. The two looked so cute together, Tommy couldn't help hoping they made it through.

"It seems weird that I don't have a soul but you do now," Tesmarie told Elebell. "Does it feel different? Seem different? And will I get one?"

"Maybe you should ask Sena," Tommy offered. "With her rebuilding the entire church, I bet she could whisper a prayer in Wren's ear for a favor."

They turned a corner, the end of the road almost upon them. Devin's house came into view, and as if on cue, the door to it cracked open. Devin stepped outside in preparation for his nightly patrol, and he did not see them at first, for his back was turned as he shut the door while trying to hold his pistol belt and tricorn hat in his free hand. Tesmarie zipped toward him, and she tried sounding calm as she called out to him, but the speed of her words belied her excitement.

"Hey-there-silly-human!"

Devin slowly turned, then froze in place. His hat slipped from his numb fingers. His mouth opened, closed, then opened again as tears trickled down his bewildered face. The joy that lit his eyes was so bright, Tommy felt his own tears start to flow.

"Tes?"

Tesmarie flung herself against his chest, arms open to accept his embrace, his tears, and his eventual laughter.

A NOTE FROM THE AUTHOR

As always, I chatted at the end of *Ravencaller* about my reactions to different parts of the book, and in that author's note I talked about the death of one of my favorite characters: Tesmarie. It's a sentiment that I've written shades of several times before, where I discuss my reaction anytime I kill beloved characters. There was a time when I thoroughly enjoyed it, a sadistic pleasure in knowing I was pulling on the heartstrings of my readers. As I mellowed with age, as well as continued fairly deep into various series of mine like the Half-Orcs, I started to lament how every character death meant an end to telling more stories with that character. It was a denial of possibility, and it meant I needed to be sure, absolutely sure, that I wanted a character's story to end at that moment.

So in that letter, I lamented how it hurt killing off Tesmarie, but it was the right tragedy for that moment in the story. Saying this felt a little cruel, though, for me to look at my readers at the end of *Ravencaller* and tell them, "I was just as sad as you, I swear! But this was what the story demanded, and so it had to be."

I still believe that, by the way.

But to recap a bit of what I discussed on Twitter during *Ravencaller*'s release, this story of the Cradle was meant to be, above all things, one of hope. Its heroes looked upon a changing world that frightened them. They faced challenges that seemingly have no good solutions, such as who deserves Londheim, the dragon-sired who were banished or the humans who have lived there for centuries afterward unaware of what their Goddess had done. The world itself would be one of infinite shades of gray, with complicated problems and damaged characters all struggling to do what is right for their friends and family, be they human and dragon-sired. But hope was meant to win out. Peace was to be the endgame. The villains and monsters were those who would perpetuate hatred, those like Janus, who would refuse to even entertain the possibility to an end of continuous violence. Devin embodied this fully, a hero not because he had the strongest sword arm or the most powerful magic, but because he was a friend to all in need, who would hold faith in his sister even at the end of the world.

And yet...and yet...

If there was one character who embodied hope and joy, it was Tesmarie. And I killed her.

I often joke that I am god of my worlds I write. I can kill anyone (and often have, just ask those who read and loved/hated the Shadowdance books). I'll pull off the most insane stuff. I'll split open the sky and send down angels, bring back villains only to redeem them, and bring back heroes only to turn them into undead abominations. Yet when asked questions like "Why did so-and-so die?" it feels like I am often abdicating my responsibility. "The story demanded it," I'll say. "That's just how things happened," as if I am not able to rewind the pages and edit away every single aspect of my story.

So the cold truth is that sometimes I make calculations of the impact of a death. Villains are easy in this regard. The hero finally triumphed, the villain is defeated, a sick bastard got what he deserved. Pump a fist, crack a smile, and move on. Except sometimes I won't move on. I'll have a villain survive, such as Logarius, so I might take a second bite at that apple. The story beats for *Ravencaller* flowed better with him defeated, and the thematic impact of being killed by his mother fit everything I wanted with *Ravencaller*, but my personal desire for how the story progressed wanted him alive, because he was fun, he was cool, and I could do more with him in *Voidbreaker*. Whenever I do this, there's always a little worry that I'm tweaking a story to give myself exclusively what *I* want, not necessarily what *the story* wants.

Yet there again I go acting as if *the story* were some cosmic thing separate from myself, as if I read that Tesmarie was meant to die written on a wall in gold no different than Janus left messages to Adria. But to say I was conflicted about what to do with Tesmarie is putting it mildly. I had more than a few conversations with my editor about ideas, ways I could manipulate time/space/events. I wouldn't cheat, I swore, because there's always a fear of undoing major, impactful events, or making people feel like their emotions were unfairly manipulated. Even worse, a risk of having readers simply no longer trust me as a storyteller. A lot of that worry kept me from writing that final epilogue you just read. Leave it be. The story's been told.

And then one day, when I was feeling particularly down, I did something I very rarely do since I started writing professionally a decade ago: I wrote a story solely for myself. I wasn't going to give it to my editor. I wasn't going to use it. At best, I thought I might throw it onto my website as a little side gift for anyone who wanted it. I crafted a little tale that I needed at the time, and it was what you just finished reading, of how Tesmarie was pulled through time and spared the death that claimed her. And at that final moment, when I imagined Devin freezing in place as a joyful Tesmarie slammed full-speed into his chest for a hug, I bawled my eyes out.

The Keepers was meant to be about hope. And I realized then and there, that was the hope I needed. If you disagree, I pray you forgive me. If you feel I cheated or manipulated you, I ask you to understand it was all done with absolute honesty. These characters mean the world to me, as do the trials they face, the spaces they inhabit, and the messages they convey through their heroic deeds and abysmal failures. And with this series of books, filled with some brutal tragedies, violent deaths, and seemingly impossible differences, I knew the last image I wanted to leave, the image that would convey what I myself hoped would be the future of these characters, and this world in general.

A friend embracing another friend, once lost, now returned, so sorrow might be replaced with joy.

David Dalglish
April 27, 2020

extras

orbitbooks.net

about the author

David Dalglish currently lives in Myrtle Beach with his wife, Samantha, and daughters Morgan, Katherine, and Alyssa. He graduated from Missouri Southern State University in 2006 with a degree in mathematics and currently spends his free time grinding tomestones in *Final Fantasy XIV*.

Find out more about David Dalglish and other Orbit authors by registering online for the free monthly newsletter at orbitbooks.net.

Prologue

You stand on a rocky outcrop, riddled with tunnels like the other hills, and look over Guerdon. From here, you see the heart of the old city, its palaces and churches and towers reaching up like the hands of a man drowning, trying to break free of the warren of alleyways and hovels that surrounds them. Guerdon has always been a place in tension with itself, a city built atop its own previous incarnations yet denying them, striving to hide its past mistakes and present a new face to the world. Ships throng the island-spangled harbour between two sheltering headlands, bringing traders and travellers from across the world. Some will settle here, melding into the eternal, essential Guerdon.

Some will come not as travellers, but as refugees. You stand as testament to the freedom that Guerdon offers: freedom to worship, freedom from tyranny and hatred. Oh, this freedom is conditional, uncertain – the city has, in its time, chosen tyrants and fanatics and monsters to rule it, and you have been part of that, too – but the sheer weight of the city, its history and its myriad peoples always ensure that it slouches back eventually into comfortable corruption, where anything is permissible if you've got money.

Some will come as conquerors, drawn by that wealth. You were born in such a conflict, the spoils of a victory. Sometimes, the conquerors stay and are slowly absorbed into the city's culture. Sometimes, they raze what they can and move on, and Guerdon grows again from the ashes and rubble, incorporating the scar tissue into the living city.

You are aware of all this, as well as certain other things, but you cannot articulate how. You know, for example, that two Tallowmen guards patrol your western side, moving with the unearthly speed and grace of their kind. The dancing flames inside their heads illuminate a row of carvings on your flank, faces of long-dead judges and politicians immortalised in stone while their mortal remains have long since gone down the corpse shafts. The Tallowmen jitter by, and turn right down Mercy Street, passing the arch of your front door beneath the bell tower.

You are aware, too, of another patrol coming up behind you.

And in that gap, in the shadows, three thieves creep up on you. The first darts out of the mouth of an alleyway and scales your outer wall. Ragged hands find purchase in the cracks of your crumbling western side with inhuman quickness. He scampers across the low roof, hiding behind gargoyles and statues when the second group of Tallowmen pass by. Even if they'd looked up with their flickering fiery eyes, they'd have seen nothing amiss.

Something in the flames of the Tallowmen should disquiet you, but you are incapable of that or any other emotion.

The ghoul boy comes to a small door, used only by workmen cleaning the lead tiles of the roof. You know – again, you don't know how you know – that this door is unlocked, that the guard who should have locked it was bribed to neglect that part of his duties tonight. The ghoul boy tries the door, and it opens silently. Yellow-brown teeth gleam in the moonlight.

Back to the edge of the roof. He checks for the tell-tale light of the Tallowmen on the street, then drops a rope down. Another thief emerges from the same alleyway and climbs. The ghoul hauls up the rope, grabs her hand and pulls her out of sight in the brief gap between patrols. As she touches your walls, you know her to be a stranger to the city, a nomad girl, a runaway. You have not seen her before, but a flash of anger runs through you at her touch as you share, impossibly, in her emotion.

You have never felt this or anything else before, and wonder at it. Her hatred is not directed at you, but at the man who compels her to be here tonight, but you still marvel at it as the feeling travels the length of your roof-ridge.

The girl is familiar. The girl is important.

You hear her heart beating, her shallow, nervous breathing, feel the weight of the dagger in its sheathe pressing against her leg. There is, however, something missing about her. Something incomplete.

She and the ghoul boy vanish in through the open door, hurrying through your corridors and rows of offices, then down the side stairs back to ground level. There are more guards inside, humans – but they're stationed at the vaults on the north side, beneath your grand tower, not here in this hive of paper and records; the two thieves remain unseen as they descend. They come to one of your side doors, used by clerks and scribes during the day. It's locked and bolted and barred, but the girl picks the lock even as the ghoul scrabbles at the bolts. Now the door's unlocked, but they don't open it yet. The girl presses her eye to the keyhole and watches, waits, until the Tallowmen pass by again. Her hand fumbles at her throat, as if looking for a necklace that usually rests there, but her neck is bare. She scowls, and the flash of anger at the theft thrills you.

You are aware of the ghoul, of his physical presence within you, but you feel the girl far more keenly, share her fretful excitement as she waits for the glow of the Tallowmen candles to diminish. This, she fears, is the most dangerous part of the whole business.

She's wrong.

Again, the Tallowmen turn the corner onto Mercy Street. You want to reassure her that she is safe, that they are out of sight, but you cannot find your voice. No matter – she opens the door a crack and gestures, and the third member of the trio lumbers from the alley.

Now, as he thuds across the street in the best approximation of a sprint he's capable of, you see why they needed to open the ground-level door when they already had the roof entrance. The third member of the group is a Stone Man. You remember when the disease – or curse – first took root in the city. You remember the panic, the debates about internment, about quarantines. The alchemists found a treatment in time, and a full-scale epidemic was forestalled. But there are still outbreaks, patches, leper colonies of sufferers in the city. If the symptoms aren't caught early enough, the result is the motley creature that even now lurches over your threshold – a man whose flesh and bone are slowly transmuting into rock. Those afflicted by the plague grow immensely strong, but every little bit of wear and tear, every injury hastens their calcification. The internal organs are the last to go, so towards the end they are living statues, unable to move or see, locked forever in place, labouring to breathe, kept alive only by the charity of others.

This Stone Man is not yet paralysed, though he moves awkwardly, dragging his right leg. The girl winces at the noise as she shuts the door behind him, but you feel an equally unfamiliar thrill of joy and relief as her friend reaches the safety of their hiding place. The ghoul's already moving, racing down the long silent corridor that's usually thronged with prisoners and guards, witnesses and jurists, lawyers and liars. He runs on all fours, like a grey dog. The girl and the Stone Man follow; she stays low, but he's not that flexible. Fortunately, the corridor does not look out directly onto the street outside, so, even if the patrolling Tallowmen glanced this way, they wouldn't see him.

The thieves are looking for something. They check one record room, then another. These rooms are secure, locked away behind iron doors, but stone is stronger and the Stone Man bends or breaks them, one by one, enough for the ghoul or the human girl to wriggle through and search.

At one point, the girl grabs the Stone Man's elbow to hasten him along. A native of the city would never do such a thing, not willingly, not unless they had the alchemist's cure to hand. The curse is contagious.

They search another room, and another and another. There are hundreds of thousands of papers here, organised by a scheme that is a secret of the clerks, whispered only from one to another, passed on like an heirloom. If you knew what they sought, and they could understand your speech, you could perhaps tell them where to find what they seek, but they fumble on half blind.

They cannot find what they are looking for. Panic rises. The girl argues that they should leave, flee before they are discovered. The Stone Man shakes his head, as stubborn and immovable as, well, as stone. The ghoul keeps his own counsel, but hunches down, pulling his hood over his face as if trying to remove himself from their debate. They will keep looking. Maybe it's in the next room.

Elsewhere inside you, one guard asks another if he heard that. Why, might that not be the sound of an intruder? The other guards look at each other curiously, but then in the distance, the Stone Man smashes down another door, and the now-attentive guards definitely hear it.

You know – you alone know – that the guard who alerted his fellows is the same one who left the rooftop door unlocked. The guards fan out, sound the alarm, begin to search the labyrinth within you. The three thieves split up, try to evade their pursuers. You see the chase from both sides, hunters and hunted.

And, after the guards leave their post by the vaults, other figures enter. Two, three, four, climbing up from below. How have you not sensed them before? How did they come upon you, enter you, unawares? They move with the confidence of experience, sure of every action. Veterans of their trade.

The guards find the damage wrought by the Stone Man and begin to search the south wing, but your attention is focused on the strangers in your vault. With the guards gone, they work unimpeded. They unwrap a package, press it against the vault door, light a fuse. It blazes brighter than any Tallowman's candle, fizzing and roaring and then—

—you are burning, broken, rent asunder, thrown into disorder. Flames race through you, all those thousands of documents catching in an instant, old wooden floors fuelling the inferno. The stones crack. Your western hall collapses, the stone faces of judges plummeting into the street outside to smash on the cobblestones. You feel your *awareness* contract as the fire numbs you. Each part of you that is consumed is no longer part of you, just a burning ruin. It's eating you up.

It is not that you can no longer see the thieves – the ghoul, the Stone Boy, the nomad girl who taught you briefly to hate. It is that you can no longer know them with certainty. They flicker in and out of your rapidly fragmenting consciousness as they move from one part of you to another.

When the girl runs across the central courtyard, pursued by a Tallowman, you feel every footstep, every panicked breath she takes as she runs, trying to outdistance creatures that move far faster than her merely human flesh can hope to achieve. She's clever, though – she zigzags back into a burning section, vanishing from your perception. The Tallowman hesitates to follow her into the flames for fear of melting prematurely.

You've lost track of the ghoul, but the Stone Man is easy to spot. He stumbles into the High Court, knocking over the wooden seats where the Lords Justice and Wisdom sit when proceedings are in session. The velvet cushions of the viewer's gallery are already on fire. More pursuers close in on him. He's too slow to escape.

Around you, around what's left of you, the alarm spreads. A blaze of this size must be contained. People flee the neighbouring buildings, or hurl buckets of water on roofs set alight by sparks from your inferno. Others gather to gawk, as if the destruction of one of the city's greatest institutions was a sideshow for their amusement. Alchemy wagons race through the streets, carrying vats of fire-quelling liquids, better than water for dealing with a conflagration like this. They know the dangers of a fire in the city; there have been great fires in the past, though none in recent decades. Perhaps, with the alchemists' concoctions and the discipline of the city watch, they can contain this fire.

But it is too late for you.

Too late, you hear the voices of your brothers and sisters cry out, shouting the alarm, rousing the city to the danger.

Too late, you realise what you are. Your consciousness shrinks down, takes refuge in its vessel. That is what you are, if not what you have always been.

You feel a second emotion – fear – as the flames climb the tower. Something beneath you breaks, and the tower sags suddenly to one side, sending you rocking back and forth. Your voice jangles in the tumult, a sonorous death rattle.

Your supports break, and you fall.

[illegible]

[illegible]

[illegible]

[illegible]

[illegible]

[illegible]

[illegible]

Chapter One

Carillon crouches in the shadow, eyes fixed on the door. Her knife is in her hand, a gesture of bravado to herself more than a deadly weapon. She's fought before, cut people with it, but never killed with it. Cut and run, that's her way.

In this crowded city, that's not necessarily an option.

If one guard comes through the door, she'll wait until he goes past her hiding place, then creep after him and cut his throat. She tries to envisage herself doing it, but can't manage it. Maybe she can get away with just scaring him, or shanking him in the leg so he can't chase them.

If it's two, then she'll wait until they're about to find the others, hiss a warning and leap on one of them. Surely, between herself, Spar and Rat, they'll be able to take out two guards without giving themselves away.

Surely.

If it's three, same plan, only riskier.

She doesn't let her mind dwell on the other possibility – that it won't be humans like her who can be cut with her little knife, but something worse like the Tallowmen or Gullheads. The city has bred horrors all its own.

Every instinct in her tells her to run, to flee with her friends, to risk Heinreil's wrath for returning empty-handed. Better yet, to not return at all, but take the Dowager Gate or the River Gate out of the city tonight, be a dozen miles away before dawn.

Six. The door opens and it's six guards, all human, one two three big men, in padded leathers, maces in hand, and three more with pistols. She freezes for an instant in terror, unable to act, unable to run, caught against the cold stone of the old walls.

And then – she feels the shock through the wall before she hears the roar, the crash. She feels the whole House of Law shatter. She was in Severast when there was an earth tremor once, but it's not like that – it's more like a lightning strike and thunderclap right on top of her. She springs forward without thinking, as if the explosion had physically struck her, too, jumping through the scattered confusion of the guards.

One of them fires his pistol, point blank, so close she feels the sparks, the rush of air past her head, hot splinters of metal or stone showering down across her back, but the pain doesn't blossom and she knows she's not hit even as she runs.

Follow me, she prays as she runs blindly down the passageway, ducking into one random room and another, bouncing off locked doors. From the shouts behind her, she knows that some of them are after her. It's like stealing fruit in the market – one of you makes a big show of running, distracts the fruitseller, and the others grab an apple each and one more for the runner. Only, if she gets caught, she won't be let off with a thrashing. Still, she's got a better chance of escaping than Spar has.

She runs up a short stairway and sees an orange glow beneath the door. Tallowmen, she thinks, imagining their blazing wicks on the far side, before she realises that the whole north wing of the square House is ablaze. The guards are close behind her, so she opens the door anyway, ducking low to avoid the thick black smoke that pours through.

She skirts along the edge of the burning room. It is a library, with long rows of shelves packed with rows of cloth-bound books, journals of civic institutions, proceedings of parliament. At least, half of it is a library; the other half *was* a library. Old books burn quickly. She clings to the wall, finding her way through the smoke by touch, trailing her right hand along the stone blocks while groping ahead with her left.

One of the guards has the courage to follow her in, but, from the sound of his shouts, she guesses he went straight forward, thinking she'd run towards the fires. There's a creak, and a crash, and a shower of sparks as one of the burning bookcases topples. The guard's shouts to his fellows become a scream of pain, but she can do nothing for him. She can't see, can scarcely breathe. She fights down panic and keeps going until she comes to the side wall.

The House of Law is a quadrangle of buildings around a central green. They hang thieves there, and hanging seems like a better fate than burning right now. But there was a row of windows, wasn't there? On the inside face of the building, looking out onto that green. She's sure there is, there must be, because the fires have closed in behind her and there's no turning back.

The outstretched fingers of her left hand touch warm stone. The side wall. She scrabbles and sweeps her fingers over it, looking for the windows. They're higher than she remembers, and she can barely reach the sill even when stretching, standing on tiptoes. The windows are thick, leaded glass, and, while the fires have blown some of them out, this one is intact. She grabs a book off a shelf and flings it at the glass, to no avail. It bounces back. There's nothing she can do to break the glass from down here.

On this side, the sill's less than an inch wide, but if she can get up there, maybe she can lever one of the panes out, make an opening. She takes a step back to make a running jump up, and a hand closes around her ankle.

"Help me!"

It's the guard who followed her in. The burning bookcase must have fallen on him. He's crawling, dragging a limp and twisted leg, and he's horribly burnt down his left side. Weeping white-red blisters and blackened flesh on his face.

"I can't."

He's still clutching his pistol, and he tries to aim it at her while still grabbing her ankle, but she's faster. She grabs his arm and lifts it, pulls the trigger for him. The report, that close to her ear, is deafening, but the shot smashes part of the window behind her. More panes and panels fall, leaving a gap in the stained glass large enough to crawl through if she can climb up to it.

A face appears in the gap. Yellow eyes, brown teeth, pitted flesh – a grin of wickedly sharp teeth. Rat extends his rag-wrapped hand through the window. Cari's heart leaps. She's going to live. In that moment, her friend's monstrous, misshapen face seems as beautiful as the flawless features of a saint she once knew. She runs towards Rat – and stops.

Burning's a terrible way to die. She's never thought so before, but now that it's a distinct possibility it seems worse than anything. Her head feels weird, and she knows she's not thinking straight, but between the smoke and the heat and terror, weird seems wholly reasonable. She kneels down, slips an arm beneath the guard's shoulders, helps him stand on his good leg, to limp towards Rat.

"What are you doing?" hisses the ghoul, but he doesn't hesitate either. He grabs the guard by the shoulders when the wounded man is within reach of the window, and pulls him through the gap. Then he comes back for her, pulling her up, too. Rat's sinewy limbs aren't as tough or as strong as Spar's stone-cursed muscles, but he's more than strong enough to lift Carillon out of the burning building with one hand and pull her through into the blessed coolness of the open courtyard.

The guard moans and crawls away across the grass. They've done enough for him, Carillon decides; a half-act of mercy is all they can afford.

"Did you do this?" Rat asks in horror and wonder, flinching as part of the burning buildings collapses in on itself. The flames twine around the base of the huge bell tower that looms over the north side of the quadrangle.

Carillon shakes her head. "No, there was some sort of . . . boom. Where's Spar?"

"This way." Rat scurries off, and she runs after him. South, along the edge of the garden, past the empty old gibbets, away from the fire, towards the courts. There's no way now to get what they came for, even if the documents that Heinreil wants still exist and aren't falling around her as a blizzard of white ash, but maybe they can get away if they can get out onto the streets again. They just need to find Spar, find that big slow limping lump of rock, and get out.

She could leave him behind, just like Rat could abandon her. The ghoul could make it over the wall in a flash; ghouls are prodigous climbers. But they're friends – the first true friends she's had in a long time. Rat found her on the streets after she was stranded in this city, and he introduced her to Spar, who gave her a place to sleep safely.

The two also introduced her to Heinreil, but that wasn't their fault – Guerdon's underworld is dominated by the thieves' brotherhood, just like its trade and industry is run by the guild cartels. If they're caught, it's Heinreil's fault. Another reason to hate him.

There's a side door ahead, and if she hasn't been turned around it'll open up near where they came in, and that's where they'll find Spar.

Before they can get to it, the door opens and out comes a Tallowman.

Blazing eyes in a pale, waxy face. He's an old one, worn so thin he's translucent in places, and the fire inside him shines through holes in his chest. He's got a huge axe, bigger than Cari could lift, but he swings it easily with one hand. He laughs when he sees her and Rat outlined against the fire.

They turn and run, splitting up. Rat breaks left, scaling the wall of the burning library. She turns right, hoping to vanish into the darkness of the garden. Maybe she can hide behind a gibbet or some monument, she thinks, but the Tallowman's faster than she can imagine. He flickers forward, a blur of motion, and he's right in front of her. The axe swings, she throws herself down and to the side and it whistles right past her.

Again the laugh. He's toying with her.

She finds her courage. Finds she hasn't dropped her knife. She drives it right into the Tallowman's soft waxy chest. His clothes and his flesh are the same substance, yielding and mushy as warm candle wax, and the blade goes in easily. He just laughs again, the wound closing almost as fast as it opened, and now her knife's in his other hand. He reverses it, stabs it down, and her right shoulder's suddenly black and slick with blood.

She doesn't feel the pain yet, but she knows its coming.

She runs again, half stumbling towards the flames. The Tallowman hesitates, unwilling to follow, but it stalks her, herding her, cackling as it goes. It offers her a choice of deaths – run headlong into the fire and burn to death, bleed out here on the grass where so many other thieves met their fates, or turn back and let it dismember her with her own knife.

She wishes she had never come back to this city.

The heat from the blaze ahead of her scorches her face. The air's so hot it hurts to breathe, and she knows the smell of soot and burning paper will never, ever leave her. The Tallowman keeps pace with her, flickering back and forth, always blocking her from making a break.

She runs towards the north-east corner. That part of the House of Law is on fire, too, but the flames seem less intense there. Maybe she can make it there without the Tallowman following her. Maybe she can even make it before it takes her head off with its axe. She runs, cradling her bleeding arm, bracing herself all the while for the axe to come chopping through her back.

The Tallowman laughs and comes up behind her.

And then there's a clang, the ringing of a tremendous bell, and the sound lifts Carillon up, up out of herself, up out of the courtyard and the burning building. She flies high over the city, rising like a phoenix out of the wreckage. Behind her, below her, the bell tower topples down, and the Tallowman shrieks as burning rubble crushes it.

She sees Rat scrambling over rooftops, vanishing into the shadows across Mercy Street.

She sees Spar lumbering across the burning grass, towards the blazing rubble. She sees her own body, lying there amid the wreckage, pelted with burning debris, eyes wide but unseeing. She sees—

Stillness is death to a Stone Man. You have to keep moving, keep the blood flowing, the muscles moving. If you don't, those veins and arteries will become carved channels through hard stone, the muscles will turn to useless inert rocks. Spar is never motionless, even when he's standing still. He flexes, twitches, rocks – yes, rocks, very funny – from foot to foot. Works his jaw, his tongue, flicks his eyes back and forth. He has a special fear of his lips and tongue calcifying. Other Stone Men have their own secret language of taps and cracks, a code that works even when their mouths are forever frozen in place, but few people in the city speak it.

So when they hear the thunderclap or whatever-it-was, Spar's already moving. Rat's faster than he is, so Spar follows as best he can. His right leg drags behind him. His knee is numb and stiff behind its stony shell. Alkahest might cure it, if he gets some in time. The drug's expensive, but it slows the progress of the disease, keeps flesh from turning to stone. It has to be injected subcutaneously, though, and more and more he's finding it hard to drill through his own hide and hit living flesh.

He barely feels the heat from the blazing courtyard, although he guesses that if he had more skin on his face it'd be burnt by contact with the air. He scans the scene, trying to make sense of the dance of the flames and the fast-moving silhouettes. Rat vanishes across a rooftop, pursued by a Tallowman. Cari . . . Cari's there, down in the wreckage of the tower. He stumbles across the yard, praying to the Keepers that she's still alive, expecting to find her beheaded by a Tallowman's axe.

She's alive. Stunned. Eyes wide but unseeing, muttering to herself. Nearby, a pool of liquid and a burning wick, twisting like an angry cobra. Spar stamps down on the wick, killing it, then scoops Cari up, careful not to touch her skin. She weighs next to nothing, so he can easily carry her over one shoulder. He turns and runs back the way he came.

Lumbering down the corridor, not caring about the noise now. Maybe they've got lucky; maybe the fire drove the Tallowmen away. Few dare face a Stone Man in a fight, and Spar knows how to use his strength and size to best advantage. Still, he doesn't want to try his luck against Tallowmen. Luck is what it would be – one hit from his stone fists might splatter the waxy creations of the alchemists' guild, but they're so fast he'd be lucky to land that one hit.

He marches past the first door out onto the street. Too obvious.

He stumbles to a huge pair of ornate internal doors and smashes them to flinders. Beyond is a courtroom. He's been here before, he realises, long ago. He was up there in the viewer's gallery when they sentenced his father to hang. Vague memories of being dragged down a passageway by his mother, him hanging off her arm like a dead weight, desperate to stay behind but unable to name his fear. Heinreil and the others, clustering around his mother as an invisible honour guard, keeping the press of the crowd away from them. Old men who smelled of drink and dust despite their rich clothes, whispering that his father had paid his dues, that the Brotherhood would take care of them, no matter what.

These days, that means alkahest. Spar's leg starts to hurt as he drags it across the court. Never a good sign – means it's starting to calcify.

"Hold it there."

A man steps into view, blocking the far exit. He's dressed in leathers and a grubby green half-cloak. Sword and pistol at his belt, and he's holding a big iron-shod staff with a sharp hook at one end. The broken nose of a boxer. His hair seems to be migrating south, fleeing his balding pate to colonise the rich forest of his thick black beard. He's a big man, but he's only flesh and bone.

Spar charges, breaking into a Stone Man's approximation of a sprint. It's more like an avalanche, but the man jumps aside and the iron-shod staff comes down hard, right on the back of Spar's right knee. Spar stumbles, crashes into the doorframe, smashing it beneath his weight. He avoids falling only by digging his hand into the wall, crumbling the plaster like dry leaves. He lets Cari tumble to the ground.

The man shrugs his half-cloak back, and there's a silver badge pinned to his breast. He's a licensed thief-taker, a bounty hunter. Recovers lost property, takes sanctioned revenge for the rich. Not regular city watch, more of a bonded freelancer.

"I said, hold it there," says the thief-taker. The fire's getting closer – already, the upper gallery's burning – but there isn't a trace of concern in the man's deep voice. "Spar, isn't it? Idge's boy? Who's the girl?"

Spar responds by wrenching the door off its hinges and flinging it, eight feet of heavy oak, right at the man. The man ducks under it, steps forward and drives his staff like a spear into Spar's leg again. This time, something cracks.

"Who sent you here, boy? Tell me, and maybe I let her live. Maybe even let you keep that leg."

"Go to the grave."

"You first, boy." The thief-taker moves, almost as fast as a Tallowman, and smashes the staff into Spar's leg for the third time. Pain runs up it like an earthquake, and Spar topples. Before he can try to heave himself back up again, the thief-taker's on his back, and the stave comes down for a fourth blow, right on Spar's spine, and his whole body goes numb.

He can't move. He's all stone. All stone. A living tomb.

He screams, because his mouth still works, shouts and begs and pleads and cries for them to save him or kill him or do anything but leave him here, locked inside the ruin of his own body. The thief-taker vanishes, and the flames get closer and – he assumes – hotter, but he can't feel their heat. After a while, more guards arrive. They stick a rag in his mouth, carry him outside, and eight of them heave him into the back of a cart.

He lies there, breathing in the smell of ash and the stench of the slime the alchemists use to fight the fires.

All he can see is the floor of the cart, strewn with dirty straw, but he can still hear voices. Guards running to and fro, crowds jeering and hooting as the High Court of Guerdon burns. Others shouting make way, make way.

Spar finds himself drifting away into darkness.

The thief-taker's voice again. "One got away over the rooftops. Your candles can have him."

"The south wing's lost. All we can do is save the east."

"Six dead. And a Tallowman. Caught in the fires."

Other voices, nearby. A woman, coldly furious. An older man.

"This is a blow against order. A declaration of anarchy. Of war."

"The ruins are still too hot. We won't know what's been taken until—"

"A Stone Man, then."

"What matters is what we do next, not what we can salvage."

The cart rocks back and forth, and they lie another body down next to Spar. He can't see her, but he hears Cari's voice. She's still mumbling to herself, a constant stream of words. He tries to grunt, to signal to her that she's not alone, or that he's still in here in this stone shell, but his jaw has locked around the gag and he can't make a sound.

"What have we here," says another voice. He feels pressure on his back – very, very faintly, very far away, like the pressure a mountain must feel when a sparrow alights on it – and then a pinprick of pain, right where the thief-taker struck him. Feeling blazes through nerves once more, and he welcomes the agony of his shoulders unfreezing. Alkahest, a strong dose of blessed, life-giving, stone-denying alkahest.

He will move again. He's not all stone yet. He's not all gone.

Spar weeps with gratitude, but he's too tired to speak or to move. He can feel the alkahest seeping through his veins, pushing back the paralysis. For once, the Stone Man can rest and be still. Easiest, now, is to close eyes that are no longer frozen open, and be lulled into sleep by his friend's soft babbling . . .

Before the city was the sea, and in the sea was He Who Begets. And the people of the plains came to the sea, and the first speakers heard the voice of He Who Begets, and told the people of the plains of His glory and taught them to worship Him. They camped by the shore, and built the first temple amid the ruins. And He Who Begets sent His sacred beasts up out of the sea to consume the dead of the plains, so that their souls might be brought down to Him and live with Him in glory below forever. The people of the plains were glad, and gave of their dead to the beasts, and the beasts swam down to Him.

The camp became a village in the ruins, and the village became the city anew, and the people of the plains became the people of the city, and their numbers increased until they could not be counted. The sacred beasts, too, grew fat, for all those who died in the city were given unto them.

Then famine came to the city, and ice choked the bay, and the harvest in the lands around wilted and turned to dust.

The people were hungry, and ate the animals in the fields.

Then they ate the animals in the streets.

Then they sinned against He Who Begets, and broke into the temple precincts, and killed the sacred beasts, and ate of their holy flesh.

The priests said to the people, how now will the souls of the dead be carried to the god in the waters, but the people replied, what are the dead to us? Unless we eat, we will be dead, too.

And they killed the priests, and ate them, too.

Still the people starved, and many of them died. The dead thronged the streets, for there were no more sacred beasts to carry them away into the deep waters of God.

The dead thronged the streets, but they were houseless and bodiless, for their remains were eaten by the few people who were left.

And the people of the city dwindled, and became the people of the tombs, and they were few in number.

Over the frozen sea came a new people, the people of the ice, and they came upon the city and said: lo, here is a great city, but it is empty. Even its temples are abandoned. We shall dwell here, and shelter from the cold, and raise up shrines to our own gods there.

The people of the ice endured where the people of the city had not, and survived the cold. Many of them died, too, and their bodies were interred in tombs, in accordance with their customs. And the people of the tombs stole those bodies, and ate of them.

And in this way, the people of the ice and the people of the tombs survived the winter.

When the ice melted, the people of the ice became the people of the city, and the people of the tombs became the ghouls. For they were also, in their new way, people of the city.

And that is how the ghouls came to Guerdon.